Inertial Observer

Archeons, book 4

by James L. Steele

I0575456

Inertial Observer (Archeons, book 4)
Copyright © 2020 by James L. Steele

This is a work of fiction. All characters and events are products of the author's imagination. Any resemblance to real persons or events is coincidence. Do not view or redistribute appendix G, in whole or in part, without presidential authorization.

Cover art by **Royz**, www.artstation.com/ilyar

Editing by **Alex Phengsavath**, polyglotprose.blogspot.com/

Published by KTM Publishing

Print edition set in Fanwood, Exo, Courier Prime, and Playfair Display, all royalty-free typefaces

Print edition ISBN: 978-1-7322824-3-8

Buffalo

The water poured over Stephen as he crouched on the rocks. His eyes were closed, taking in the feeling of millions of gallons washing over his back with enough force to flatten anything that wasn't solid rock, or a Krone.

This was their fifth visit to Niagara Falls, and the thirtieth time they had stood under a waterfall somewhere in the world. They had flown to Zimbabwe to stand beneath Victoria Falls, to Argentina for the Iguazu Falls, then in the dead of winter they had flown to Iceland for the Golden Falls.

Stephen had loved them as a child but never visited any of the big ones until he left the Army and took trips to Buffalo with Brenda. He frequently talked about how he wanted to come here every year and someday they would bring their children to experience this. He had looked up many waterfalls and made plans to travel the world and visit them, but between the job and saving money, it never happened.

He had only made two trips to Niagara Falls with Brenda before cancer began to take her. She didn't want him to cancel their next trip, but as treatment progressed, she had worsened. Stephen had not been back since she passed away. Without her to share the wonder, there had been no point in returning.

When the Relians had safely arrived on Earth, and the humans seemed comfortable standing in the presence of large theropods and foxlike canines as tall as grown men, Stephen took flight and immediately went to the first place he wanted to go: Yosemite Falls.

At first he had been content to stand and observe, as a human, but then Norh took control of their body and flew them underneath the falls. There they stood, letting it wash over them. It reminded Stephen that he didn't have to observe something beautiful. He could touch it now, and it wouldn't hurt him.

Under the first waterfall they shared, a strange feeling enveloped him. As the water flowed over him and the spray rose around him, he realized he only felt the water covering the parts of the body he controlled at that moment, which happened to be the head, neck, and forelegs. Stephen could not feel the water flowing over the parts of the body Norh occupied.

Norh realized it at the same time, so he shifted to the forelegs, pushing Stephen into the head and neck alone. Stephen had the sensation of not feeling his own body directly. He still felt the water in the sense that his body was aware of it, but clearly the signals were being felt before they reached him, and by the time he felt them, they had degraded somehow.

They played chase within their own body. Norh would push Stephen around, Stephen would push Norh around, and the sensation would change. It was a physical reminder that two minds occupied this body.

Since then, they had been touring the world, visiting waterfalls and even active lava flows. Letting lava flow over them produced a similar sensation.

For the most part, Norh had been content to let Stephen remain in control of their body. Norh only asserted himself when Stephen needed to push a limit his human mind imposed on him. Without that, he never would have ventured into an active volcano.

Now Stephen stood under the American side of Niagara falls, on top of the pile of rocks, turning this way and that, letting the water cover him. He opened their eyes. A boat chugged past them, full of tourists with yellow raincoats aiming waterproof cameras in his direction and clicking away. Stephen laughed, lifting their wings up and making an umbrella for the water. The cameras continued clicking away, little children clung to the rails, jumping up and down and pointing to him. Stephen smiled wider, which lifted his wings more.

"The tourists got their money's worth this time," Norh said.

"We should've agreed to take up residence in the cave," said Stephen, grinning wider with their wings. "The schedule wasn't unreasonable."

"I let him talk because I was curious. They really believed that they had something we needed, and we would be willing to give up our freedom for it."

"Oh, come on, it would've been fun! Just like old times. We'd have a cave to ourselves, and all we'd have to do is walk around the tourist area and pose for pictures in front of the falls a few times a day!"

Norh took control of their mouth. "I was intrigued by the nature of the offer. One person sees another person can be used to increase his own status, so he agrees to meet that person's basic survival needs in exchange for that. The offer is insulting. No person in the contacted universe would hold another person's survival for ransom, and yet it is normal here. I have witnessed things of this kind many times before, on other uncontacted worlds, but never as widespread."

"I had to make a living, too, when I lived here."

"I remember. I hope the Relians really can show them another way."

"Even if not, at least you're having a good time."

Norh now raised their wings a little, their dark-yellow scales shining in the sunlight in what Stephen hoped would be a photogenic pose. The little boat passed by. Stephen turned their head and watched. He raised a foreleg and waved to them. The people on the boat shouted and waved back.

"We should masturbate," Stephen said. "Give them a real show."

"I am still surprised CNN hasn't aired that footage," Norh replied. "Or announced they have it."

"I hoped *someone* would air it. I thought it would help people see us as something other than a monster. They figured it out about the foxes, so why not us?"

"We should do it again."

"During a live broadcast this time!"

Norh's libido had not calmed since the Pryip had moved Stephen's mind into Norh's body. Even after a year, Norh still marveled at how it felt to be in heat all the time, and Stephen enjoyed indulging the lizard.

Norh spread their wings and took off from beneath the falls. He soared through the air, circled the Canadian side of the Falls a couple times, then dove straight into the horseshoe and perched on a rock. Some of the people on the boat waved to them and snapped more pictures. A few of the people on the boat huddled at the rear, holding their children.

"If this tourist boat is a good sample," Stephen said, "I think we can say only twenty-two percent of the population is still afraid of us and the Relians."

Norh did not reply, but Stephen could tell he had focused on the small group of terrified individuals at the rear of the boat.

"What are you thinking?"

Norh took control of the mouth. "I do not like that they are still afraid."

"It's a work in progress, and we've made a lot of progress in just a few months. The Relians have homes. Deka, Kylac, Rive, and Sonjaa did a great job making sure they wouldn't be segregated on their own land. They were going to do that, remember? Congress was going to create reservations for them in the national parks. Pretty soon, everyone will be comfortable with aliens."

Norh did not respond. The boat held position in the middle of the horseshoe. The tourists admired the curtains of water spilling in all directions, and the Krone sitting underneath it, seemingly untouched by the force. The boat began to turn around and drift away. The terrified people pushed their children to the front of the boat.

Norh asserted control of the body. He spread their wings and took off over the boat and across the river to the shore just beyond the American side of the falls. The dock for the tour boats came in sight, and Norh set them down just off to the side. The people waiting for the next boat to leave turned to face them. About half of the people ran toward them, stopping fifty feet away. Those with cameras pulled them out and started snapping away. The rest of the tourists stood as far back as they could, holding their children close.

Norh lowered their head to the ground, trying to appear as small as possible. They waited there as the boat docked. Many of the people onboard gawked at the Krone, wide-eyed and smiling.

The collective scent coming from half of the people was wonder and joy, precursors to pheromones. The collective scent coming from the other half was terror and suspicion. Even Stephen disliked their scent, but he fed off the excitement.

The tour boat docked. Passengers walked down the ramp. Some of the fathers and mothers quickly led their children away from the Krone, not looking back even as their children did. Norh lifted their head and observed them flee.

Stephen took control, turning to onlookers that had gathered. Stephen rolled over, showing their underbelly and spreading his wings. He didn't exactly loom over the masses—he was only as large as a bus, not including his neck, tail, and wings—but he still dwarfed everyone there.

After a few minutes, Norh rolled them back over and stood tall, wings spread in a smile.

Stephen waved to his audience. "Nice to meet all of you. Safe trip!"

They took off, soared to a hundred feet over the river, and flew south.

"More than a year of being visible in public," Norh said, "and half the people are still afraid."

"It really bothers you, doesn't it?"

"A civilization only moves as far as the most fearful people will allow it. Fear is a precursor to violence. Violence leads to more fear. I lived my whole life with uncontacted species afraid of me. They either worshipped me or tried to destroy me. Now they're all dead. Nobody in the contacted universe is afraid of the Krone. It brings back memories I wish I could leave in the past."

"It's only been a year. Anyways, it's not us they have to get used to, it's the Relians, and so far that's going very well. Everyone has a home, Kylac is recovering, Sonjaa has recovered. Mostly. Deka has his fox back and he's trying to be a fox for his mate. Rive even has a White House job. We're doing great."

"I have witnessed many civilizations fall. All the signs are here. I do not wish to witness it again. That is why I hid in my cave for the last three centuries. I was weary of trying. I allow this for your sake, Stephen."

"Oh, cheer up." Stephen tried to laugh in mid-air, and they wobbled. "This isn't an infant species we're dealing with. They've been around for about ten thousand years, and things are different now. The Relians are here."

"Far more advanced species than this have died off. Some of them had histories going back twice as far."

"Really? Care to tell me about them?"

"Perhaps I will share the memory with you. I do not wish to relive it now. This is no different, but your optimism is refreshing. This fondness for your homeworld and native species. It is an alien emotion to me. I enjoy it."

"Glad to hear it. Now let's find an NBC news crew. See what they do with X-rated footage."

Norh laughed in midair.

Washington D. C.

I

Sonjaa woke up to someone nuzzling her stomach. She took a deep breath as she stretched out on her side, giving Deka even more scales to rub. She cherished his touch more than ever now.

Deka moved his muzzle up her belly and to her neck. She moaned, stretched, and exposed her throat. Deka lightly mouthed it. She reached up and dragged her claws down the front of her mate's neck. She smelled Deka was out of his slit, but this room would not be an appropriate place to do that.

The green raptor opened her eyes and lifted her head. Her mate crouched to be at her eye level. His scent had changed since the disaster. He was older, hardened to tragedy, and yet emptier, as if the disaster had drained his sense of wonder.

"We're due in the West Wing in an hour," he said in Vietnamese.

"I don't know why," she responded in Japanese. "Doesn't the president already know all the Relians have homes now? What else is there to discuss?"

"Probably the future," Deka said in Icelandic.

Sonjaa replied in European Spanish. "I don't understand why these people insist on having formal meetings to discuss the obvious."

"That's the point," Deka answered in Russian, "to learn how things work here. Someone has agreed to take us in."

"Agreed?" Sonjaa said in Zulu as she rolled to her feet. "Have we met this person?"

"Not yet," Deka said in Portuguese. "Staff promised me he would be a good host."

In German: "I just started to enjoy it here."

Deka clicked his claws. "Eway antcay stay niay hetay Valoay Fficeoay oreverfay."

Sonjaa tapped Deka's claws with her own. She nipped him on the side of the snout as she rolled to her belly and stood up. She stretched again, worked a kink out of her neck. Deka turned away and leaned over Kylac. His fox was already awake but still lying on the blanket.

Sonjaa looked around as her neck popped. Relians had been sleeping here in the Oval Office for months. She remembered when blankets covered the whole floor, as sleeping on the floor had been far more comfortable than the furniture. The president had even held meetings in here while the Relians slept just to show his support for the refugees. Now it was just the four of them sleeping here.

Sonjaa turned and watched as Deka pulled Kylac off the blanket and held him upright. The disaster had changed Deka's fox, too. Kylac used to be a typical Relian canine, full of energy, eager to meet people and sleep with everyone. Now his face had numerous scars across it, one of his ears had been cut off, and his fur hid the claw and teeth marks that still covered his body.

Eventually Kylac stood on his own and walked with Deka to the door and down the corridor. They passed staff, saying hello by bobbing at the neck and the waist. Sonjaa disliked the scent of this place. It was friendly but formal, the air full of opinions not spoken and feelings buried just under the surface. There was so much she was not allowed to say in this society, which irritated her.

Another thing she did not like was how everyone spoke the same language here. She felt that her mind was wasting away from disuse in this environment, but she was grateful for the stability. After everything she had witnessed, she craved it.

Rive joined them in the hall on the way to the West Wing. She was last to rub necks with him and share a smile. Sonjaa winced at his cold metal. Nobody had survived the disaster and come out as the same person, and Rive had been through the largest physical change. Rive's metal skin was all the humans seemed to notice, but the first thing she had noticed was his lack of a fox. He looked so lonely, and it seemed so wrong, and yet Rive did not smell disturbed and anxious.

A short walk later, they entered a meeting room in the West Wing. Several members of the cabinet were already here, shuffling papers and muttering amongst themselves.

Relian canines could sit in the human chairs, so Kylac took a seat at the table. Deka stood beside him, hands folded to hide his claws. Rive stood on the opposite side of the table next to CJ Rhine, of the newly-created Department of Relian Relations. Sonjaa stood in the corner, relaxing her hands, refusing to hide her claws.

More men trickled into the room. She knew from past meetings that only a handful of women would be here, and that was another thing she disliked: the lack of female scent.

She could tell the role each gender played in a society by analyzing its language. In English, she had noted expressions such as "man up," and the insult "pussy," and easily determined what kind of society it was.

Whenever certain individuals boasted about their country's progress in giving women more opportunities, or treating women more equally compared to other countries and time periods, Sonjaa pointed out she knew more than thirty species who did not use different pronouns in the third person singular. No "he," no "she," not even "they." Just a single collective word referring to a person. That was how she knew a society in which the sexes were equals, and that was what she respected: species who had matured to the point of not even thinking to call attention to the differences.

Even her own culture had not progressed that far, though they would still never think to make decisions so important in an all-male or all-female environment. The exclusion of half the species convinced Sonjaa that any decision the president's cabinet made would have to be wrong simply for this alone.

Eight minutes late for his own meeting, Mr. Clinton arrived. Everyone stood. Kylac stood with them, his scent empty, his eyes unfocused. Sonjaa's hands sagged.

Sonjaa was prepared to stand here and be bored as usual. For some reason, the humans here seemed to think the Archeons were the only ones worth talking to. She overheard someone say a long time ago that they only allowed her to attend these meetings because Deka refused to attend if she was not allowed to be there. She did not like being treated as extraneous. She knew the kind of society this was, and everything made sense, but unlike other worlds, everyone expected her to be bound by it.

Still, watching the decision-making process had been fascinating. The more meetings she attended, the more she came to view them as lesser males appealing to the dominant male for approval, status, resources, and direction.

Though they had been appointed by the dominant male to deal with specific tasks, they still did things as they believed the alpha would want them done. But the lesser males still had a primitive drive to protect their own interests and advance themselves in the social hierarchy, so the alpha male's role was to direct that to a different, larger goal. Meanwhile the lesser males fought against this and found other ways to sneak their own agenda in by saying things which were not true, or distorting the truth to make themselves appear better in the opinion of the alpha in the hopes of raising their status. Sonjaa had tried to tell them this so many times, but nobody listened to her observations.

Another thing that bothered her about this society was that the humans regarded the raptors as the only Relians worth speaking to. They seemed to consider the foxes pets with no mind of their own. As a result, people in these meetings directed all questions to Deka, and he did most of the talking.

One of the men was asking Deka to ask Kylac something about the foxes. Sonjaa growled quietly and spread her hands further apart. The implication was so insulting. Deka had stopped pointing it out months ago, as explaining why everything they said and did was an insult took too much time.

Deka told them about the foxes now living in the homes of Americans around the country, what to expect, what they required, and why they could not be separated from their raptors. He had answered this question several times, but nobody believed him. Sonjaa had not understood this when she first arrived on Earth. If someone told her something, she believed it because it was the truth. Here, everyone assumed everything everyone said was not accurate, which defeated the point of communication itself.

The meeting dragged on and on. Sonjaa knew the code. She knew what each male was doing. It never changed, but she had to give the system some credit: it succeeded in molding things to the alpha's larger goal so long as the alpha maintained respect. Now that the conventions were over, and integration was finally at hand, attention focused on more pressing matters.

Sonjaa scanned the room. Secretary of war, secretary of the interior, secretary of state, secretary of this or that. All of them waiting for the right opportunity to make a plea to the alpha for more resources, or approval of some task they wanted to achieve, or seek his approval of the job they were doing. So long as the alpha effectively diverted everyone's ambition into tasks he wanted, the system worked.

Sonjaa looked at Rive as he watched the president speak. A raptor with no fox beside him. That's how she looked. Lonely. She thought of Rupi, her fox. Sonjaa had raised Rupi, and they helped one another grow up. She couldn't remember the last thing she said to her before the disaster took her.

Now she had no one. No fox to goad her into taking the hatchlings to this planet or that planet. Everything in Sonjaa wanted to stay on Rel as close to the hunting grounds as possible, but Rupi wanted to go everywhere and do everything. Rupi could have been an animal controlled by instinct to keep other scents away from her. Sonjaa helped her tame her animal side, and watching her live for more than her latent scent anxiety filled Sonjaa with affection and pride. They had lived for one another, bringing each other higher. Now...

She had taught the surviving Relians the languages of Earth back on Gaow, and then here in the White House. It had been so relieving to be back in reality, catching scents and talking to people again, and she never wanted to stop meeting new people. She had been so busy learning languages she had barely noticed at the time, but now her hands sagged thinking about all those raptors who had foxes. Many raptors had lost their foxes, but they had found new canines to nurture. Sonjaa stood alone. Sonjaa walked alone. It was starting to become real at last.

Deka had been so concerned for her, eager to hear what it was like in the Lake—to be trapped in that realm outside the universe no one understood but had merely glimpsed on a mathematical level. Sonjaa had tried to tell him, but every time she started to think about it, her abdomen tightened and she began to convulse. Focusing on all the new languages this planet had to offer kept her mind off of it, but every now and then her thoughts drifted back to those years floating somewhere she did not understand, and her mind and body seized up.

Now that the survivors of the disaster all had homes, she wondered what would happen to her. She missed Rupi so much. Deka had taken it upon himself to try to replace her fox as a companion. She was grateful for the help, but he could not be this person to both her and Kylac. A mate was a poor substitute for a fox, and Sonjaa felt like she was intruding on Deka's relationship with Kylac. That was all she could do now. Intrude. Hang on like a parasite. Rupi was gone. Sonjaa had returned to this universe only to be alone. She scented Rive from across the table. Rive smelled so normal without a canine at his side. Sonjaa wished she could adjust like that.

Her eyes wandered to one particular man. He wore a muted blue suit, and though Sonjaa identified him as secretary of labor, something seemed off about him. He met Sonjaa's gaze, smiled and nodded, then turned back to listening to the president speak about the future of the Relians. Sonjaa stretched her neck out, scenting him. The scent was human, and her mind told her it was familiar, but something else told her this man should not be here.

Sonjaa stepped out of the corner and stalked around the table. The secretary of labor followed her with his eyes. The president continued speaking with the rest of the cabinet. Deka interjected. Kylac sat still and stared through the others in the room, including this man sitting where the secretary of labor should have been.

Her killing claws rose. Her hands spread. The man threw his chair down and backed away. Sonjaa had cut off his retreat to the door, so he pressed himself against the wall and walked along it, behind Mr. Clinton.

The more she focused on his scent, the angrier it made her. She opened her mouth and hissed at him. The man's scent did not change, which enraged her even more. She jumped onto the table and lunged at him. The man ran for the door. Sonjaa leaped over the secretary of energy and landed in front him. His scent gave off neither fight nor flight, which confirmed her suspicion. She screeched at him, flashed her claws.

He backed away, trying to hide behind the president. Sonjaa charged him, climbed over Mr. Clinton, leaped off his head, sailed over the table, and landed on the man's shoulders. He collapsed under her weight and crumpled to the floor. Sonjaa grabbed him, flipped him over, and looked him in the eyes. They were full of panic, but his scent was not. Sonjaa screamed at him, raised her hands, and dug into his torso. She tore his flesh off with his clothes, ripped into his guts, pulled them out, and threw them every which way while her killing claw split him open from crotch to ankle. His blood smelled so good. She hadn't hunted in months, and it felt good to take something down at last.

The man choked on his own blood, but his scent had not changed. She reached into his chest with her snout, tore his heart out, and swallowed it whole. She took a mouthful of entrails and gulped them down as well. The man was still breathing. She hated that, so she reached under his ribcage with her muzzle and yanked a lung free. She didn't eat this; she threw it aside, slapping the secretary of transportation on the forehead.

She grabbed an arm in her jaws, twisted it free, and cast it across the room. It hit the opposite wall and fell with a clunk behind the secretary of education. She ripped off his other arm and chucked it across the room as well. She grabbed his leg at the thigh and snapped it off. She let this one drop on top of the man. He was still breathing. Sonjaa screeched at him and raked his body with her hands and feet, spreading blood and entrails everywhere, screaming for the man to die.

When she ran out of breath, she stood up straight and looked out over the table. Mr. Clinton still sat in his chair, telling the attorney general to partner with the legislators to draft laws specifically for the Relians. They had to plan for their population to expand, and the Civil Rights Act needed to include them. Laws would also have to be passed that would protect humans from property damage caused by...

Sonjaa stood ankle deep in the body of the secretary of labor, snout dripping in blood, the room splattered with blood, body parts strewn across the table and the floor.

The attorney general was taking notes with pencil and paper for what the new legislation needed to accomplish and was telling Mr. Clinton whom she would need to speak with.

The new Secretary of Relian Relations, CJ Rhine, spoke up next. They would have to encourage states to expand the indecency laws to allow foxes to walk around without clothing.

This sparked the first real debate of the morning. Did the foxes have a right to flash their genitals everywhere, or were they subject to the same rules of decency as a human?

CJ argued that the foxes were covered in fur and thus should not be subject to extra clothing requirements. Some laughed at that and said the canines needed to cover themselves as any other American would. A pair of shorts and a tank top would not make them uncomfortable.

CJ disagreed, and so did Deka. Kylac sat still, eyes scanning the faces at the table. He looked in Sonjaa's direction, but his gaze went straight through her.

A piece of bloody flesh fell from Sonjaa's snout and spattered on the floor. Sonjaa dashed to the door and threw it open. She leaped outside and slammed it shut, then leaned on it, panting.

She smelled herself. She looked at her claws. No blood. Her fingers were green, and her claws were black with a thin streak of yellow running up them. A decorative mirror hung just down the hall. She trotted up to it. Her muzzle was clean. She looked back the way she had come. She hadn't even left bloody footprints.

Sonjaa couldn't catch her breath. Her gaze rose to the door. Slowly, deliberately, she walked back down the hall, never taking her eyes off the door. She expected someone to bolt out of it any breath and scream at her. Twenty steps later, she stood before it. She slowly raised her hand, depressed the handle, and pushed inward.

The body was gone. No blood or pieces of intestine anywhere. The secretary of labor sat in his place, scent normal. Mr. Clinton was shouting over the other cabinet members.

"Foxes are not dogs! They should have to cover themselves just like everyone else!"

"With respect, Mr. President," said Secretary Rhine, "they're already covered in fur. They're warm enough. Making them wear clothes will only make them uncomfortable."

"And what about the people who have to look at that?" said several people at once.

"I don't want my kids seeing that."

Kylac remained silent, still staring at the opposite wall. Deka stood quiet as he observed the people in the room. Rive stood beside Secretary Rhine, watching the others, sniffing the air.

Sonjaa's hand shook as she held the door handle. The shaking spread to her entire body. She backed away, gently closing the door, and retreated to the Oval Office. She missed Rupi now more than ever.

2

Madame Secretary CJ Rhine scooped up her papers and held them under her arm. She pushed her chair backwards and left the room. She was first to leave. Metallic footsteps followed and quickly caught up to her.

"Mr. Clinton was pleased," said CJ.

"They spent twenty minutes arguing about whether foxes had to cover themselves." Rive's voice always had a metallic echo to it. CJ was used to it, but it made her wonder if only half his vocal chords was still flesh.

"And the president decided to leave the matter to the states. Probably a smart choice. He was happy everyone was settled and we can move on from the conventions. I'll bet you're happy, too."

"Move on to what?"

CJ turned to Rive. He kept pace with her as they walked to her office, head perfectly level while the rest of his body moved.

"This is a new cabinet position, Rive. My job will be to resolve conflicts quickly and without press. Nobody's sure what to expect. What did you think of the president's offer?"

"It is what I have already been doing."

"Except for one small thing. Mr. Clinton said no more portals leading to other nations. All portals that do so must have his signature first."

Rive clicked his claws, the Relian way of laughing. "Is there a form to fill out, or am I supposed to wake him in the middle of the night and ask?"

"That is a good question. I'll get back to you on that."

"Will congress have to be involved, or will this be entirely executive order?"

"Another good question."

"What are the consequences for breaking this request?"

"That is also a good question."

Rive held his fingers together, rubbed his claws. "What makes your country's leaders think they can presume to tell me where I can and cannot go?"

"That I can answer." She faced him. This was the side of his face made mostly of real skin, which looked far less imposing than his metal side. "As long as you are living in the United States, you recognize that contact with other nations may compromise national security."

Rive clicked his claws loudly, laughing harder now. "This request to limit portal travel is purely for the leaders of your society to create the illusion of control over something they do not understand. I wish you knew how unnatural it is to me, restricting portal travel for no reason other than the whim of someone who claims to be able to tell me what to do."

"Is it really that strange?"

"Just the idea of someone else placing restrictions on me. I will abide by the rules of this society as best as I can."

"Good. That means no more trips to Japan for sushi."

"I already thought of that. I overheard a number of people talking about this earlier, so I asked the chef to prepare us something to celebrate every Relian in America having a home."

CJ smiled. "Is that where you were all morning? Bothering the kitchen?"

"I wanted to make sure they had enough. I do not ask for this often. I am aware of how difficult it is to make."

They had reached CJ's new office. She turned the handle and led them inside. CJ was just glad to have an office. She had been improvising storage for months, but now everything was official.

She sat down in the chair behind her desk and faced the metal and flesh theropod. Moments later, a small sphere opened over the surface of the desk. It was just large enough to fit a serving tray through, open over a section of the White House kitchen. Rive reached in, picked up the tray, and pulled it through. CJ reached into the other side of the portal and picked up the plate. It was like reaching into a bubble of room-temperature water, but she did not feel wet when she withdrew her hand. When her arm and the plate were safely out of the sphere, the portal winked closed, and Rive set his tray on the desk.

Months ago, when Relians began seeking homes around the world, sushi chefs in Japan had taken it upon themselves to create a dish raptors could eat. They created sushi without using rice or seaweed, wrapping one type of fish inside another, sometimes mixing as many as six different species into one roll, making it large enough for a raptor's mouth. It was the only form of human food preparation that seemed to impress the Relians. The White House chef had learned how to prepare it especially for Relian guests. Rive had grown fond of it.

The eight sliced sections on the plate were the size of baseballs, and CJ imagined if he were to order it at a restaurant it would be several hundred dollars for one meal. Rive picked up one of the rolls between the tips of two claws and plopped it in his mouth. He growled gently, which sounded like a big cat purring. CJ smiled as she picked up the fork and dug into her fettuccini.

Rive chewed the fish. CJ had seen raptors hunt before, and they never chewed their food. As with many carnivores, they gulped it down whole, but when it came to human-prepared food, they chewed gingerly.

"Do you do that to make me feel more comfortable, or are you really enjoying it?" CJ said.

Rive swallowed, met her eyes. "My taste buds do not work the way yours do. Most of the flavor comes from the hunt. Some raptors prefer fast prey, some prefer prey that fights back. I knew a few carnivores who liked to hear prey screaming in agony. Eating scavenged food, or something that was hunted and prepared by someone else, has very little flavor. It is not satisfying. I chew my food to experience it the way you would."

Somehow the Archeons always seemed to know where she was going with something, even if she asked a question completely out of context without warning. CJ had long ago stopped being surprised.

"You said you didn't enjoy hunting."

"I didn't until after the disaster. I enjoyed what my fox killed because my fox hunted it without reverting. That was special. The disaster was a turning point in my life. Fish is generally not a part of a raptor's diet. We have to rely on other people to catch fish for us. Eating multiple species wrapped together is truly exotic."

He picked up another roll and dropped it on his tongue. He chewed it nine times before swallowing.

"This is indeed something to celebrate with a very expensive meal," CJ said. "Everyone has a home."

"Including Deka, Kylac, and Sonjaa."

"They're leaving the White House?"

"A man is waiting for them in the Map Room. I overheard him talking about taking them in. They will go with him."

CJ shook her head. "I was hoping they'd stay. The White House needs resident aliens. What about you? Where are you going?"

"It doesn't matter. I can live anywhere I want, though if I am to help you resolve matters of Relian conflict with humans, I should stay close. I will probably remain here."

"That may be wise. I'm not sure how this is going to work yet. Can we expect Deka and Kylac to help with these matters?"

"Maybe. Deka is devoting his time to Kylac and Sonjaa. He found his mate... only to lose his fox."

"Yes, Kylac does not seem well. What happened to him? Nobody's said."

"He witnessed many horrible things during the disaster, as did everyone, but Kylac had it worst of all."

"That's saying a lot coming from someone whose body was ripped apart and then rebuilt by living metal."

Rive clicked his claws together as he dropped another piece into his mouth. CJ watched him chew. His lower jaw somehow flexed and bent as if it were flesh. She swallowed her pasta.

"You're not a very typical raptor, and I don't mean because of the metal. You don't like to hunt, you don't have a fox or a wife. You strike me as an intellectual."

"Stephen once called me a bookworm. I was never interested in taking a mate. Nobody's scent ever caught my attention. My fox found a mate, and they were about to raise a child. I wanted him to, but... I never wanted eggs." He picked up another roll, slurped it up with his tongue. "I have heard a number of people mention their spouse, but not you. Do you not have one?"

CJ sat back. "No. Not anymore."

Rive chewed the roll a few more times and swallowed. "Did you part ways?"

"I used to be married. Years ago. I lost him to pneumonia not long after I was first elected to the House."

"I am sorry."

"Albert was a wonderful man."

"Pneumonia is treatable. Why did he succumb?"

She laughed once. "He didn't know he was sick. Thought it was just a bad cold. By the time I convinced him to go the hospital, it was too late. He loved boating. Was out on the water during a storm. Too cold. Too wet. I almost didn't run again after that, but my career was all I had. I had just turned forty. It was either that or go back into private practice."

"Why did you not want to return to private practice?"

She forked her pasta a few times, then looked up at the raptor, who was chewing on his last piece of sushi.

"I was bored with the reams of paperwork and miles of red tape. It wasn't why I went to law school, or ran for congress, or started my own law firm with Albert. There was no room to experiment or try anything or do anything special. Just rules and procedures. I wanted to be in something that had no rules yet. To be the one writing the rules. Now here I am. No forms. Everything is typed up on the fly, and nothing even has to be. There is no process. No forms that have to be filled out just right. Something needs to be done, I inform the president, and I do it. I have never had this kind of freedom in law. I hope this office never becomes a bureaucracy."

"Where I come from, that is all I know. If something needs to be done, I do it."

"From what I gather, the Archeons are the only ones who need to do anything."

"We maintain the portals between worlds and to different regions on the same planet. If we need to make another way, we simply make it. No need to wait for authority to sign permission and file the form with the proper person for it to happen. Everyone knows the right thing to do, and they do it. Why should anyone behave differently?"

"Sounds like heaven."

Rive did not speak immediately. His hands were apart, and he was staring at her. CJ paused chewing and waited for him. Finally, he spoke.

"I have great empathy for your loss. I hope you do no blame yourself for Albert's death."

"I did for a while. For months it was all I could think about. Always something I could have done different. Could have pushed him harder to be seen. It was almost a year before I stopped doing that to myself. Took me that long to accept that sometimes things just happen."

Rive folded his hands and looked down at his feet. "You spend so much time going over the past, wondering what happened, what you did wrong, what you could have done differently. No matter how many times you think back you still feel that maybe if you had recognized the signs sooner you could have prevented a whole lot of suffering and agony and you wouldn't have to watch everyone you care about still suffering from your mistake."

CJ blinked. "What do you mean?"

Now Rive met her eyes again. "I lost my fox, too, and I still wonder if I could have done more to help him."

"You haven't really mentioned him that much. All the other raptors who lost their foxes talk about them constantly. Is it something you need to talk about?"

"I will tell you someday, but I'm still figuring out what went wrong."

"You're right, now is not the time to open old wounds. This is a time to celebrate. Aliens are in America, and they are blending in. We're making history. Speaking of that, I remember browsing the archives of former slaves a while back. People went out to record their voices before their stories were lost forever. I want to do the same for the people living with Relians. Start recording their experiences living with aliens."

"A good idea. No one trusts anyone's memory on this planet, let alone someone else's word."

"We'll need a crew to go around the country. I need to hire a numbers guy to check our budget. I need to get with someone on the budget committee to find out what our budget is—"

"You should conduct the interviews personally."

"Me?"

"It's history. You should have a direct part in it."

"I don't know. I have a feeling I'm going to be busy enough."

"You will want to hear their stories firsthand. As many of them as possible. I will help you with that."

"I'm not sure that is very practical."

"I can take us anywhere in the country at any time, and it will be easier with just two people on the task. The fewer involved in the project, the less of a process it will have to be."

CJ thought about that for a moment with a noodle hanging from her mouth. "I'm all for that for as long as we can keep it that way. But that's later. We're probably going to have our plate full mediating between humans and Relians."

"It will make everything easier." He stepped backwards from the desk one pace. "I enjoyed the meal. I do not think I will ask for it again, as it is very difficult to make."

"Don't worry about it. The president's chef is paid very well for what he does, and he is the best in the country."

"Nonetheless, I will consider it my last. Is there anything you need from me today?"

"I am mostly getting things in order and determining what else needs to be done to help the Relians adjust to their new life in America."

"When you need me, I will either be here or with Deka."

The raptor backed away and walked out, closing the door behind him. CJ forked her pasta a few times, set the fork down, and then opened one of the drawers in her desk. She pulled out a packet of paper and leaned back in her chair.

It was as thick as a book, as were most government documents, meant to deter unauthorized persons who stumbled upon it from getting too much out of it at a glance. She had only read a little bit before the meeting, and now she wanted to know what the experts thought of the theropods and canines now living around the world.

Joint Subcommittee Report on the Relian Refugees: A Collaborate Effort Between Members of the House of Representatives, the Senate, and the Appointed Experts in the Fields of Zoology, Medicine, Paleontology, Faith, and Biology.

Report issued 15 June, 1997

It has been nearly a year since the "Relian" refugees arrived. This report constitutes everything we have learned about them, everything the experts have deduced, and issues recommendations and precautions as well as warnings for proper course of action.

For the purpose of this report, "raptor" shall refer to the Relian theropod and not the family of dinosaur; "fox" shall refer to the Relian canine, not the species of animal *Vulpes vulpes*; "portal" or "sphere" shall refer to the spacetime gateways the "Archeons" are capable of opening (§ 4); "Krone" and "dragon" may be used interchangeably to describe the large flying reptile answering to the names of "Stephen" and "Norh."

Section 1 — The Relians

Recall that on 31 July 1996, the Krone named Norh appeared on Fort Drum, NY, and announced he would be touring the world, preparing the people for the arrival of refugees who went by the name Relians, after the planet Rel, which he claims was destroyed in an event called the Disaster (§ 7).

Shortly after the arrival of the Relians on 18 August 1996, numerous physical, biological, psychological, and aptitude profiles were conducted. Out of 250 Relians in total, we were able to do physical examinations of 64, and mental evaluations of 21 (including the ones who call themselves the Archeons, see § 4).

1.1 physical

Average height of the foxes is 5' 4'', relaxed (height is difficult to measure because they are hunched over, and if standing fully upright can equal the height of a raptor, but this is an uncomfortable position for them). Average weight is 204 lbs. Average height of the raptors is roughly 6' 3'', although their necks can move about, and they frequently crouch to be at different heights. They tell us it is an evolutionary leftover, originally useful to keep prey guessing as to the size of the creature stalking it and thus less able to assess the threat it poses. Average weight is 782 lbs.

Experts in zoology and veterinary medicine have examined the foxes and determined them to be biologically similar to terrestrial canines. *Vulpes vulpes* has 34 chromosomes, while the Relian canine has 48. Genetically, they have nothing in common. The name "fox" is used because of the superficial resemblance. The genetic sequence is unlike anything found anywhere on Earth. It represents, in the view of the panel, a DNA structure that can only be classified as extrater-restrial.

Paleontologists and zoologists have examined the raptors and determined them to be endotherms (warm-blooded), and therefore not dinosaurs. Earth dinosaurs may have been ectotherms (cold-blooded), but the planet was so warm at the time they did not need to produce their own heat, which made them behave as if they were endotherms. It is also possible dinosaurs were warm-blooded, as this is a trait of modern birds. Scientists are still divided on the issue.

The theropods have 52 chromosomes, and are clearly not related to the Earth dinosaur species *Utahraptor* (the panel was adamant that they resemble the species Utahraptor, not *velociraptor*). Our panel of consultants asserts that, despite their depiction in popular movies, many Earth dinosaurs likely had feathers to varying degrees. On the planet Rel, we are told, the avian order (birds) never evolved. Avian and reptile never split, meaning the raptors display traits of both, but feathers never evolved.

The foxes have several peculiar physical abilities, including 1) the ability to function as bipedal or quadrupedal, and 2) opposable thumbs. Raptors also have opposable digits.

It deserves particular note that the foxes were very eager to show the experts how their reproductive organs work. In the category of reproduction, foxes are similar to canines on Earth, but do not "tie" their mates as terrestrial canines do (they lack a *Bulbus glandis*). Instead, the entire penis swells in several stages, still remaining mobile in the orifice, and greatly increasing in sensitivity.

Only one male and two female raptors were willing to be examined in this manner. More details can be found in appendix G.

1.2 mental

Standard IQ tests were performed on 16 individuals, including the 3 Archeons.

The Archeons deserve special mention here, as their IQs were off the scale, and their observed capabilities are incredible. They can "photoread" by taking in entire pages of information at a glance without having to read individual words. They can take in information from multiple channels at once (audio, visual, olfactory, etc.). This is to say nothing of their ability to learn new languages in minutes, retain all information to which they are exposed, and the spacetime spheres they are capable of opening, which facilitate travel over long distances anywhere in the world, and, we are told, the universe (§ 4).

The other Relians, while less capable, are no less remarkable. Their IQs are near or above genius level. Every one of them learned a second and/or third language within a matter of months. To say they are more intelligent than the average human is an understatement. To call them "superior" may not be appropriate.

1.3 behavioral

The canines are sexually promiscuous, while the theropods are highly protective of their canines and encourage them to take sexual partners. A raptor is always paired with a fox, and always of the same gender. It resembles owner/pet or parent/child relationship.

We have only their word on this matter: they tell us the bond is instinctual for raptors. Foxes used to be a violent species, and it was only by taking personal control of individual canines that raptors were able to survive on their planet. The raptors tamed the foxes. Foxes would still be violent if not for the theropods, which is why they allow themselves to be dominated by the raptors. Every fox has "reverted" to their "old ways" at least once in their lifetime, so they know the consequences of being apart from their raptor.

Because of this, the canines do not hunt. The raptors do this for them. The raptors are predators, and are exclusively carnivorous. The panel of experts observed them in a controlled hunt of wild elk. Though the raptors had no leader, they were able to function as a unit to bring down the entire herd with ease. After the hunt, many asked if there was anything bigger and more challenging they could hunt next.

The raptors were observed to feed their foxes. After the meal, the foxes would clean their raptors of the blood. Some raptors were observed to clean one another after the hunt, as well, but never another raptor's fox.

During the meal, raptors conversed while touching hands and clicking claws. We are told it is their means of smiling and laughing. They lack facial muscles, so they express the emotion in this manner. The normal way they converse looks strange to human eyes, with entire groups holding hands and touching claws. During very amusing parts, one raptor will often swipe his claws down the other's flank or even the neck as a bonding gesture.

Meanwhile the foxes were having sexual intercourse with one another, with raptors often directing their fox to a particular partner. We are told a raptor teaches his or her fox to do this shortly after puberty, and by the time he or she is an adult, the behavior is automatic. This is as it should be, otherwise the fox would become violent to the point of madness. (See § 9 for more anecdotal accounts of a fox's "old ways.")

Same-sex (and interspecies) pairings can happen almost automatically for adults, but for opposite sex pairings the raptor will often keep the fox from coupling. If a female is in heat, other raptors with male foxes will keep them away from her. None of this has been directly observed; the analysts have deduced all of this from interviews.

The foxes have a strange effect on people they meet. They are seductive, able to coerce people into intercourse who would otherwise not be willing, including homosexual encounters. We are told foxes have "universal pheromones" which appeal to many species, and these pheromones merely "advertise" willingness and availability. At first this panel was going to suggest that foxes have the ability to project their bisexual tendencies onto others, but Relians insist their scent merely encourages humans to act on impulses that already exist but were repressed by culture. Indeed while interviewing the foxes, many members of this panel became involved with them and requested to be removed from the project.

The word "love" appears to mean something different among the Relians. Rather than describe the affection one feels for one's husband or wife, the word describes the feeling a raptor and a fox have for one another.

Among foxes, mated pairs exist only for as long as it takes to raise a child. There were no mated pairs among foxes, as the Disaster tore families apart, and none of the children survived.

Among raptors, there were only 3 mated pairs. Raptors are devoted to their mates, but the basic unit of their society appears to be the raptor/fox pairing, not the husband/wife. The researchers were not aware of the mated pairs until they were told simply because both partners had been with their foxes the entire time, and the mated pairs did not stand close to one another or act as couples even after making this fact known.

1.3.1 notable exceptions

(Regarding the Archeons, see § 4.)

There are several notable exceptions regarding the raptors. Though we are told they are intensely loyal to their "spouses," a number are promiscuous, even displaying bisexual tendencies. We are also told it is something of a taboo among their kind for the canines and theropods to intermate. Raptors are not supposed to have sexual relations with their foxes, but a small number of them do. The practice seems to be unusual but not explicitly forbidden. One exception of particular note is a raptor named Ratash, who was the only male willing (some would say eager) to demonstrate how his reproductive organ worked and to let it be photographed and examined (see appendix G). ...

1.4 integration with human society

Raptors do not seem to understand authority, or the chain of command. They recognize it as a concept, and they understand human society is organized as a hierarchy, but do not understand why they should be subject to it as well. They do not take orders well, which means recruiting for military purposes will be difficult.

The foxes understand authority, but they obey only his or her own raptor. While they are highly intelligent, their sexual tendencies make them poor workers and even worse soldiers. It remains to be seen how the foxes will fit in with the employment market, if they can be utilized as workers at all.

This calls into question whether raptors can fit in with a capitalist society, as the raptor refuses to be separated from his or her fox for even a brief interval, to say nothing of an eight-hour workday. A structural change in their mentality may be necessary if they are to integrate into American society.

Relians do not understand the concept of money, or profit motive, or incentives. We are told planets with carnivorous species (including their former homeworld) reserve entire continents full of game which the carnivores may hunt as they please, facilitated by portals leading to many different regions. They are used to a sort of communal living in which they are free to come and go as they like, and where resources are plentiful and not owned by any particular person.

34

```
    With proper education and the right in-
centives, this panel believes the raptors can
be convinced to allow for brief periods of
separation from their foxes, but this change
in mindset will have to be achieved in grad-
ual steps spread out over multiple genera-
tions.
    Relian social structure itself will have
to change to meet market needs, and public
education should be implemented to achieve
this end in the form of special classes for
the adults, and in the future, the children.
Special incentives can be introduced into
legislation in the form of high hunting li-
cense surcharges, frequent renewal require-
ments, and mandatory safety courses and
equipment to facilitate participation in the
labor market. (§ 10.)
```

All of this was nothing CJ hadn't figured out from working with the Relians for so long, or from hearing her fellow human beings talking about them. She flipped to the section she was most interested in.

3

Deka walked beside his fox out of the West Wing and into the White House proper. He had been told their new host was waiting for them in the Map Room. Deka was intrigued, but Kylac remained unmoved. Nothing reached Kylac anymore. Nothing surprised him, nothing interested him, nothing frightened him. Even now, as Kylac walked down the corridor, his scent remained distant and neutral. When he spoke, he sounded disconnected from reality, and it hurt Deka to watch.

Deka turned his head and scented the hall for Sonjaa, but he smelled no trace of where she had gone. Deka had not seen her leave the room, and now her scent seemed to have vanished.

Sonjaa had worried him since they returned to Gaow and rejoined the survivors of the disaster. He had tried to talk to her about the Lake and her experiences in it, but not only was it mentally painful for her to remember but physically painful as well. Rather than face it, she had thrown herself into the task of teaching Earth languages to the Relians, up to twenty different languages in a day, forgoing sleep for days at a time to prepare everyone as quickly as possible.

When the president received them at the White House, Sonjaa latched onto various diplomats and shadowed them, learning their languages, building up a reserve of different ones to try on the Relians. If anyone showed even the slightest interest, Sonjaa did not rest until those raptors and foxes had learned it and decided if that was the place they wanted to live.

Deka had not pressed his mate to talk about the Lake, but he worried what would happen to her now that she had nobody to teach. She seemed much better in recent weeks, and she had adjusted to reality, but no matter what Deka did, he could never be there for her in the same way Rupi had.

He hoped Sonjaa would be able to face what the disaster had done to her, but beyond that, he could do nothing. He hoped Kylac would be able to adjust to his new life with a subconscious, and he did all he could to make Kylac feel welcome in reality.

Deka had his mate and his fox back, but it had been no happy reunion. The disaster had scarred both of them beyond consolation, and all Deka could do was watch helplessly while everyone licked their wounds.

Kylac slowed his pace and walked behind Deka. The raptor stepped into the Map Room, fox at his tail.

A thin man with light-colored skin dressed in casual clothes that looked more expensive than the suit the president himself wore sat in one of the chairs. On the other side of a table sat a woman with skin so pale Deka wondered if she was ill. She wore formal women's slacks and a matching blouse. Her hat had a mesh veil that covered her face. They both stood when Deka entered the room.

"My word," said the woman. "As many times as I've seen you on television it's still hard to believe you're real."

She had a slight southern US accent. Her scent betrayed no fear or surprise, even as she stood in the presence of a theropod taller than she was.

The man walked toward both of them and held out his hand to Deka. The red and blue raptor shook the hand. The man then turned his head to the side and bent at the waist. Deka stretched his neck forward and did a raptor greeting as best as he could with a human. The gesture was reassuring; he had obviously been prepared for this.

But his scent was awful. If Deka were to meet him on another planet, he would not remain anywhere near this man for long. If his scent was bad, it could only mean conflict would result, but this was human society, which often required forcing oneself to get along with people who had unpleasant scents.

"It is nice to meet both of you," said the man. "My name is Jeff Morton—Jeff *Mitchell* Morton, and this is my wife Penny."

"I am delighted to meet both of you at last. I have heard so much about you. Oh, where is your wife, Mr. Deka?"

Deka blinked once. It bothered him that he had not noticed her leave the meeting. "I don't know."

"Ah, well I'm sure she'll be along soon." Big smile. "You know how us ladies are. Oh, excuse us, we should all be sitting to get to know each other, but I told Jeff that would be rude in this case."

"Penny is right about these things. She always is. Anyway, you're probably wondering why we're here. I own a number of businesses, a good deal of stock in others, not a controlling interest of course, but enough to have some pull with the owners. This means I have a lot of friends in the business world, and consequently a lot of friends in Washington, Mr. Deka."

"Mister is not necessary. My name is Deka."

"Very good. I heard through some of my connections that the three of you were the only ones who had yet to find lodging."

"Now we're both sure you would love to stay at the White House," Penny said. Her mouth was laughing, but her scent was everything except mirthful.

"But that won't work forever," Jeff continued. "Rather than force you to comb through all the cities in the country again looking for a place to stay, I told my associate I would volunteer. I have a summer house in Boston and winter homes in California and the Bahamas, all with plenty of space to run around."

"We would be delighted to have you," said Penny. "We have two girls, six and fourteen. They're in school right now; they go to a private school year-round, and we told them to expect special guests."

"We have a car out back waiting to pick us up, and then we can leave by private jet when we're out of the DC area. I asked to land a helicopter on the White House lawn, but they wouldn't allow it this time, so I had to hire a driver for the trip here."

Deka turned to Kylac. His scent was distant and wounded, as usual, but it still confirmed that he and Deka were thinking the same thing.

"There is plenty for you to do in Boston," said Penny, "and there's lots of room for you to make your ways if you need to."

"And I should mention I'm a bit of a hunter myself. I have a number of friends who would certainly allow us to hunt on their land, and I mean things bigger than deer, Deka. Exotic game, wild horses. Maybe other things."

Every word out of their mouths made Deka want to piss in front of them and leave. Kylac, too. Their scents were equally repulsive, but Deka and Kylac both realized the opportunity. Deka caught Sonjaa's scent at the door and turned to face her.

"Ah, there she is," said Penny.

Sonjaa's adrenaline was far too high for being in the normally calm and formal White House atmosphere. Deka walked to her and wrapped necks with her as he touched her claws.

"Are you all right?" he asked in Italian.

Sonjaa answered in Gaelic. "No. How was the meeting?"

"Fruitless but informative," Deka said in Navajo.

"Nothing unusual happened?" she said in Hawaiian. "Nobody died?"

Deka's neck curled back. He answered in Esperanto. "No. What happened to you?"

She answered in Relian. "I don't know. I'll tell you later."

Sonjaa stepped forward and stood next to Kylac. Deka turned around and squeezed between both of them. Jeff and Penny were staring, both of their scents high on amazement with a hint of intimidation.

"Wow," said Jeff. "I speak a little Mandarin and French myself, but that's miles beyond me."

Penny smiled at him and then turned to the Relians. "Our oldest daughter is studying Chinese and Hindi. I think you'll get along with her well. She hasn't cared for any of the tutors we hired for her, but she might like you, Mrs. Sonjaa."

Sonjaa winced at their scents. She turned to Deka and spoke to him in Hindi. "I hate them, but we're going to live with them aren't we?"

Deka also answered in Hindi. "This man was sent on purpose. We should learn why."

Sonjaa growled. Deka touched claws with her and then stepped forward.

"Yes, we will be your guests."

Penny clapped. "Wonderful. I'll send word to prepare the extra bedrooms and set extra places at the tables. I am told you cannot eat plants, Deka, is that true?"

Deka was tired of everyone on this planet, no matter what nation or culture, asking him if things they had heard were true. Deka thought it should be something that was taken for granted, not the exception. Stephen had prepared them for it, but after nearly a year it was wearing on all of them.

"I am a carnivore, not an omnivore."

"Do you like the sushi? Our cook is not a sushi chef, but I am sure he can prepare something similar."

"Rive likes the sushi. I prefer beef."

"I see. Excuse me for a moment, please." She walked to the window as she pulled out a cellular phone from a tiny purse and extended the antenna.

Jeff sat down in one of the chairs. Deka walked closer to him, Sonjaa at his side. Kylac sat down in the other chair, facing Jeff. The human met Kylac's eyes.

"I hesitate to bring this up now, but I think I should. I am told you went through some kind of mental trauma, Kylac. I know a very good psychiatrist. I can ask him to talk to you about whatever it is you're going through."

Kylac held his stare for a few seconds before answering. "Talking about it will not help me."

"You'd be surprised what talking can do. He helped me get through some troubling times. Man's a miracle worker. Expensive, but you get what you pay for."

"No, thank you. What I need is to forget, and to have as many people around me as possible."

Jeff laughed in his voice but not in his scent. "You won't be in want of that, let me tell you. There's the four of us plus six staff including the chef, and there's always business friends coming and going. Penny entertains a lot. Sometimes I come home and it's a madhouse."

Kylac did not answer. Mentally, he folded back into himself. Deka's hands sagged at the change in his scent. Jeff spoke to Deka again.

"I think we'll have a lot to talk about. There are so many places in Boston I'd like to show you. Place has a lot of history. Do you know anything about American history?"

Deka straightened his neck. "I've read sixteen books on the history of this nation, plus another twenty-four on world events."

Jeff blinked. "No kidding?"

"No."

"I heard the... uh, portal masters could read fast, but I didn't know you were—oh my goodness."

The Relians caught the scent at the same time and turned to the door. Rive stood in it. Penny had stopped speaking on the phone and gawked at the metal and flesh raptor, mouth hanging.

"Have fun in Boston," Rive said. "I will remain in the White House. Secretary Rhine will need help, and I seem to have been volunteered for the job. President's orders, so I must obey." He rubbed his claws together.

"They're letting you stay?" Deka said, also laughing.

"They haven't thrown me out yet."

"I-i-if they do," Jeff stammered, "uh, ask for me. I have enough room in my house for you as well, Mr. Rive."

"Thank you, but I will be more useful here. Where is your house, in case I need to make a way there. And where is the best place to make one?"

"I'll come back and show you later," said Deka. "Will you still sleep in the Oval Office?"

Rive backed out of the room and turned to leave. "For now. I think I could sleep anywhere and nobody would disturb me."

Jeff was still trying to form coherent words. "Let me know if you change your mind. I would be happy to have you, too."

"Thank you," Rive said.

His tail slipped out of sight. Jeff and Penny were silent for several seconds. Finally Penny held the phone up again and resumed talking. Deka listened as she spoke to someone about the spare rooms and the menu as Jeff began again.

"He's the one who looks alien," Jeff said. "You three don't look like you're from another planet, but him..."

"Even Rive doesn't understand what he is," Sonjaa said.

Jeff took a deep breath and stood up. "Well, if there's nothing else, I think it's time we left. There's so much I want to talk to all of you about, but that can wait. Do you mind flying in a private jet?"

4

Section 4 — Archeons, Their Associates, & Portals

4.1 Deka
    The raptor named Deka is a medium-build theropod with blue scales that are nearly

black, and a red stripe running up the center of his snout and down his spine all the way to the tip of the tail. His species resembles the "raptors" in the movie *Jurassic Park*, but with more colorful scale patterns, and in possession of thumbs. ...

4.2 Kylac

Deka's fox. Appearance is typical of the species (thin build, red and black fur, bushy tail, backwards doglike legs, hunched posture). Exhibits all symptoms of "battle fatigue" or "Post-traumatic Stress Disorder." He does not seem interested in sex at all, unlike the other foxes, in spite of his raptor's urgings. He lacks the energy the others exhibit and is often aloof and introverted. He claims to have suffered a great trauma but will not give more details, and neither will his raptor. ...

4.3 Sonjaa

The raptor named Sonjaa (she insisted it should be spelled with a j, despite it making the sound of a y) is green in color with yellow coloration on her fingers, shoulders, thighs, and neck. She is mated to Deka. Though not an Archeon, she displays a talent for learning languages on a similar level. She educated the common Relians in human languages prior to their arrival on Earth, and she continued to educate them in the early months of their arrival. The Relian refugees chose the country they wished to settle based on its language, and it was her work combined with the other Archeons that enabled them to make this decision.

She claims her fox was killed in the disaster and has yet to find one in need of a raptor. Unlike Rive (§ 4.4), the loss of her fox clearly upsets her and makes her a poor asset beyond a translator. ...

4.4 Rive

In physical appearance, this raptor is the most extraordinary. Half his body is made of tan-colored scales, and the other half is composed of some sort of flexible metal unknown to mankind. He tells us his body was torn apart during the disaster and then rebuilt by a sentient species of metal, which is why he will not allow it to be analyzed. This extraordinary claim can neither be verified nor disproven.

He is the other raptor without a fox but does not seem lost without one. He claims his fox (named "Friend") perished during the disaster but will not provide details. ...

4.5 Stephen / Norh

The "Krone" resembles a mythic dragon of European depictions. He claims to have been human at one point, named Stephen Penarrow. Taken from Earth several years ago for a "tour" of the contacted universe, his body was torn apart by an unknown event, after which a race of sentient plant life transferred his memories into the body of a willing Krone. The Department of Defense and Federal Bureau of Investigation have independently confirmed a man named Stephen Penarrow lived at the address in upstate New York the Krone provided, and has been missing since late 1994. His social security number matches the one the Krone gave as well.

He cannot be coerced to do anything, and appears to have no allegiance to any nation. He wanders the world and creates portals anywhere he pleases. He has refused physical and mental examinations, and should be considered a threat. His flight may interfere with airlines, or set off satellite and missile monitoring stations in foreign nations. The United States has coordinated IFF measures to ensure false alarms caused by the Krone in flight do not start an international war.

He shows a fondness for the United States but does not display any interest in helping American interests.

 ...

Interviews with Relians regarding the Krone species all say the Krone are "the most

evolved life form in the contacted universe."
Norh has been observed bathing in molten
lava, standing under Niagara Falls, and sitting casually on the peak of Mt. Everest.
These corroborate the anecdotal accounts of a
Krone's capabilities: their scales are so
well armored they are not vulnerable to pro-
jectile weapons, missiles, or physical harm
except for the eyes. If there is breathable
air, they can survive there.

   ...

4.6 overview of portals

The Relians claim they do not know what a
spaceship, or Unidentified Flying Object, is.
They also claim real extraterrestrials do not
travel using them. Instead, certain members
of the population are able to travel the universe using spheres, or portals, or "ways."

These portals are always spherical, but
we are told they can be made into any three-
dimensional shape, including cubes, planes,
multi-sided figures, and even torus (donut)
shapes. They claim spheres are simply the
easiest to calculate and hold open for long
intervals.

   ...

The Relians explain that these portals
are created by a person becoming capable of
comprehending a special kind of physics. The
subconscious mind merges with the conscious
mind, and the person is then able to perceive
the universe as it truly is, not how it is
filtered through the body's limited senses.
This allows their minds to form connections
between points in spacetime and hold these
connections open in the form of a wormhole-
like sphere through which people can cross
light years instantly.

They claim it is a natural thing which
has happened hundreds of times in the "contacted universe": two intelligent species
evolve on the same planet. When they meet,
both species then embark on a quest to understand this intelligence, and the journey
helps them understand themselves from the

point of view of someone else, which allows some people of both species to transcend their understanding of reality itself and become capable of manipulating spacetime. Eventually they use this power to journey beyond their homeworld, and their planet becomes part of the contacted universe, a community of over five hundred other planets all networked together by Archeons maintaining spacetime portals to and from numerous other planets. Everyone uses these portals to travel across the universe as they please, apparently without restriction of any kind.

Attempts to assess how they open these portals anywhere in the world have been unsuccessful. They claim not to use machines, only the power of the mind understanding the universe. It can be surmised that this is beyond human ability for now, though this has yet to be tested. The executive branch shall have authority to investigate this matter by whatever means necessary.

. . .

They claim "lone species," intelligent life forms that develop on a planet without another intelligent species, never become capable of opening portals and joining the contacted universe. Their animal instincts eventually destroy their civilization.

. . .

While there are no immediate plans to utilize the portals for military purposes, the option should not be allowed to slip by. It is not recommended asking the Relians directly, and they cannot be ordered to do so. Representatives from other nations express strong concern that the United States may take advantage of the Archeons in this manner, so any attempt to utilize their abilities for American interests must be done with utmost care and secrecy.

It is unlikely the Archeons will agree to do something overtly military or hostile, but this panel believes they can be convinced to use their abilities if they believe innocent lives are at stake, or if the consequences of

not intervening are more severe than remaining neutral. (See § 12 for more detailed
analysis of this opportunity.)

...

Still nothing CJ hadn't learned from working with the
Relians. She flipped to the back of the report.

Section 17 — Recommendations & Warnings

This section outlines worst-case possibilities and solutions. While ideal cases are
preferred, this committee's mission is to assess all the outcomes and come up with a consensus for action should the need arise.

17.1 worst-case scenarios & solutions
The Relians are highly intelligent and
potentially dangerous. Both possess claws and
teeth, and though they appear civilized,
there is no way to know what may trigger violence. If they feel threatened, they will not
hesitate to defend themselves.

The Archeons in particular are a concern-
ing threat to national security. The portals
they open can lead to other countries, which
can let people into the United States who
would do us harm. In addition, they can also
expose the United States to diseases that
otherwise would never reach American shores.

Military staff recommended confining
them, but such proposals were dismissed, as
the Archeons can easily escape from any confinement.

The committee recommends being as
friendly to them as possible. Though the Relians have chosen to settle all over the
globe, the Archeons remain here, and with
enough time can be educated in American
virtues and values and thereby persuaded to
our side.

In the event they show signs of defection
or compromising American interests, termina-
tion may be the only option. The Relians are
like any biological creature and are suscep-

tible to bullets and poisons the same as a human.

The Archeon Rive represents the biggest unknown. He is not a machine per se, but conventional weapons (i.e. firearms, missiles) will likely not have an effect on him. Biological agents that attack the central nervous system (which he freely admits is still intact and not metallic) are the best option. It shall be up to the executive office to determine how to allocate the responsibility of such a contingency.

The ideal course of action is coercion. The Archeons remain here in America and not a foreign land, so this must be leveraged. While the common Relians are being naturalized at a local and state level thanks to noble American citizens willing to share a home with them, the Archeons must be handled at the Federal level. They must be educated in the best interests of the United States and convinced to ally with the Federal Government to those ends. Failure to do so will risk foreign powers seizing the Archeons and hurting American interests abroad and at home.

17.2 creation of a Department of Relian Relations

Matters dealing with conflict between Relians and humans are more delicate than usual at this critical time of adjustment. At the insistence of the Archeons, the Relian refugees are living in the homes of ordinary Americans across the country. Conflict and unrest have already resulted, and the President has created a new cabinet position with the goal of resolving these matters peacefully, and with as little attention as possible. This office has jurisdiction to go anywhere in the country at any time by way of Archeon-created portals to resolve all situations that may arise.

Currently, 84 Relians are living in the country (see appendix A for names and addresses of all registered households with Relian guests). They are still adjusting to their new life in America. Initiatives to educate the Relians in the ways of American society are still being explored, but in the meantime, citizens are showing them how to live productive lives in pursuit of the American dream.

Even in light of this, precautions must be taken in case the Secretary of Relian Relations cannot resolve a conflict. Law enforcement in the neighborhoods shall be equipped with special tools to handle a raptor or a fox who is out of control.

...

17.3 the special case for hunting

As for the hunting needs of the raptors, each State where Relians are living shall been given the option to accommodate the raptors as it sees fit. Solutions include extending special hunting licenses and creating hunting reserves. The creation of carnivore "theme parks" is possible in the future as population increases. These options are favorable to manufacturers, as they allow for streamlined privatization, and special safety equipment will have to be designed for this potential new market of customers that is sure to grow in the future.

17.4 the Krone as a random element

If the stories are to be believed, the only harm that can be done to the Krone is to the eyes, but a precision shot would be nearly impossible, and would likely not be fatal. If a means were devised to trap him in an oxygen-starved environment, this could be a solution should he turn on the United States, but restraint would be a difficult task, as there is no way to tell how long it will take before asphyxiation occurs, and he may be capable of breaking out of confinement in the meantime.

Since he has refused mental and physical examination, this panel cannot make recommendations. Ideal course of action is to con-

tinue coercion and hope he can be won over to
US interests in some capacity.

17.5 conclusion
     The Relians value freedom and personal
choice, which makes them an ideal fit for the
American lifestyle. Every effort should be
made to help them adjust to their new home.
     Every precaution should be taken to pre-
pare for conflict, as an unarmed human would
not survive a violent confrontation with a
raptor or a fox. They have exhibited no ulte-
rior motive as far as the panel has determined, and seem genuinely interested in
learning about our culture and how to function within it. Local and State officials
shall be empowered to help them further these
objectives.
     On a Federal level, efforts should focus
on the Archeons and how they can be convinced
to hold American interests to the utmost importance. It shall be up to the President and
his appointed officials to decide how this is
to be done, and to determine if dire measures
must be taken should the worst case scenario
arise.

CJ closed the packet and slipped it in a drawer. She
leaned back in her chair, stared at the far wall. Her office
was modest, but it had enough room for the files she was
generating. There were no official forms or reports she had
to file for anything she was doing. She simply typed everything up as it happened, submitted it to the president for re-
view, then filed it in a cabinet here, with a copy going to an
archive in a secret facility for preservation until the end of
time.

CJ realized when she took this job that she was going
down in history as the first Secretary of Relian Relations.
Everything she did would set a precedent for future cabinet
members. History was watching.

She had had a lot of help over these first few months. Rive, Deka, Kylac, and Sonjaa had been invaluable while CJ handled these events personally. As the population of Relians expanded, she foresaw the creation of local offices in every major city that would resolve conflicts between Relians and humans. There was so much that needed to be done to prepare for the future.

Until recently, her primary job had been arranging special conventions around the country. The Relians told her they needed to find people willing to take them in, but they needed to physically meet people. They would know the right person by scent, and CJ had arranged for the group to tour the country. More than a dozen convention centers and hotels had to be booked on very short notice. It had been a logistical nightmare, but she had the power of the Federal Government at her disposal, and she was able to arrange them quickly, sometimes cutting certain events short or canceling them altogether to make room for the Relians.

The three Archeons could take the group anywhere with ease at only an hour's notice, sometimes less. The first time CJ saw it, she could not believe it was that easy. She was able to book a convention center for a whole week and have the Relians across the country within an hour.

Sonjaa had been invaluable as another language instructor. She learned languages as quickly as an Archeon, and she, along with the Krone, had taught the people new languages. These last six months had been a frenzy of booking, traveling, scenting, and learning. Just last week the final convention had been held, and every Relian pair had a home now. They were in thirty-seven states, including a single pair in Alaska, of all places.

Although Deka, Kylac, and Sonjaa had been helpful, it was Rive who became CJ's primary helper. He stood alone among the raptors with a metallic body straight out of a science fiction movie, and yet he preferred to converse with the mathematicians and biologists and physicists in the local universities while the other Relians were off hunting.

The tan and grey raptor was intimidating at first, but the longer CJ worked with him, the more he reminded her of one of her college roommates. He was a socially inept clean freak, soft spoken, always lost in thought, focused so much on the big picture he forgot to notice the small stuff. Viewing him this way, he was not so alien after all. She could imagine herself in law school with this man.

She was a little relieved he would be staying in the White House. As long as he continued to be part of this team, she would not have to create a bureaucracy. She took out her day planner and made a note to follow up on where the other Archeons were living now.

Pittsburgh

I

Malcolm climbed the escalator to the second floor of the convention center. His heart raced, and he felt tingly in the fingertips. He had driven three hours to be here, arrived what he thought would be early enough to avoid the traffic, but downtown Pittsburgh had been more crowded than he thought. He was lucky to get a spot in a parking garage.

The line of people waiting to get in reached the top of the escalator. He breathed easier now, knowing that he arrived early enough to get a decent place in line. He stood behind a family of three, and patiently waited for it to move.

Aliens were on Earth, in America, touring the country so people could meet them. Malcolm had to beg for the day off, and he couldn't believe everyone within a three-state radius had not taken time off to meet the aliens. How could people continue working at a time like this, he wondered. Then again, how could church still go on even when something obviously not part of God's Word was staring them in the face? How could guys in the clubs continue to argue politics when they should be looking at these people instead?

The world had not stopped spinning since the revelation that aliens were real. Life had continued exactly the same as before, and the whole thing disgusted Malcolm.

For months he had been watching their progress on television. It had been the lead story on the news every night, but even by the sixth month the press had become bored with it, and the Relians were often fourth or fifth down the list. Malcolm had never read a newspaper before, but when broadcast news stopped reporting on what was happening with the alien refugees, he began buying them. The stories were often buried in the middle. Malcolm thought it shameful how quickly it had become old news.

The line began moving. Malcolm ended up walking fourteen steps before it stopped again. He thought this was a strange setup. Why would the Relians not simply wander the halls so the people could mingle with them? Were they afraid of assassination or something? He wondered if the Archeons were here. He wondered if they would demonstrate one of their spheres.

Half an hour later, the line moved again, and the entrance was in sight. Three armed marines guarded the door. Malcolm gulped. He looked around again, and he just now noticed marines holding firearms every fifty feet around the hallway. All of a sudden this place felt less like a convention center and more like a fortress.

Malcolm was also the only black man in line he could see. He smirked at that. It wasn't the first time, but right now he wished he blended in with the crowd, and that he could sneak in a cigarette.

He took the pamphlet from his pocket and skimmed the announcement. It was only a single page announcing the Relians would be at the David L. Lawrence convention center in Pittsburgh from January sixth through the ninth. Day one was a general meet and greet. Day two would be a series of Q&As in a lecture hall. Day three was to be announced, and he cursed his boss for only letting him have today off.

The line moved again. At this rate, Malcolm figured he was only an hour away from finally seeing the aliens in person.

He daydreamed about what the third day would be. The press had been very quiet about what was actually happening at the conventions, and the official lists of events at the panels seemed mundane and thoughtless, which made the *X-Files* fan in him squeal with paranoid delight. He had stopped at three gas stations on the way here to run to the bathroom, and he wondered if he was the only one who was this nervous.

He looked back. The line reached down the escalator and out the door. It probably went halfway around the block by now. He wondered why they let it go out the door instead of snaking through the convention center.

He'd done everything the announcement told him. He was not wearing perfume, cologne, or deodorant. He dressed lightly while in the convention center. He brought proper identification and proof of residency. All were in his coat pocket and ready to present upon request.

The line moved again, and it stopped just a few paces from the door. Now he saw inside. They had velvet ropes boxing off an area in the center of the large interior space. Merchants and other presentations set up in here, but now the crowd was meant to stand on the outside, behind the ropes, and the Relians were inside. He saw a fox shaking hands with someone. Another was sniffing a baby. A good deal of conversation happened within that box. Malcolm's heart skipped a few beats. It was exactly what Malcolm hoped for. Not just to see them, but to meet them.

Twenty agonizing minutes of waiting later, an armed marine unclasped the velvet, and the line moved again. Malcolm walked inside the open hall. It was a huge interior space lit by skylights. The floor was cement and inelegant, and the aliens' claws clicked on it as they moved around in the square, talking to the people behind the rope.

"Papers, sir," said a uniformed man at a table.

Malcolm removed the papers from his jacket and handed them to the man. He wrote some information down in a thick binder, gave his papers back to him plus one extra.

"Please abide by the rules of this convention. You have up to an hour. If you are escorted out, please cooperate with military personnel. There is no re-admittance until tomorrow. Enjoy your visit."

"Thank you."

Malcolm walked into the hall. He followed the line to the last checkpoint, where another marine patted him down. Cameras were not allowed in here, as were knives, guns, or any other weapons. He passed the checkpoint quickly and then walked under the skylights.

The humans pressed right up against the ropes. Malcolm now noticed armed marines standing inside this box, facing outward. He shook his head and then skimmed the new paper the marine had given him. It stated basic rules of conduct. No touching unless the Relian makes the first move, no inappropriate conversation—there were children here, after all—do not cross the rope, etc. He pocketed his papers, unzipped his jacket, and walked to an empty space against the velvet.

A marine stood impassively just a couple steps to his left, arms behind his back, holstered weapon plainly visible. Malcolm smiled at him. The marine did not smile back. Malcolm looked the other way.

There they were.

Aliens.

Actual fucking creatures from outer space.

At least fifty of them, an equal number of raptors and foxes. Many were at the ropes, shaking hands. The raptors were touching people's fingers, rubbing their claws against their bare skin. Malcolm wondered how many people knew that was their gesture for smiling.

Some of the raptors attempted to wrap necks with the people. The gesture didn't work at all, but Malcolm recognized what it was. He loosened his coat and tried to pull his shirt down to expose more skin, just in case.

Most people looked much more comfortable with the foxes. Children were trying to pet the foxes, and parents scolded them. Malcolm couldn't help but notice the foxes all wore boxer shorts.

Nobody was near him, but Malcolm didn't mind. Just looking at them was enough, watching them move, seeing how they interacted with one another. The raptor/fox pairings were easy to spot. Though foxes often left their raptors, they always returned to one another's side eventually. One could easily mistake them for married couples.

Malcolm's attention settled on the left side of the roped-off area. A raptor knelt to be at a six-year-old's eye level. He could just barely make out the raptor's voice, harsh and growly; he could only tell what gender she was because her fox wore a shirt. She was asking the boy about school. The boy was not afraid but still having a difficult time thinking on the spot. Malcolm smiled thinking about what effect an experience like this would have on a child.

Sniffing sounds came from right next to his face. Malcolm turned and bumped noses with an orange-colored raptor who had green water-wave stripes running up his snout and down his body. The raptor's snout reached over the rope, sniffing Malcolm's face. The muzzle moved down his chest and under his shirt. Malcolm lifted an arm, glad he had followed the rules. The raptor's nose probed underneath his arm, sniffing him harder than ever.

Malcolm now noticed the fox next to the raptor. The fox wore a pair of black boxers and was obviously male, which meant this raptor was also male. The fox's nose nudged Malcolm's arm up and now probed his other armpit. Malcolm smiled and blushed.

"Uh, hi. Good to meet you, too. I'm Malcolm."

They scented him so intensely Malcolm drew a small crowd of his own. Little children giggled in his direction. The stone-faced marine watched but did not move a muscle.

The raptors and foxes in the enclosure started to notice what was going on. They looked over their shoulders, clicked claws with one another. Even the Relians were laughing at this.

The fox lifted the rope with one hand and crouched under it. His raptor did the same with his snout, and they stood outside the enclosure, with the con-goers, sniffing Malcolm like police dogs looking for drugs. Malcolm had his own invisible rope separating himself from the rest of the people now. He felt the need to say something for the benefit of the viewing audience.

"Um... Hi. What's your names? Is... Is something interesting about me?"

They had moved on from his armpits and jointly removed his coat and scented every piece of bare skin they could find. Malcolm was surprised none of the marines in the box had made a move, including the nearest one, who remained as impassive as ever, and Malcolm was tempted to gesture to him for help.

They must have sniffed him for five whole minutes. Every human, raptor, and fox stared at him. The hall echoed with the sound of raptors clicking claws. The foxes in the enclosure wagged tails. Malcolm looked at that marine again. He was smiling.

Finally, the raptor lifted his head from under Malcolm's shirt and looked him in the eye.

"My name is Ratash. This is my fox, Irus. You're compatible."

"Um..."

The marine on the other side of the rope stepped over the barrier and placed a hand on Malcolm's shoulder, gripping him hard.

"Sir, please come with me."

The clicking claws echoed louder. The raptors now shouted to him in some other language. The raptor, Ratash, shouted back, clicking his own claws together. The marine walked Malcolm by the shoulder around the barrier to the far side of the hall. The raptor flanked Malcolm on his right with the fox on his left.

He really needed a cigarette.

A cubicle divider occupied one corner of the hall. The marine herded Malcolm to it. Behind it was a desk, and sitting at that desk was the same marine who had checked Malcolm's papers earlier. He grinned at the sight of Malcolm flanked by Ratash and Irus.

"Have a seat, sir. Malcolm, was it?"

"Uh, yeah."

He opened a drawer, took out a few forms, and slid them across the desk. Malcolm sat in the only chair on this side of the desk. Ratash took position on Malcolm's right, and the fox stood on his left. Malcolm glanced to either side of him, surrounded by dog and reptile smell. He glanced behind them. Their escort was nowhere to be seen.

"You're sure?" the man at the desk said to the raptor.

"Yes."

The marine half-smiled. "Very well. I need to see your papers again, please, sir."

Malcolm wasn't wearing his coat, and he turned in his chair but then saw the fox was carrying his coat. He reached in, fished out his papers, and presented them.

"Thank you, Mr. ... Patton. Please fill out these forms. The first is an application for food stamps. The second is contact information and registration. The third is general survey information. All questions are required."

"Wha— Stop!"

Malcolm had shouted it. It echoed. Claws clicked in the distance.

"What the hell is going on?!"

The marine leaned on the desk, folded his hands. "I forget we're keeping it out of the press. These conventions, sir. They're not rock concert tours. The Relians need homes, and they refuse to be put into one area of some big city. The Federal Government has been arranging conventions so the Relians can meet the people, and it seems our favorite couple think you're compatible."

"Compati...b..."

"I know it's a lot to take in, sir, but that's what the food stamp form is for. Congress expanded it to include all households with Relian guests to compensate for the expense. At the end, I'll give you a packet with useful information and phone numbers to call in case you need help."

Malcolm looked up at the fox. He turned and looked up at the raptor. He faced the marine again.

"I just came here to see them."

"You'll be getting roommates, sir, and they'll be mostly paid for. You'll be doing a great service, giving them a place to stay, teaching them how to live. Where do you live, Mr. Patton?"

"Columbus, Ohio."

"Not too far, not a bad place. What do you say, sir? Did you just want to see them, or would you like to take a couple of them home?" He grinned.

Malcolm sat with his jaw hanging. For several seconds he couldn't speak. Then he felt a hand on his crotch. The hand had only three fingers, and it squeezed his dick through his jeans. Malcolm looked up at the raptor. His face was impassive. The hand slid away from his crotch and found his own. Claws rubbed his fingers, and then the raptor stood normally.

The marine smiled and tried not to laugh. "Maybe you'd like some time to think about it. I've been authorized to book you a hotel room so you can get to know these two a little better before signing."

"A room?" Malcolm looked up.

"Trust me, you'll need one."

"I'm only here today. I have work in the morning."

"Put your work number down. The government will make sure you get a week off, paid. This counts as a life event, similar to adoption. We're keeping it out of the press, but it's legally binding. Your work can't touch you. Hotel room is taken care of as well."

"I haven't signed anything."

The marine nodded. "No, sir, you have not."

Malcolm had the feeling someone told a joke and he was the only one in the building who hadn't heard it.

The marine slid a small packet of paper to Malcolm. "This is what will be required of you should you decide to sign. It basically states that you're to help them live life in the United States. Since they chose you, you must be perfect for the job."

High heels clopped across the cement, headed straight toward them. A middle-aged woman wearing formal slacks and green blouse rounded the corner. Two raptors and a fox were right behind her. Malcolm recognized them immediately as Deka, Kylac, and Rive. The dark blue raptor met Malcolm's eyes. He clicked his claws. Rive was also chuckling with his hands. Kylac's tail waved a little.

"Mr. Patton?" said the woman.

Malcolm rose from the chair and held out his hand. She shook it quickly.

"I'm CJ Rhine, White House secretary of Relian Relations. This is your hotel key. Room nine-oh-six."

"Thanks, but I don't need a room."

"Yes, you do." She smiled as she took his hand, slapped the key into his palm, and closed his fingers. "You're doing us a great service. This is payment."

"In fact," said the marine, "you should go now. Must have been a long drive."

The marine who had led them to the cubicle now stood behind Malcolm and nudged him forward.

"O—Only three hours."

"Very long. You'll receive marine escort."

"Escort?! I didn't sign anything!"

The blue and red raptor was in his face. "You're perfect for them. Have fun." He rubbed his claws against Malcolm's fingers.

"Wha—?"

With the Relians flanking him, the marine led them out the opposite door up a set of stairs, into the adjacent hotel, and into an elevator. The ride was long and bizarrely silent. Malcolm wanted to speak, but he couldn't think of a thing to say. He wasn't even sure if he was really here.

The elevator dinged, the doors slid open, and the marine led him to the correct room number. The door opened, and Malcolm walked inside, followed by the two Relians. The raptor walked past him to one of the twin beds. Malcolm turned back. The marine was smiling at them. The door closed, and Malcolm was alone with aliens.

"What the hell is going on?"

He heard the sound of tape peeling off. He turned. The raptor lay on the bed, tearing something from between his legs. It looked like he had duct-taped a maxi pad to himself. It was soaked, but there was no blood. When he removed it, clear liquid leaked out from the slit between his legs.

Ratash tossed the thing onto the other bed as he rubbed his slit with his fingers. The way he squirmed, and the growling noises he made... There was no mistaking what that was coming out of his slit. It was bright red, already half the length of his arm and still growing, and so slick Malcolm could see his reflection in it from across the room.

The raptor looked at him from the bed sheets. "I could smell you before you walked up to the ropes. Take off your clothes and get over here."

Malcolm suddenly came to life. He pulled his shirt off. The fox was behind him, unbuttoning his pants. The raptor was still on the bed, rubbing himself, growling. In seconds Malcolm was naked and on the bed. He grabbed the raptor with one hand. Ratash reached up with his free hand and fondled Malcom's testicles. He growled. Malcolm felt fur on his back. Irus was behind him, holding him by the stomach.

2

Malcolm woke up on the carpeted floor, lying on his side on top of a pile of blankets and sheets. A warm fox was spooning him. Ratash lay at his feet, head and neck between his legs with Malcolm's balls dangling over the raptor's muzzle. He shifted his muzzle, shaking Malcolm's junk around, and grumbled.

"Damn..." said the human.

The orange and green raptor slipped his head from between his legs and rested his muzzle on Malcolm's hip. Malcolm just now noticed the raptor's eyes were slitted.

"You shot four times," he said. "You must've had fun."

Malcolm stretched, mostly just to make sure his legs still worked. Irus was now awake, and he clutched Malcolm's stomach and pulled himself even closer. He felt a canine sheath poking his ass.

"Wow, that was good. What time is it?"

Ratash lifted his head, then rested it on Malcolm's hip again. "Just after four in the afternoon."

"We've been fucking for... God, we've been in here five hours."

"I know what kind of person you are. I can smell it a mile away. Even after you finish, it doesn't go soft half the time. You whack off ten times a day and it never seems to be happy. Women don't do anything for you, and it's so hard to find a man who can keep up."

Malcolm was so relaxed he couldn't remember how to agree. Ratash and Irus had taken turns on his ass. They each got him twice. Malcolm got each of them back once thanks to the complimentary bottle of lotion in the bathroom. At some point during the day, they determined the bed could not support their weight, and just did it on the floor. He barely remembered it.

"You two are... Wow."

"That was just a taste of what we do. You're a prey species. Prey loves me. I know how to take your fear of predators and twist it into bliss." He rubbed his claws. "Deep bliss."

"What? No, I'm not prey. I eat meat."

A clawed hand reached up, gripped Malcolm's balls. Ratash licked his lips. "Oh, you have all the instincts of a species that spent most of its time hiding from predators. Didn't take me long to figure out how to use them."

"What do you mean? I really... don't remember very much."

Ratash squeezed his scrotum and growled. Malcolm's heart raced. Ratash rolled to his feet and crouched over him, growling louder, deeper. Irus held Malcolm tighter, rubbed his muzzle against his neck. The raptor crouched over him. He lowered his muzzle to Malcolm's eye level and opened his mouth. Malcolm's heart was in his throat. The raptor raised a foot and stood on Malcolm's flank. The enormous killing claw poked him under the ribs.

Malcolm was hard. Ratash's head swung down to his cock, opened his mouth, snarled, and then suckled on it. He did this for a minute, then opened his mouth wider and took the balls. The killing claw poked him harder, coming close to breaking the skin, and the whole time he was growling. It rumbled so deep Malcolm felt it rolling through his chest.

Ratash opened his mouth, and released Malcolm's junk. The human raised his head and glared at him. Ratash stared back, brought his hands together and rubbed his claws.

"Prey instinct," he said.

"That... that scared the piss out of me."

Ratash lay on the floor, facing him. He looked like a chicken roosting, and it would have been funny without the claws and teeth.

"And it gets you hard as a rock. Every prey species has that reaction. Your mind knows I'm a predator, but I'm also making you feel good. The brain doesn't know how to react, so the impulses mix. There are lots of ways to exploit it."

Irus was rubbing Malcolm's stomach, feeling his cock.

"Humans are a surprise to be with," continued the raptor, stretching his neck forward, closing the distance. "You don't know you have these impulses. You've never been around a predator before, so that makes all of you virgins. It's almost too easy. Even the marines they gave me only lasted a few days before they were too tired to keep up with me."

"They were scared," Irus said.

Malcolm laughed, rolled to his back. The fox now draped an arm across his chest and buried his muzzle in Malcolm's neck.

"You like fucking with your prey?"

"Not just prey. I fuck predators, too. Sometimes I let them believe I'm their prey. They have a whole different set of impulses to use." He clicked his claws. "Sometimes I let the prey dominate me. Give them a taste of what it's like to be the hunter."

He rose, stepped over to Malcolm's junk, reached down and fondled his scrotum again.

"*This* is what I want."

As he fondled Malcolm, the human heard something dripping and sliding. He smelled it, too. He was on the floor, so he had a front row seat to Ratash's cock emerging from his slit.

"I've had a thing for mammals since I hatched. There's something about external junk. Nothing gets me going faster. Never fucked anyone of my species. Female scent never did anything for me either, but this. This is what I get out of it. And you, Malcolm, have a nice set on you. I like how there's almost no fur covering it."

He growled as he bent down and licked Malcolm from tip to base. He did it again. He lifted a leg and stepped over him, straddling Malcolm's face. Malcolm couldn't believe this thing had been inside him just a couple hours ago. He grabbed it and started licking.

3

Malcolm remembered a lot more this time. Now that he understood what was happening, his mind retained more. He wiped his face. It was covered in whatever dripped from the raptor's slit. It smelled weird, but it was the slickest liquid he had ever seen.

He rolled out from under the fox's arm and stood up. His legs wobbled. He pulled himself up onto the bed and sat there for a minute. Ratash and Irus were asleep on the floor, but he had enough room to get up.

The clock on the nightstand between the beds read six minutes after nine at night. He crab-walked over the bed, picked up his coat, and wobbled to the bathroom. He sat on the toilet, panted for a few minutes, pulled the pack of cigarettes out of his coat, and lit one up. He didn't know if this was a smoking room or not, and he wasn't sure if he cared.

He could barely walk, and he felt filthy, but he had never felt so good in his life. He savored the cigarette, ran it under the faucet, then tossed the butt in the trash. He wiped, flushed, and did the one thing he knew never to do after a night of fucking and looked at himself in the mirror.

He laughed. He was covered in raised lines where fox and raptor claws had been. He found a few vague mouth impressions, too. He leaned over the sink and looked at his face. It was dry and crusty. He ran his hand under the faucet and wiped his face clean. He wiped the rest of it off with a hotel towel. He still didn't feel clean, but at least he looked clean.

He stuffed the pack and lighter in his coat pocket and wobbled out of the bathroom, leaning against the wall. He stopped at the corner. Ratash and Irus were up on the beds now. Irus was kicking his legs, bouncing up and down, tail waving around.

Ratash lay sprawled out on the bed. The position was alluring, revealing, and even a little slutty. Malcolm noticed the thing on the bed covered in duct tape. He walked over to it, picked it up. It really was a maxi pad covered in duct tape. He laughed, met the raptor's eyes.

"What's this for?"

"Ratash drips a lot," said the fox.

"My slit makes lube," said the raptor. "All male raptors do, and they drip when they're horny, which for me is fucking always. Sometimes if I'm walking my middle claw slides out and I walk around hard and dripping for a few hours. They don't want people to see that. I don't know why. It's biology. Why does everyone want to hide it? Even Irus has to wear shorts. One person told him to cover his shame. What kind of people are you to call it that?"

Malcolm laughed. "Middle claw?"

"Relian slang for cock." Irus said. "It translates well into this language."

"Good name," Malcolm said. "That thing could kill someone. And who has the lucky job of changing your pad every day?"

He rubbed his claws. "Four or five times a day! They're paying for the room to thank you for taking me off their hands. I already broke three marines. Can't afford to lose too many. I hear they're expensive. If I stayed in the White House any longer I'd embarrass them, since I was always fucking around with Irus and everyone could hear us. Only thing louder than a fox with a human is a fox with a raptor."

Malcolm smiled as he leaned on the bed and laughed. "I only came here for one day. I planned on meeting everyone, staying for lunch, then leaving before dark. That's it! What the hell?"

Irus rolled upright and nuzzled Malcolm. "We're gonna get along great. We were scenting for someone we can get along with personally. Before you know it, you'll forget there was a time you didn't know us."

"I hope you're right 'cause... Jesus, I can't believe this."

He laughed again and fell face first into the bed, kneeling on the floor. Irus nuzzled him and licked his face. The human turned to the side and faced Ratash on the other bed.

"I thought raptors were supposed to be intensely loyal to their mates, never did anything with their foxes, and foxes were the ones who fucked everything in sight. What happened to you?"

Ratash clicked his claws. "Stereotype." He gestured with his snout to the other bed. "He is. I'm not. Yeah, I play around with my fox. I understand why most raptors don't, but me and Irus have a different relationship."

"And he's not enough?"

"We play together. It's more fun that way."

"Well, I'm here for the whole convention now. I hope to fucking God they're serious when they say work won't fuck with me."

"They won't," said Irus. "Everyone who found a raptor and fox got the same thing. Nobody asks questions when people in suits show up and tell the bosses where you're going to be for the next week."

Malcolm smiled, pounded the bed, straightened up. "All right! We're here, and I'm starving! Let's find somewhere to eat."

"Uncle Sam is catering," Ratash said. "No hunting allowed, but they have meat, and the Archeons bring it in as fresh as possible. Last time it was still warm and hadn't even been skinned."

"Closed to the public, so no pants required!" Irus jumped on the bed a couple times. He leaped off and landed on all fours on the floor. "Everyone'll want to meet you!"

"Yeah," said Ratash, rolling off the bed and touching down on the floor, rising to full height. "Deka especially."

He walked around the bed toward the door. As large as he was, he was very light on his feet.

"The Archeons are still here? Why would they want to meet me?"

"Everybody wants to meet the human equivalent of me," said the raptor, walking behind Malcolm, giving his ass a squeeze. "Half the marines didn't think I'd find someone. Deka didn't think they'd find another me on this planet."

Irus slipped into the bathroom. Ratash walked in after him. They did not close the door. Malcolm leaned on the bed. His body couldn't remember how to laugh, but inside he roared like a hurricane.

4

The second day he not only sat in the audience on two of the Q&A panels, but had his own private Q&A with the Archeons, the Relians at this convention, and half the marines assigned to guard it. They treated Malcolm as if he had saved each of them from a grenade blast and earned their undying respect. Once the con-goers left, the off-duty marines mingled with the Relians as though they were brothers.

The Archeons had talked to him, and Malcolm did not freeze up. He asked them everything he had wanted to ask over all these months following the news: what other planets have you been to; what's the most interesting world you've been to... He asked what the Disaster was, but they were surprisingly dodgy and secretive.

Other raptor's foxes left him alone, and to his surprise he wasn't even tempted to go with them to hotel rooms, as he saw many of the marines doing. Malcolm wondered how they had recruited these people.

The surprise event on the third day turned out to be a dodge ball game, marines verses Relians. They took a walking field trip across the river to the baseball stadium, humans and Relians flanked by armed marines. The con-goers watched from the stands. Malcolm and the other humans who took in Relians got field seats.

Dodge Ball was not meant to be played outdoors, so they were only using the infield. The marines had set up plywood barriers on both sides so the game would be more confined and dynamic. It felt good to be out in the open, even though it was cold.

Ratash and Irus participated for a few rounds. Malcolm could tell this game wasn't just for entertainment but an outlet for the raptor's hunting instincts. The raptors kept chasing the balls and popping them, but the marines seemed to have a never-ending supply, so the game continued uninterrupted. Watching the raptors use their mouths to catch and throw had been so interesting Malcolm didn't even glance at the bulges on some of the soldiers.

He wondered why dodge ball and not basketball or football or something. Then he realized how that would look to outside observers, so this was probably the best option. The game lasted all day, and it never became tiresome. Watching the raptors move was astonishing. As big as they were, they could turn on a dime, dash at lightning speed, and yet they could also be measured with their claws and teeth. The foxes were just as agile, and they had the advantage of being able to switch between running on two legs and four. It kept the marines guessing. Malcolm had even joined them for a few rounds. There wasn't a dull moment.

Thirteen pairs of Relians also found compatible humans, and Malcolm compared notes with them. He was the only one fucking around with the raptor. The others freely admitted to fooling around with their new fox. In all other instances, the raptor merely lay off to the side and watched. At first Malcolm was embarrassed, but as the convention progressed, he owned it, and now he felt like a million bucks.

Malcolm climbed into the driver's seat. Irus sat in the passenger seat. Ratash took up the entire back seat, and Malcolm was glad his shocks were in good shape, as the theropod tested the limits of what a car could haul.

He held the steering wheel and caught his breath. The Archeons knew his name. The secretary of Relian relations knew him by first name. Every Relian and marine in that convention center knew who he was and what he had done.

"It's only a three-hour drive." Malcolm adjusted the mirror so he could see Ratash in it. "I dunno how the neighbors are gonna react."

"We'll get along," Irus said.

"It's just an apartment, but there's enough room for us. Columbus is a pretty good city. Got a few days before I have to go to work again. I'll show you around. Make sure no one is surprised when they see you."

He had called his work on the second day of the convention, and sure enough they had been informed, so he was clear for the next week. Malcolm had no idea the government could be so efficient. He wondered if aliens had changed the world after all.

"Buckle up, Irus. Uh, Ratash, I don't think seat belts will work for you, so just hope we make it out of Pittsburgh alive."

A scaly muzzle hovered close to his ear. "I've been in a car before. Didn't even get sick."

"Good. Well, here we go. Good thing I have a Caviler and not one of those cheap foreign cars. I didn't expect to need room for hauling my kids around."

The muzzle moved even closer to his ear. "That's no way to talk to your daddy."

Malcolm laughed. "Where did you learn to talk like this? Didn't you just learn English a month ago?"

"Three months. I liked English way more than the other languages I sampled. It's rigid, it's direct, and the slang is delicious. Took two months for Sonjaa to teach us. I've only been fluent for one. The rest I learned from the marines and the secret service. They got us pay-per-view between conventions. A bunch of them had porn tapes, too. Quite a few of them were fetish videos."

Malcolm hid his face in the steering wheel. "Oh, God."

Ratash growled and clicked his claws. "I know what it means. It's all exaggeration meant to stimulate an impulse. Once I learned which one it does, and what works for someone, it's easy to use. Audio cues are just one thing to learn. Did you notice how formal the Archeons were?"

"Yeah, I did. They sounded like politicians, actually."

"They enjoy language on an intellectual level. It's what happens to people who become Archeons. They think of everything as information to process. One reason Sonjaa stuck with languages and didn't learn how to open portals, or if she even can. I dive right into the sewers of a language. Worked great on my last marine. I forgot to ask if he's all right."

Malcolm grinned as he lit a cigarette. "Well, this relationship started off in the gutter. Can only go up from here."

Irus leaned over and rested his head on Malcolm's shoulder. The human rubbed his ear, then rubbed Ratash under the chin. He growled. Malcolm got hard. He took the car out of park and backed out. Columbus felt so far away, and when he got back he had one hell of a story for everyone at work.

Wilmington

I

Lucy poked her head around an office door.

"Rob, do you have it yet?"

The suited man on the phone covered the mouthpiece and whispered loudly across the office. "Not yet, I'm still waiting on Richard."

"Tell him eight million dollars is on the line, so move it!"

Rob nodded, held up his finger, spoke into the phone again. "Yeah, I got Ms. Schrifton here. She's telling you to earn your thirty thousand dollar fee and move it."

Sounds came from the receiver. Rob turned in his chair and faced Lucy. A dark brown raptor with white splotches across her body and a single green stripe running down one flank stood next to her, and next to that stood a two-legged red fox wearing a pair of blue shorts and a thin, loose-fitting t-shirt. He stared for a moment while Richard talked on the other end.

"Uh, he says he's waiting on word from his subordinates. As soon as he hears from them, he'll call us with the analysis."

Lucy walked in. She wore a white blouse with beige slacks today, but no high heels. She leaned on his desk, looking down at the man. The raptor and the fox remained by the door. The raptor lowered her body a little and tilted her head as she watched. Lucy held out her hand.

Rob handed her the phone, and she raised it to her ear. "Richard? This is Lucy Schrifton. Yes, you remember me. I'm the woman who recommended your consulting firm. We have been waiting for three weeks now. The contract stated ten business days. I shouldn't have to remind you there's a clause that allows us to—"

Panicked sounds came from the phone. Lucy interrupted.

"Listen, Richard, no more excuses! No more dragging your feet! I want something by the end of business today, even if it's incomplete! Am I clear? I hired you, I will fire you. This is an eight million dollar tax deal. We are negotiating with the Federal Government! If it fails, our client's stock price is going to drop, I will take the blame, and I will take you down with me if that happens!"

More panicked voices. She handed the phone back to him and then walked to the door. "Make sure he delivers. Call him every hour if you have to."

"Yes, ma'am," he said, lifting the phone back to his ear. "You heard her. That's from the boss lady herself."

Lucy left the office. The raptor was still at the door, watching him. The fox walked behind her and followed Lucy. The raptor bobbed her neck and then walked out of sight.

"Yeah," Rob said, "and she has an attack raptor with her now. That's right, honest-to-God aliens are in the building. You better give us something today, or she might just pay you a personal visit. You'll be lucky if they wait till you're dead to eat you."

The voice became low and more measured.

Rob laughed. "I'm serious! She has a pair of Relians living with her! She was on mandatory leave about a month ago."

The tone changed. Rob smiled. "End of business day, Richard. Goodbye." He hung up, still giggling. He wondered how many times that would work.

Down the hall, Lucy walked with a raptor and a fox just a few paces behind her. People emerged from offices as Lucy passed to confirm what they had seen from the corner of their eye.

Lucy turned and walked into another office.

"Paul, what's the status?"

The young man at the desk looked up from a computer. "The defense declined the plea deal."

"What? We practically handed them a victory!"

"They want more money."

"Of course they do. What are they asking?"

"Six million."

"Six mil." Lucy wrote that down in her planner. "I've got a meeting with the brass in one hour. Let me check in with what's-his-name to see if we can meet that. I think he'll go as high as four-point-five just to end it, but you never know."

"They want an answer now."

"Tell them I'll have it in about two hours."

He was staring at the raptor and the fox on either side of Lucy. They stared back at him.

Lucy turned to the raptor and spoke. "All right, only three more check-ins, and then you get to meet the people in charge."

The raptor stood with her hands apart. "You have ten cases at the same time?"

Lucy noticed Paul's eyes widened when Vae spoke. "Twenty-seven, actually. I'm in charge of a certain group of cases."

The raptor made a chirping noise followed by a grumble. Lucy recognized it as bewilderment. She wondered how it sounded to Paul. She walked out, Relians at her heels.

They stopped at another office two floors down. Lucy stood in the room and spoke on the phone with two other lawyers on a conference call with some other law firm. It was on speaker phone, and the Relians stood by and listened.

Lucy and the other lawyers argued for twenty minutes with the other firm over a seventeen million dollar settlement. The other firm was trying to talk them down to twelve, but Lucy had researched it herself and she wanted everything the law entitled her client.

The lawyers on the other end reminded her that this company was much smaller, and a settlement that large was not realistic. They had already shown the patent infringement had not been intentional, so she could not show criminal intent. Lucy did not stay for the entire call; she left the bulk of the arguing to the other lawyers, who now knew what she wanted and could argue in that direction in her stead.

Another office on another floor had Lucy arguing with members of her own staff for whether or not to take another case to trial and risk a judge reducing their winnings, or to settle out of court.

The argument wasn't over by the time she left. She promised to get back to them, and then speed-walked to the elevator. She led the Relians into a large meeting room on one of the top floors. Twenty men, all of them wearing suits, sat in the plush seats around an oval table. Nobody was smiling, but when the Relians followed Lucy into the office, every man in the room gasped, voicing concerns at the breach of protocol.

Lucy took a place at the foot of the table.

"Gentlemen, thank you for coming to this meeting. I see a couple new faces, so let me introduce myself. My name is Lucy Schrifton. As some of you have heard by now, yes, I have Relians living with me. The raptor is Vae. The fox is Tema. They're women. They have been on Earth for less than a year, so naturally they were curious what I did for my nine-to-five. Or, in most cases, my eight-to-eight."

The men in the room laughed. It sounded like fake sit-com laughter.

"So I contacted our chief executive, Mr. Brendon, and he gave special permission for them to shadow me for a day." She turned to the Relians. "Tema, Vae, these are the directors of my legal firm, and some of their personal and professional assistants. This is a privately held company, but it's still run like a little government. This is congress, and that man at the end of the table would be president. It's only been a few hours, but tell them what you think of what you've seen so far."

Vae straightened her neck, standing at full height and scanning the men in the room. They were all old and white, with the younger ones clearly the assistants.

"Everyone here smells of adrenaline. I believe the term in your language is fight or flight. I haven't smelled this much of it from so many people at once since the disaster ripped my homeworld apart."

The laugh track played again.

"It is a high-energy environment," one of them said.

"I dislike the smell," said Tema, the fox. "It's oppressive."

"After a while, you can't live without it," said someone else.

The man at the head of the table leaned forward. "Very well, gentlemen. I call this meeting to order. We'll begin with Ms. Schrifton. I've spoken with the shareholders of several of our clients. They are especially interested in the progress of…"

Lucy addressed the group, Relians in the background watching her and the men. She gave a lengthy report on all the cases she had checked in with earlier, and quite a few more. Someone mentioned 8-K filings were coming up, and she was to summarize their information and fax it to each company's finance department within the week. Lucy replied that she already knew to do this and was working on those summaries.

As she turned to leave, one man toward the head of the table told her the client would settle for five million on the Brenner case. Lucy thanked him and promised to relay the offer shortly.

They exited the office, and Lucy walked to the elevator. She pressed the button and waited. The raptor caught up to her.

"I didn't like any of those men," Vae said.

"Nobody does, but they run the firm."

"They said they were fine with the status on the cases, but their scents all reeked of impatience."

"They're eager to get on with the agenda. Some of them probably had golf with important people this afternoon and needed to be out of there in less than an hour."

"I smelled distaste," Tema said. "They don't like you."

"I've long suspected it."

"Why don't they? Don't you do good work for them?"

"Nothing is good enough for those people. They answer to the shareholders of our corporate clients. Shareholders are never happy. Stock price could always be higher, cases can always be settled faster, for less money, less press. If I win and stock price doesn't move they say it was a waste of effort. No matter what I do, they find a way to criticize."

The elevator opened. It was empty. Lucy walked in, faced the door. Vae and Tema stepped in and stood on either side of her. Lucy glanced up, noticed the maximum weight capacity was nine hundred pounds, and yet the elevator still worked. She wondered if this was a good thing or not.

"I think it's because the last person to have my job was a man," she continued. "I've earned more money for this firm than he did, but that man had a lot of friends in the legal world."

"They dislike you because you're doing the job better than the previous person?" Vae said.

"I think so, but don't tell anyone here I said that. Everyone else thinks it, too, but don't say it."

"Why are you not allowed to say this?" Tema asked.

"It's not professional."

"Even if it's the truth?"

"I can show the stock prices of six different clients going up six times since I came on, all directly related to a press release of a case we won, or settled for below what was expected. I'm here because the guy at the top respects me, but if he ever goes, the rest of the board will probably get rid of me."

"That makes no sense," said the raptor.

"Welcome to the business world."

The elevator dinged. Lucy walked out, and so did the Relians. She returned to Paul's office and stood at the door.

"Good news, Paul. Board says they will offer five million."

"Bad news, Lucy." He turned in his chair, holding a pencil between both hands. "The lawyers just threatened to add an obstruction charge to the suit."

"For what?"

"Now they're claiming our client is withholding documents."

"They seemed happy with what we gave them last year."

"I know."

"It's a play for more money. Call them."

Paul swiveled, hit speed dial, and then the speaker button. The line rang twice, a secretary picked up. A couple secretaries later, she was on the line with the same lawyer Paul had spoken with a couple hours ago.

"Hello, this is Lucy Schrifton. I'm calling to inform you that my client is willing to settle this case for five million."

The man on the other end sounded impassive, and far too young to be this detached. "As I said earlier, my clients suspect they have not been provided all the information relevant to this case."

"Our clients insist you received everything they had."

"My clients are not convinced. A subpoena is being drafted now. This one has a scope for the last ten years instead of five and includes more categories."

"Are you prepared to go to trial? If you issue this subpoena, I guarantee we won't settle."

"My clients are prepared to go to trial, yes."

"It may take six months to gather those documents. Plus another three to ensure there is nothing proprietary in them. Are you prepared to wait that long?"

"That does not sound like a reasonable timeframe."

"The judge in this district will declare otherwise, as he has many times in the past. The case will be tried in this district if it does go to court. Consider my client's offer. Five million."

There was silence on the other end for a few seconds. Then he spoke again, "I will take it up with my clients."

"Please get back to Paul with your answer tomorrow. Good day."

She pressed the end call button so hard she pushed the phone against the wall, then she turned to Paul. "Don't let them intimidate you like that again. You know what happens if we go to trial. The client's last financial statements all but declared we will avoid one."

"I wasn't sure what you'd say."

"You know damn well what I would say—you've been here six years."

She turned, walked past the Relians and out of the office. Vae and Tema had to run to catch up to her. As soon as they were by her side, Lucy talked.

"They know we can't go to trial. They read our client's last quarterly report, so they know we're expected to settle this case, and they're trying to scare us into offering more money, so I'm threatening to drag the process out. They're a smaller law firm, and their clients don't have as much money as ours does. They know they won't survive that long. It's a classic staring contest. If we go to trial, we can win, but that's not the point. Company doesn't want the attention. Just pay these people so they go away. Nobody reports on settlements, but if we go to court, it will make the news."

"All of this sounds unnecessary," said Tema. "Who is right?"

"They are. The company who hired us to represent them has hurt a lot of people. They want to settle to make the issue go away."

"They are in the right?" Vae said. "Then why not admit that and pay what is owed?"

"If they did that, they'd be out at least fifty million, and they'd have the government on their backs slapping fines on them. That's out of the question. They hired us to avoid that, and if we just pay them directly, they'll go away, nobody has to admit wrongdoing, everyone is happy."

They walked silently beside Lucy for a few paces.

"I dislike the scent here more and more," Vae said.

"Believe it or not, it's what keeps me going."

They walked down the hall. Fewer people came out of their offices now to look at the aliens.

2

It was past nine o'clock at night as they drove south to Dover. Her commute was usually an hour, but this late at night she often made it home in forty minutes. Lucy drove a Mercedes, and now she was glad for getting a four-door sedan, as she had a dinosaur in the back and a fox in the front.

Lucy looked in the rearview mirror. Vae did not show emotion as a human would, so she was difficult to read if her hands were hidden, but even now Lucy thought she looked distressed. She turned to the fox in the other seat. Canines had some facial expressions, and Tema definitely looked like she had seen a battlefield.

"You okay?" she said. "Or are you just tired?"

Tema whimpered. "That was traumatizing."

Lucy nodded. "It's a stressful job. Lot of pressure. Lot of money at stake. Pretty much everyone works on the assumption that they're one mistake away from losing it all. If you're not successful, you're in danger of losing not just your job, but your career. If you are successful, you're under pressure to succeed bigger and bigger, or no one will want to hire you. I started out as a peon here. I did good work, happened to make some friends in the corporate world, and they got me this post. Been here for nine years."

"It's a horrible place," Vae said. "It smells like a hunt in there, and everyone is both predator and prey."

"You like hunting."

"The scent is misplaced. Animals have to live that way. People are not supposed to. That's why civilization exists."

"Even animals don't live under that kind of stress for so long," Tema said.

"I know, but it's a living, and it's good money. That's actually why I'm so glad you two came along. Since you've been here, it's nice having someone to come home to."

"Why not seek a husband?" said Tema.

Lucy laughed. "As if anyone has time for that. Most of the people there are single. They won't admit it, but companies like this tend not to hire married people for jobs this high up. And if you have kids, forget it. Family takes time away from work. Can't have that with million-dollar cases pending."

Lucy focused on the road for about a mile. Vae and Tema remained quiet, and their body language still betrayed how horrible they felt. Lucy continued.

"Today was pretty typical for me. Ten hours, work through lunch. Meetings pretty much are break time. It's all but policy. I haven't had time to date since I passed the bar. After a while, this job teaches you to see your fellow man as opponents. Everything everyone says is some kind of play, and it's your job to figure out why they said this, or why they said that so you can figure out where they're going, and use it against them. That's the whole point of knowing law. What law are they trying to use? Can they use it like that? Who's the judge, and will he allow it? Every time I talk to a man, that's all I hear. Even talking to cashiers at the store I'm thinking that."

Tema slowly turned to Lucy. She watched the fox from the corner of her eye.

"Vae and I weren't on Rel when the disaster hit. We were on a planet called Abaxy. Their climate was changing, so to keep their land from flooding, they used portals to divert the rivers away from them. They had six portals to Rel. Their Archeon died in the disaster, and all the portals collapsed. Days later, the land began to flood."

Vae picked up where Tema left off. "The people there are desert creatures. They can't swim, or dig, or climb trees. The water pushed them to higher and higher ground for months. Thousands died when the water took them. Rive and Deka restored the portals, and the water began to subside."

"For nearly a year, Vae and I were on the run with them. The people had that same scent. Panic. Stress. Fear. It was constant. That is why we are distressed. It was enough for us to live with it for that year, and we never want to experience that again, but you have been living with it for nine years."

"Close to fifteen if you count the jobs I had before."

"Fifteen years," Tema repeated.

"Do you enjoy it?" Vae asked.

"At first, no, but now I feel lost without it. On the rare years I can take a vacation, I don't know what to do with myself. That's why I'm so glad you two are here. I feel so much better coming home to someone. It's just what I needed. No building a relationship, no dating. You just knew I was right for you. I wish it were that easy for all of us."

"There are many species who are not scent-based who find other means of recognizing companions," Vae said. "What's remarkable about the people we've met so far is that they make every effort to hide what they are."

Tema continued. "So why should they be surprised when relationships do not work out? If both people are trying to be what they assume others expect of them, deception is expected."

"It's required if you want to get anywhere in this world. I used to be very different person before I had fifteen years of practice under my belt."

Vae shifted, wiggled, stretched her neck forward to be close to Lucy's ear. "That is the person we smelled at the convention. The person we smelled in that building was not you."

"It's what I have to be."

"I do not like what you became in that building, Lucy," Tema said. "It's only now you smell normal again, but there's still the lingering odor. It's like you keep stress in reserve so it's easier to become stressed again."

"It's how we all survive in that building."

Lucy felt a scaly muzzle against her neck. "I like you this way. Is there another way to earn money?"

"Lots of other ways, but if you want to make a decent living, you have to put in these kinds of hours."

Vae rubbed Lucy's neck with her muzzle. "So the more money you make, the less you're allowed to live?"

"Yup."

"Why bother earning money if you never have time to enjoy it?"

"Maybe when I retire at age seventy-five."

"Another forty years?" said Tema.

"Unless I win the case of a lifetime and someone showers me with millions of dollars, yes."

Vae retracted her neck, watched the road.

"Other species also require work for a time," Vae said. "The Selts and the Zjr. The Zjr are canines, and the Selts are feline. Both are quadrupeds. The Zjr are the only ones fast enough to hunt the animals on the world. They hunt for two of their years, providing food for the whole population, and then they are allowed to pursue their own interests. They still must hunt, of course, as they have to eat, but they are allowed to pursue their own goals on their terms. It's a mutual relationship. The Zjr hunt, the Selts heal their bodies."

"Makes sense. Get as much work out of them as you can while they're young, build up a surplus, then they can retire after two years. Sounds nice."

"Her point is the Selts do not force the Zjr to hunt their entire lives," Tema said. "Those first two years are to channel the new hormones after maturity, not to make them hunt extra for the Selts' benefit. The Zjr are not very capable of conscious thought until their hormones level off."

"If humans were in control of their society," Lucy said, "the board of directors would force the Zjr to hunt more and more every year to keep the Selts happy. The Selts would be the investors and managers of course."

"The Selts consider it a companionship," said Tema. "Humans view this kind of relationship very differently."

"It's how the world works. And it's Monday. Got four more days of that. At least lawyers don't work weekends. Officially."

"I do not wish you to be yourself only on the weekends," said Vae. "I want the woman I smelled at the convention center all the time."

Lucy smiled, reached back, held Vae's muzzle. "I would like to retire, too, but this is what you have to do to survive."

Tema leaned against Lucy's shoulder. Lucy stroked her head. It always felt wrong to pet the canines, but foxes thrived on physical contact of any kind.

"Why do you live so far away?" said Vae.

"Nobody wants to live in Wilmington. Dover is so much nicer and cheaper."

"You spend two hours every day driving to and from a place where everyone fears for their lives."

"The long drive helps me decompress. Sometimes the traffic is hell, but overall it's worth it."

The raptor in the back seat shifted. "I disagree."

"Wait until you get a job. I can imagine you as a trial lawyer. You standing in a courtroom, appealing to the jury's humanity." She laughed. "There's an obsolete word. Humanity meaning compassion, concern, dignity, mercy. All things warm and good about a person, including their ability to make mistakes and have feelings. I wonder if the politically correct crowd is pushing to stop using the word that way. What do you think we should use in place of it? It has to be clunky, unmusical, and completely inconvenient to say. Thoughts?"

"Sentience," said Tema, rubbing against Lucy's shoulder.

"That's a good one. Ladies and gentlemen of the jury, I urge you to look deep into your hearts and remember your sentience. He's a sentient creature just like all of you. Don't send this man to death. Try another. We need options. I know some people in universities; I'll ask if they can try these out on the students. Maybe something will stick."

"I do not want to be a lawyer," Vae said. "Not if everyone smells like that. Not if I have to spend my entire life hunting."

"But you like hunting."

"I hunt for mine and Tema's survival because I enjoy it. I do not hunt to draw criticism from the managers. I do not want to defend someone who is clearly wrong. I do not want to hunt my fellow sentient creatures. I do not want to be hunted by them. I do not want to do well and my only reward is anxiety."

"You don't have to be a trial lawyer. Most lawyers aren't cut out for that. I tried it in college. I suck at it. Honestly, you can get a job anywhere, doing anything. You learned English so fast. I think you can learn just about anything quickly. But if you want to make enough to live comfortably, you're gonna have to give up half your waking hours to it."

"That does not sound like a happy prospect."

Lucy listened for clicking claws. She heard none. Tema rubbed against her shoulder. Lucy stroked Tema's arm and held her close. Breathing her air always made Lucy feel better. She was surprised Tema hadn't pulled anyone in the office aside and made love on someone's desk. She was going to ask about that but figured the fight-or-flight smell in the place did not make her want to find a partner.

"Mammalian nature," said Vae.

"Excellent!" Lucy shook Tema. "Ladies and gentlemen of the jury, the man sitting before you today is guilty as sin, but I urge you to find your mammalian nature and realize he has one, too. Except for you reptiles, you have a different nature, so don't look into yours." Lucy laughed again. "That's a good one, but think of terms that apply to everyone, not just mammals. Keep 'em coming—oh, that reminds me! I heard some people calling you a dinosaur behind your back. I think that should count as a racial slur. What do you think? And should 'fox' count as one, too? Tema, you look like one, and Vae, you do look like a dinosaur, but where's the line between that and an insult?"

Vae clicked her claws. They were only fifteen minutes from home. Lucy wished the drive would last forever.

Boston

I

Jeff Morton lived on an estate on the outskirts of the city covering ninety acres with twenty-seven rooms, including eight bathrooms, a pool, a formal dining room, two informal dining rooms, and even an old-fashioned drawing room on the ground floor. Outside was a patio and a wooded yard which concealed a helipad, all fenced in.

Kylac wore purple boxer shorts. He sat on the couch in the drawing room, the largest and most-used room in the house. Though it had been decorated Victorian-style as a tribute to the house's age, it had everything a modern home could want: entertainment center, a pool table, dart board beside a fully-stocked bar, several pinball and arcade machines, and a place to practice a golf swing.

Only four people lived here, and guests were always coming and going. They tended to congregate in the drawing room, which was perfect for Kylac. The fox needed scents and sounds and movement around him at all times.

He was watching the three television sets in front of him. The big-screen inside the entertainment center against the wall was hooked up to a satellite service, laserdisc player, and VCR. The television had a switch to play a Nintendo Entertainment System, Super NES, a Sega Genesis with CD and 32X attachments, a 3DO, and a Nintendo 64. Hidden in a cabinet, not hooked up to anything, rested a CD-i, a TurboGrafx-16, and a Neo-Geo. The TV was currently set to Comedy Central.

The other two televisions were thirteen-inch sets on TV stands with rabbit-ears extended. The one on the left displayed a PBS station. The one on the right showed a local network.

Kylac heard a door close across the house. He heard everything going on in this house. He knew where everybody was at all times, and even after all this time he still caught himself trying to peek at their numbers to figure out what they were doing, thinking, and what they would achieve in life before they died.

He couldn't forget what he had learned about the universe. As hard as he tried, it never left him alone. Deka had been successful helping him come home and handle the scent anxiety, but the knowledge remained: the universe existed inside something else, like foam floating on a Lake, and this medium created the universe everyone knew. Understanding this meant reality became easy to calculate. People became mere numbers in the equation, which had triggered his scent anxiety as nothing else had. Kylac's mind had probed the numbers and equations that made up the universe automatically, and the scent anxiety always threatened to come back.

When they had arrived on Earth, Kylac calmed down. Deka and Kylac knew what was happening, and Kylac allowed it to happen because by the time they held the first convention, he realized there could be no other way.

His mind had built a new subconscious to confine the information he could not handle, keeping it from his conscious mind so he would not perceive people for what they really were—so his old ways would not use the information to justify destroying them all.

He wasn't an Archeon anymore in the sense that he could not open portals, but only the knowledge of the Lake hid behind the new barrier. All the information he needed to create a portal within this universe still hit him constantly. He was aware of the size of this room, the atomic vibrations in the wood, the amount of gravity pulling him down into the cushion, the chemical structure of the molecules of dust he kicked up, the x-rays humming just behind the glass inside the televisions. Now his mind blocked him from using this information. Before, it had been a river an infinite distance across, and he caught every drop of water in his mouth. Now it flowed off the cliff and drowned him, and he often found himself crushed by his perception of the universe instead of floating in it.

Deka had not told the humans about this. They believed Kylac could open portals as well as any Archeon. As far as Deka was concerned, Kylac still was an Archeon, and he would be had Friend not taken it away from him.

Kylac felt helpless, and now he sat alone with the guilt of the planets he had destroyed and the lives he had ended. Instead of screaming in his face day and night, now it merely burrowed through his fur and made him uncomfortable. He could never forget what he did. He could only ignore it, and that allowed him to rejoin civilization.

He wasn't used to his own mind hiding things from him, but he was too dangerous to trust with knowledge of the Lake. The continuing existence of every form of life in the universe far outweighed one Relian canine. He had to believe that, or he would go insane.

Bombarding his mind with stimuli had been the best way to draw attention away from knowledge of the Lake that threatened to resurface. Scents and sounds reminded him he was a living creature, and that living creatures mattered and were not merely equations wiggling through a universe that didn't actually exist.

He was glad nobody said much to him, preferring to speak to Deka instead. He would rather watch TV. It was a strain on the eyes, as the refresh rate on the sets was so slow he could see the lines being scanned, but it distracted him well. Three sets weren't enough anymore. He wondered if someone could rig a television that would change the channels fast enough for him to watch all of them at once, but he figured the limits of the equipment probably prevented that.

Since they had arrived in this house three weeks ago, it had been a nonstop march of visitors. Business associates, social gatherings, local politicians, federal politicians, investors, entrepreneurs seeking funding, and on and on. Kylac enjoyed hearing Jeff talk to them. He liked it when Penny had people over, too. It was new auditory stimulus to keep his mind busy so he didn't have time to think.

Kylac heard another door close, this time the front door, and the footsteps belonged to the six-year-old. She trotted in, climbed on the couch next to Kylac, and cuddled into his fur. At first her mother had tried to stop her from doing this, but Kylac wanted the physical contact. He missed those years when he enjoyed it. Now he enjoyed the idea of a person's touch, but actually experiencing it did not meet expectations.

"Tell me about the Gliss and the Faln again."

Kylac held her, smiling with his tail. "I've told you about them three times. Don't you want to hear about the Hypsil, or about the people of Xce? I haven't told you about them. They live on a shallow ocean where it's always raining."

"I wanna hear about the Gliss."

Kylac told her about the predator and prey species on the planet Ashen. Both were intelligent, and in their society predator still hunted and ate prey. Amy was fascinated by this. To put it in human terms, it was as if snakes and mice found a way to live in harmony. The mice had enough children for the snakes to eat, and the snakes often came to the mice's burrow for tea, biscuits, and a drawing room play. Kylac did not tell her about how he and Friend almost ended their civilization when they visited.

When Kylac finished, he reminded her she had homework to do, and she reluctantly trotted upstairs to her room.

A few minutes later, Helen, the fourteen-year-old, arrived. She greeted him in Mandarin. Kylac answered her in Hindi, and she tried to reply with her limited vocabulary. Kylac spoke again in Mandarin. She struggled, but Kylac had noticed a spark of enthusiasm in her since his arrival. She had watched Kylac learn both languages in just a few minutes, and that pushed her to try harder. Kylac knew it was an inferiority complex, but she was doing the right thing with it, and he, Deka, and Sonjaa used it to help her learn.

They had a broken conversation with three television programs on in the background. After half an hour of going back and forth between the two languages, she went upstairs to start on her homework.

An hour later, the front door opened again. The weight of the footsteps told him Jeff, Deka, and Sonjaa had returned. Jeff and Deka entered the drawing room. Deka nuzzled his neck with his nose and then lay on the floor beside his fox, facing the televisions.

"Where did you two go?" Kylac asked.

"To the zoo. Jeff wanted me to see it. Plus, he was meeting an executive there. It was a business meeting."

Kylac's tail twitched in weak laughter. "Everything is some kind of business opportunity."

Jeff had moved to the other end of the couch and stood over the empty seat.

"Of course. He was in the neighborhood, and it's important I use my time wisely. He's offering me an ownership stake in a Mexican mine. I'm intrigued. I called my finance guy and told him to look at the prospectus and all the details. Never trust a sales pitch, even if it comes from someone you know."

He sat down sideways on the couch, facing Deka and Kylac.

"Speaking of business opportunities, there's something I wanted to ask you. I have a number of friends out west in Hollywood."

When Jeff said "friends," he often meant people he had met at business meetings, or dinner parties, or executive retreats, or some other social function, and they were merely acquaintances he collected for later use. Deka and Kylac disliked how he used the terms interchangeably.

"Don't tell anyone I told you this, but a third *Jurassic Park* movie is in the works. Of course they want to cast Relians to be raptors in the film. Computer-animation can never do what you guys can do, and it will save the studio a lot of money. They even want to make the movie more raptor-centric. But the problem is none of the Relians have agreed to be in the film. Now this is a little confusing because they're offering the Relians quite a bit of money for the parts, even though they would technically be considered extras, but nobody is saying yes."

Kylac focused on the televisions. Many people hated it when Kylac did this, as he did not seem to be paying attention, but Jeff was used to it.

"Nintendo is also floating the idea of a *Star Fox* movie," Jeff continued. "Naturally, since there are actual two-legged foxes living on this world now. I've heard they approached a number of Relians living in Japan, Europe, and California about the idea, but nobody will do it. My friends asked me if I could talk to you two and see if you can persuade your people to open up to the opportunity. Maybe they don't know what a movie is, or what's expected of them. Maybe they're nervous about the exposure. Video game movies are going to be huge in the coming years as soon as they find their stride, so I can see a *Star Fox* franchise taking off quick. They might even want you for the part, Kylac. My associate told me you have a good voice for it, and you can do the dubbing for all languages. It's win-win for everyone."

Deka snorted. "I have seen the *Jurassic Park* films. I am not interested in portraying a monster."

Kylac continued. "Real aliens do not fly around space in battle planes shooting lasers that behave like bullets. I will not be part of that fiction."

Deka finished. "We're here to help humanity rise above that, not encourage you to sink further into your own distorted vision of reality."

"That's... fair," Jeff said, "and it's pretty much what my friends told me they were told by the Relians, but perhaps others are more willing but they're just following your lead. If you could be persuaded to inform the other Relians that they are free to be more open—"

Deka curled his neck. "You think we're telling them what to do?"

"You are the Archeons. You must have some influence."

"We are not leaders. Those Relians know what the best thing to do is, so they do it. We are not telling them anything."

Jeff laughed a little, but he was clearly covering his discomfort. "Honestly, that's a little hard to believe. These people seem pretty united. You're trying to tell me they got there on their own, completely independent with no direction?"

"Humanity divides itself into leaders and followers," Deka said. "In primates, a dominant person rises to the top of a group and compels the less aggressive ones to fall in line or starve. The others comply because they cannot survive apart from the group."

Kylac continued. "You are so used to it you can't imagine aliens being different. We don't command the other Relians. They are simply doing the right thing for themselves and for others. The only reason anyone needs direction is to do something that accomplishes the opposite."

Deka finished. "And only another human being trying to break out of another human's dominance will act in ways that are contrary to what is best."

Jeff laughed again. "I hate it when you guys start talking that way. So what should I tell my friends out west?"

"Stop wasting your time trying to cast raptors as monsters and foxes as cartoon caricatures," said the raptor. "You don't need our help to create your distorted pictures of reality."

Jeff stood up. "All right. I'll tell 'em, but they won't be happy." He left the room. Deka and Kylac heard him climbing the stairs.

Deka faced the televisions. He winced at the canned laughter coming from one of them.

"How 'bout a game? This time you can be the hedgehog."

Kylac laughed with his tail as he rose from the couch.

2

Sonjaa turned off the fan and walked out of the bathroom. Using the fan was hardly necessary, since Relians didn't have nearly as much bacteria in their guts as humans did, but Sonjaa was used to being among sight-based creatures, so she knew how to interact with them. Human noses regarded odors of any kind as either good or bad, and the scents contained no other information for them, so it was good courtesy to turn on the vent.

Her only complaint was the toilets were too small, and situated in such tight places she often had a difficult time maneuvering her ass over one. This bathroom was the largest in the house, and the toilet was off by itself, not crammed between a shower and a sink, so it had become the Relian's restroom.

Marissa walked up the hall, two armfuls of cleaning supplies and spray bottles in her gloved hands. Sonjaa bobbed her neck and spoke to her in American Spanish.

"Is your son feeling better today?"

She smiled, nodded. "Much, madam, thank you."

Sonjaa, Deka, and Kylac had all tried to convince the staff to stop addressing them as sir and madam, but they could not seem to break the habit, even when speaking their native language.

"School is over now, and I am grateful." She paused in the hallway and stood eye to eye with Sonjaa. "I can't afford to miss more work, and neither can my husband."

"Why would they hold that against you?"

"They say they won't, but they always do. And there is no bargaining. You miss this many days and they get rid of you!" She smiled, removed one glove, reached for Sonjaa's hand, and rubbed a claw between her index and middle fingers. She nodded and then walked onwards down the hall. "Good talking with you, Sonjaa. You have a wonderful evening."

Sonjaa stood still for a moment, watching her disappear into the next room. She grumbled at the thought that Marissa had been working for this man for almost ten years and Jeff still did not speak her language. In the contacted universe, that would have been one of the first things they did.

Jeff did not deal with most of his staff directly. If he needed them to do something apart from their usual routines, he called their employer, who did speak English, and his orders were relayed to the staff through them.

Sonjaa had watched Jeff, Penny, and even the girls around their employees. Just the other day Sonjaa had stepped between Penny and Marissa to translate, but Penny was not interested in speaking to someone she saw every day. Sonjaa realized the language barrier was encouraged here, as it meant these people could treat the ones who worked for them as if they did not exist. As if they were tools to be used instead of people to understand. The only members of staff who spoke English worked in the kitchen, and the housekeeper rarely interacted with them outside of taking out their trash.

Marissa was so used to being invisible she treated herself as though she had always been. Sonjaa did not want to let Marissa leave with that. She walked down the hall after her.

Jeff exited the room Marissa had gone into. He approached Sonjaa, face down, looking at a packet of papers in his hand. Sonjaa stopped. Eyed him. He looked up, nodded, and returned to the papers as he passed.

She turned her head and followed him as he walked down the hall. His scent was perfect. His gait was normal. His hair was perfect. Sonjaa growled at him.

Jeff stopped, turned and looked over his shoulder at Sonjaa.

She growled at him again, though she didn't know why.

"Sonjaa?"

At the sound of his voice, her toeclaws rose and her hands fanned. She turned around and screamed at him. Jeff dropped the papers and ran down the hall. Sonjaa let him run a few steps and then dashed after him, tearing strips out of the carpet with her claws.

His panicked scent felt wonderful—something she hadn't smelled in years—the rush of the hunt—and above all she hated that she didn't have anybody to hunt for and every breath of this man's scent she took in reminded her that he was the cause of that. He took her fox away. That scent. His!

He glided down the stairs. Sonjaa leaped over the railing and landed on her feet on the ground floor, cutting him off. He skid to a stop halfway down the stairs and began to turn around.

Sonjaa stalked him, savoring the scent, imagining how his meat would feel in her mouth. She had tasted it once and it had given her no pleasure but this time would be different. This time it would feel so good Deka would pick up on it and fuck her on top of the body. She missed doing that. She missed all of it, and this scent would pay for it!

She charged him up the stairs and flattened him on his stomach. She flayed him open with her killing claw from neck to asshole, speared him with both hands, and flung him down the stairs.

As he rolled, Sonjaa smeared her muzzle with the blood on her hands. When he stopped, Sonjaa leaped off the staircase, sailed through the air, and landed on him. His back snapped. Sonjaa smelled Deka and Kylac in the drawing room. She hopped off the moaning human, picked him up in her jaws, and carried him there.

Deka and Kylac were playing a video game. No wonder they hadn't heard her. She walked in front of the television, dropped the screaming slab of meat in front of Deka, and waited.

They held the controllers and narrated the action as if they were playing out a story on another planet. They did this often when they played a game, imagined it as a planet they traveled to. They were either fixing the damage from the disaster or imagined they were meeting human-style aliens who used spaceships and were on the warpath.

They seemed to look straight through her. Sonjaa looked down at herself. A path of blood from her feet led to the stairs. Sonjaa's mouth, hands, and feet dripped red. Deka and Kylac laughed as they tried to stop the humanoid alien Robotnik from turning the helpless forest creatures of the planet Genkai into machines.

Sonjaa ran from the drawing room and paused at the staircase. The blood on her claws was gone. She turned and looked back. The drawing room had no blood in it either, and the body of Jeff Morton was nowhere to be seen.

Sonjaa ran up the stairs, down the hall, past the bathroom, and into the next room. Marissa was in Jeff's office, cleaning a window. Jeff also stood in here, on the phone, talking to someone about video game movies.

"Marissa," Sonjaa said.

The housekeeper turned and regarded her with a painted smile.

"Did you hear anything just now?"

Marissa looked puzzled. "Other than Mr. Morton, no."

Sonjaa stood there, hands apart and sagging, staring at Jeff. Her hands began to shake.

"Is something wrong, Sonjaa?"

"I don't know."

Sonjaa walked out of the room. She stopped halfway to the staircase. This would normally have been when Rupi would have been there to help her make sense of things—to help her calm down after a hunt. Sonjaa had a particular problem of staying enraged after unsuccessful hunts, and Rupi had always been there to bring her back down. Every raptor had a fox to help them make sense of moments like this. Now she could only stand here and let the echoes of her own breath bring her down. Sonjaa moved her feet again. Staring blankly ahead, she descended the stairs and entered the parlor. She lay next to Deka in the drawing room as he and Kylac sped through this level.

"Don't leave me behind, Kylac," the raptor said. "I'm just a fox."

"Now you know how it feels," his fox replied. For a brief moment, he was his old self again.

Sonjaa leaned against him, rubbing her neck against his. "Deka, it happened again."

"Just now?"

"Yes. I killed Jeff Morton at the staircase. I presented the body to you about three minutes ago, and you didn't see me. Jeff is still alive upstairs."

Deka gave the hedgehog on screen a lift. "What did you smell that made you want to attack?"

Sonjaa shook a little. She didn't remember, and that scared her more than anything.

3

The formal dining room had been decorated in an eclectic mix of Colonial and Victorian styles. The oak table sat twelve people, and since it was not covered in some foul-smelling chemical meant to preserve the wood, it was pleasing to Relian noses.

Deka and Sonjaa stood on opposite sides of the table. Kylac sat in a chair next to Deka. Multiple people were seated, all of them emitting a scent that said they did not want to be here, but they still pretended to be enthusiastic, all dressed in formal eveningwear. Two business associates and their wives, plus one entrepreneur who had a friend who arranged a meeting with Jeff and was about to beg Jeff for money, as all the other entrepreneurs who came to this house did.

Formal dining was a strange concept for both the raptors and the foxes. Humans went out of their way to make it as ceremonial as possible. So desperate were they to convince themselves they were more than animals that they made everything natural a social crime.

The raptors had to eat their food in small bites, and most of the blood had been cooked out of the meat. The foxes had to refrain from having sex with any of the guests while the others ate, or even after the meal. It had been awfully confining and went against everything Relians were used to.

The entrepreneur made his pitch to Jeff, who pretended not to want to laugh at it but conversed with the young man anyway for the sake of civility. The other two business associates joined in with conversation of their own, and their wives interjected something obvious for the sole purpose of not allowing the other guests to forget they existed.

Mostly, the men talked business. Investments were up or down. Certain laws were pending in state or federal houses of congress that needed to be killed or encouraged, and Jeff said he would make a note to give his senators a call and make sure of their stance on those issues. He assured his business partners that the bills would be dealt with, for the senators' campaigns depended on his money. Everyone laughed at that, but the Relians smelled no amusement.

When the dinner concluded, Penny, seated at the end of the table opposite her husband, stood.

"Ladies and gentlemen, I have an announcement. As most of you know, the Relians have been here for almost a month. Well, last week Kylac told me there were a good many fruits and vegetables he had yet to try. Apparently the White House chef doesn't stock everything."

Everyone at the table laughed, raised a glass, and drank.

"So I had my assistant call around to various stores, looking for these things. I'm proud to announce she found them all. Oh, Lisa. Lisa, it's time."

A young Korean woman wearing a lot of makeup came from the kitchen carrying a large platter full of produce.

Kylac leaned over the table, scenting it. Deka watched the other guests, and from their reactions, sniffing in this way was one of those unwritten social crimes. He expected someone to tell Kylac to stop, and he even hoped someone would try it, but it was the nature of these gatherings to keep everything hidden and only present what everyone expected to see.

Lisa took Kylac's plate and replaced it with the platter. Kylac still sniffed it. Even Deka craned his neck over and took in the new odors.

"A Relian's opinion on some of the less common fruits," Mrs. Morton continued. "Now, no telling. Nobody say what anything is until he's had a bite."

Kylac's tail wagged. It was good to see Kylac laugh again. The fox was about to pick up a slice of something white and seeded with his claws, but he caught himself and used a fork. A few guests looked mildly amused by this.

He poked the slice and chewed it. His ear perked up. The guests laughed.

"Well, what do you think?" said Penny, still standing.

"It's very mild. A lot of flavor underneath the sugar. It reminds me of fruit that used to grow on Rel. Remember those," he turned to Deka, "the Gr'laise?"

Deka clicked his claws. "He used to throw them at me when we were young."

Everyone at the table laughed, the first genuine laugh of amusement all evening.

Deka continued when it quieted down. "They grew in large groves of trees, and before they ripened they were hard as rocks. Young Relians would often go down there and throw the fruit at each other."

"My goodness," said one of the wives, full of exasperation in her voice but not in her scent. "Was anyone hurt?"

"Of course not," said Kylac. "His scales were thick enough and so was my fur. I remember one time we managed to get a bunch of predators together. It turned into predators verses prey. Prey won."

"Which side were you on?" asked the young entrepreneur.

"I jumped between both sides."

That earned another hearty laugh and a drink. Deka clicked claws and took a swig from his water pitcher. None of the Relians could drink alcohol, and they refused to touch soda or anything artificial, so they always drank water.

"That was dragon fruit," said Penny.

Everyone at the table applauded. Deka knew why Penny had done this. Nobody else had Relians living with them, so the Mortons used them to impress business partners. Deka understood what it meant, but it had been amusing, and they had met a lot of people who claimed to be important this way, so he allowed it.

Kylac picked up the fork and placed something else on his tongue. He chewed a few times and then swallowed.

"This reminds me of darfon. It's a fruit on Xce that only grows underwater. The natives don't eat it, but other wildlife does."

"What is Xce?" asked Jeff.

"A planet that has a special ocean only about two to four feet deep," Deka said. "It's raining constantly on that part of the planet. A species of salamander as tall as humans lives there, as well as theropods like me, but they lack forelimbs."

"Fascinating," Jeff said. "Such creatures really are out there."

"They're predator and prey," said Sonjaa. "During the disaster, they almost destroyed themselves. Predator gave up hunting prey generations ago when each realized the other was intelligent. They live in harmony now, but for a while the birds started hunting the salamanders again.

Deka and Kylac prevented it from happening. I remember. I saw it. I lived it. I created a life for myself there. It was the first time I managed to gather around Deka while I was outside the universe..."

She looked down and took a few breaths. Deka wanted to stand beside her and rub necks, but it wouldn't have been the same as having a fox. Deka knew Sonjaa would only see that he had to leave his fox to be with her. He wanted to do it anyway, but etiquette forced them to be on opposite sides of the table, so Sonjaa had to deal with this alone.

"Also interesting about them," continued the fox. "They're not sight-based or scent-based. Their primary sense is hearing. You could be standing in front of them and they will not know you're there until you make a noise."

"Amazing," said the businessman sitting opposite Kylac. He did not act amazed.

"All that from a starfruit," Penny said, applauding.

Deka was aware of Lisa's scent. She stood behind Deka and Kylac. Deka did not wonder why nobody offered her a seat at the table, despite there being room.

Kylac forked a red berry on the table and munched it. He gagged, spat it out. Deka scanned the table but nobody looked as if Kylac had done something rude. In fact, they seemed genuinely amused.

"That is awful." The canine forked another bite of the dragonfruit and chewed it instead.

"I'm not surprised," said Penny. "That was a cranberry."

Everyone laughed, and their scents did match the action. They even applauded.

"Nobody likes cranberries," said Jeff. "Not plain anyway. They're always mixed with something."

Kylac had just swallowed. The people at the table expected another amusing story, so Kylac gave it to them.

"Reminds me of the berries that grow on some of the trees on Ixcy, but worse. Do birds on this planet eat these berries?"

A few people nodded and muttered.

"They taste like berries that evolved for avian tongues. There's a species of bird on Ixcy. They're about as tall as a human. They are one of the intelligent species on that world, and they eat those berries. They began eating them more when they found out their main source of food was intelligent. A fish. Someone in the past had the idea of hollowing out the tree trunks so they can talk to the fish in the water. The tree trunks carry the vibrations from the water to the air and back, making it possible for them to talk to each other. Birds will often eat the berries while in those trees as they converse with the fish."

"Really?" said one of the businessmen. "Do you think they'd like cranberries?"

"I think they would. They taste similar. A few other species would also like them."

"I see." He tapped his knife on the table in thought, then turned to Jeff. "I know the CEO of Ocean Spray. I think he might want to hear this."

"I was thinking the same thing. He's been looking to expand for quite some time."

"Oh, Jeff," Penny said, "let's not spoil the occasion with business." She laughed but was clearly annoyed.

"Have to think of things like this," her husband retorted. "It's how money is made. Conversations like this, moments like this." He turned to Kylac. "It's another thing I've been meaning to talk to you about. Cranberries, for example. There's over five hundred planets in the contacted universe, you say. How many people do you think would eat those berries?"

"There are ninety-seven species who might like them," said Deka. "Total population is about four hundred thousand."

Jeff blinked a couple times. "That's it?"

"Is what it?" Kylac asked.

"I was expecting advanced civilizations to have more people."

Kylac's tail wagged. "Do you believe size is proportional to importance?"

As a group, the dinner guests around the table laughed and clinked glasses.

Jeff had not. "That could be a problem, but it's the very early stages. I'm going to put this plainly. There are millions of people beyond Earth. We have things they might want, lots of untapped markets, and the two of you can get us into them. Cranberries are only the start, but let's focus on that as an example. You set up a few portals, we arrange export, and in return they send us something back."

One of the businessmen at the table picked up the thought and ran with it. "Start with trade at first, and once they get a taste of what the market has to offer, it's only a matter of time before they want more. They'll let industry and commerce in, they'll get jobs, start earning money, and that's when the market economy takes over."

Deka and Kylac glanced at each other. Deka met Sonjaa's eyes and then spoke to everyone at the table. "They're happy just as they are. The fish can swim anywhere. The birds can fly anywhere. There's plenty of food growing on the trees, and there are plenty of things to eat on other planets. The only work they do is to maintain the trees."

The men laughed. Even the women laughed, including Penny, who was now sitting. Lisa was not standing behind them anymore. Penny had silently dismissed her to the kitchen while Jeff had been speaking.

"All that time is wasted," Jeff said. "It benefits no one. When they learn the reward of a hard day's work, they'll wonder what they did with all their time."

"And those trees," someone else said. "How much time does it take to maintain them? We have sonar equipment, stereos, and microphones that can do two-way communication underwater. They'll have lots more free time once they don't have to do that anymore."

"Time they can spend in the new factories we install making that equipment," said the other businessman.

"Then forget the trees. We'll sell everyone their own personal communication devices."

"Once they have jobs," one of the wives said, "and all the benefits of the market, they'll want to work more. I'm sure even the fish you mentioned need things. Where there's want, there's a market. Maybe they can be useful to someone."

"The same will happen to other worlds," continued another businessman. "Once they see what other planets have because of the market, they will beg us to move our factories there so they can have money and buy our goods. If things are as you say they are, and there's no government, it won't take long at all for the people to be converted."

Everyone laughed, clinked glasses, and took a drink.

Sonjaa growled.

The laughter stopped. Everyone gave off fight-or-flight scent as they stared at her.

"No," she said.

Jeff met her eyes. "No what?"

"You're always going on about hard work and self-sufficiency as a virtue, but when you hear about people who are self-sufficient and work hard, you abhor it. You hear about civilizations on other planets, and this is your first thought. How to destroy them."

Jeff cleared his throat. "I believe there's been a misunderstanding. Nobody's going to hurt them. We'll be helping them by spreading employment to their land, gradually lifting them out of poverty."

"It really is your first thought!" she continued. "How to turn them into servants. They have portals to other planets. They can get their food and water anywhere. They don't need you or your microphones."

"Yes, we would have to form an association with all of the, uh, Archeons," said the young entrepreneur. "Someone would have to be in charge of restricting portal access. A toll system would be easy to set up. Same for the birds flying. We'll have to set up a license system to restrict that. We'll say it's for safety or something. With all that out of the way, we can bring cars or boats to that world. Besides, it can't be healthy, all those people going to and from other planets. Think of the diseases they must be spreading."

"There is no disease," Deka said, looking at him directly. "Our populations are low enough that disease is rare, and most species have much stronger immune systems compared to yours. You're the only ones in danger of epidemic."

"You *want* to inflict it on them," said Sonjaa, a growl rumbling under her voice. "Factories make pollution. Cars make pollution. It will make them sick, and the people who work in the factories will be around chemicals."

The businessman sitting nearest Jeff laughed. "It creates a new market for healthcare services. We'll have to make sure the government doesn't step in and provide it for the people. Would be a shame to let that profit slip away. Any problems that show up, the market has an answer."

The entrepreneur nodded in Deka's direction. "And there's also the question of what the Archeons are getting out this whole deal. From what I hear, you guys maintain portals all over the universe. But for what? Sounds like you're doing all the work and you get nothing back. People enjoy free access to other planets at your expense."

"I think once the Archeons realize this," continued one of the businessmen, "they'll see their society for what it is, and they'll join us. They'll make the people pay them for their work, and if the people don't, they'll cut their portals entirely. That's as it should be. A person's wealth is a good measurement of their value to society, and pretty soon they'll be able to recognize the Archeons as such. Nothing for free. Nothing for freeloaders."

Sonjaa snarled at everyone. She backed away from the table and stormed out, letting her killing claws tap the floor. Deka heard the front door open. He backed away from the table as well and regarded everyone.

"One of my closest companions lived on that world. His name was Chreeb, and you're talking about destroying his culture so you can make money. Relians only share a kill with people they get along with. I will not pretend to get along with you."

Kylac stood up, turning to Penny. "I will be happy to try the rest of the fruit later, but I will not indulge you with more stories. I'm speaking of real civilizations that thrive just fine without you. They're not fuel for fantasies of how to acquire more subordinate humans working on your behalf."

Kylac followed Deka out of the dining room. They walked down the long hall. Conversation continued in their absence. Host and hostess tried to cover up what just happened with more formalities, and they continued the discussion of how the contacted universe can be converted to a market economy. They walked out the front door, following Sonjaa's scent into the trees.

4

Sonjaa growled as she walked. She paused at a tree and slashed it and stabbed it with her killing claw. It did little damage, so she walked on. Deka and Kylac caught up to her. Sonjaa was snarling.

"Where are all the good people Stephen told us about?" she shouted.

"That's why we're here," Deka answered. "To find them."

"I hope the others are, because the only people in this house I like are the servants! *Those* fuckholes have no idea what they're saying! We're telling them about cultures on other planets, and that's all they can think about! How to enslave them!"

Deka clicked his claws whenever Sonjaa cursed. Everyone had told her she could make any vulgar word sound musical.

"It's great insight into their society."

"Let's leave! We can live anywhere! I can't put up with these people anymore!"

"Sonjaa—"

"I know, I know. We're not here for ourselves, and the other Relians aren't finished." She took a few breaths. "I'll tolerate them, but I will *not* apologize."

"They won't ask us to," Kylac said. "We're too important. They know they can't make us do anything, so they're trying to tempt us with money and status so we'll do as they wish."

Sonjaa was about to answer when a scent caught her nose. It came from just behind Deka. She snarled and chased it. Deka turned and followed, Kylac not far behind.

She was vaguely aware it was happening again. That scent made her want to kill. She blamed it for the loss of her fox, for dozens of planets, millions of lives. She channeled the anger of the dead, and they wanted that scent snuffed out. She wanted to do it for them, for Rupi and the children she would never have!

From the trees, she saw him. It wasn't Jeff this time, but that same man she saw in the White House. She snarled, sprinted toward him. He smiled at her, turned and ran. Sonjaa picked up speed. The man dashed out of the trees and onto the giant slab of concrete with the letter H painted on it. The helipad was unoccupied at the moment, illuminated by a light at each corner.

The man now gave off a panicked odor. Sonjaa caught up to him on top of the H and jumped on him. He fell to the concrete and slid. Sonjaa slipped a killing claw into his back, shoved a hand under his spine, and pulled upwards, screaming.

Deka and Kylac caught up and stood on either side of her as she hacked the man to ribbons. The more she hacked, the weaker the scent became, and she felt better. She began to slow down. Finally, she slouched, stepped out of the hollowed-out body cavity, and faced Deka.

Deka and Kylac glared at her, tails still, hands far apart. Kylac's remaining ear had turned backwards against his head. Sonjaa just now realized what she had done.

"You saw that?" she gasped.

Deka blinked. His scent spoke for him. So did Kylac's.

"Sonjaa..." said her mate. "Who was that?"

Sonjaa swallowed something warm and bloody. It was the best meat she'd ever tasted, but her stomach felt empty. "I don't know."

"Shit," Kylac said.

The body moved. The three Relians leaped back. The raptors crouched, toeclaws raised, hands splayed. Kylac also crouched, fur standing straight up, teeth bared. The body stood, blood pouring from every hole, his back wide open with pieces of organs still falling out. He turned to face Sonjaa, still smiling.

"Feel better?" he said.

Sonjaa backed away another step.

"I did not expect you to notice me," he said. "Maybe this will help."

His body morphed from a human's to a Relian canine's. Now instead of his body being hollowed out from the back, his chest and stomach were flayed open, and his organs were missing. Sonjaa could see his spine from the front.

"Friend?" she whispered.

Friend laughed with his voice, imitating a human sound. "This is how I looked and smelled the last time we met. Raptors haven't tasted fox meat for centuries, so I hope you enjoyed eating me."

He turned around and met Deka's and Kylac's panicked scents. "And you two—"

"Friend, what the fuck!" Sonjaa screamed.

Friend spun around again. "I'll explain in just a moment. Not everyone is here yet. I hope you got most of the anger out of your system, Sonjaa. I'm here to talk. Believe it or not, the three of you are the most interesting people in the universe. I will tell you why as soon as the rest of the guests arrive. They will be here any second."

A Krone-sized sphere opened up just off to the side of the helipad, and Norh stepped through. As soon as his tail was on this side of the sphere, it shut. Norh stared at Friend as he walked toward the concrete square.

"That's one," said the half-eaten fox. "When Rive makes his way here, we'll be ready to begin. Until then, I have just enough time to tell you that those men mean exactly what they say. If they ever got off this planet, that's the first thing they'd try. Build factories, isolate the people, get them into the market economy, and force the avians and the fish on Ixcy to do work. Everything that had once been plentiful and free would now be scarce and cost money, but most important, it would be under their control. I can predict how they will make it happen. Gradually they start to convince young Archeons of the benefits of the market. Men like them elevate those Archeons to exclusive positions of power, and in return the Archeons monetize and restrict portal access. They repeat the promises to the people of other planets, and the people believe them. If the people don't, the Archeons threaten to close the portals unless they are paid for the service of maintaining the ways, which forces the people to go to work. The people give up their freedom for the stuff the market produces. Portals close, huge tolls are enacted, passage is regulated. The businessmen set up new governments on those planets to enact policies that keep the people desperate, hungry, and thirsty, and now the people have to rely on men like that for their survival. They will support corrupt governments who oppress the people because a lack of services creates markets to profit from, and without isolation, the market would never exist. As long as the people actually have free choice to accept the terms of the work or chose to live their own lives, their idea can never succeed. You will be relieved to know every Archeon in the contacted universe is smart enough to realize all of this and does not share these primate-derived creatures' sense of values. They will never let it happen, but hypothetically, that's how it can."

A Relian-sized way opened up and Rive emerged from it, straight from CJ's office. The sphere closed, and Rive stared at the walking, dissected fox on the helipad.

"Welcome, Rive," said Friend, spreading his arms.

Rive smelled as confused as everyone else. He walked onto the concrete and joined the circle that had formed around the gutless, walking corpse shaped like a Relian canine.

"I appeared to both of you while Sonjaa was hunting me. Now was the time to talk, but first Sonjaa had to purge some anger. She surprised me in the White House. I did not expect her to recognize me."

He addressed Sonjaa to her face now. "I believe you can sense me because you used to be in the Lake. I don't understand how or why, and I did not anticipate it, and that is rare. Oh, but you want me to start at the beginning. Yes, you're still in the universe and need linear reasoning to comprehend anything, so I'll begin with the day you ripped me apart and ate me.

"I had spent years figuring out the equations that proved something exists beyond the universe. Yes, I destroyed some planets in the process, but eventually I figured it out. It took me that long to stabilize the portals that led outside the universe. Then you three cornered me on Reyno and ended my life because you were afraid I would kill more people. In my last breaths, I figured out what Sonjaa had done, and how she managed to survive outside the universe for so long before coming back. It was a puzzle I had yet to contemplate because the equations had kept me so busy.

"I once thought the conscious mind cannot exist outside the universe, but I was wrong. The conscious mind is the *only* thing that can exist there, in the Lake. I believe that's what makes up the real universe. Consciousness itself. I simply moved my mind into the Lake just before my body died in this universe.

"Sonjaa showed me it was possible, but she is not an Archeon, so the perspective overwhelmed her. I am now where Sonjaa was. I think that's why she recognized me in the White House. She can sense my projections subconsciously because she used to make them when she was trapped here. I understand what she did while she was in the Lake, and I have perfected it. I'm not actually here right now. I'm projecting myself into this universe, just as she once did. I can change reality around me as I want because I am outside the universe, everywhere at once, past, present, and the calculated future."

He paused, clearly not for his own benefit. Stephen spoke first.

"So you're Q?"

Friend suddenly had a tail again, and it wasn't saturated in blood. It wagged.

"Yes, yes, the human inside the Krone body understands! Excellent metaphor! Deka, you think fiction is a waste of time, but this is exactly why lone species create it: to help them understand impossible things. But I'm not omnipotent. I know exactly how this universe works, and I can change things within it, but the Lake is still a mystery to me. I'm in it, but I don't fully understand where I am. I have not been brave enough to travel too far from this universe. I am afraid I won't be able to find my way back here, and then I will be lost in oblivion, so to speak."

"Then what brings you here?" Deka said.

"And how have you not destroyed the universe by now?" Kylac said at the same time.

"I am here because of you three." He turned and pointed to Deka, Kylac, and then Sonjaa. "I can tell you where every atom in the universe was when it began, what life forms it will be part of, and where it will be when the universe spreads so far apart no atoms will ever touch again, but you... You are three little holes in the universe. You have no numbers. That can only mean one thing. At some point in the future, you will come into contact with the Lake."

Friend turned around and faced Rive just as the metal raptor opened his mouth.

"Nobody else?" Rive said.

Friend suddenly had internal organs and a beating heart. "No. You, Norh, and Stephen will never find the Lake. I asked you to come here so you would be in the loop, as they say here. It's a little annoying, coming down to this level. I never would have bothered if I didn't keep seeing these three holes reaching through spacetime. Everyone else has a clear, calculable path from beginning to end, but not Deka, Sonjaa, or Kylac.

"Just before I died on Reyno, I realized I was about to overpower Kylac. I would have won, but Sonjaa stepped in and changed the future. For a while, you three did have numbers. That's why I waited so long to come here and tell you I'm still alive. But then something changed. Anything that comes in contact with the Lake can alter the universe. It's the only place where it can be altered.

"You three are the only ones who surprise me. Everything else is predictable, but not you. I want to be close to that. I think if I am trapped in a reality where I know everything, I will go insane, which brings me to Kylac's question."

He turned, faced the other fox. Friend now had skin and fur covering his body. He didn't resemble walking carrion anymore, but much of his fur was still blood-soaked.

"You were right, Kylac. If you hadn't stopped me, I would have satisfied my scent anxiety. Being able to calculate the universe and everyone inside it meant I felt everyone's scent close to me. I had never experienced uncontrollable panic before. My instincts distracted me from my goal. I can admit that now, and I would have killed everyone to calm them. Why not? They aren't people, just collections of atoms that technically don't exist anyway. Without knowledge of their scents bothering me, I would have been free to work out the remaining equations alone in peace.

"So as soon as I moved myself into the Lake, I separated my old ways from my higher mind. Now I am free of my old ways, and I am certain of how the universe works. Once a conscious creature understands the Lake, this medium where the universe resides, that creature can create a new reality. A new universe. One they can control and manipulate. I'm not there yet, and that is the mystery I'm working on now. Once I understand the Lake, I will be free to travel from this universe to any of the others. Then I can return to mine whenever I want. I'm reasonably sure that's how it works.

"In the meantime, I can be everywhere in this universe at once. It is portal physics in reverse. Instead of opening up multiple ways through the universe at once, I send myself to multiple places in the universe. I know hundreds of planets the contacted universe has yet to meet. Some of them are still primitive, and some will eventually make contact. Others are lone species even a Krone has yet to discover. I will tell you about some of them when you have more time to listen."

The others breathed. The blood in Friend's fur disappeared, and his fur was now pristine, fluffy red, black, and white. Friend continued.

"Rive is terrified that I'm still alive and free and have such power over everyone. Norh is not confident anyone can separate their animal nature from their higher thoughts. Stephen is still trying to figure out what the hell I'm talking about, and Norh will share the memories with him shortly."

He turned and faced Deka, Kylac, and Sonjaa.

"I can't calculate what the three of you are thinking. I'm drawn to this. Something in the universe I can't trace from beginning to end—even the atoms in your bodies are unpredictable! I have to know why! I have to be close to this! It might be important. As soon as I figure this out, I'll make a new universe, and then I will be able to journey away from this one completely."

Deka sat down on the concrete, a hand over one eye. "Shit."

"Don't worry, Deka. I haven't destroyed any planets or people. I got rid of my old ways before I was even tempted to do that. Kylac was right. I had untamed animal instincts. I wasn't convinced of that until my last moments; everything I was doing didn't feel like old ways—I just wanted to be calm so I could figure this out. Opening portals on everyone was the easiest way to do it, but I was fully aware of myself so I thought it couldn't be instinct. I'd never reverted before. Rive never had to bring me back from anything, so I didn't think I had animal ways to tame, but it happened. I realized it just before I entered the Lake. All of you were right to stop me. I heeded Kylac's warning, and my reward is a perspective Archeons have only imagined."

"Can you restore what we destroyed?" Kylac said.

"No. I can't change the past. I tried that many times and it didn't work."

Kylac's lips curled in a half-snarl. "Then what's the point?"

"Discovery. I took the next leap—the one I wanted to make with you. That's why I took you with me, Kylac. I wanted to share this with someone. The solution! A way to leave the universe and enter the Lake! I would never have figured it out if not for Sonjaa showing me how it could be done."

"I should have eaten you faster," she said.

"You wanted me to suffer for all the pain I caused. For the planets I destroyed and the lives I ruined as I worked on discovering what lies outside the universe. I understand that. I have been watching all of you for some time." He turned, approached Kylac. "I know the pain you're in. You don't think you can handle what you know. What you had to do to acquire the knowledge. You have hidden from it, so now it's an insect burrowing under your skin. It's not too late, Kylac. You can dive into the Lake, too. You can join me here. I know my way around. I will show you how to survive."

Kylac growled, his single ear flattening against his head. "You abducted me! You forced me to learn about the Lake! I destroyed entire planets because of you!" He turned and walked up the sidewalk that led to the house. A few paces later, a second Friend appeared on the path in front of him.

"You can handle it," he said. "I can show you how to separate your higher mind from your old ways and be free of them forever."

"I will never forgive you." Kylac walked past him toward the house. The second Friend watched from the sidewalk.

The others at the helipad looked from one instance of the fox to the other.

"I did not expect him to walk away from me," said the Friend on the H. "This is so exciting!"

"My God, I don't believe this," said Stephen.

The first Friend turned. "You'll be interested to know that I am where God would be. Just being here shows that the universe had a creator, and whoever that was had reached a level of knowledge to create your universe. But this person doesn't seem to be around anymore. I presume this person moved on. Decided to explore the Lake and learn what other universes are out there. That's what I want to do, but I don't think I can do it alone."

Deka rose and walked up to him. He opened his mouth, grabbed Friend by the neck and twisted his head off. He chewed the skull, cracking it, spilling blood and brain matter out, and spat it aside. The headless fox stood in place for a few seconds. A new head appeared where the old one had been, and the blood and gore ceased to exist.

"That was so wonderful!" Friend said, ears blooming, mouth parted in a human-like smile. "I didn't expect that! I'll be around, but nobody else will be able to see, smell, or hear me. I won't interfere with anything that happens. Not that I would want to. This planet is on a path to a clear end, and I understand it means a lot to the collections of atoms who inhabit it. The three of you are all I want."

Deka's killing claws rose. "If you touch my fox again, I will kill you every time I see you."

Friend's tail waved about. "You will grow tired of that quickly. I won't leave without Kylac. I'm sure I will succeed in convincing him to come with me eventually. You and Sonjaa, too, but I don't know how, and that is breathtaking."

Sonjaa huffed. "I wish I could have swallowed you whole." She turned around and dashed up the sidewalk.

Deka growled at him, then turned to Rive and Norh.

"If you want to come in, I'll warn you the house is full of assholes, and they would love to discuss their plan for enslaving the contacted universe with you. They're very proud of it."

He turned around and sprinted to the house. The first instance of Friend walked casually up the sidewalk. He joined his second self, and they walked together up the path. A third instance of Friend appeared on the helipad facing Rive, and at the same time a fourth appeared in front of Norh.

The one in front of Rive said: "You and she will be very happy together, but you will outlive her by a long time."

Simultaneously, the one in front of Norh said: "The two of you will change the world, but not the one you expect."

Both foxes winked away like portals, leaving the metal raptor and the Krone alone on the H. They stared at the empty landing pad for a moment.

"He barely looked at me," Rive said.

The Krone turned to Rive. Norh spoke. "Or us." Stephen took over. "Your fox."

Rive looked down. "He destroyed fifty-six planets, millions of lives, and Kylac. I would have been happy never to talk about him again. Now... He's alive."

"If he is correct," said Norh, "and he can predict everyone in the universe, then he will not be interested in us."

Rive looked at the house in the distance. "I'm glad. I should want to kill him again, but I feel nothing."

Stephen spoke again. "Who was he talking about? Who is she?"

"I don't know. But that was his final word to me. He has nothing to say."

Stephen's wings lowered, and he turned to the building. So many lights were on in a house with so few residents. He turned back to Rive.

"Shall we go inside?"

"I deal with a lot of assholes these days. I can handle this."

The Krone's wings stretched out, then folded back against his flanks. "Please tell them I'm making a way into the drawing room between the pool table and the window. It will be large enough for my head and neck."

"I'll warn them." Rive walked up the path.

The Krone stepped off the helipad and lay in the grass.

"How long should we wait?" Stephen asked.

"Ten minutes should be enough time. And Stephen... What is a Q?"

Stephen laughed through their wings and fed Norh the entire series.

5

The Krone's head and some of his neck protruded from a small sphere near the pool table. The metal and skin raptor stood off to the side, facing the other way. Half the people stood around the sphere and chatted up the Krone, holding glasses of liquor or wine. The others had gathered around Rive.

Jeff had taken position beside the talking Krone head, acting as if he had summoned Norh here and the others had to go through him to get to the Krone. Sonjaa was sure it wasn't a conscious act on his part, but it had the desired effect. The guests acted impressed by the company Jeff kept, and the mood had lightened.

Friend sat on the ceiling, looking down at the conversations, smiling like a human. Kylac sat on the couch and watched the televisions. Sonjaa and Deka lay in front of the couch on either side of Kylac's legs. Sonjaa tuned out the noise and listened to the people chatting up Rive and the Krone.

They asked Stephen and Norh about the various cultures that existed across the contacted universe, and as Norh spoke, the businessmen brainstormed about how they could convert these cultures to capitalism. The Krone played along, indulging their fantasies, obviously to find out how far they would go with the ideas. Sonjaa found it disturbing how often they laughed at topics such as the destruction of culture and monetary servitude and pollution creating demand for other markets.

The group around Rive wanted to hear some horror stories of Relian Relations and general updates on how things were really going with integration. Most did not trust the media's liberal bias and wanted the truth. Rive's answers seemed to disappoint them. There had been no serious incidents thus far, and the people the Relians had chosen to live with had been eager to learn about a new species. Everyone had adjusted well to aliens living among them. With no dirt on the Relians, the guests found other things to laugh at, such as details about the foxes' promiscuity among humans.

Friend's muzzle manifested next to Deka's, Sonjaa's, and Kylac's ears and whispered. "This was a bad idea, you know. All these people believe Jeff keeps company with a Krone, which has raised his status in their eyes. They'll take any business venture he suggests. It will cause several million people a lot of anguish years from now."

"How?" Deka growled.

"A mine in South Africa he wants to invest in. He'll convince others to join him, the mine will have funding, and it would not have happened at all if not for them coming inside."

"You told them to come here," Deka growled. "If you don't like the results, just leave."

"This is why I'd rather all of you come with me now. The longer I'm here, the wider the effects of my actions spread."

Now Sonjaa growled. She wanted to tell Friend to leave the universe so he could figure out the Lake, but as soon as her mind neared it, she felt nauseated and she forgot the rhythm of breathing. She swallowed stomach acid and slinked away from the thought. She watched Rive.

The metal raptor looked so comfortable standing alone. She craned her neck, cutting through the other scents to find Rive's. He smelled so peaceful in the midst of these people. She shivered with envy. She noticed Deka had turned to her. He nuzzled her neck and met her eyes.

"What's wrong?"

Sonjaa shivered for a few breaths. "It's Friend... I was just thinking... about where he is. What he can do..."

Deka leaned closer. "What can he do?"

Sonjaa opened her mouth. She convulsed harder. Her mind felt as if it would fall into the abyss again if she thought about it too hard. She almost uttered a syllable, but her stomach lurched. She tucked her muzzle into her chest and convulsed as she took conscious control of her breathing and came back down.

Deka placed a hand on her neck, leaned close. "Sonjaa, you have to face this eventually."

"I can't. It hurts. I'm never doing that again."

"It's there. It's in your subconscious. You're thinking about it all the time. You just don't realize it. If you bury it too deep, it will hurt you."

Sonjaa leaned on him and shivered as she breathed and cleared her mind. His warm touch was so nice and comforting, but it wasn't Rupi. She could soothe Sonjaa with just her scent. Deka felt concerned and caring, but she hadn't been with him as a hatchling; she hadn't grown up helping him tame his animal side and become a thinking, happy person. Her fox was gone. Sonjaa was alone.

Deka wrapped his neck around hers while she convulsed. She didn't hear the rest of the conversation, but some time later, Rive took his leave of the party, and they now congregated around the Krone head. Norh was telling them about vast mineral deposits in the caves of Kronia, and someone began floating ideas for road construction and who to contact for mining. Sonjaa looked up from the floor and turned to the Krone. She saw Norh's wings fluttering behind the portal. The humans did not know the Krone was laughing at them. Rive walked to the bar, filled a glass of water, and took a long drink.

Friend's muzzle appeared in the carpet in front of Sonjaa. "Don't feel bad. I don't understand where I am either, and I'm an Archeon. Must be even more difficult for you to come to grips with where you were. What you were doing... How you came back..."

Sonjaa gasped a few times, and yet no air entered her lungs. Deka growled at the carpet and stabbed it with his hand-claws. It did not affect the face in the carpet at all. Sonjaa rose from the floor and walked around the couch to the bar, still struggling to breathe, wishing Rupi were here, wishing she could find a way beyond this block in her mind that made her censor every thought. She stumbled up to the bar and faced Rive.

"Bartender..." She gasped. "Do you have any helpless herbivores back there that will scream for mercy as I slice them apart and devour them?"

Rive clicked his claws. He gestured with his muzzle toward the group around Norh. "The man wearing the green necktie claims to be vegan."

She rubbed her claws as she turned her head and looked at Deka. His fox was also shivering. She wondered what Friend had said to him. Deka looked desperate to comfort him, but Kylac had also been beyond reach since the disaster. She turned to Rive again, head low, hands limp. Rive's posture and scent were full of confidence. She almost growled at him.

"Rive..." she began. The metal raptor waited a few beats for her to finish. "How do you do it? Your fox is here, and he wants nothing to do with you. How can you be so happy?"

Rive held his hands apart as he set his empty glass down. He took another glass from under the counter and filled it with water. He slid it to Sonjaa with his metal hand.

"I've been asking myself that for some time, too. I noticed you haven't been yourself without a fox. But I..."

"Maybe you're hiding in your work."

He curled his neck. "I do sleep in the White House and wait for CJ to come back. I answer the phone while she's home."

"I wish I could adjust like you have. I miss my fox so much. I want to talk about the Lake, but every time I get—"

The word carried weight in her mind, and she thought she felt her mind separating from her body, sinking into a hole. She braced her arms on the bar and held herself upright, shaking and dry-heaving. When the wave passed, she picked up the glass and threw the water into her mouth. She set the glass down again and continued panting to calm herself.

"Every time I see him... He reminds me of... Of where I was."

She lost her voice.

Rive tapped her claws. She turned her eyes down to the polished countertop and tried to clear her mind. The people in the group around the Krone began talking all at once. Their voices sounded so loud, and their words hit her all at the same time. She felt her mind sinking into the abyss, and this time she had not thought about the Lake. She looked up at him. She growled.

"Rive, I would kill to have my fox back and here you are pretending yours isn't even here."

Rive's hands sagged. Sonjaa continued.

"Talk to him! He's right there! How can you let this pass?"

Rive looked down.

Sonjaa growled louder and sprinted out of the parlor and down the hall to the front door. The further away she ran from the voices, the happier she felt. She threw open the door and ran to the porch. She breathed easier now that walls muffled the conversations.

Friend's head floated in front of her. "Deka is trying to decide who needs help more. You or Kylac. Should I tell him you do?"

Sonjaa's killing claws rose. "You killed my fox and you don't even care! You could be with Rive again, but you're pretending he doesn't exist! Why you?! Why couldn't *my* fox come back? Why do I have to be alone?!"

Friend's muzzle vanished. The night air cooled her scales. She shivered. Her legs wobbled her down to a sitting position. She held herself and caught her breath. It was hard enough living with the Mortons. Now she had to live with Friend.

Maggie

I

"Yes, we were at the grocery store an hour ago," Sors said.

The officer at the door did not look at the raptor. He spoke to the human standing next to the raptor. "The station received a number of phone calls about your dinosaur."

"He's not a dinosaur, officer," said the young man.

"I know, but that's what the calls were."

"Did we do something wrong?" Sors said.

The officer did not look at him or the fox just behind him. "Accusations of threatening gestures, eyeing children, that sort of thing."

"The store has cameras," said the human. "Did you check with them?"

"That's my next stop, but I wanted to get your side first. What happened, Mister...?"

"James Summit. This is Sors, and his fox Prael. We were shopping. Sors spent some time at the deli counter. We passed a lot of people. Nobody acted threatened then."

The officer's uniform read *Officer J. Athens, township of Maggie, California.*

"Did anyone give you three any looks?"

"All the time since I came back from the convention," James answered. "We try to say hello, but everyone walks away. Even the military guys."

"Did you approach or pass any small children?"

"We did," Sors answered. "A boy came running up to me yelling 'Yoshi, yoshi'."

Officer Athens held eye contact with James. "How old was the boy, Mr. Summit?"

"Five or six. Why don't you ask Sors? It'll be faster."

"This will only take a moment more. What happened then?"

James narrowed his eyes and looked at Sors.

"He asked for a ride," said the raptor. "I lowered my neck to be at his eye level and told him I'm not for riding. He started crying and walked away."

Officer Athens wrote on the pad. He addressed his question to his pen. "Why do you think he did that?"

"Teeth," Sors said. "The boy wasn't expecting to see them."

"His voice is awfully gruff, Mr. Summit," said the officer. "Could've scared the kid, too."

"I heard him," James said. "He was doing everything he could to be as nonthreatening as possible."

"There was something else. Something about an altercation at the cash register?"

James was happy to answer that one. "The cashier turned out her light and left right as we got up to her. There were two more people in line behind us, and she left."

"Was it her break?"

"I worked as a cashier. Everyone knows you don't walk away while people are in line. She left because of us. It's the third time someone did that, so I yelled at her to get back here and do her job."

"That caused a scene?" said the officer.

"Of course it did. I called her out on what she was do-ing. Lots of people have been doing that. Walking away from us, turning around when they see we're in the aisle. I try to go up to them and say hello, but they avoid us. Hon-estly it's scaring me, and I've had enough of it."

"I understand this is the fourth time you've had the po-lice called on you, Mr. Summit?"

"Yes, unfortunately."

"What were the first three incidents?"

"Someone called on us because they thought Sors was stalking them. The second call was about Prael walking outside without shorts on. The third… I don't know what that was about. Someone complained about Sors making noises and thought I was in trouble. We hadn't made a sound all day."

The officer took a moment to catch up, then he clipped the pen to the board and held it at his side.

"Thank you, Mr. Summit. That's all I need. I'll be pay-ing that store a visit shortly. I suggest you be a little more careful around town."

"What's that supposed to mean?"

"Be a little less confrontational. Stay away from peo-ple's children. That kind of thing."

"The child approached me," said Sors, "and that girl left her lane while there were people still in line."

"She rang out the four people in front of us," James said. "No. That's not right, and I'm not going to take it."

"We'll be in touch, Mr. Summit. Thank you for your time. Have a nice day."

The officer turned around and walked down the steps. His car was still running, so he drove off as soon as he climbed in. James closed the door.

"Did we do something wrong?" Prael said, adjusting the pink shorts which belonged to Beth.

"No, we're not doing anything wrong, but I'm getting worried. I was wondering when they'd knock on the door. Have you noticed the police have been following us a lot?"

"Not that I've seen," Sors said.

James walked to the kitchen and poured himself a cup of coffee. "Cop cars. I see them rolling down this street several times a day. They drive by these apartments real slow. They were just waiting for an excuse to walk up and talk to us."

Sors walked in, hands apart, looking at him with his head tilted. "Is it bad that he talked to us? Now he knows what happened."

"I don't get that feeling. It's like when I was middle school. Bullies ask you to explain yourself, so you do, and they just wanted more stuff to laugh at." He took a long swig from the cup. "I don't know what's happening. Everybody I know was talking about the aliens on Earth. They were so interested in them on TV. Well, here you are. Now they're calling the police."

"We should make more of an effort to meet them," Prael said.

James shook his head. "I don't think it's gonna work."

"We have to try."

"They'll take it as aggression. Another excuse to call the police."

"We'll be as nonthreatening as possible," Sors said.

"That's the problem. You have claws and teeth. There's no way you can't look threatening unless you wear boxing gloves and a veil. A big veil."

The doorknob turned. Beth walked in, dressed in work clothes and smelling like a deep fryer. Prael pranced away from his raptor and hugged her, licking her face. She closed the door, rubbed him between his ears.

They walked to the kitchen together. She kissed James, holding him around the waist. Prael nudged James's mouth aside and snuck his mouth where James's had been. Beth continued kissing him as though nothing were different.

After a few seconds watching, James growled at Prael. The fox pretended to be intimidated, whimpered and slinked away. Sors clicked his claws. James replaced his mouth where it had been. Beth hadn't moved the whole time and continued kissing whoever happened to be in front of her. Finally she laughed, smacked James on the arm, and walked to the refrigerator.

"Have a good day off?" she said.

"No. Got the cops called on us."

"Again?"

"Hopefully the last time. We're not going to try anything from now on. Won't talk to anybody, won't look at anyone. Don't give them a reason to be afraid of us."

Beth closed the door. She had a beer in her hand. "What? You're going to let them win?"

"The cops are on us now. It's different. I don't think they're on our side."

"That's ridiculous." She twisted the cap off, tossed it in the trash. "This is California. We're the most liberal state in the country. We have aliens in our house! We're not gonna hide them from our neighbors because they don't have the guts to talk to them."

"Not just them. The whole freakin' town."

She walked across the kitchen, past James. "We're gonna parade them around like we always do. If they don't like it, that's their problem. If we give in, they win, right Prael?"

She put an arm around him and leaned on the fox. The fox leaned on her, grinning with his muzzle, suddenly not wearing shorts.

2

James woke up in the middle of the night. Beth lay in the middle of the bed. He peeked over her. Prael lay on the other side. James smiled.

The day he brought the Relians home from the convention in Monterey, he somehow ended up buried to the hilt in the fox. Beth had come home from work later that day, since the restaurant wouldn't give her the time off. She knew he had slept with the fox. She had later told him he acted differently around him, being closer than she had ever seen him next to another guy. Beth had assured him it looked adorable.

She found Prael enticing as well, and she wanted to try it. The news was true: foxes had a smell that could make anyone do anything, it seemed. To James's surprise, there had been no feelings of jealousy. In fact, the Relians knew it could ignite those feelings, so they had called attention to them, played with them, made fun of them. It had actually been fun. He had done things he never knew he would do, and she had done things she had long sworn she would never do, and it seemed to have opened things up even more.

James sat up. Sors lay at the foot of the bed, on the hard floor. James did not understand how he found the floor more comfortable than the bed, but it had worked out, as he didn't know if the bed could handle his weight.

The clock read two in the morning, and he was cold and thirsty. He threw on his bathrobe and walked to the kitchen. He picked up the coffee pot and filled his cup. As he leaned over the sink and took a sip, he heard claws clicking on the floor.

"Are you always awake?" James said.

"Lately, yes," Sors said. "Are you sure you don't have insomnia?"

"I dunno if it's that. I just wake up at two a.m. every night. Kick around for a couple hours, go back to sleep."

"Maybe if you wouldn't drink so much bean water."

James giggled, turned around and leaned against the counter. The only light came from a nightlight plugged into a wall socket behind him. All James could see was Sors' white underbelly and the yellow stripes that ringed his arms. The rest of his body was dark green, a shadow on top of the darkness. Now that he thought about it, he really did look a little like Yoshi.

"I never get wired on coffee. It's soda that makes me hyper." He smiled. "What's your excuse for being awake?"

"I haven't hunted in months."

"That makes you restless?"

"Yes. The last time I hunted was under human supervision. That was the first hunt I had been on in a very long time. The planet Rive moved us to after the disaster did not have anything I could hunt. Food only tastes good when I have to take it down. Some prey is like coffee to me. Other prey is like pizza. The flavor is in the hunting."

"I remember you said that. What's pizza to you?"

"Do you mean what my favorite kind of kill is?"

James nodded.

He shifted. His hands were together. "There's a species of carnivore on Apotha I like called the Esi. Quadrupeds, horns everywhere, covered in thin fur. They're predators, and they don't run. When they're being hunted, they fight back." He growled a little, bobbing at the waist. "That's where these came from."

He turned his right flank. The dim nightlight highlighted the scars across it. James had noticed them at the convention in the hotel room, but didn't ask about them. In this poor light, he looked like a creature straight out of a horror film.

"I joined six other carnivores one hunt. Four different species, none of them mine. There's something about being among hunters. We cornered it, took it down. It caught me down the side with its claws. It was painful, but the pain felt so good, and when we brought it down, that meat tasted so good. Mounted three of those hunters over the body while the blood was still running down our necks. Prael cleaned the wounds for me and shared the meat. Other carnivores know who the foxes are and they always let the fox eat. That was my first Esi. Went back to Apotha dozens of times after that to take one down. Every time the meat gets better. The more it fights back, the better it tastes."

James laughed, pushed away from the counter, and walked into the living room. "What's your idea of coffee?"

"If by that you mean a species that's good for a quick meal to perk me up, I would choose a species of mammal on Lant. The locals don't have a name for them besides *hopping mammal*, so that's what we call them, too. They're huge, about half my size, but harmless. They run fast. I love it when they run. It's not as good when they don't fight back, but running still makes me excited. It's what I hunt when I'm not in the mood to fight for my meal. They taste better when they're still alive."

"You eat them alive?"

"Only the Lant mammals. They might escape if I don't start eating them right away. I tried doing that to an Esi, and it ruins the flavor. Best to wait until they're dead before eating them. But the Lant mammals taste better when they're screaming."

James picked up the remote. "You must laugh at coffee."

"Actually I often wonder what it would be like not to have to chase down and kill everything I eat. Sometimes I look at Prael and wish I could just reach up to a tree and pick something. My body is built for killing, so I think nothing of it when I do. Being around herbivores and omnivores reminds me not everyone is like me."

"What's it smell like to you?"

"Plant water. Not something I want to drink. Just information."

"And what about the beef and pork I buy?"

"It is bland and unexciting."

"Like eating plain pasta every day."

"Something like that. To enjoy something, I need to kill it. Not every raptor likes prey that fights back. Some prefer the runners, some prefer prey that eludes predators, leaves false trails, climbs trees. Others really like to hear prey scream as they eat it. Some don't. To my race, it's the difference between someone liking pizza instead of lasagna."

Sors rubbed his claws.

James was about to sit down and watch a western. There was usually one on TV this time of night. James had had a thing for westerns ever since he was a kid, and they had become a late-night companion for him as an adult.

A gust of wind blew through the open window. The venetian blinds swung inward slightly and clapped against the window frame, drawing James's attention. He saw something through the blinds and straightened up. He walked up to the window, pulled a slat down, and peeked outside. A police car sat across the street, hidden in the dark but just barely visible by the light of a nearby street lamp.

"Oh God."

"What?"

"Now they're watching us."

Sors walked across the living room and peered through the window blind. "Why is he out there?"

"Trying to get something on us. Shit, they might have our phone tapped—they might have a bug in the house—the cop may be listening to us right now."

"I thought that was not allowed."

"That kid might've given them probable cause. If they think you and Prael are dangerous they'll have every right to watch us. Shit, they're waiting for us to do something."

Sors backed away from the blinds and turned. "Let's go meet him."

James let the blind go. "What? No!" The raptor was already at the door and turning the knob. "No, don't go out there!"

Sors paused with the door cracked slightly. "Do you not want to find out if he is listening? If he wants to know us, we should invite him in. He might need coffee to stay awake."

"If we go out there, he'll call it a threat."

"I'll keep my claws hidden." He opened the door the rest of the way and then walked outside.

"Damn." James leaped to the door, stepping into Beth's flip-flops. His had broken a long time ago and he hadn't bothered to buy a new pair yet.

Sors had reached the bottom of the steps by the time James made it outside. He ran down the stairs and jogged after the reptile as fast as he could in these shoes. He noticed the raptor had curled his hands as far as he could, trying to hide the claws. His killing claws were down but there was no hiding those things.

James didn't catch up until Sors was in the middle of the street. The officer in the car watched them approach. It was Athens, the same man who had talked to them earlier, but not wearing sunglasses.

James figured he should speak before the raptor. "Hello, officer. Something going on in the neighborhood?"

"I can't discuss that, sir."

Sors stopped at the window and crouched at the knees to be eye level with the officer. The officer looked like he wanted to raise a hand and shoo a fly away. He turned his cheek aside just enough to avoid looking at him, and James noticed he was holding his breath.

"Would you like to come inside?" Sors said. "James has insomnia, so he made coffee to help himself sleep." He clicked his claws, keeping them hidden from the officer's view.

"Please back away from the car."

Sors pulled his muzzle out of the window and stood just outside of it. "Is this a stakeout? Are we the ones you're watching?"

The officer looked at James. "Sir, if you don't keep your dinosaur under control, I will have to arrest both of you for obstructing an officer."

James was at the window. The streetlight lit the car just enough for him to see the remote sound amplifier on the passenger seat. It looked like something out of a spy movie, resembling a satellite dish attached to a revolver. He had not known they really existed until now. James lay his arm around Sors' neck and guided him back from the car a step.

"I think you should answer him," James said. "Do you have a warrant to use that?"

"Sir, this is the last time I'm warning you."

"We're not doing anything, officer."

The officer opened the door and stepped out. He had a hand on his side. James backed away, pulling the raptor with him. They were in the middle of the street, slowly retreating. The officer stood with a hand on his holster.

"I can smell the fear on you," Sors said. "It comes out in your sweat. I came down to say hello."

Officer Athens unbuttoned his holster and took out the gun and aimed it. James couldn't tell who he was aiming at.

"Get back inside."

James and Sors walked backwards.

"Get back! Get inside, and do not approach a police officer in the line of duty again!"

James turned them around and walked them up the stairs to the apartment, Sors keeping pace. He had left the front door open, so he let Sors go in first. The officer was still pointing his gun at them. He closed the door and flicked off the light.

James walked to the window, shut it, and peeked through the blinds. The officer climbed back into his car. The car did not move.

"James, I—"

The human touched a finger to his lips. Sors had long ago learned it was the gesture to stop speaking. James pointed to his ear, then to the cop. Sors peeked through the same blind.

James's heart raced. He wished he could speak. Sors was still learning how to read, so he couldn't even write down what he wanted to tell him.

3

Local grocery stores were harder and harder to find these days, and Beth was positive this place stayed open purely because of Sors. The owner hadn't accepted food stamps until she told them how much meat their raptor needed. Beth practically begged them to start accepting because she knew they had the best meat in the county. It was all local, the butcher was an actual person, and the cuts were fresh. No preservatives, no processing, as close to killing it personally as the Relians would get.

The tiny store was maybe twice the size of the apartment living room, with just three aisles full of essentials, and it was so close in here the shoppers had no choice but to talk to each other.

Beth stood at the counter in the back. She heard the butcher around the corner chopping the cow apart. Sors stood next to her, neck stretched, as if trying to see what was happening with his ears. He had walked around back many times and the butcher had been glad to let him watch what he did. One time he even let Sors help him cut the meat. It was then that Beth finally saw exactly what those claws could do, and even she had to admit it was intimidating and yet fascinating.

Prael stood next to his raptor, ears forward, also listening. They didn't go back there this time. After James and Sors told her about the cop a couple nights ago, she figured it wouldn't be a good idea to draw attention to themselves.

The bell rang twice. A couple people walked in. Their shoes didn't sound normal, and they had stopped just inside the door. Beth turned and looked down the aisle. Two uniformed police officers stood by the door, one with his arms folded, the other with one hand on his hip near his holster. They watched her.

Sors and Prael snorted. The raptor turned to Beth.

"The one on the left," he whispered.

"Just ignore them. Don't give them a reason to do anything."

The officers didn't move, but they held eye contact with Beth. She turned away and listened to the butcher in the back. A couple minutes later, footsteps approached. The officer walked to Beth's other side and leaned on the counter.

"Afternoon. Bethany Black?"

"That's right, Officer Athens."

"You live with James Summit. Wife?"

"Girlfriend."

"You live with him and you're not married?"

"No, not yet."

The officer laughed a bit. "Some might call that a sin."

"Aiming a gun at someone who hasn't done anything could also be."

The man shifted positions, leaned closer. "Getting screwed by a dog definitely is."

Beth turned to him. "Your wife must really be in trouble then, in bed with a pig every night. Now what the hell do you want?"

The man smirked. "Touché. I'll let that one slide. I was hoping to talk to Mr. Summit again today, but since you're his girlfriend and he trusts you with his aliens, I'll talk to you about this. How often do you come here for their food?"

"A couple times a week."

"I think it would be a good idea if you found someplace else to buy their food. Someplace out of town."

"Where I shop is my business."

"The safety of this community is part of mine, and I don't want there to be any trouble."

"There hasn't been any trouble, officer."

"I intend to keep it that way. Don't let us catch you in here or anywhere else in town with them again."

"Officer," said Sors, "what's the problem?"

As soon as Sors opened his mouth, Athens unbuttoned his holster and rested his hand on his sidearm. Beth looked him square in the eyes.

"I didn't come here expecting trouble. Don't make any. Station has received a dozen more calls about your aliens. If they were pit bulls, Animal Control would have taken them away weeks ago, but your pit bulls are federally protected. This is the last meal you're going to buy for them here or anywhere in town. We will find out if you do it again."

He turned and walked down the center aisle. He opened the door, let the other officer out, and he followed.

Beth leaned on the counter. "Pit bulls..."

Prael walked behind her and stood where the officer had been. He leaned against her, rubbed his muzzle against her cheek. Sors turned and waited for the butcher.

4

James's car was much too small for a pair of Relians, but Sors didn't seem to mind riding either with his head out the window or with it curled back around his body.

They were on the state route out of town, and James drove exactly the speed limit. Two miles out. Four. Five. James checked his side view mirror, and the police car was still there. He kept telling himself the cop wasn't following him. Police cars drive these roads all the time, so this was just paranoia.

James skipped Salinas and drove all the way to Prunedale just to be safe, but the cruiser remained three cars behind him. He took the exit. So did the police. James thought he felt safer being outside their jurisdiction, but he still had a sour feeling in his gut that such ideas were the work of Hollywood, like getting fingerprints off a gun or enhancing a photo.

He had found a grocery store in the phone book that took food stamps and agreed to sell fresh cuts of meat to him for the Relians. It was a chain grocery store, so the meat had been processed, but it would do for now. James was concerned that the people didn't seem all that excited at the idea of alien creatures coming to visit, and he hoped it was just more paranoia.

A few turns down two-lane roads and he pulled in. Two police cars were already parked in the lot.

"That can't be good," James said.

"We're doing exactly what they asked," said the fox as he unbuckled his seatbelt.

"Yes, we are." James got out of the car.

Sors had climbed out of the back seat and closed the door.

The cruisers were empty, and by the time they reached the sliding doors, the cop car that had been following them since they left Maggie pulled into a space.

The meat counter was in the back of the store, and James led the two Relians down the aisles to the rear. When they left the aisle, James noticed four police officers in uniform with different county emblems on them. They stood in pairs about twenty feet past either side of the meat section. James looked back. Another police officer stood halfway down an aisle. James wondered how many more there were.

He walked up to the counter, told them who he was and pointed to whom he was ordering for. The woman nodded and went to the back. James waited patiently. The Relians scented the air in all directions. The officers glared at them.

"Stop that," James said. "Stop sniffing."

"I can't," said Prael. "Their scents are interesting."

"They'll take it as a threat."

"How?"

"They just will."

"That's like asking you to stop sweating."

"I know, but stop it anyway. Be calm and still. And if any kids walk up to you and ask for a ride, let me do the talking."

Sors' hands remained apart. He leaned closer to James and spoke in his ear. "I can speak for myself. Is this how we are to live for the rest of our lives?"

"I hope not."

"When will it end?"

"It will blow over soon enough. Just comply and eventually they'll go away."

"Even when we are home, we can't go anywhere. Police are always following us. People hide from us. Store employees won't talk to you if we're with you. This has to end, and it can't unless we speak to people. The whole reason we are with you and not in some segregated part of a large city is so people can meet us and not be afraid."

"Look, I don't know what else to do. Let's just get your food and go home. Maybe if we stick to the rules, we'll have a chance to meet people after everyone calms down."

The Relians continued scenting the air but tried to be less visual about it. The officers surrounding them stood in place. James noticed a new one at the top of another aisle. He wondered how the shoppers felt about so much blue and black in here.

A few minutes later, the woman returned with several paper-wrapped packages of beef specially cut for them. She weighed them. James handed over the food stamps, picked up the containers, and turned to leave.

A police officer stood in his path. James pretended to be brave and walked in an arc around him. The policeman stepped sideways to be in James's path again. James stepped aside. The officer did not move. James stepped further aside and walked down the aisle. The officer moved as James neared, standing in front of him.

From the corner of his eye, James noticed all the policemen closing in. Sors and Prael scented the air in all directions, the raptor trying very hard to keep his claws folded and invisible.

"Find everything you needed, sir?" said the policeman.

"Yup, everything."

"Stay out of trouble. Have a nice day."

He did not move.

James walked around him, and this time the officer let him pass. The Relians clicked across the tile down the aisle. It wasn't often James outpaced Sors and Prael.

5

James didn't like this. Driving anywhere with the Relians was scary enough but going for a walk through town could have been enough to give him a nervous breakdown. Beth kept insisting they couldn't let the cops win, so they were going out whether the boys in blue liked it or not.

Everything in this town was pretty much down two main streets, and downtown was where all the lawyers, doctor's offices, and decent restaurants were. Beth had decided they would walk there, sit down and eat, and then walk back like perfectly ordinary people were free to do.

Beth led the way with Sors beside her. Prael wore a pair of James's workout shorts and walked behind Beth. James brought up the rear, flanked by Sors' tail. They passed a parked police car, and another one on the other side of the street as they came into the restaurant district. Again, James tried to convince himself they weren't here just for them, but the less rational side of his brain knew that was wrong. James didn't know what to do now that the unreasonable side of his brain made more sense than the rational side.

They'd had the sidewalk to themselves the whole walk thus far. Everyone walked on the other side, and James's paranoid side told him it was because of them. He wondered if the entire town really had turned against them.

They entered the old section of town, where all the buildings had unused living areas above the shops. A few people exited the fancier restaurants on this side of the street. One man looked their way, took his wife by the shoulders, and led her and their two children across the street. James sighed. It couldn't be good for the health to have one's paranoid side proven right too often.

"James," Beth said over her shoulder. "I changed my mind. I don't want a burger. I want something good. We never go out for anything good. Let's go here."

She stopped them in front of the restaurant the family had just exited, an Italian place called *al dente*, an absolute cliché of a name, but they served good food, and they weren't part of a national chain.

"I don't think we…" James started to say, but Beth had already opened the door.

Sors looked at him. James shrugged and followed her inside. Sors and Prael filed in after them, and they stood at the sign that read *please wait to be seated*.

James scanned the dining area. A number of people had noticed them, and the looks they shot his way disturbed him. A couple mothers held their children, as if discreetly trying to hide them from view. One father gestured to his two-year-old daughter to get under the table.

It took an unusually long time for someone to come and seat them. James had a bad feeling about this. Moments later, a man accompanied by three women approached them.

"Hello, all of you, I am the manager, and I'm afraid I have to request you leave."

James sighed and shook his head.

Beth leaned on her hip. "Excuse me?"

"I'm sorry, but we can't serve you here."

"If this is because of the cops, you can tell them the Relians won't be eating. They're just dining with us."

"We just don't want our customers to be disturbed."

"If we do something disturbing, feel free to throw us out. Until then, we're paying customers."

"Please, ma'am, we can't serve any of you."

James narrowed his eyes at the man, tugged Beth by the shoulder. "Come on, Beth. If they don't want our business, they don't have to take it."

"This isn't right, you son of a bitch," Beth whispered to the manager's face. "Go to hell."

She turned around, and now James led the way back out the door. They stood on the sidewalk. Beth was the last one out, and as soon as the door closed, she spun around and flipped off the manager through the window. She turned back to James.

"Somebody in this town will let them in."

James clenched his fist. "Plenty of places on this street."

He led the way now. Sors walked beside him, followed by Beth and Prael. They walked a little ways. Two people were walking down the street on their side. They looked up, saw them, and crossed to the other side.

"This won't end," said Sors.

"We'll keep walking until we find a place to eat."

"We can give in to every one of their demands, but they will not be satisfied until they can forget we exist."

An elderly women with a cane opened a door and stepped out of an antiques store. She began walking their way, then she looked up and froze dead in her tracks. She turned and walked between two cars and began crossing the street.

"This ends now," said the raptor.

He broke away from James and Beth, dropped to the street, and squeezed between two cars. He was out in the street, walking to intercept the lady.

"Greetings, ma'am," he called as he approached. "My name is Sors. I just moved here a couple months ago and I'd like to get to know everybody in town."

The woman walked faster. Sors stood still in the middle of the street, hands tucked in as far as he could.

"Ma'am, I think there's a misunderstanding. I want to say hello."

"You! Get down on the ground! Now!" A police officer stood about ten paces away from Sors in the middle of the street, legs apart, gun aimed straight at him.

Another officer appeared behind the group, firearm drawn and aimed at all of them. "You three! Face down on the ground!"

"What the hell?!" Beth shouted.

"Get down!"

The old women had crossed. Sors turned around to face the officer.

A police car with rollers flashing pulled out of an alleyway a block ahead of them and parked in the middle of the road. Two officers dove out of the car and ran toward them, guns drawn. James looked back. Another police car blocked the road at the other end, lights flashing. Pedestrians dove into stores and then peered out the windows.

"On the ground! Last warning!" the officer confronting Sors shouted as the others neared.

"All of you, get down!" repeated the policeman behind the humans and the fox.

James crouched and knelt, raising his arms. So did Beth. Prael was still up, looking at Sors. The raptor was looking at the officer, head tilted. He saw what James and Beth were doing and bent at the knees and lowered himself, keeping his claws hidden.

The officer fired. Sors shrieked, bucked left and teetered over. Blood spilled from his shoulder.

Prael turned to the cop that had fired. He snarled as he dropped to all fours. He then hopped on top of the car and leaped off it. He came down on the asphalt, running to the officer. The policeman who had fired approached Sors, gun aimed at his head, screaming at him to be still. Sors writhed on the ground, growling.

Prael leaped onto the officer, knocking him to the ground. The gun flew from his hand and landed on the sidewalk. Officers converged. Some had holstered their guns and now extended batons.

Prael leaped off the officer and ran to Sors. He made it to him and began licking the wound as the officers arrived. Four of them raised their batons and brought them down on the fox one after the other.

"Son of a bitch!" James shouted as he jumped to his feet.

Something hit James on the side of the head and sent him to the concrete. Beth fell a second later, also clutching her head. Another strike hit James on the arm. Then the shoulder. Then the hip. Then his shin.

When the policeman was done with James, he started hitting Beth.

"Goddamned pigs! Pigs! Motherfucking pigs!"

She continued screaming it even when the cop struck her face.

6

The portal opened over the sidewalk in downtown. Rive stepped through, followed by CJ immediately after. Rive quickly closed the portal and scented the air. Several people had seen them arrive. They stared for a moment but quickly crossed the street or turned around and walked the other way.

"They said this is where it happened," said Secretary Rhine. She was dressed like a government official but wasn't wearing high heels, as she predicted she would have to do a lot of walking. She opened the folder at her side and read the file.

"I can smell the blood," Rive said. He looked both ways, crossed the street, and scented the asphalt up to a particular spot.

"According to the briefing, multiple officers witnessed the raptor attempt to hunt down an elderly woman. Police intercepted, and the raptor refused to comply with repeated orders to stand down. He began to turn on the officer in charge. Officer fired one shot to the shoulder, whereupon his fox attacked the officer. Supporting law enforcement officers attempted to control the fox, but he did not comply and was subdued only by a police officer's baton. At the same time the two humans with the Relians became unruly and threatened officers nearby. They were controlled with batons as well. An ambulance was summoned, perpetrators were treated, and they are now being held at the police station, pending transfer to a more secure facility. This was yesterday evening."

Rive had been scenting the whole street. The road was still blocked off as a crime scene, so no traffic had been through. He now moved to the sidewalk.

"I smell where the two humans were."

"Police station is a couple blocks away," CJ said, opening the briefcase in her other hand. She stuffed the folder inside. "We'll speak to the chief first, then to the Relians and the humans involved. The statement says his girlfriend also lives with him and she was present as well."

CJ walked down the street. She ducked under the yellow tape blocking off the sidewalk and turned the corner. Rive trotted to catch up and walked at her side.

"What do you think so far?" she said.

"I want to hear from them what happened."

"You think Sors would hunt an old lady?"

"I would rather wait to hear what the humans said happened before I say anything."

"Not even a hint? These are serious charges. Lots of witnesses. Evidence on tape."

"Not until I know everyone's perspective."

CJ shook her head as they walked. "This isn't what I was trained to do. Lawyers don't solve crimes or investigate anything, but here I am. It's my job now."

"That didn't stop Matlock," Rive said, clicking his claws.

CJ wasn't laughing. "Another crime-solving lawyer. Television gives millions of people the wrong idea about what lawyers do."

"Perhaps if lawyers had to solve the cases they were involved with, your justice system would be more efficient."

"And every case would be solved in an hour. If only."

The station was in sight. CJ picked up the pace. They received the call less than an hour ago, and the station had faxed them the reports only twenty minutes ago. Rive had made the way while the faxes printed. CJ wasn't used to things happening so fast.

She ascended the steps, opened the door, and walked inside. An elderly woman sat at the front desk, typing away on a computer, wrist braces on both hands. CJ stopped at the counter. Rive stood next to her.

"Morning. I'm here to see the chief. I'm White House Secretary CJ Rhine of Relian Relations."

The woman did not seem impressed by the title. "Just a moment. I'll let him know you're here." She turned away from the computer and picked up a phone. "Chief, Ms. Rhine is here." She nodded, hung up. "He's in his office. Down that way, on the right. R. Noland printed on the door." She pointed with a pencil.

"Thank you."

CJ led them down the hall and knocked on the door. She pushed the door open a crack, and then the rest of the way. A caucasian man about ten years CJ's senior sat behind the modest desk. A dozen cassette and VHS tapes and a thick folder had been stacked to his left. He did not stand when she and Rive entered.

"Mr. Noland," she said, extending her hand over the desk and setting her briefcase next to the chair. "Madame Secretary Rhine."

"The secretary herself." He gave her hand a weak shake. "Didn't expect you to show up. Thought the whole town would be flooded with feds by now. Is it just you?"

"And Rive, my assistant." She sat down. "You have evidence to show me?"

"It's supposed to be for their lawyer. I understand our president signed an order extending the civil rights bill to include Relians."

"He did that last year," said CJ. "It was an emergency measure until congress can make it more official."

"Good idea. Have to make sure everyone knows they have equal rights and all that. Well, all the evidence is right here." He gestured to the pile of tapes and papers. "The boys compiled a highlight reel last night. Would you like to see it now? It has both the video evidence and the audio from those tapes."

"Yes, please, and would you mind if Rive had a look at those documents?"

"Four hundred pages. Knock yourself out." He slid the pile of manila folders Rive's direction.

The tan and grey raptor opened it and began flipping through the documents at about one every couple of seconds. Noland stared at him.

"Is he really reading those?"

Rive did not look up at him as he flipped through the pages. "I am. I will be done by the time the two of you are. Then I will listen to the tapes."

"There's nineteen hours worth of audio. Most of it is rubbish. The good parts are up here."

He rolled the chair over to a television on a rolling stand, switched it on, and popped the tape in. The VCR began playing immediately. He rolled back to his desk, facing the television, hands folded over his belly.

"It's our investigation, step by step. We'd received multiple complaints from people in the neighborhood prior, but this was the first incident caught on camera."

The tape showed security camera footage from a grocery store. A little boy pranced up to Sors. The raptor lowered his neck and body to be at his eye level, and the child ran away. Even with no audio and from such a high angle, the child was obviously crying.

"Mother said she heard him growling at her son. This footage and the sworn testimony was enough to convince a judge to get us a surveillance warrant. We tapped their phone and had an officer stationed outside the residence with sound enhancing equipment."

The screen switched to California's state flag as the audio evidence played.

Sor's voice: *"They run fast. I love it when they run. It's not as good when they don't fight back, but running still makes me excited. It's what I hunt when I'm not in the mood to fight for my meal. They taste better when they're still alive."*

James Summit's voice: *"You eat them alive?"*

Sors: *"Only the Lant mammals. They might escape if I don't start eating them right away. I tried doing that to an Esi, and it ruins the flavor. Best to wait until they're dead before eating them. But the Lant mammals taste better when they're screaming. To enjoy something, I need to kill it. Not every raptor likes prey that fights back. Some prefer the runners, some prefer prey that eludes predators, leaves false trails, climbs trees. Others really like to hear prey scream as they eat it. Some don't. To my race, it's the difference between someone liking pizza instead of lasagna. I haven't hunted in months."*

James responding: *"That makes you restless?"*

"Yes. The last time I hunted was under human supervision. That was the first hunt I had been on in a very long time. The planet Rive moved us to after the disaster did not have anything I could catch. Food only tastes good when I have to take it down. Some prey is like coffee to me. Other prey is like pizza. The flavor is in the hunting."

The screen changed to another security camera video.

"That audio prompted us to step up security," Noland said. "This next bit is at a local grocery store. The girl is Beth, James's girlfriend slash roommate. The owner has a few cameras in there hooked up to VCRs. Very basic, but it did capture this moment."

An officer approached Beth at the counter and started talking to her. Seconds later, Sors stretched his neck in the officer's direction, and the policeman placed his hand on his sidearm. Beth backed away, pushing the Relians back.

Noland narrated. "The officer here says the raptor growled at him for being too close to Beth. We figured it still wouldn't be enough to apprehend because, like with humans, threatening is not a reason for arrest by itself, but human laws apply to aliens now, so we had to wait."

More security camera footage from other stores followed. Sometimes the Relians were with James. Other times with Beth.

Then the view switched to side-by-side dash cams. This one did have audio. It showed the Relians on the sidewalk with James and Beth. An elderly lady crossed the street, and Sors left the sidewalk and walked to intercept. He was saying something, but the audio was distorted. Officers got out of the car, aiming firearms at him. Several times they told him to stand down. Sors crouched low, and a shot went off. Prael leaped from a car off camera and tackled the officer who fired the shot. Multiple policemen showed up and clubbed the fox. Just visible off to the side, an officer clubbed James and Beth as she screamed bloody murder at the officers.

The screen went blank. Noland hit the stop button and then rewind. He turned in his chair and faced them. Rive closed the folder.

"That's what we can show a jury," said Noland. "Everything is documented, just as it would be if humans were involved. We almost had to let a woman die before we could apprehend, but luckily that didn't have to happen."

CJ leaned forward. "It took six officers to club a Relian canine into submission?"

"We have no idea what we were dealing with or what these people are capable of. My officers reacted to an unknown threat. That fox attacked an officer. Firing a shot was too risky to bystanders, so they used batons."

Rive spoke. "Prael attacked the officer because the officer attacked his raptor."

Noland swiveled in his chair and faced Rive. "And had Sors done what the officers asked and stood down, he wouldn't have been shot. Maybe you should have taught your people respect for authority before sending them all over the world. Not to mention respect for human life."

Rive walked behind CJ and picked up one of the audio cassettes. He flipped open the case, stooped down, and unlocked CJ's briefcase. He pulled out a cassette player and a pair of ear buds.

"Nineteen hours," said Noland. "I just showed you the best parts. The rest is worthless chitchat."

"He will listen to the tapes," CJ said. "Hopefully these aren't the originals."

"They are copies. Take all the time you need. They'll be transferred to a state prison in a couple days."

"In the meantime," CJ said, standing up, "we'd like to interview James, Beth, the Relians, and any others who were involved in this investigation. Are any of the officers present today?"

"A couple. They're out on patrol, but I'll have them recalled if you like."

"Please call them. We'll be here for a while. And also, is there a car rental service around here?"

"Closest one is in Salinas." He swiveled back and forth in his chair and smiled. "Ah, tell you what. You can use one of our patrol cars while you're here. You're a federal official. I trust you not to go around flashing the rollers just to get through red lights."

"Thank you, Mr. Noland. I promise."

He smiled, pointed with a finger. "Talk to Sandy at the front. She'll give you a key."

Rive had finished loading the cassettes into the briefcase. Noland smirked at the setup the raptor had: a belt around his neck, tape player clipped to it, ear bud taped to one of his earholes.

"Thanks," he said, rocking in his chair. "That made my day. I'll let everyone know you're coming. You'll have as much time with the perps as you need."

CJ led the way out of the room, carrying a heavier briefcase now. They turned and walked down the hall to the holding cells.

"Read anything interesting in there?"

"The police reports are similar. Forty-seven people claim Sors was stalking them or stalking their child and about to attack or growling at them. Some of them also claim Prael licked his lips at the sight of them or their children. Some reports mention excessive sniffing in their direction, which the people took to mean they were being hunted. A judge did consider the incident with the boy in the grocery store enough evidence to warrant surveillance, so the tapes will be legal to use against them."

"Yes, those tapes. Did Sors really say that?"

"The audio quality is poor, but his voice is recognizable, as is James Summit's. But the audio has been edited. I'm listening to the tapes now to find out what the rest of the conversation was."

"It sounds pretty damning. 'The flavor is in the hunting.' If I were a judge, I'd allow police to tail anyone who said that."

"It is a normal thing for a raptor to say, especially in the company of another predator, or a prey species well-acclimated to the company of predators."

"What about James and Beth's testimony?"

"They claim police harassment, accusations not unlike racial profiling."

"Give me more details later. I want to hear it from them."

They reached the back of the station. The officer at the door nodded, unlocked it, and let them in. She walked in with them and stood by.

The jail had four cells against the far wall, and everyone was in their own cell. At the sight of Rive, Prael leaped to his feet and stood at the bars. Prael's bruises showed even through his fur. The raptor's gunshot wound had been dressed and bandaged. The humans, Beth and James, stared at him from their cots on the floor.

"Rive, what's going on?" Prael said. "They're not telling us anything!"

Rive and CJ looked at one another. CJ walked to the cells with the humans while Rive took the side with the Relians.

"Tell me what happened," said the metal raptor.

Rive expected both of them to speak at once, since they knew he was an Archeon and could understand them at the same time, but only Prael spoke. Sors sat on the concrete, staring at the floor.

Secretary Rhine stood between the two cells. James and Beth were bruised and bandaged. Beth wore a nose splint.

"Those fucking pigs!" Beth yelled, trying to be quiet. "They stalked us! They were waiting for Sors and Prael to do anything just to pull guns on them and shoot!"

"It started with patrols," James said. "I knew they were watching us, but then they wouldn't leave us alone. Any time Sors would try to talk, they took that as aggression and pulled a gun on him. If they even looked at an officer wrong, that was a reason to use force."

"Rive read your testimonies," CJ said. "You realize you're claiming entrapment. That's nearly impossible to prove even in the best of times."

"God damn it, it's what happened!" James shouted. "Sors was doing exactly what the officer said, and they shot him anyway! Prael was defending his raptor after they shot him for no reason! They were looking for an excuse to take them out. Figured if they followed us long enough they'd get one."

"Or make it," Beth said. "Fuck, I've never been arrested before."

"It started with the boy in the grocery store," CJ said to James. "From your point of view, what happened?"

"The little boy thought Sors was Yoshi and wanted a ride. Sors got down at his eye level and told the kid he wasn't for riding, and the kid walked away crying. It was the teeth. It had to be. Sors wasn't stalking the kid. People have just seen too many movies and they won't even go up to him."

CJ looked sideways at Sors. She smirked. "He does look like Yoshi."

"Yeah," said James. "That's when they started listening in on us. Sors and I saw them that night. We went out to the police car to say hello. Sors was nothing but nice to him, and the cop pulled a gun on us and told us to get back in-side. It only got worse from there."

On the other side of the room, Prael was finishing up their side of the story. Rive walked in front of Sors' cell. The raptor hadn't said a word so far.

"Sors, are you all right?"

The green raptor raised his snout and met Rive's eyes. "Nobody has ever been afraid of me before. I thought I was doing the right thing, meeting people, trying to talk to them. James and Beth wanted us to stay submissive. They figured if we did what they said things would be better, but I knew the demands would never stop. Did I do something wrong?"

Rive turned his head to Secretary Rhine, the tape player hanging by the belt jiggling. He turned back to Sors. "We're trying to figure out what went wrong. It will not be the only time something of this kind happens."

"What do we do?"

"Don't make trouble. We're working on it."

"Do you know what's happening?" Prael said.

"I knew what was happening before I made the way here, but the people on this planet do not trust one another, so I must find evidence of it."

He walked away from them and met CJ at the other end. James and Beth stopped talking and stared at Rive.

"I was listening to both of you as well. Please con-tinue."

They smiled at his tape player.

Six hours later, CJ and Rive were in a vacant office used for interviews. CJ sat behind the desk and looked up at the ceiling. They had just interviewed the last officer in-volved in the apprehension yesterday. Their testimonies were so consistent they had to have been rehearsed. It felt like a horrible waste of time, but Rive had listened to six tapes during the process, so it hadn't been a total loss.

"We won't get anywhere like this," CJ said. "All right, what do we have so far? Video evidence of children running from the Relians, endless testimony of aggression, audio of the raptor talking about the pleasures of killing, multiple videos of Relians attacking police officers. There's testimony that the officers were the aggressors but not enough to go against the word of law enforcement. Rive... Unless you have anything else, I think we're screwed. All of the evidence points to the Relians."

Rive tilted his head. "Do you believe the officers?"

"Hell no, this whole thing is shady beyond belief but that's not the point."

"I think we need to visit one of these officers at home."

"At home? Why?"

"They will behave differently. I should do the talking while we're there."

"Where are you going with this?"

7

The front door opened. Rive's muzzle was the first thing officer Jerry Athens saw. The scent of repulsion and fear was so thick Rive was surprised CJ couldn't smell it. It had come from every officer they had interviewed but especially this man.

"Officer Athens," Rive said.

Athens looked past Rive, but CJ was not around. Athens had no choice but to speak to Rive, and the raptor could tell it was a fate worse than death for him.

"What do you want?"

"Just a couple questions, sir. May I step inside?"

Athens smelled as though it were the last thing he wanted to do, but Rive figured he did not want to behave suspiciously with federal officials in town.

"Sure, for just a moment."

Rive stepped over the landing and walked in just far enough for half of his tail to hang out the door. He wiped his feet on the rug.

"Finished listening to the tapes?" Athens nodded to Rive's bare neck.

"I listened to seven of them. I have heard enough. Chief Noland tells me you recorded some of them."

Jerry Athens still held the doorknob, waiting for Rive to walk all the way in so he could close the door. "That's right. What's your point? I'm eating dinner."

"Jerry, who is it?" called a woman's voice from the next room.

Rive smelled two children, a boy and a girl.

"Just a federal investigator with a few more questions."

"My name is Rive," the raptor shouted, making sure he could be heard throughout the whole house.

"Rive," she said. "The Archeon Rive?"

"Yes, honey."

Little footsteps dropped to the floor and bounded to the front door. Two children, both about eight years old, peeked around the corner. Their eyes were full of wonder even as Mr. Athens' heart raced.

"Kids, stay in the dining room. Mr. Rive is just here for a moment to ask me some questions about what happened the other day."

Rive clicked his claws and lowered his neck and body to be at their level. "Hello, children!"

"Holy crap," said the boy. "He *is* a robot!"

"Benjamin..."

Both children walked closer. Now the mother stood in the hall, looking on, worry in her scent but also confusion.

Rive kept his hands apart. "I'm not a robot. My body is made of a living metal."

"So it's true!" said the girl. "The metal is alive! Is it eating your flesh?"

Rive was finding it so difficult not to laugh. "No, it doesn't eat me. It keeps me alive. It's actually another alien species."

Both children had walked right up to Rive's snout and were touching the metal.

"Can it say hello?" said the girl.

"Not directly. It's getting better at learning my language."

"Can I ride you?" said Benjamin.

"Ben!" said Mrs. Athens.

"Ben, Mary..." Jerry began, still holding the door open just a hair wider than Rive's tail.

"Sure, climb on," Rive said before the parents could stop them.

Rive lay on his stomach. The girl climbed on him first, and then the boy climbed up behind her. Rive rose to full height.

Officer Athens smelled and looked livid. "Kids, get back to the table!"

"It's all right," Rive said. "I like mixing business with pleasure."

"Let's go!" shouted Benjamin, trying to spur Rive. "The princess is in trouble and we gotta save her!"

Rive backed out of the door, wedging it open the rest of the way with his hips, spun around on the porch, and bolted down the steps. He stopped in the middle of the front yard and jumped a few times, kids holding on to him and laughing.

"Where's the princess?" Rive said.

"She's over there!" said Ben, pointing to a tree on the left side of the yard. "The dragon's got her in the castle!"

"Dragon?" Rive trotted around the yard. "Dragons aren't dangerous, but you know who is? Princes barging in and stealing princesses away from their dragons."

"But the prince loves her!" Mary said, holding onto Rive's neck as hard as she could.

"What if the dragon does, too? Does the prince even ask the dragon?"

Both kids giggled.

"Dragons can't love a princess," said Benjamin.

"Then why did he take her?" Rive hopped from foot to foot. He didn't normally bounce this much when he walked, but the children enjoyed it more. "Before I ride in there and help you slay that dragon, we need to think this through. We should ask the dragon why he took that princess, and why her? Why not some peasant from the fields? What makes the princess so special? He must have had a reason to take her and not someone else."

Rive heard a click. He stopped and turned around. Officer Athens stood on the porch, legs apart, aiming a handgun at him.

"Stop right there!"

"Dad?" said Mary.

"Let my kids down."

Rive lowered himself to his belly. His kids slid off, ran up the porch steps and behind their mother, who took them inside and closed the door. Rive rose to full height, keeping eye contact with officer Athens.

"What the hell do you think you're doing?" said the man.

"Teaching your children to question whether the dragon is a monster that needs to be slain." He clicked his claws. "It is an assumption in your culture that anything bigger than you and different is a threat to your lives and will steal your females and offspring, evidenced by monsters in movies always threatening them or carrying them away. These are very primitive impulses—a deep-seated desire to win your chance to mate by challenging the dominant male. The story of the dragon and the princess is a cliché even in your culture, but it persists, so it's important to introduce new perspectives to prepare them if they ever meet a real dragon. Or an alien creature."

"Get off my yard." He gestured away with his gun.

Rive stood still, looking up the porch at the man with the gun. "I have a couple questions, sir, and then I'll be gone."

"Get off."

"I read the testimonies on file at the station. There were four official complaints prior to the 'Yoshi' incident, and none of the people had met Sors or Prael. Statements describe perceptions of stalking, feeling as though they were being hunted or growled at from at least thirty feet away, and indecency. The reports don't start getting closer and more frequent until after the encounter with the young boy in the grocery store, which was when the police started following the Relians."

"This is your last warning! Get off my property!"

Rive backed away slowly, raising his voice to be heard as he opened the distance.

"Statements came from people at a variety of stores and public places both before and since that day. They range from vague feelings of uncertainty to outright terror, yet the people had been shopping in those stores or walking in the museum the whole time. Some of them state the excessive police presence is what scared them. If they were truly afraid of the Relians, they would have taken their children and left in a hurry, but footage does not show that."

Rive felt grass change to the concrete, so he planted his feet on the sidewalk and stood at full height.

"My first question, officer Athens, is why did you and your fellow officers walk around places where the Relians had been and solicit statements when no event had occurred?"

"Get off my property!"

"I am off, sir. My second question: is it possible people became afraid because the police officers in this town told them to be afraid? Statements were collected from people before the encounter in the grocery store, and they only became more frequent and closer to the Relians after. The more officers asked people about the Relians, and the more officers followed and harassed them, the more afraid of them people became. Two of the police reports even state this. Two different people wrote that if the police were making such a big deal about Sors and Prael, they must be dangerous, so yes, they were scared of them. Statements such as these were used to justify even more scrutiny. My next question is why was the recorded conversation between Mr. Summit and Sors on tape five? You told us at the station that it had been the first piece of evidence you recorded. My last question: why was the conversation edited on the video presentation? James and Sors were talking about a raptor hunting animals on other planets, not humans, but the two are placed side by side to compel listeners to make that connect—"

Officer Athens fired. The bullet made a metallic *chank* sound. Rive backed away another step. Athens fired again. This time Rive turned, and the bullet struck metal again. Rive stood tall, staring at officer Athens.

Police rollers switched on and bathed the yard in flashing red and blue light. Jerry Athens lowered his gun and faced the patrol car parked askew in his driveway. The door opened. CJ stepped out.

"Mr. Athens, can I trust you to meet us at the station?"

8

The dashboard camera had captured almost everything. What it didn't pick up, the tape recorder Rive had planted by the front door had. Rive played them as close to synchronized as the equipment would allow. All the audio the dash cam had missed was on the cassette tape, and both played before Chief Noland.

Rive, Secretary Rhine, officer Athens, and chief Noland had gathered in Noland's office. Athens had just fired the shot. Noland flinched at the duel sound from the television and the tape player. Then the second shot rang. CJ stopped the tapes.

Noland swiveled around in his chair to face CJ. Athens stood at attention in front of the desk.

"Thank you, officer. Please wait outside."

Athens's face remained neutral, but he reeked of fight-or-flight. He nodded, opened the door, and then walked down the hall to the vending machines.

"What do you want me to say?" Noland said as soon as the door shut. "Your raptor touched a man's children without his permission, was told to leave the premises repeatedly, did not comply, the officer perceived a threat, so he fired. The raptor did not fall, the officer assumed he missed, so he fired again."

CJ leaned on Noland's desk and looked him in the eye. "Officer Athens invited Rive inside. His children touched him. He was in full view of the parents and never left the property. When asked, Rive let his children go, and he did back away to the sidewalk. He was nothing but cooperative, but officer Jerry Athens fired on him, twice, the second time while he was backing away!"

Noland sat with his hands folded under his chin. CJ continued.

"I don't need a grand jury, chief Noland. I am authorized to get the FBI involved. They will investigate your station, find evidence of discrimination and police corruption, and remove all of you from the force."

Noland rocked back and forth a few times. "What they'll find is a community scared to leave their homes because of these creatures. They will find a community who hates the federal government for forcing them to let these dangerous people live here. They will also find a police force that did everything they thought was necessary to protect the people."

"There were no incidents. None! You created the fear and then used that to justify hounding the Relians until they did something you could frame as threatening."

"It's because of me and my officers nobody got killed. Nobody got maimed or eaten alive. Have you heard the tape of that raptor talking about eating things alive because it tasted better? What would you do? Would you wait and see what happened, or would you protect people from it?"

CJ stood up straight. "The FBI will be here in the morning. I'm keeping these copies of the evidence, including recordings Rive and I just made. In the meantime, let those people out of there."

"They resisted arrest and assaulted an officer. They're not going anywhere."

"I can have the president on the phone in five minutes. All he has to hear is my story about what happened in this town, and he will want to talk to you personally and ask why they were arrested for a crime your boys caused. Let's just skip the middle step, can we?"

Noland chuckled, but he was fuming. "This is exactly what the federal government does. You think you own everything. That you can tell the people how to live their lives, how to look out for ourselves. The press would love to see that evidence tape."

"You are not authorized to go to the media with this, Mr. Noland. The president made a personal request to all the media outlets to refrain from reporting on things like this."

"I'm not surprised to hear you say that. Don't want the people to know the truth about what the federal government is putting in their neighborhoods. Don't want people to know anything about them, but they want them to believe that they're just the same as you and me."

Rive walked to the VCR and ejected the tape.

CJ reached into her pocket and set a key on his desk. "He wants them to take time to let things sink in and put them in context instead of jumping to conclusions. Thanks for the car. We'll be leaving shortly. Destroying evidence, or accidentally losing it, will make you look more guilty. Going to the press will show that you manipulated evidence. I'm keeping these copies as insurance. I suggest you get some sleep. You'll have to explain all of this to the FBI soon. Maybe you'll get lucky and they'll let you keep your job. Good night, chief."

Rive had placed the last tape in the briefcase, packed full of tapes plus the manila folder of statements and testimonies. Rive picked it up as he turned to the chief.

"Seven of the police reports were taken in places the Relians hadn't been to in a week. Police were going around asking people who had merely seen them in the past. The notes the police took suggest the questions they asked were meant to elicit the responses they wanted. Try talking to the Relians instead of projecting your fear onto others."

Noland scowled at him. "Go to hell."

Rive followed CJ out of the office.

9

Al dente was still open this late at night, as they would be, since they served alcohol. James and Beth had been scared to go in, but to their surprise they were seated right away. According to the waitress, the police had been in there the day prior to their arrival and told the manager the Relians were dangerous and not to serve them. No police had been here today, so they got a table. The raptors did not sit, but there was plenty of room to stand while the omnivores waited for their food.

"He shot you twice?" Beth said.

"What would you have done had he not hit you in the... metal?" James said.

"My skin is infused with it. It would have healed quickly."

"But you would've been shot," said James.

Rive rubbed his claws. "Not fatally. I would have felt it, but it would not have hurt."

"Damn," said James. "That's... That's... Wow. It's a life form, and it bends and moves? How does it know how to do that?"

"I'm still learning how to communicate with it. We often work on our cultural exchanges when I'm asleep. It used to shut me down whenever it had had enough of the outside world, but we have a better understanding now."

"There's no dent or scar from the bullets," CJ said.

"It knows what it's supposed to be, so it keeps that form. Same for my skin."

CJ noticed Prael leaning on Beth. CJ smiled. "So, Columbo, would you like to explain what you knew before we arrived?"

"Sure. Just from the police reports we received at the White House, I knew Sors would not have done it. I know what kind of prey he prefers, therefore he would never hunt an old woman or a little boy. Neither can fight back nor run very fast, so it would never have happened, but that is not evidence in this culture. We needed to know what the humans claimed. Reading the rest of police reports confirmed what was happening: a few people in authority were scared, so they used their positions to make others afraid, thereby confirming their own fear. It's how the human mind works. Most of the time you're not conscious of it, but you can find it working in other aspects of life. Whatever the boss's attitude is, the employees adopt the same attitude, even if they disagree in private. Authority has means to spread that perception to others. Not just fear, but positive things as well."

Sors stretched his neck to be closer to Rive. "So you think the town won't be afraid of us once those officers are gone?"

"It will take time to undo the damage, but I think you will discover a lot more people were comfortable with you than you thought. I suggest you keep going out in public, keep meeting people, and if a child asks you for a ride, just give it to him."

The humans laughed. The raptors reached across the table and clicked claws. The fox wagged his tail and discreetly rubbed Beth's leg.

"You were great with those children," CJ said. "You're sure you never wanted kids?"

"I like other people's children. To have one of my own... No. I picked him because he was the officer who made that first recording, and he had children. I figured the best way to make him break out of his rehearsed testimony was to interact with them. He hadn't taught them how to be afraid of Relians yet, as I hoped. He panicked, and it was on camera. Should be enough to call everything into question."

The waitress came with their food. The omnivores at the table had ordered pasta and breadsticks with sauce. The raptors had ordered special meatballs with no spices and minimal preparation. James looked at Sors and Rive. When Sors took a bite, James made a little screaming noise. Rive took a bite, and Beth did the same thing.

"Thanks, but it's just not the same," said the green raptor.

"Would it help if I grabbed one and threw it across the room?" James said.

"We're trying to make people less afraid of us!"

"If you did it with a dog toy, they'd think it was funny," said Beth.

The raptors held hands and shared a laugh. CJ noticed the waitresses across the room were giggling, too. She breathed easier as she took another bite.

10

CJ and Rive stood side by side in the middle of the street still blocked off as a crime scene. A cool, midnight breeze blew in. The Relians and their humans were walking home. CJ waited for Rive to make a way back to the White House.

"The government should be paying you, Rive. A normal investigation would have taken months to sift through all those papers and tapes and figure out what happened. The story would have gone national, and by the time the truth came out, millions of people would have been influenced. You'd make one hell of a detective."

"I'm an Archeon. I'm good at noticing things. That is the only quality your fictional super-sleuths have. They are good observers. I am good at making connections, but I am not here to solve crimes. There is a larger goal."

"Yes. Integration. America sure failed at it after the Civil War, and a long time before that, too. This is our chance to get it right."

"Not only that. The general attitude in this country states everyone must adapt to American ways and values, even those who do not live here. Relians are here to show you that it is you who must change."

"I saw the tapes Stephen made when he first arrived. I don't see how you think Relians will change anything. It's hard to change people."

"It's the most difficult thing in the universe to do, and this is coming from someone who calculated where a planet that had lost its star would have ended up in its former solar system. It will be particularly challenging for your species because as Stephen once told us, you are smart as individuals but not when you gather in groups. I meant what I said earlier about authority. There are men in this country who change people to suit their needs. That is what it means to be in authority, but it is not absolute. The Relians are unknown elements. As soon as the dominant humans in this society realize Relians cannot be controlled, they will start spreading an attitude of fear among the people. The people will believe they chose to be afraid of Relians on their own, never realizing that their minds had been manipulated by someone they regard as authority. What happened here can easily happen on a national scale."

"I doubt that," CJ replied. "The White House is working hard to keep the peace and help the people adjust to Relians being here."

"The police officers here did the work, but the chief wanted it done. So it is with the government itself. It is analogous to the police force here, doing the work on the ground but on behalf of someone else. Things are calm for now, but as soon as it suits the metaphorical chief, opinion will suddenly turn, and it will be as if the people were never comfortable around Relians."

CJ looked at him and chuckled. "No wonder you never had a date."

Rive clicked his claws. "My mind will not let me rest. It continually turns these kinds of thoughts over and over. My fox was the same way. He was all I needed."

"I wish I could have met him. He must have been an incredible person."

"He was," Rive said. "We were so synchronous with one another. The things we discussed were so hypothetical, so beyond the realm of possibility, and yet we lived there together. Years we would inhabit these ideas as if they were reality, one flowing into another without effort. Was... Was any of it real? Did we really inhabit these places together? Were we... Did we share those years, or was he pretending? Did he mean any of it?"

CJ looked at him. After a lengthy pause, she spoke up. "Rive, what are you talking about?"

Rive fidgeted and looked in every direction except at her. He did not respond. CJ couldn't stop looking at his face.

"Rive, there's something I've been meaning to ask you for months. Do you mind if...?"

She held out her hand.

Rive stared at her. His body language was hard to read. He hesitated, but she couldn't tell why. He stretched his neck and held his muzzle out. CJ reached and touched two fingers to the metallic side of his face. It was cold. She pressed on it, and it felt as unyielding as it looked. Her fingers moved downward to his jaw. It, too, was solid and did not give a millimeter to the touch, and yet it flexed and moved when Rive spoke.

"How does this work?" she said.

"I am not sure."

"What is it made of? How does it move like this?"

"The metal is alive, and that really is all I know."

CJ's hand wandered down to the raptor's neck, and she felt the seam where the flesh met the metal.

"Does that hurt?"

"No."

"How did they do this? How can metal be alive?"

"I am curious of that myself."

CJ tapped his metal neck with a fingernail. Rive winced.

"You can feel that?"

"The metal reconstructed the nerve endings. They connect to my brain. Yes, I have feeling in the metal."

"I've been staring at it for months... Now you've been shot twice and there isn't a mark on it."

Rive reached for CJ. She flinched, seeing three claws as long as her fingers coming toward her, but she held still. Rive touched her cheek with the fingertips just below the base of his claws. He felt her cheek, felt the cartilage of the nose, her face down to her neck. He let his hand drop.

"People in this culture seem afraid to touch one another. Raptors and foxes do all the time. It's good for bonding."

CJ smiled. "It's all foxes seem to do."

"We teach them to do that. Foxes need it. Well.. most."

A sphere opened in the middle of the street. CJ stared at it. Portals had not ceased to be a wonder yet, and she hoped they never would.

"Sleeping in the Oval Office again?"

"There's a press conference tomorrow. I think I'll sleep there tonight. Find out if anyone has the courage to ask me to leave the stage, or if they'll hold the conference with me on it."

Rive stepped through the way. CJ followed him. The sphere shut, and the street became quiet.

Boston

I

The video wall in the drawing room now had seven televisions: four hooked up to VCRs playing tapes, two on different channels over antenna, and the largest screen on satellite.

Kylac also had the stereo playing a CD of *Einstein on the Beach*. He listened to this often, as well as other recordings by similar composers. Penny once asked him why he listened to such repetitive, unmusical noise, and Kylac replied that it was an auditory representation of his state of mind. She did not ask a follow-up question.

It had been a week since the dinner party, and many more guests had come and gone since. Kylac had been in here most of the time, listening to Jeff talk business with dozens of people. Investment opportunities, the state of the labor market, the state of politics. It had become the Morton Channel.

Jeff stood at the bar behind the couch with a politician for the state of Massachusetts. Senator Sattle was his name.

Jeff was asking him about the upcoming vote for funding unemployment benefits.

Sattle said it was coming up soon.

Jeff wanted him to block it until someone made concessions to reduce funding to something else.

Sattle promised he was working with fellow senators to form a block against it until the other side agreed to some spending cuts elsewhere.

Jeff asked him about the bill for school funding. He wanted to know if his income was in danger of going to public schools.

Sattle said he had already inserted a provision into the bill that would exclude capital gains income at his level from the tax.

Jeff said that was good and to make sure it passed with that clause intact.

Kylac had something new in the background of conversations like these: Friend standing against the wall.

The older fox appeared just as he had been in the prime of life. He never seemed to follow Kylac anywhere, choosing to appear in whatever room he happened to be in. Kylac knew he was actually in all rooms at once, only making himself visible to keep the younger fox from forgetting he existed.

"Don't worry about him," Friend said from against the wall. "He's irrelevant, not just to the universe but to this nation. Whatever he wants done won't last forever."

"I have no choice but to worry about him." Kylac didn't know how Friend did it, but whenever he spoke to Friend, nobody else in the room seemed to hear.

Friend yawned. "I know every word that man will ever say. I know exactly where the carbon atoms in his asshole were when the universe formed, and I can tell you where they will end up when the universe ends. Trust me when I say he is not important."

Kylac smelled Sattle was drinking wine, an Amarone, and Jeff had a bottle of some local beer. Sattle talked about an upcoming bill that hadn't been introduced to the senate yet, one that would create new funding to improve the bus system in the city.

Jeff asked what was wrong with it.

Sattle said some people seem to think it needed to be updated.

Jeff laughed and said if people didn't like the bus system, they were free to buy a car like everyone else.

Sattle promised to unite his allies to vote against it.

Jeff took a swig and said state money could be used in a much better way.

Sattle also took a sip. He asked if there were any further matters he wanted to discuss. His voice changed pitch, which meant he was now facing Kylac's direction.

Jeff set his bottle down. "Nothing else. Yes, of course you can meet him."

Friend wagged his tail. "How's it feel to be a centerpiece?"

Jeff walked around one side of the couch and sat on Kylac's right. Senator Sattle stood at the other end, wine glass in hand. Kylac smelled cigar smoke on the senator's clothes.

"I trust you were listening?" said Jeff.

"I hear everything that happens in this room. Sometimes even the house."

"Excellent ears," Jeff said to Mr. Sattle.

The senator smiled as he swirled his wine. He took another sip.

"Senator Sattle wanted to meet you. I promised he could."

The senator sat down next to Kylac on the edge of the cushion, glancing at the khaki shorts Kylac wore. "I've heard so much about the aliens but have yet to meet one. I must say how privileged I feel."

Kylac did not look away from the televisions.

"I plan to retire soon. A number of people have offered me a job in their corporate sectors, thanks to the numerous contacts I've nurtured over the years, but I don't think I'm too interested. I may be too old to work for someone else."

He and Jeff chuckled.

Senator Sattle and Jeff stopped moving and froze in mid-laugh. Friend pushed away from the wall and approached the couch. He examined the two men visually up and down from multiple angles. The pictures on the TVs had frozen as well. The world had stopped. Friend often did this just to show he could. He had explained time and motion were linked, so he couldn't actually stop time, merely adjust the rate different parts of the universe moved. Time seemed to stop in one section that moved slower while moving normally in the other.

He turned to Kylac. "Would you like to know what they're going to ask so you can have a response ready?"

"It won't be a surprise. Jeff's friends all want one thing. Deka and I are an untapped resource. They want to use us to make more money."

Friend's tail waved wildly. "I can predict exactly what they're going to say next, so your side of the conversation should be obvious by solving for x, as they say here, but I still can't calculate it. It's blank to me. I have to watch it in real time."

"Must be so demeaning for someone with a brain the size of the universe."

"You could be here, too."

"I destroyed twelve worlds to know what I know. I murdered over three hundred thousand people. Not again."

"I'm living proof things can be different."

"You're not even sorry about the fifty-six planets you destroyed, or the two million six hundred and forty-one thousand nine hundred and three people you killed. That doesn't include the people who died indirectly because the portals went out."

"I think about them all the time. I am determined not to let their deaths be wasted. Being able to leave this universe is the larger goal, and it's more important than any planet."

"Why, Friend? You were willing to kill everyone in the universe to understand it. Why do you want this so badly? Whatever happened to pondering theoretical physics with Rive? The two of you created entire realities together out of it and you lived there more than you lived in the real one."

For the first time since his return, Friend had to think before he answered. "Call it an itch. Maybe I'd had enough of theory. Enough talking about it. This is discovery, Kylac. Other universes exist, and we have a chance to go there. Don't you feel an itch? Don't you want to know what else it out there?"

"Of course I'm curious, but it wasn't worth millions of lives."

"If I'm right, Kylac, it will be. I'm still working on the math, but it suggests leaving the universe is more important than any lives lost along the way. Nobody except for me seems to understand that. It still baffles me you threw away your chance to be part of it just to crawl back to Deka."

"That's not why I trapped you on Reyno."

"I showed you how to control your old ways yourself, and you begged your raptor to tame you again. Deka can't. You're still here."

"What about Rive?"

"What about him?"

"And Taris? Have you once thought of your mate? Of the child she would have had?"

"She would have had a son. I know what his life would have been had he been born. He would have achieved nothing but having another child who passed on my stable mind seemingly free of old ways."

Friend crossed Kylac's line of sight. He examined Jeff from head to toe.

"Atoms aren't real. These people aren't real. It's all shockwaves. Reality is somewhere else causing all of this to happen. Since realizing that, it's hard to remember why I once thought any of this matters."

"And you wonder why I don't want to be in the Lake. If I end up like you, then I will destroy the universe."

"I haven't, so you won't either. Let the collections of atoms fritter about, chasing the excess energy they need to stay together and hold the conscious mind within. There's another goal to chase. I will show you how to separate your higher mind from your old ways. Then together we can figure out what the Lake is and how to leave the universe."

"No, and I don't know of anything that will change my mind."

"It will happen."

Jeff and Sattle and the televisions began moving again. Friend walked to the far wall and leaned against the big screen.

"I am thinking of starting a hedge fund," the senator resumed. "Jeff has already agreed to provide some initial funding. I will provide the rest, and I will be running the fund, of course. I hear you and your raptor are outstanding at finding patterns and trends."

"I am very good at it," Kylac answered.

Friend mouthed Sattle's next words perfectly.

"You would be perfect to work the stock market. Do you know what a hedge fund is?"

"Other people pay you to invest their money."

Friend mouthed Sattle's words again.

"Exactly. We would be the only hedge fund with an Archeon picking the stocks. I think people will throw their money at us faster than we can spend it. So here's the proposal. All you have to do is what you already do. Watch monitors, look for trends, comb the news, look for other connections in the world that might affect the stock price. It would be an ideal job for you."

Friend's tail wagged. Kylac turned and met the senator's eyes for the first time. Mr. Sattle could not have been older and whiter had he been painted that way.

"And what would I get out of this?"

"You would get ten percent off the top. If we're right, that will add up to a substantial amount of money."

"So I do all the work, you take ninety percent of what I earn, and only give me ten?"

"It is my money I'm risking, as well as Jeff's and the other investors."

"But I will have done all the work."

"This is pretty generous for a hedge fund."

"I understand why. We are not here to solve your human problems. We are here to help you understand the root cause of your problems."

Sattle looked at Jeff. Mr. Morton leaned closer to Kylac. The fox turned to him. Friend crept up behind Jeff, opened his mouth, and mimed going for the throat.

"This is an excellent opportunity for all of us, but especially you, Kylac. You and Deka need to start earning money. You can't live on my dime forever."

"Actually, we can," Kylac said. "You have enough money for eight hundred and forty-seven people to live off of for the rest of their lives, even accounting for inflation."

Friend dropped to his knees and pretended to unzip Jeff's pants.

"That's not the point," Jeff said. "The point is that you must earn your own."

"And how are you earning your money?"

Friend was miming giving Jeff a blowjob. Kylac hadn't thought of Friend as a Relian canine in a very long time.

"Investments, mostly," Jeff answered. "I'm on the board of directors for several companies. I own a number of offshore mines. I'm part owner in a few factories and other funds."

"Your father was also rich. Sent you to private schools, introduced you to all his business friends, got you a good management position at a hedge fund. That's all you do. Last week one of your business associates said nothing for free, nothing for freeloaders. You expect a lot of money for no work."

"I'm risking my money on someone else's work. Of course I expect a return."

"You don't want to learn about me, and you don't care. All you want to do is use me. No, I will not manage other people's money."

Jeff shifted and looked at Senator Sattle, who had finished his wine and was setting the glass on the end table.

"Kylac," Jeff said. Friend now sat on his lap, pretending to ride his cock. "Let me make something clear. You, Deka, and Sonjaa cannot live off of me forever. I won't allow it. You will need to start working soon. I have presented you with outstanding offers for employment. Offers that would allow you to avoid the drudgery of labor. You're being foolish refusing them."

Friend rose from Jeff and walked to the big screen television. He leaned on it. Jeff and Mr. Sattle paused again.

"Oh, this is wonderful!" said the other fox. "He's about to threaten to cut off your food and water and throw you out in the cold if you don't work for him! This is the standard means they use to control other people! I can't wait to hear how he's going to react when it doesn't work!"

Kylac turned to Friend. "Should I not say it? Will it put the others in danger?"

"Not yet. Right now they still think it's just you and Deka who can't be reasoned with. They haven't made the connection that it's everyone."

Kylac looked at Jeff again. "Good. Resume, please."

Jeff and Mr. Sattle unpaused.

"I'm grateful for you taking us in, but I think you misunderstand this arrangement. We're not here because we have nowhere else to go. We're here because we want to be. Why would I work for you when I can go anywhere I want?"

"You haven't gone anywhere since you arrived. You have been living off me this whole time."

"Deka and I can hunt food anywhere, not just on Earth, but on any planet we please. You can't convince me to make you more money, so now you threaten me with starvation and exposure. People like you own the food, water, and shelter purely to make others work so you don't have to."

Jeff raised his hands. "Let's not make this personal. You have to start earning money. Nothing in life is free."

Senator Sattle inserted a calm word. "Listen, Kylac, you have brains. You're smart. I know you're watching all these shows and listening to this CD at the same time you're listening to us, so put those talents to good use. You can earn a lot of money with the things you can do."

Kylac turned to the senator. "I used my talents before the disaster. I maintained portals across the universe so people could travel between planets and live their lives as they wished."

"And now you're here, jobless. With that attitude, you'll be living poor."

"Living poor," Kylac said. "You say that as if it's a choice."

Jeff and Sattle laughed. The sight repulsed Kylac, so he turned to the televisions.

Friend pretended to whisper at Kylac from across the room. "This is good! I can't wait for him to say it!"

Jeff answered. "People are poor because they're lazy. You, me, Mr. Sattle, and Deka though, we're above that. Any idiot can inherit, but I've made more than my father did. If they would turn off their televisions and get off their couches, they'd have money, too. They'd get an education, get out of those neighborhoods, but no, they want me to pay taxes to fix those neighborhoods and keep buses going to them and keep the schools open. Instead of doing what they should do and get out, they stay there and live off welfare, and then want *me* to pay for their choice."

Friend was on all fours running up and down the walls and across the ceiling. "Excellent point! How will the fox answer? I can't take the suspense!"

"You charge people for that education," Kylac said, turning his head slightly in Jeff's direction. "You charge them to relocate, to eat, to sleep, to be warm. You charge people for the privilege of improving their lives. The only way to earn money is to work, but you cut the workforce so machines can take over. Then you move jobs elsewhere. You deprive people of the very thing they need to do what you say they should. Then you blame them for being lazy."

Jeff and Sattle looked at one another. Sattle's expression was *silence your dog*. Jeff's face said *he's not my dog*.

"Those bills you were talking about earlier," Kylac continued. "All of them were meant to help people, but you want to kill them. Why?"

"If you help people," Sattle said, "they'll become dependent on that help. The best way to provide public assistance is to stop helping them so they will get off their rears and help themselves."

"If they have what it takes to get out of trouble, they will," Jeff said.

"You didn't start where they are and rise up to where you are now. You started at the top and brought yourself higher. Where I come from, everyone starts at the top because nobody owns other person's food and shelter. Nobody forces another person to work so people like you don't have to. That's what employment is—it's implied in your language, to work *for* someone else, implying the burden has shifted to another person."

"Hmpf," snorted Mr. Sattle. "From what Jeff tells me, you were okay using your talents to maintain corridors across the universe, and you never expected anything in return for that. Picking stocks is bound to be a lot less work, but you want something for that?"

Kylac turned to face the senator. The contents of the TV screens still flowed into his mind, as did the music.

"I maintained portals throughout the contacted universe because it enabled entire civilizations to live the lives they wanted. I used my talent to give people freedom. I helped join the universe in one community. You use your talent to keep people separated and bickering amongst each other in pointless competition for the resources you control. Helping you will only benefit a few investors."

"That sounds boring, actually," Sattle said. "Nobody competing for anything, nobody needs to do work. Why do anything?"

"We do as we please."

"But without conflict," Sattle said, "people will become lazy. They need opposition and adversary. That's where creativity comes from. That's where innovation comes from."

"There are problems. Just not the same ones people like you create."

"You can't just let people do whatever they want," Sattle said, holding eye contact firmly. "They'll hurt each other and throw their lives away with sex and drugs. If their lives don't have some kind of structure and discipline, they won't do anything with them."

"You'd be surprised what people will do if they have the freedom to live. The difference is whether they have to survive or not. If you give people unlimited freedom but don't satisfy their need to survive, they will have to step on one another to achieve it. Take care of that, and there is no reason to hurt each other. That is what Deka and I did. Portals relieve everyone of the burden of survival. They free everyone to live for their own benefit, not for people like you, and certainly not for the sake of investors.

"Someone has to assert dominance over another person to force them to do something they won't benefit from directly. That's what you are. So you need managers and systems to make the people to do that work, those systems have problems, now you must create jobs for people to maintain those systems, and so on, layer upon layer until you eventually have your society: a bunch of horny males asserting dominance."

Jeff was about to speak. Sattle held his finger up. The senator locked eyes with Kylac.

"You seem to have things upside down, Kylac. People like me and Jeff. We do the work in this country. Take people like us away, all of society will collapse. Who do you think creates all the jobs the people need to buy food? Who do you think does all the innovation those people out there enjoy? People like Jeff do. What we do is for their benefit, and all they can do is complain about it. I am proud to have represented Jeff in Washington all these years. If not for me, the looters would have sucked Jeff dry by now. *That's* what happens when you give people unlimited freedom. I'd rather help him any day of the week because I know if I give him a dollar, he'll invest it and turn it into five dollars. Give any of them a dollar and they'll use it to get into debt, and then they'll want me to make Jeff get them out of it."

Kylac leaned close to Sattle until he touched noses with the man. "You think it is righteous to keep your fellow creatures in bondage to you instead of letting them live their own lives. You disgust me."

Kylac turned back to the televisions.

Senator Sattle stood, picked up his wine glass, and walked back to the bar. Jeff shot Kylac a dirty look as he followed. Friend was suddenly sitting next to Kylac, not depressing the couch cushion in any way. Jeff and Sattle stood at the bar and discussed the hedge fund they wanted to start.

"They still don't understand," Friend said.

"No, and that makes me so angry."

"Do you realize I could make them understand?"

Kylac looked at Friend. The other fox smiled with his muzzle instead of his tail.

"It might even change some things for a few people, but that would also make things worse for others. That's the problem. Any change I make will have other effects. This is why the Krone give up trying to help lone species. It's not worth the effort. No matter what I do, without constant maintenance, the planet moves toward the same end anyway."

"What hurts me is these people are in control of so much."

"They could say the same of you. You controlled a lot of portals, which in their minds translates to controlling a lot of people's food and water and safety, and yet you did not charge for it. You squandered your power. That's what they don't understand. Why you would devote your life to that and get nothing in return."

"Being a useful part of the contacted universe is reward."

"They can't put a price on that. To them, it's just work for no reward."

"They have no problem with reward for no work as long as they're the ones benefiting."

"They consider their position of wealth a job in and of itself."

Kylac sighed. "Do they really think the people on Earth are free to do as they please?"

"They believe what they were taught, too. Most don't even realize they are in control of anything and their decisions affect people's lives."

"Dominant individuals who are not even aware they are in control. Nothing can be more dangerous."

Friend was quiet. He pretended to watch TV with Kylac. Several laugh tracks later, Kylac turned to Friend and met his eyes.

"Should I have said all that?"

"It's all on your mind. Why not let it all out?"

"If I say the wrong thing, they could do something that will hurt a lot of people, and they might not even know it."

"That will happen, but not because of you. Don't worry."

Kylac held Friend's gaze for a moment. His tail wagged.

They both turned to the televisions. The rabbit ears on one of the sets needed adjusting. The antenna adjusted itself, and the snow lessened.

"Thanks," Kylac said.

Friend's tail wagged.

The lady on the stereo went on and on about a prematurely air-conditioned supermarket. A moment later, the CD changed, and *Music for 18 Musicians* played.

Kylac blinked. "This is the wrong disc."

Friend's tail wagged. "Penny switched the discs around while you were in the bathroom. She's trying to tell you she's tired of this music."

Kylac's tail twitched.

2

One of the men in Jeff's upstairs office wore a suit. The other wore shorts and a Hawaiian shirt. The man in the suit had not introduced himself, but he did introduce the man in the shorts as Martin. No last name.

The men sat in the office chairs in front of the computer desk. Deka and Sonjaa sat on the floor in the middle of the room. Friend sat on the desk behind the two men, mouthing their words as they spoke.

The suited man had done most of the talking. He had brought numerous papers with him, all schematics and drawings and technical outlines. He had shown them to Deka, periodically forgetting Sonjaa was even in the room. Right now he held up an oversized sheet depicting a missile defense system.

"The hardware is pretty much finalized. But the software... Oh, the software is shit. Take a look at this."

He took out some leaves of normal-sized paper, pages and pages of printed computer code.

"It is so long, so confusing, so complicated nobody can find all the bugs in it. It's spaghetti. Pure spaghetti. Now, Deka, you don't know computer code, or engineering, or any such thing do you?"

"No."

"But you can learn, and I'm told you learn very fast. Once you're up to speed, you can read all of this code in just a couple hours. It would take months for any one person to read it, and they can't hold the entire program in their mind. My friend Jeff said you can help us get back on schedule. I can promise you'll be paid very well for your service, and you'll never be without work. These engineers get paid top dollar, but then they load the code with bugs so the company has no choice but to keep them on the payroll so they can fix it."

"Actually," Deka said, "your company is cutting back. I checked into it when Jeff told me you were coming. It's loading more work onto fewer people, constricting deadlines and hiring subcontractors in India, so the engineers are forced to create their own job security."

The suited man smiled. "Exactly! It's that kind of analysis we need!"

"You want me to replace seven hundred engineers and programmers?"

"Hell no, you won't be replacing them. Obviously we don't expect you to design everything yourself. Just debug what others have done."

"I am not an idiot," Deka said.

Martin and the suit had already paused. Friend danced on the desk.

"Damn it, Friend, stop that!"

Friend rolled around on the desk and then looked at them upside down. Deka and Sonjaa could not see how he fit up there without knocking things over.

"You should know this is not a real missile project," he said, tail waving wildly. "That's not real code. A bunch of engineers made up dummy papers for this presentation. The real projects are much different, but the problems he describes are real, and they are on systems like that."

"Shut up," Deka said.

"His bosses plan to hire you to debug everything, but they never plan to tell you what the code is for or what the projects are supposed to be. All of that is classified. They'll tell you it's for missile defense systems, and that's true, they can be used defensively, but they can just as easily be used as offensive weapons. They plan to load them onto remote-controlled airplanes. They will use your work to oppress people, but the whole time they will tell you they're for defense."

"I was going to tell them that!"

"Were you? That's so interesting! I forget how smart you are. Both of you. They don't care about you, Sonjaa. They're letting you hear this because they know Deka won't listen without you."

"I'm used to it," she said.

"You're a woman, so they think you're driven by emotion and won't be able to make the kinds of decisions needed in leadership."

"I know. I've only lived here for a year and I fucking know."

"They see you have talent for languages," Friend continued, "but that's it. They'll have a job for you in the future, but interpreters aren't really necessary when obedience is all they want from people in other countries."

"Just let me talk," Deka said.

"You should hear the conversation Kylac is having with Jeff and his senator downstairs. Would you like to go down and listen? I'll keep time paused in this room so you can."

"No. Resume."

The suit unpaused. Martin leaned on the desk, hand on chin, watching them.

"I'm not an idiot," Deka said. "As soon as you hire me and I start doing the work of a hundred engineers, your company will fire most of the staff and expect me to do their work."

"I doubt very much the company would let that many talented people go," said the suit.

"You just said they were milking payroll. It's only because the company is squeezing them that they're responding in this way. Your friendship with Jeff gave your company a way to replace those jobs."

The suited man smiled. "He told us you'd be a hard sell. That's why they got me. All right, you can see right through me. Yeah, they'll cut a lot of jobs when they take you on. Even more if your fox comes. But so what? You have more brains between you than all of those people put together. You can handle the work. They can't. Just take the money and run."

"I don't want money, neither does Sonjaa, and neither does Kylac."

"You really think Jeff is going to let you live here for free forever? He told me he's getting frustrated with all of you. He's bringing you job after job, but you won't work. Push him too far and you'll be out on the street."

They paused. Friend leaped to his feet and stood proudly on the desk. "Jeff's senator and Kylac are having the same conversation downstairs."

"Really?" said Sonjaa. "This meeting must be special. We can expect a change in Jeff after this."

"Definitely. It's only been a month, and you three have managed to piss off your host. If you weren't Archeons, you'd be in trouble. You have no such worry, but the other people who can't make portals do. If they lose their government aid, they'll have nowhere to hunt. Nowhere to find food. Everything is owned, and the laws are set up to protect the owners, not people who are trying to live independent lives."

"I know how this society works," Deka said.

"You ready to tell them that?"

"I don't need your help preparing an answer."

The man in the suit unpaused. Martin also resumed, but he hadn't moved much, so it was hard to tell. Deka answered the suited man.

"Why would I work for your company knowing other people will lose their livelihood? Companies are predators, but unlike any I have met before. People create predatory entities to hunt their fellow creatures. Real predators don't hunt their own kind. I don't hold other raptors in bondage to me. I don't control their food to make them hunt for me. I will not be part of that, so I will not help your company make weapon systems designed to keep people part of that."

"These weapons are defensive," said the suit. "The United States has enemies, and these systems keep us safe from them."

"The United States has enemies because this country has invaded other nations so corporations such as yours can move in and take their resources. The United States installs oppressive governments that keep the people down so you can operate without opposition, and then you give nothing back to the people but the pollution. If the people are enemies, it's because they're fighting back against something that subjugates them. You demonize them for desiring freedom. Your company is very much part of this."

Martin sat up. He seemed to be paying attention now. "Yup, you're not stupid."

Friend climbed onto Martin's head and perched on his scalp. "Give him the Archeon test." His tail waved wildly.

It was the first thing Friend had said that interested Deka. He checked with Sonjaa, then started talking.

"There is a species named the Zalh. They also have a companion species named the Weban. The Zalh realized what they were, and the alphas started using their position to take their whole species higher. They consider it a privilege to be in such a position. The Weban, however, have a solitary social structure."

At the same time, Sonjaa spoke: "They live on the planet Dulet. They have a similar social structure to yours. Dominant males rise up to the top of the group. The Zalh live in the trees, much like you once did, and the Weban are mammals on the ground, similar to kangaroos, actually."

Martin smiled. Friend smiled with his mouth as well, imitating his human grin.

"The Zalh are primates like us," Martin said. "The Weban are kangaroos. The Zalh's alphas use their position to take their species higher. The Weban have a solitary social structure."

Deka rose and approached Martin. He scented him. Martin seemed oddly comfortable being examined like this.

"That was the first Archeon test," Deka said. "You passed. What else can you do?"

"Quite a bit of the same things you two can. I can read like that," he snapped his fingers, "and follow a few dozen conversations at once, watch ten TVs at once. But I can't remember everything, and I can't learn languages like you. I definitely can't open doors to other planets."

Deka stopped, looked at him. "So why aren't you debugging the code?"

"I am, but even I can't hold an entire program in my head at once. I can do a few modules, but you... You'd put me out of a job." He rocked in the chair and smiled. "So let's be real here. Other people have things we need, everyone in the world has a role to play, we're on top, they're not. Enjoy it while it lasts. You've got a sweet setup here with Jeff Morton. You know if you don't cooperate with something, he can make a few phone calls and raptors and foxes will suddenly find themselves without food stamps. No hunting grounds. If they try to hunt, they'll be arrested, and the press will demonize them for trying to eat. Suddenly they have to work. Then states will pass laws forbidding raptors and foxes from working together, so now they have to leave their foxes during the working day. Kinda funny how it will happen, ain't it?"

Deka rose to full height. He looked past the fox perched on Martin's head to the man in the suit.

"This is how you use the smartest people in your society? Making weapons? Designing new ways to oppress people?"

"It's good money," Martin said. "I need it. Still paying off student loans. No jobs outside the military for someone like me. Skill like this is pretty useless in normal jobs."

Deka walked back to Sonjaa's side and sat down. "Money is the tool other human beings use to control you. They squander the smartest people in society, making your skills useless except to help the people in power keep everyone else from rising up to challenge them. The Zalh would have done the same thing if not for their companion species. Mature societies want everyone to be smarter. Your society goes out of its way to keep the people thoughtless and weak so they have to buy things. No demand for car repair if everyone knows how to maintain their own vehicles. Ignorant people will also never ask why things work the way they do. Mature species want everyone to have freedom to live as they choose."

"Things might improve," said the suited man. "You said Martin passed the test. I'm sure there'd be an enormous reward if you taught him the secret of those spheres you can open."

Everyone paused. Friend jumped off Martin's head and stood on all fours before the two theropods. Deka hesitated, turning from Martin to Friend several times. Finally he focused on the fox.

"What do you know about him?"

"He is one of hundreds on this planet who are mentally capable, but humans lack a companion species, that one little element that keeps them from understanding what the universe really is. Or what you think the universe really is. Enough to allow his mind to open portals. You can teach him all you want, but he will never understand."

"I thought so."

Martin unpaused.

"You show the potential," said the raptor, "but even if I explained how to create portals, you would not comprehend. If you could, you would use them as weapons, and then you would take the military to other worlds and take their resources, just as your nation does to others."

"It's how the world works," said Martin. "You can fight it all your life and live paranoid and helpless in the gutter, or you can work with it and live easy. Make your choice. Pretty soon, the other Relians around the world won't have one."

"We represent people who are free," Sonjaa said, "and all you want is to destroy it. Every person who comes to this house has the same reaction. It makes me sick."

"Free." Martin snorted. "You dominate your foxes and you call that being free. You outright admit you control their reproduction, force them to be at your side the whole time, tell them where they can and can't go, who they can sleep with. What right do you have to tell foxes they can't have children or they can't live *their* own lives?"

Friend wagged his tail as Martin spoke. "I like this guy!"

Sonjaa straightened her neck. "Our social structure is different from yours. You don't even want to understand us. Your first thought is to change us to suit your needs."

Martin laughed. "It's still fucked up. You sit there and judge us, but you do the same damn thing to your dogs. No human being would ever submit to that kind of treatment."

Deka answered. "Actually they do. Every human submits to the control of someone else. Their boss, the police, the community, someone is always in control, and everyone hates it. It's an entire planet of people who don't want to be told what to do, but they spend their entire lives that way, and you're surprised when they fight back."

Sonjaa growled at the word *dogs* and then spoke at the same time: "Rupi submitted to me because she knew she needed me to keep her instincts under control. I needed my fox to help me break away from my family ties and hunting instincts. Our relationship with our companion species is mutual companionship, not dominance or submission the way you know it. Stop trying to define it in your terms."

"Bullshit," said Martin. Friend was rolling on the floor, imitating human laughter. "Absolute bullshit. I've seen how foxes are around raptors. They check their raptors for everything they want to do. If they had a taste of freedom, they'd get out."

"I love this guy!" Friend shouted.

"Foxes know what they are apart from us," Sonjaa said, killing claws rising. "We are using our position to bring our foxes higher, which is something I don't think you are even capable of understanding. This is why there is no crime or war in the contacted universe. Nobody is oppressing one another, and nobody is trying to break free from it."

Martin smelled indignant. "Are you saying criminals and terrorists are righteous for trying to kill us?"

"Not at all," Deka answered. "People rebel against someone else's control; it is human nature to do so. It comes from the animal instinct to rise up in the group to achieve the right to mate. Here, they are punished for doing so, which goes against their nature. Crime and terrorism are inevitable results of your social structure."

"People who don't want to work," Martin said. "People who will bomb buildings just to rack up a body count and take our stuff. Hypocrites, all of you. We're doing the best we can with the system we've got. It ain't perfect, but it's a hell of a lot better than what they've got elsewhere. I'd rather be here designing weapons to keep people like that away from me than over there working in a factory for pennies a week."

"I have read your history," Deka said, hands sagging. "Humans do not only have an instinct to dominate. You also have an instinct to nurture and care for one another. It's another trait from before you achieved sentience, when groups banded together for mutual survival. I have read there are cultures in the world that emphasize these impulses. All of them have been swallowed up or annihilated by the current culture, which means the instinct to dominate is taking over. Because you have no companion species —another intelligent creature sharing the planet with you to teach you how to understand yourselves from another perspective, this instinct has gone unchecked. It will destroy your species eventually."

"If you want peace in the world," Sonjaa said, "stop oppressing other people. If you want your enemies to go away, don't build more weapons. Just stop forcing them to do things they don't want to do."

Martin huffed. "Who wants peace? Nobody would have jobs if we were at peace. What the hell good is my talent without military contracts?"

Deka stood. "This is why you'll never be an Archeon."

He walked to the door. Sonjaa followed.

The man in the suit rose from his chair. "You two really need to change your attitude. I'm warning you. The honeymoon won't last."

Deka paused at the door and turned to him. "Not if we get through to the right people first."

"Jeff is the right people," said the suit. "Disappoint him and he will ruin the lives of every single raptor and fox in the country. They'll end up ditch diggers in Mexico."

"You can't threaten a predator."

"One phone call," said Martin, holding up his index finger, "and there will be an incident. A murder, maybe, a mass killing. Doesn't matter who causes it or why, or if a fox or a raptor was just defending himself. The press will claim people are clamoring for raptors and foxes to be declawed and de-toothed. Politicians will use that as an excuse to pass a law making it happen. All because people like Jeff decided it needs to happen. Don't think it can't. I've seen it."

"We are a threat to their position," Deka said. "They don't want things to change, and Relians represent the first real change on Earth since the last ice age."

"You're lucky Jeff is patient," said the suit. "Most rich guys aren't. If they can't use you, they ditch you. You want a second chance, you have to beg. Hell, if you want a first chance, you have to beg."

Sonjaa stretched her neck toward him. "He's lucky we're indulging his offers."

Deka turned the knob and walked out the door, Sonjaa following. Deka closed the door behind them. Another instance of Friend frolicked in the hallway.

Sonjaa curled her neck as she watched. "What happened to you? You never acted this way when you were alive."

"I am *happy*! For the first time in my life, I feel joy! Real joy! I don't know why—maybe being in a place where only a conscious mind can exist has something to do with it. Theoretical physics is real, and I'm living it at last!"

"We've gone from friendly business offers to threats, and you're dancing like a cartoon."

Friend jumped, landed on the ceiling, and stared down at them. "I can't predict all of this! I know what they're doing, but I can't tell how either of you will react! This is... Do you have any idea what it's like to be trapped where you can see everything all at once? Where you know everything, and nothing can surprise you? No wonder the god of this universe moved on!"

"Actually, yes," Sonjaa said, twitching and shuddering. "I know exactly what it's like."

Friend fell from the ceiling and landed upright on the floor but did not make a sound. He rose to their height. "Go downstairs. I paused Kylac's conversation for you."

"You what?" Deka said.

"I even rewound it to the beginning so you can watch the whole thing. You should know Kylac was watching your conversation with a version of me."

"Time travel is impossible," Deka said, walking down the hall to the stairs. Sonjaa and Friend were at his side.

"You saw it when I brought Rel back. We're not actually traveling through time. I'm just holding pieces of spacetime back from moving with the rest of the universe and moving you to different points where the universe has already been. I can't influence anything, but manipulating spacetime is easy for me now."

"This can't be safe," Sonjaa said.

"Just watch and enjoy. I'll bring the whole house together in its proper time shortly."

They walked down the stairs and paused at the drawing room. Sure enough, everything was frozen. Deka grumbled and took position in a corner. Sonjaa stood behind the couch and looked at Friend.

"Helping us doesn't make up for all the people you killed. Your attitude about life isn't much different from those men."

Friend had perched on top of the entertainment center. "That was before I sent my old ways out of the universe. Those men are living by their old ways, so to speak."

"Where did you send them?" she asked.

"Between the universes. I wish I had known how to do it when the antispheres first started, but this is how progress happens."

Sonjaa rubbed her claws. "I never saw you this happy when you were with Rive. I wish I could be that happy without a fox."

Friend tilted his head. "Having a larger goal helps." His tail wagged.

Dover

I

Vae liked this city. It was small, and to its west lay wilderness, back roads, and family farms. Plenty of places to roam and hunt where nobody would notice her. She sped through the night across the road and onto the next plot of farmland, tracking a scent.

Before the disaster, she had taken Tema to planets that had small prey which eluded predators. Some left false scent trails, others jumped from tree to tree, others had blunt feet that left no scent marks, forcing her to search for other places where the scent would be. Nothing made her blood flow like tracking.

Right now she had the scent of one of this region's most elusive herbivores. The locals considered it mundane, but they were not predators, so they could not appreciate what a beautiful creature a deer was. They had hooves on their feet, perfect for leaving no scent marks. They were fast, which was usual for a species that had to run from threats all the time. They were cautious. Fearful. Designed by evolution to be chased.

She went on these hunts once every couple of weeks at first, but as time went by, the anxiety did not go away. Lucy worked longer and longer, came home more and more exhausted, and her scent only became worse. Lucy was herself on the weekends, but her job often bled into those as well.

In the contacted universe, there was always something to do, somewhere to go, something new to discover on one planet or another—something special they had not witnessed. New people to know, new perspectives on what it meant to be alive. On this world, there was nothing to do if one was not working. Vae and Tema were bored of the television. Recorded music had such a narrow range it felt like listening to a clipped voice no matter how busy the composition was. Vae swore this society had been designed to be boring in order to force people to seek employment just to pass the time.

Vae followed hoofprints across the field and into a bank of trees. She caught the scent against a trunk and followed it in the most likely direction. The vibrations of the distant traffic distracted her, but that was part of the challenge of hunting here.

The raptor ran down the faint trail. The buck's scent was in full flight mode, and it smelled delicious. A few hundred strides later, she saw him cutting across a field toward another cluster of trees. The buck was in the open.

She bolted. Running at full speed reminded her what her body was capable of. She was much faster than the buck, so she closed in on him in no time. The creatures on this world were not adapted to her, so catching prey was almost too easy, but they remained elusive enough to be invigorating.

Moments later she leaped on top of him, and her bulk knocked him to the ground. Her killing claws sliced his abdomen open, and at the same time she reached for his neck and snapped it in half. The crackling sound made her feel like a predator again. She let the buck's head drop, bent down, tore a few hunks of meat from the carcass, and swallowed them whole. The meat did not taste good.

She stared at it. Everything in her wanted to take this back to Tema and Lucy so everyone could eat. So Tema wouldn't be so listless. So Lucy wouldn't smell so bad all the time.

She realized it wouldn't work here. Vae knew what was happening. She knew her impulses well enough to realize what she was trying to do, and knowing it didn't work on this planet made her angry. Everything logical and natural was futile here.

She left the carcass to rot and trotted home, following her own scent trail across the fields and through the trees. After crossing a couple roads, she came back to the city. A sidewalk replaced the bare ground, and with it the smell of everything artificial. Asphalt, concrete, synthetic rubber, car exhaust. The first few paces made her cringe.

Lucy lived in a housing development that bordered the outskirts of the city. She turned down their street. She turned again and set foot on the driveway, Lucy's car parked in it. Vae preferred to be home when Lucy arrived, but this hunt had taken longer than usual.

Vae hopped the step to the front door and turned the knob. The television was on some late-night program. Lucy and Tema's scents came from the couch. Another odor in the air told her Tema had been helping Lucy relax, and she was glad one of them was able to do that.

She noticed new papers on the table. She walked to the pile and looked them over. Bills for doctor's offices, receipts for prescription drugs. She picked up a new bottle beside the papers. She didn't know what the name meant, but the directions said to take one pill every twenty-four hours to reduce anxiety. This was the third new bottle in the last month.

The raptor turned the corner and walked into the living room. Tema and Lucy lay cuddled up on the couch.

Lucy's clothes lay crumpled in a pile on the floor. A studio audience laughed at a comedian on television.

Tema turned to her raptor, scenting in her direction. "How was the buck?"

She crossed the living room and then lay in front of Tema. The fox began cleaning the blood off her muzzle. Lucy watched, still curled into Tema's fur.

"Long. Unsatisfying."

"Not difficult enough?" asked the fox.

"It was, but something else is bothering me."

"You really should wash that off before you come back," Lucy said. "It's risky enough going out hunting at all. Someone sees you, they'll call the police on you."

"What's bothering you?" Tema said between licks.

"There's no reason to hunt. I can't bring it back, and it's not even allowed. It won't solve the problem."

"What problem?" said Lucy.

Tema had finished cleaning off Vae's snout. Now she took one of her hands and began licking the claws.

"The buck's scent. He was in flight. The stress hormones make his body pump extra power into his muscles so he can move faster. Anything to preserve his life from a threat."

"That's normal," said Lucy. "Isn't it?"

"Normal for a buck but not for you."

Lucy cuddled into Tema deeper. She smelled so relaxed now, but underneath it Vae smelled latent anxiety. She stretched her neck to be nose to nose with the human and continued.

"Stress is how the body deals with threats. The body is not supposed to be under stress for long periods of time. The effects of it over entire years are unpredictable. I saw you have new medicine."

Lucy nodded. "Doctor gave them to me today. I'll start them in the morning. Maybe they'll help."

"You've already tried four medicines. You can't keep putting chemicals into your body and expect that to solve the problem."

"Is that why you're so restless lately?" Lucy said, smiled. "Are you worried about me?" She reached up and lay a hand on Vae's muzzle. "Don't let yourself get stressed over me, now."

"My first instinct is to hunt," Vae said. "This place makes me restless because hunting won't help you. Everything I normally do is suppressed here."

"It's so sweet of you to want to help, Vae. But you have to get a job. A damn good one."

Tema had finished with one hand. Now she took the other and licked the claws one by one.

"That is what irritates me. To help, I must hunt someone else's way, hunt their prey with tools they charge me money to use, and then I must hunt surrender my kill to them and be satisfied with the scraps they leave me."

Lucy laughed. She let her hand fall from Vae's muzzle and buried it in Tema's fur again. "You've only been here six months and you're already griping about taxes."

"Not that! I'm talking about the need to work for someone else so I can buy food instead of hunting it myself."

"Isn't that what you normally did? You hunted for Tema. Others ate what you killed, too."

"The game was free for all predators to enjoy so we didn't need to fight over it. Here... Just smelling all the stress people are under shows how unnatural it is. Anything that keeps a person in a constant fight for life must stop."

Tema had finished with the claws. She curled up on the couch again. Vae stood at full height and backed away so she could talk to both of them.

"There must be another job, Lucy. Another way you can earn money."

Lucy laughed weakly. "I'm a lawyer. There's no such thing as stress-free work."

"Maybe it's time to stop being a lawyer."

"It's way too late for me to start over. I'm still in debt from my law degree. Like it or not, I'm stuck with this. I need this job to pay down my loans. They just keep growing no matter how much I pay, it seems. Plus the car, the house..."

"Do you have vacation time?"

"Too many cases pending. Half of them would fall apart without me."

Vae looked into her eyes. They were dreamy and tired, a mask covering years of anxiety, and the body had to destroy itself to handle more of it, a threat it could never defeat or escape, and Lucy was in it against her will.

That scent at the office building... She was sure it had been suffering, but pondering what Lucy did all day made her think twice. She thought she might have misunderstood. She needed to take it in again.

"Teach me about the cases."

"Mmm, what?"

"I will be your replacement while you're on vacation. We'll start in the morning. Tema and I will go with you to work. Give me everything I need to take over for a while."

Lucy sat up and met the raptor's eyes. "Are you serious?"

Vae held her hands together, rubbing her claws.

"Vae, it's not that simple. It takes years to learn how to be a lawyer. You can't just take over for me."

"I have watched you at work. Your job is telling others what to do. You don't need a law degree to do that."

"Oh, yes, you do. It's my experience that tells those people what to pursue, what we can get away with, and what we shouldn't bother fighting."

"I can learn."

Lucy laughed. "I can't afford to put someone through law school."

"Give me the books you read to learn law, and I will know what you know."

"Vae, it's still not that simple. There are channels to go through. By the time you pass the bar, I'll be on heart medicine."

Vae growled. "This is how they trap you."

"All the exits are covered."

The raptor looked away, still growling. Then she thought of something. "People had assistants there. I will be yours. Please let me help."

Lucy thought for a moment. She smiled. "I don't think anyone will stop me from doing *that*."

2

On the hunting grounds throughout the contacted universe, the scent of the hunt was everywhere, and the more predators who gathered, the stronger it became and the more exciting it felt. Vae preferred to hunt alone, but from time to time she liked joining up with others who enjoyed tracking. There was stress, there was adrenaline, there was blood and danger and death, but it smelled good. It excited her. It made life worth living.

So she wondered why it smelled so bad here.

The prey was elusive and cunning. It left no traces, and it tried to throw everyone off the track. This seemed to be exactly the kind of place she would thrive, and yet it smelled rancid. The question had bothered her since the first time Lucy brought her to work.

Now she and Tema were here again, trapped in Lucy's office as people came to her with case after case, question after question, complication after dilemma after proposal after subtle threat.

Vae took in their scents. She searched them for something familiar. Something she thought she remembered but had been too scared to face at the time. It reminded her so much of the disaster she could barely tolerate it. Now she forced herself to understand it instead of react to it. As the hours passed, and she smelled dozens of people under various degrees of stress, she realized what was happening.

This was the same exciting scent she enjoyed on the hunting grounds, but decayed with age. It was how the joy of hunting elusive prey would smell if it were years old and never allowed to rest. This was exactly Vae's kind of place, except the people in it were not allowed to stop hunting. They lived in fear of failure not because it was their own personal failure to catch it, but because they might lose access to it. Vae never doubted her own ability to kill to stay alive. Lucy's work, however, seemed to cultivate this doubt and use it against everyone to make them hunt harder. The smell of fear and decayed adrenaline was everywhere, and the ventilation system spread it around so there could be no escape, even in the solitude of the restrooms.

Vae took mental notes for Lucy. She reminded Lucy of meetings and conference calls. She reminded Lucy to call so-and-so at such-and-such time. She remembered details about cases Lucy would have had to look up. When her co-workers asked Vae where her notebook was, she replied her memory was good enough she didn't need one. Nobody believed her until she started reminding Lucy of things they themselves had forgotten.

Whenever Lucy mentioned a case precedent, Vae made a mental note to look it up and read more about it. Whenever Lucy mentioned procedure, Vae made sure to remember it for further reading. She wished she were an Archeon so she could read everything at a glance, but she had been told she was a fast reader by human standards, so she supposed she made excellent progress.

Vae's new role as Lucy's assistant felt strange but not too different from swiping her claws across a giant herbivore to slow it down so another predator could make a killing blow. Knowing she had been part of a successful hunt felt just as satisfying as closing her own mouth around its neck. It was more metaphorical in Lucy's world, but the body reacted as if it were life and death.

Vae reminded Lucy to call a law firm by this time with an answer. Lucy picked up the phone and switched it to conference so the Relians could listen. The man on the other end was elusive. Vae felt hormones rising up, blood moving into her muscles. The impulses were the same, and if not for the fear scent covering it up, this would be the hunting grounds all over again. Now that she had learned to smell beneath the fear and anxiety and search for the scent of her fellow predators, she felt as though she belonged here. All she had to learn was how to follow the scent trails these people left, and they would be hers.

This was not a good atmosphere for hunting. Had Vae smelled this offworld, she would not have hunted there. It was wrong, people's bodies pumped full of panic hormones long enough for it to rot into exhaustion and anxiety, all of them confident and yet full of doubt. If not for that, Lucy's law firm would be exactly her kind of hunting grounds.

Vae ignored the fear and anxiety and focused on the hunt. It was new prey, and it needed to be studied. She had done this countless times whenever she and Tema went to a new world. There was always new prey to track. When she studied it, she missed nothing. She forgot nothing. She was hunting again.

Vae knew this job would keep her in hunting mode for days at a time. It would wreak her health, and there was no way to tell how it would affect her in the long run, but it was how she had to hunt on this planet.

Several conference calls and debates among her subordinates later, the day calmed down enough for her to go home relatively early at six in the evening. They did not walk through the door until just after seven. Lucy went upstairs and slipped into bed with Tema.

The raptor took out the books on law and looked up the cases other people had mentioned. There was so much law, so many interpretations of it, and so much of it was contradictory, but her prey hid within it, so she had to catch it.

She went back the next day and took more notes for Lucy. Lucy left Vae and Tema alone in her office so she could have a lunch break, and Vae fielded a few questions from her subordinates. They did not seem to mind listening to her as long as they believed she spoke on Lucy's behalf.

So far, nobody had stopped them. They saw Vae reminding Lucy of meetings and calls to make and case details and prior phone calls. She excelled at remembering what people said or did not say during phone calls, and Lucy had been thrilled to have someone who could throw their own words back in their face. People accepted the reptile as Lucy's assistant. She became part of the office by the third day.

What most people did not understand was why Tema remained there. She did not seem to do anything except sit around and listen, but when it came time for meetings with other law firms, she showed everybody exactly why Vae and Lucy brought her along.

Her pheromones made everyone uneasy except for Lucy and Vae. Twenty minutes in a closed room with the fox, and the other men and women suddenly found themselves a lot more agreeable. It wasn't long before they caught on and kept Tema out of the room during meetings, but Tema did not mind. She was sure they'd ask for her eventually, and on the fifth day, during a difficult meeting with a very difficult attorney representing an even more difficult client, they brought her in. An hour later, the difficult attorney had dropped his roadblock, and the case began moving again. The office knew Tema as Vae's assistant from that day on.

Vae amassed an enormous amount of details on every pending case. She began to anticipate what Lucy would say and spoke it before Lucy did. It happened so often people began to talk to Vae first; only when she asked Lucy did her team talk to the human about the cases.

In the third week, Vae started to field questions from Lucy's subordinates. People had begun to go to Vae for things first, talking to Lucy through her raptor. The transition had been so gradual and yet so profound.

Lucy couldn't believe people were doing it. Nobody had told them to do it. The raptor had just placed herself between Lucy and them, and they listened to her. Vae was not surprised it had happened. She had been among many species that had a hierarchy of dominance before. She remembered how some individuals slipped into positions without anyone noticing. Vae had behaved as expected among these other species, so they had accepted her as one of their own.

The days began running into one another. Vae couldn't remember the last time she relaxed and enjoyed herself, but she began to see the trails in the dirt, smell where the fur had brushed against the trees, and hear the crunch of underbrush. The more the lawyers talked, the more sense it made, and she even became outraged before Lucy did at this announcement or that.

Today she reminded Lucy of a meeting with the directors, and they expected a statement from her. Lucy held her head in her hands as she sat at the desk.

"I'll take care of it," Vae said.

"You think you can?" Lucy looked up at her.

She lowered her muzzle to Lucy's cheek and rubbed it. "Absolutely."

"Would you, please? I don't think I can face them now."

Vae walked to the door. Tema took Vae's place and nuzzled Lucy at her desk. The raptor paused in the hallway, regarding them. For a month she had shared Lucy's anxiety. She had tasted it herself, so she knew exactly in what kind of environment Lucy worked. Lucy's body, and maybe her species, was not meant to handle this kind of stress for such long intervals. Neither was a Relian's, but a Relian reptile was better suited for it than any human.

She was hunting. This time it was making a difference. Now it was time to face the men who represented the people who demanded human beings endure such conditions, sacrifice their health and happiness in perpetual, miserable anxiety. She walked around the corner, took the elevator up, and stopped at the secretary's desk.

"The board is expecting a presentation. Lucy sent me to give it to them. An important development has come up in a case, and she cannot leave. I am Lucy's assistant, Vae."

The secretary could not have cared less. She pushed the button and buzzed the people in the next room.

"Sir, Ms. Vae is here with the presentation as requested."

"Send her in."

The secretary waved her though. She opened the double doors and stalked inside. All of the men in the room jumped to their feet at the sight of her. Some looked ready to walk away, but then they noticed the papers in her hands. She had the details memorized, so she didn't need the papers at all, but had she walked in empty-handed, they would not have believed she was here to give a presentation.

Mr. Lawrence Brendon, seated at the head of the table, had been taken aback. "Where the hell is Ms. Schrifton?"

Vae approached the table. "Ms. Schrifton is busy with a case in development. She sent me to give the presentation. I'm Vae, her assistant."

"Did we hire her?" one of the men said to the other, thinking she wouldn't hear.

"No," Vae said to him. "Ms. Schrifton did."

A few of the men murmured. Vae did not give them any more time to think about it. She looked at one of the papers and pretended to read from it.

"Regarding the Ellisburg case, in which our client is plaintiff, we have managed to negotiate a settlement of forty-eight million and change, up from the original twenty. They had been unwilling to negotiate the patent infringement until we cited a case won last year for a similar infringement. Lucy herself noticed the case. Somehow it had passed under everyone's radar all these months. We must have caught them by surprise. They did not want to go to court with that kind of precedent. They agree to pay damages plus royalties, however, in exchange, they may keep using our client's proprietary software."

Several breaths passed in silence. The men sitting around the table looked at one another. None of them had been listening, but Vae wasn't interested in them. She had given that entire speech looking straight at the man sitting in the center of this. Her killing claws rose while she waited for him to respond.

"Is that wise?" Mr. Brendon finally asked. "They're a competitor."

"Lucy convinced our client to set a precedent of their own," Vae said, meeting his eyes. "They don't want to spend all their time putting out fires. They want to establish that they are willing to allow legal use through the proper channels."

The men considered that. Vae could smell detached boredom coming from all of them. They were stressed, but not in the same way. Their only worry was how the people under them performed. It took effort not to growl at them for making Lucy and all those lawyers on the floors below stay in perpetual hunting mode while they themselves reaped the benefits.

"I think that's wise," said the man at the head of the table. "How soon will we close the case?"

"Before the end of the quarter."

"Very good. How is the Genston situation progressing? I've heard a lot about that one in the press."

Vae flipped through the packet. Her fingers were not as nimble as Lucy's when it came to paper, so for this one she rested the pile on the table and parted the papers a few at a time. Becoming frustrated, she straightened up and looked over all the men in the room.

"We are still negotiating that one. We offered three million. They're asking for nine."

"A number of their shareholders have written to us about that," said Mr. Brendon. "They don't want anything over four and a half. They're afraid anything more will affect their dividends."

"We've been keeping the ceiling at five so far. Lucy and her team are still working on other ways to yield without money involved."

"What other ways?" said one of the men who, just a few minutes ago, didn't believe she was here.

Just as she had thought, all she had to do was convince the dominant male to take her seriously, and the others would follow. Her hunting grounds had expanded to in-clude the entire firm and everyone it represented. Her killing claws tapped the carpet under the table.

3

Vae looked at the bottles on the bathroom sink. Only one of them was missing pills, and not nearly as many as there should have been. The other three prescriptions had collected dust. She hadn't refilled any of these bottles in months. Vae lowered her muzzle and scented them, tempted to try one, but for all she knew they would be poi-son to her.

She backed out of the bathroom and turned to the bed. Lucy and Tema were curled up together. Lucy had been home by herself for the last week, and Vae could tell she had mostly been sleeping. Not the kind of sleep to delay anxiety, meant to help her rest so she could deal with more of it, but the kind of sleep in which a person knows anxiety will not come again soon, so she could drop her guard.

It had been the prey Vae had sought to capture for months. It had eluded her all this time. To find it, she had to catch other elusive animals until she had enough corpses to add up to this moment. She watched Lucy sleep past the alarm while she held Tema. Over these last few weeks, the Lucy she had smelled at the convention center had been around more often. No longer was Lucy only herself on the weekend as a mask to hide the stress.

Instead, Vae had taken the anxiety. She knew it would happen, but she had been prepared for it. Tema had told her she smelled of aged hunting by now, but the change in Lucy's scent, and seeing her on the bed relaxed and con-tent, had been worth it.

Vae approached the bed and nudged Tema with her muzzle. The fox rolled off the bed and stood up. Vae rubbed muzzles with her, and they walked out of the room together.

Tema drove to Wilmington. She had to drive; Vae couldn't fit in the driver's seat no matter how hard she tried. Otherwise she would have liked for Tema to stay home and keep Lucy company.

They walked into the office, and before Vae had even settled in, she had a line of four people waiting to update her on the status of this case or that, or ask her what they should say to this threat or that offer.

Vae knew enough about the cases to answer most of their questions. Weeks ago, they had reached a point where she only had to call Lucy a few times a day for specific guidance. This had freed Lucy to stay home and take the occasional phone call from Vae, or from one of the other attorneys.

Everyone believed Ms. Schrifton was in the building, but "somewhere else" working on "something big." Vae had worked consciously to create this image. It happened gradually as Vae and Tema became more and more visible. Lucy slipped away for longer and longer periods until finally Vae ran everything. What little she didn't know about the cases and procedures, Lucy could walk her through over the phone.

Lucy trusted Vae, and there had been many nights when she ran out of ways to thank her for the help. Some nights she just cried while curled up between the raptor and the fox as she fell asleep. Most nights, she breathed, and the air brought her calm.

Vae listened to cases. She spoke on the phone to attorneys. She answered calls from attorneys with decades of experience on equal terms with them.

After one conference call just past one in the afternoon, she had a few moments to pause. Her heart raced. Her blood was full of adrenaline. She was hunting, and the prey was worth it, but this kill lacked pleasure. The fun had gone. This hunt was for pure survival, and now she realized this is what it had been leading up to the whole time. The stench of anxiety burying the smell of perpetual hunting. It added up to what was really wrong with this place: hunting was not fun here, but frenetic, unending effort.

She did not hunt for herself or her fox now. She hunted for the sake of the firm who took on clients who made the rules, established quotas, forced her to kill for others, and those others either sat in boardrooms discussing new ways of changing the rules so they could benefit even more from the prey she killed, or they elected the people who sat on the board.

She lived in hunting mode, never allowed to relax, perpetually terrified of failure and thus losing access to the hunting grounds. She could never stop.

This introduced a whole new reaction in Vae, one she had never felt before, and now she understood exactly why Lucy's health had been in the early stages of collapse: Vae hated hunting. She had become so tired of being in this perpetual state of worry that all she wanted to do was sit at home and make someone else do it for her.

Suddenly, staring at the phone on the desk, everything made sense. She knew how everything worked, why it worked, and why humans did this to other humans.

The phone rang. Vae wanted nothing more than to urinate on it and walk away forever.

It rang again. She pondered that if she walked away, Lucy would be held responsible, the ruse would be up, Lucy would have to return to work, and all her progress would be lost. She may even lose her job over this. If they wanted to keep food on the table and a roof over their heads, she had to do this forever.

It was not right. Vae and Tema had lived anywhere they pleased in the contacted universe. If it was too cold, they went to a warmer planet. If they were tired of the game on one world, they traveled to another. Nobody told them they couldn't live somewhere, or hunt those animals, or talk to this person. Here, everything was owned, and providing for oneself was forbidden by punishment of law, the very thing Vae was helping to perpetuate. It was the only way to survive on this planet.

She went to the phone and answered it. As she listened, she felt Tema's fur against her flank. Vae leaned on her fox. She felt at home again.

"It'll be over soon," Tema said. "We can endure. Just a little while longer."

Vae needed to hear it. If she didn't hear it from time to time, she would lose her will to continue. Vae leaned harder on her fox as she talked business with the human on the other end of the line.

4

A knock at the door. Lucy rose from the couch and opend it. Mr. Lawrence Brendon stood on her front step, his assistant just behind and to the side. Lucy was still in pajamas at one in the afternoon.

She cursed herself under her breath. She had become so used to the routine she forgot nobody else knew about it. She had not discussed with Vae what they should do if this happened, but Lucy prided herself on her skill in shaping interpretations of the truth.

"Good afternoon, sir," she said, opening the door wider. "Care to come in? There's still coffee."

Mr. Brendon did not move, but he looked her up and down.

"Ms. Schrifton..." he began. He did not finish.

Lucy smiled. "This will be a lot easier to explain inside."

After a few moments of hesitation, he stepped inside, the assistant at his heels. Lucy kept the smile as she closed the door gently behind them.

"I feel privileged," Lucy said. "The head of my law firm just drops by my house unannounced. How many years have I worked for you and this is the first time?"

He had walked straight to the kitchen table and taken a seat. Lucy walked to the kitchen and took two cups from the cabinet. There was just enough coffee for two more people. She carried the steaming mugs to the dining room and set one in front of each. Then she went back to the living room to get her own.

"I do not believe this company has a telecommuting policy," he said. "In fact, I do not believe there is a way you can do your job from your living room."

Lucy had just returned. She took a seat at the other end of the table, cradling her mug. Neither of them had touched theirs yet.

"I worked out a system with my assistant," Lucy said. "After she learned the ins and outs of all the cases I worked on, she was qualified to handle some of my tasks for me."

"Your Relian."

"Right. My assistants. Vae was eager to help me. It started out as just that. She remembered meetings I needed to attend, phone calls I needed to make. Then she learned about the cases and started making recommendations to the staff in my presence. I approved. Before I knew it, she was doing most of the work. It's only on very specific matters, or when people actually need to talk to me, that she calls me here. It's a few calls a day. Used to be a few dozen." Lucy laughed.

"I see. And how long has this been going on?"

"Months. Everyone accepted her as my assistant, and they got used to going to her instead of me. Everyone assumed I was busy somewhere else in the building. Vae and

I have been taking turns. She was off last month. Now it's her turn back in the office. I still have two more weeks before I show my face again."

The two men regarded at her. Lucy could not read their faces.

"How did you find out?" she continued.

"Security cameras. Someone mentioned they hadn't seen you come in. I wanted to talk to you personally about it."

Lucy smiled, took a sip, and leaned back in the chair. "It feels so good to breathe again, sir. I was just as surprised Vae took it upon herself to do this as you are. She wasn't content to sit on her ass at home all day. She wanted to work."

"She wanted your job?"

"She hated the way I was when I came home every night. Stress has a scent, sir. They told you that. We call it a 'high-energy environment,' but it's killing us. What's the point of making money when we have to give ourselves heart disease and panic attacks to get it? Vae took some of the stress off me, and I have never felt better."

"Why didn't she find a job of her own?"

"That wouldn't have helped me any. No matter how much I make, my needs increase at just the right pace to cancel it all out. Never enough. Would have been the same thing if she had found a job. Now... Maybe we both can live with it."

"There is no policy for something like this."

"I'm still doing the work. Vae is still my assistant. I still show up, I answer her calls when she has to check in with something. All of it is under my supervision. Honestly, sir, I couldn't take it anymore. I needed to quit. I just didn't want to admit it. Vae knew what I needed, but she also recognized I was trapped. She comes home jittery all the time, and now I understand how she felt looking at me. I see the job changing her. She was such a happy person when she first came to Earth. Now she's on track to heart disease. Who knows how the stress will affect her body. We barely know how it affects ours. All the money we waste treating the symptoms. We think they're the problem. It's not until you step back and breathe a little you realize they're not."

He stared at her for a solid minute as Lucy sipped her coffee.

"I promise I'll be back in the office in two weeks. Or would you rather I come back tomorrow?"

He stared at her for another minute. Lucy cradled her cup and took a long swallow.

The most powerful man in her company picked up his cup by the handle and took a gulp while it was still steaming. He lowered just below his chin and gazed into it for a moment before raising his eyes.

"Many people wanted me to fire you years ago. I went against them because I knew you were good." He smiled. "You were gone for months and nobody knew it. A goddamned dinosaur took over a hundred million dollars worth of cases, and nobody put two and two together."

He set his cup down. Now his assistant took a sip from the mug in front of him.

Lucy smiled. "She's good at fitting in with predators."

He laughed through his nose. "Very. Think she would like to take over for me for a few weeks?"

She laughed. "By the end of the year she'd have everyone convinced she owned the place."

He smiled. "I think we'd all like to breathe." He took another swig.

So did Lucy.

Clarkesville

I

The church on the corner was huge, as was the church on the corner two blocks away, and the next, and the next. The Bible Belt was the best place to be for people of faith, and pastor Anthony Curtis stood at the pulpit looking over the pews, the seats packed with people of all colors, which never ceased to bring joy to his heart.

"I'm sure all of you have heard the news by now," he began. "You know what they say: rumor is halfway around the world before truth can put on its shoes, even among God's people."

The audience laughed.

"Yes, I went to the convention in Nashville last month, and yes, a pair of Relians chose me and my wife, and are living with us now."

There were cries of amen under the applause that followed, and some of the congregation stood. Pastor Anthony smiled, thanked them, and then gestured for everyone to be seated.

"That's why I've been absent the past couple of Sundays. Those conventions had another purpose which I only found out about when I got there: to find the Relians places to live. I only wanted to see what God had created elsewhere, and to my surprise, they told me I was a good match for them. Both me and my wife, and that was also a surprise.

"I'm sure you're all eager to hear what life has been like, but I want to begin with a question. What does alien life actually mean for believers? The Bible doesn't address it at all. Furthermore, the Bible states that we are God's creation. We were made in God's image, so who are these people? If they're not made in God's image, does that make them less than us? Why does God not mention them in the Bible? Wouldn't it have been a good idea to inform us we weren't the only ones out there? Is there anything we can glean from the Bible regarding the Relians?

"First, I think their appearance is great proof that God is out there, and He used the same template for life multiple times. The reptiles look like dinosaurs. The canines look like foxes. Is it coincidence? God was likely thinking of us and chose to make them in the image of something we know to make contact easier.

"Second, I believe God brought them to us to test our faith in Him. It encourages us to lean on God even more for answers to difficult questions. Some of you may be asking if any of God's Word applies to them. Can they be saved? Are they all doomed to the fires of hell simply because they are not made in God's image? What does 'in God's image' even mean anymore? I have been wrestling with questions like these since before my trip to Nashville, and to be honest, I have not reached a conclusion yet. We are in unusual times, my brothers and sisters in Christ. I will continue to meditate on these questions and many more, and I will let you know as soon as God leads me to an answer. In the meantime, I want all of you to meet my new guests, Teth, the raptor, and his fox, Nai."

The raptor and the fox stepped out from behind the curtain, crossed the stage, and stood beside the podium. The fox seemed on the heavy side from what most had seen on television, but still agile and spry in his white shorts. The raptor appeared to have been beaten to a pulp and then reassembled sometime later his body was so scarred. Light purple stripes ringed him from head to tail, breaking up his glossy black scales.

The congregation applauded as they stood. Some shouted praise the Lord, and welcome to Tennessee. After a minute, pastor Anthony gestured with his hands for everyone to be silent.

"There is no message this week, folks. I'm sorry, but my wife and I have been so busy adjusting to life with a pair of extraterrestrials I have had no time to prepare one. But fellowship is just as important as hearing the Word of the Lord, so rather than give you a half-done sermon, let's all meet downstairs for refreshments and fellowship. The Relians will join us there. Come and welcome them to Tennessee and to First Baptist Church of Christ. God bless."

Everyone in the pews stood and gathered in groups, chatting. Teth and Nai retreated to the curtain and waited. Pastor Anthony bent low and spoke to a few of the people who had approached the pulpit. He told them the Relians would be downstairs in a moment. The congregation gradually filed into the hall. The murmur faded. Anthony took his Bible from the podium, crossed the stage, and pushed the curtain aside.

"Are you guys ready?"

"Yes, we are," said Teth with a light Southern accent. They had both learned to speak the local dialect when they found out where they were going, which had shocked pastor Anthony and Camille.

"Are they all right?" said Nai, ears folded backwards.

"Of course they are," Anthony said. "Is something wrong?"

"They sound cheerful, and they appear enthused, but they do not smell it."

"They don't?"

"He's right," the raptor said. "They smell scared."

"That's why we're having fellowship."

"I'm used to people being afraid of me on this world. Most people show it. Why don't they?"

"These are God's people. They will treat you with the upmost respect."

He nudged them further backstage to the door that led to the rear hallway. Teth opened it, and they walked downstairs to the kitchen. The wall separating it from the rest of the lower floor had a window with no glass in it, giving them a good view of the congregation gathering around the tables. The refreshments consisted of cold cuts of meats and cheeses that belonged on crackers, warm turkey, fresh vegetables and fruit, x-brand cookies for dessert, and a choice of diluted orange juice or water.

Teth and Nai watched from the kitchen as pastor Anthony stood by. Camille had already come down here, and she was chatting up a group of women. Lots of people laughed and smiled. Men slapped one another on their backs. Women held onto one another's shoulders. Nai's tail slipped between his legs.

The raptor stood close to his fox and nudged him. "I don't like the scent in the room either, but that's why we're here. Maybe they'll smell better after they meet us."

"I hope you're right," Nai replied.

"They're just scared," said Anthony. "These are uncertain times. Some probably didn't even believe aliens really had landed until they saw you upstairs."

He moved out of the way for one of the ladies in the kitchen. She pulled out the last turkey, and set it on the counter to cool.

Anthony continued. "Some preachers on TV have been calling it a hoax designed to scare people away from

God. I never taught these people that. I taught them to embrace what is new."

One of the other elderly ladies moved the turkey from the pan to a serving dish and carried it out to a table. She paused for a few minutes to chat with some ladies her age while they discreetly took paper plates and helped themselves to crackers and meat.

"Let's go meet God's people," the raptor said.

The fox was shaking. Anthony wrapped an arm around his shoulder as he led him to the door. Nai never liked being in crowds, as they tended to trigger his old ways. Teth had kept them under control for a long time, but the fear still lingered.

"I'm not afraid of reverting," Nai said, mostly to Teth. "It's their scents..."

"I know."

They passed through the partition. Pastor Anthony smiled and spread his arms and embraced the first three people who came up to him. He shook hands with the rest and then everyone gathered around the raptor and the fox. It felt no different from the conventions except no barrier and no marines.

"Welcome to Earth!" some said through his enormous smile.

"It's so wonderful to meet you at last!" said someone else through an even wider smile.

"How has it been for y'all?"

"Are you all right? It's been hot here these last few weeks. Are you handling it?"

"Do they have churches where y'all come from?"

Half the congregation had gathered around the Relians. The other half talked in smaller groups around the fellowship hall, presumably waiting until the crowd thinned before trying to meet the Relians. Once the excitement wore off, pastor Anthony mediated, and the questions came one at a time.

"Sister Pam, I think you had an interesting question. What was it?"

A young woman wearing her best church clothes spoke. "Do they have churches? On y'all's homeworld?"

Her eyes were bright, and her smile was full of wonder, but her scent reminded Nai and Teth of someone on the edge of a cliff about to be washed away by a flood.

Teth answered. "Our homeworld was destroyed. Nobody has church."

"So aliens haven't heard of Jesus?"

"Jesus didn't visit us, no," Teth said.

Sister Pam's bright smile never faded, but she had visibly wilted.

Someone else in the congregation spoke up. "We thought maybe there'd be similar stories of a savior dying for the sins of others on other planets. That would be definite proof of God."

Everyone laughed. A few people applauded.

"That's—that's very interesting," pastor Anthony said, turning to the Relians. "Someone brought it up when the, uh, dragon was making appearances all over the world, and it's been on TV a lot. What God did here, He probably did elsewhere, too, so it would make sense."

"Press hasn't really talked about this in terms of faith," said a woman in the room.

"Would you expect them to?" replied a man. "Too afraid of offending people."

Everyone in earshot laughed.

The group smelled a bit more relaxed now that they knew they could hear the Relians from across the fellowship hall. Hearing them speak with a Southern accent must have also reassured them. They dispersed wide enough to get refreshments and stand by the tables, and the group around the Relians now encompassed the entire hall. It was far less cramped, and the Relians were free to move about. Camille had joined her husband at his side, holding a cup of water.

"Please," pastor Anthony said. "Tell us about faith among other people not on Earth. We're all eager to know."

Teth and Nai looked at one another. They read the room. Everyone was all smiles visually, but they smelled on the edge of panic.

Teth rubbed his claws. "I'm sorry, but there are no stories of that."

"None at all?" Camille said loud enough for everyone to hear.

"No. We didn't need a savior to lead us away from sin. We found one another."

The congregation was still all smiles, but they clearly did not know what to think of that.

"What do you mean?" Anthony said.

Nai raised his muzzle to the awful-smelling crowd. "Thousands of years ago, Relians were animals. The foxes lived in the northern climate, where food was scarce, and we became territorial. We killed everything in scenting distance. That's how we survived. Killing all competition for food."

"The raptors lived in the south," Teth continued. "The foxes spread across the planet in search of territory far enough away from each other not to make themselves anxious, and eventually they met us. We fought for a long time until someone realized some of the foxes weren't as aggressive as others, and they could be tamed. The raptors began killing the most aggressive ones and keeping the ones who submitted upon defeat. We chose the least aggressive canines to bear young, and we taught them how to divert their scent anxiety into something else. Over hundreds of years, we helped them become more than animals."

"And then the foxes did something for the raptors," continued the fox. "We taught them to break free of their strong family bonds and spread to new regions. Learning about one another brought us to sentience."

"We all didn't need divine help to rescue us from our animal ways," Teth said. "We freed one another from sin."

The humans feel silent again, smiles hiding uneasy, agitated scents.

Pastor Anthony raised one hand as he wrapped the other around Teth's neck. "I think we can see how God provides. God created the Relians to save one another, but He knew we had no one to save us, so he gave Himself instead."

Everyone in the congregation smiled wider and applauded and drank to that.

"But without faith," some gentleman called out, "how do aliens handle the idea of death?"

Teth looked straight at him. Direct eye contact with a predator clearly shook these people to the core, but hearing him speak helped with that. "We don't need to handle the idea of death. People are allowed live a full life of their choosing."

Nai finished. "They don't fear an end because the journey was so good."

"What about others?" said a woman by the tables, holding a plate of turkey and trying to eat daintily without utensils. "God must have had to sacrifice Himself for someone else out there."

Teth rubbed his claws. "There are no such stories."

"None at all?" one of the elderly ladies said.

"We've been to seventy planets," Teth answered. "Not a single culture tells of a supreme being who sacrificed Himself to save everyone from their animal ways."

"Jesus died to save us from sin," someone said.

"We've listened to pastor Anthony talk about what Jesus did," Nai replied. "Sin is just a word y'all use to describe y'all's animal ways. That's why all y'all feel tempted into it. It's natural to behave that way sometimes. Taking control of it is a lifetime goal for everyone in the contacted universe."

"But without God," Camille said, mouth wide and eyes bright, "how do people manage? What keeps them on the path of righteousness?"

Nai turned to her. "Every species in the contacted universe has a companion race. We keep one another from descending into our animal ways. It's actually the usual way things happen: two intelligent species grow up on a planet, and when they find each other, they bring each other higher."

Camille kept eye contact with the fox for a few seconds, then her smile fell and she turned away. Nai smelled hormones coming from her. Less than a second later, Camille left her husband's side and walked straight to a table. Nai watched her go.

"Nobody else needs the Almighty to do that?" someone in the back shouted.

"No," Teth answered. "Normal species find one another."

The congregation hall fell silent for a few beats. A man in the rear beamed from ear to ear. "Well, that just makes us special then!"

"Amen!" someone else said.

Pastor Anthony applauded. The congregation followed his lead, drowning out more cries of "amen."

Anthony whispered into Teth's ear. "They're all yours."

He stepped away from them and followed his wife, who stood by the water dispenser, gulping down cup after cup. She was sweating, but she smiled to everyone who came to talk to her. Her eyes never lost their brightness.

Teth led Nai around the fellowship hall. Everyone mixed freely. Many walked up to the Relians to shake hands and wish them well in their new home. The Relians were used to shaking hands as a formal greeting by now, and a great many people smelled uneasy shaking hands with Teth, let alone standing close to him and his mouthful of sharp teeth.

A light-skinned woman approached and embraced the fox. Nai arched his back to keep from pushing on her midsection. She was about six months pregnant, and the scent she gave off made that obvious as well.

"I am so thrilled to meet y'all at last. Will y'all be attending service now? Other community events? Y'all are practically the pastor's sons now, so I'd expect he'd want both y'all to get involved."

Nai sniffed her from a distance for a second and then turned to her. "May I scent you?"

She looked at him, smile frozen on her face even as she was puzzled. "Do what now?"

"You're only the second pregnant human I've met. The first so late in term. I'm curious how the scent changes."

She still smiled, but her stance indicated she did not want to say yes. "If it makes you happy, you go right on ahead."

Nai circled her and took in her scent from every angle he could. She pretended not to be uncomfortable.

Teth spoke to fill the silence. "We probably will get involved with the church, as much as we can. We want to get to know the place."

She smiled. "I hope so. Me and my husband lead the youth groups. I teach Sunday school for the teens. Maybe y'all'd like to join us for an event I'm tryin' to put together later in the year."

As she spoke, a man joined her at her side. Nai's nose led him to the man, and he scented his exposed skin as thoroughly as possible. The man seemed puzzled.

Teth rubbed his claws. "Sorry. We're not used to asking for permission to scent someone. Where we come from, it's just expected."

The man smiled and laughed. The woman just now noticed him.

"Oh, this is my husband, Charlie. I'm Mary. Mary Kentworth."

Charlie shook hands with Nai, and then with Teth. His scent changed upon touching Teth's claws, but both still held up the smiles.

"Charlie is very active in the community. He leads the charity construction projects the church supports a few times a year."

"I'm a foreman," he said. "It's my calling. We've been married four years. This is our first child."

Nai had just finished scenting both of them. He looked at each of them in turn, then at Teth. The raptor sensed Nai needed to say something but did not know if it was a good idea to do so now.

"So what do y'all do, Mr. Teth, Mr. Nai?" Charlie Kentworth said.

Teth spoke for both of them. "Do?"

"I mean, what do y'all plan to do in terms of a job?"

"We haven't thought that far ahead. We only just arrived. Give us some time to get to know this place and then we'll figure it out."

Charlie smiled warmly. "Good idea. Figure things out first. Pastor Anthony is a good man. He'll help y'all, and if he can't, God surely will."

He raised his cup and took a drink from it, as if congratulating himself for what he just said.

Mary nudged him. "There's Tommy."

"Oh, finally." He turned back to the Relians. "Excuse us, please. Tommy doesn't attend Sunday School and we need his help for something. So nice to meet both y'all. Till next week!"

They walked away. Nai turned to Teth, words on the tip of his tongue, but another couple approached the Relians before Nai could speak. The woman embraced them. The man shook hands. He did not smell so agitated at the touch of Teth's claws.

Nai indiscreetly scented both of them. He looked at Teth again. Teth spoke for them about what they were going to do now that they were here. After ten minutes of small talk, they parted ways. The Relians looked at one another. Both had smelled the four men were all smiles and appeared to be pillars of stability, but none of them had been very stable or happy. The Relians very much wanted to ask what was wrong, but there was no time in this arrangement—only enough to exchange a few words and then part company to trade meaningless words with someone else.

Nai's scent told Teth he smelled something more between them, but he had no time to talk about it.

The Relians walked to the water dispenser and took cups. All this talking had made both of them thirsty, and filtered water tasted so good. Men approached them, shook hands, and chatted them up. Most did not know what to say to an alien, so the Relians tried to get them talking about themselves.

Nai tried to resist the urge to scent them, but he could not stop himself. He walked around them, sniffing them from ear to ankle. He got the feeling the humans found it strange but charming. Most understood dogs, so they knew what he was doing, and it was not entirely uncalled for, even in church.

As Nai scented one man's backside, the man flushed. He smelled a lot more coming off this man than he expected. Nai sensed he wanted to say much more than he was. He stood straight, nuzzled the man's cheek with his muzzle. The man's scent exploded in hormones, and he quickly excused himself and melted into the congregation. Nai watched him go. Nai turned and gave Teth that look again. The fox's scent became more and more agitated as the day wore on. Teth was sure his own scent was just as frustrated.

Finally the hour was up. The people began going home. Everyone had met the Relians at least once, and taking in so many new scents had left them thirsty. Camille found them at the table gulping down water, and she approached them.

"Lovely congregation, isn't it? We're so blessed to have such good people here."

Nai was shivering.

"What's the matter?"

Nai did not answer. Teth spoke for him. "A fox's nose is more sensitive than a raptor's. It takes more energy for them to meet such a large number of new people in a day."

"I understand. Anthony is upstairs in his office. Both y'all should find out if he wants y'all to do anything. We're going to be here for a little while longer."

Teth scented the air coming off Nai. The fox wanted to go home badly. Teth stood close to him.

"Please stop smiling," Nai said, looking directly into Camille's eyes. "I can smell it's bothering you. It's okay to act like it is."

Her smile dropped slightly. "Later. Please."

Nai growled. Teth held him tighter.

Camille reeked of fear and turned away.

"I'm not angry," Nai said as she walked to the door. "I'm frustrated. Are you?"

She crossed the room and rounded the corner. Only a few parishioners remained in the fellowship hall now. Teth whispered to Nai.

"She wants you so bad."

"And it's making her angry. Teth, I can't do this again. Crowds are hard enough for me, but this one sends too many mixed signals."

"What else did you smell?"

Nai led them into the hallway and up the stairs.

2

Nai pulled out of Camille and lay on top of her. She held him around his back, panting and sweating. Nai took in her scent. He couldn't get enough of it. This was her real scent, the one he liked. She stroked the fur on his back all the way down to his tail.

The smile on her face was also real, not the one covering up shame. He enjoyed it while it lasted, as he knew once the hormones calmed down, she would change. For these few moments, she was the person he had come to know at the convention and during the time they spent at home, and the one he enjoyed being with.

"This is wrong," she said.

Nai panted. "You say that every time."

"I know, and I mean it every time."

"Anthony knows about it. He's slept with me lots of times. He doesn't want you to see him like that either. Both y'all should talk about it."

"What's to talk about? This is between me and God, just like whatever he does is between himself and God."

"What about me? Am I immune to God's judgment?"

She didn't answer. Her scent started to change from satisfaction to confusion. He rolled off her and lay on the bed. She rolled over and he lay beside him. She was taller than he was, so the position wasn't perfect, but she liked being close to someone like this.

"I don't know," she said. "Lot of unanswered questions now."

"Where I come from, we have answers."

"I wish things were that easy for me."

"They can be."

"Nai... I love my husband. We've been married for twelve years. Do you know how often I've been tempted to betray his trust? I resisted every time, but when I'm around you... Satan is tempting me harder than ever, and I have failed."

"Satan is not working through me. This is not some evil spirit. Teth told you about my pheromones the day we met. My scent tells everyone around me I'm eager and available, and people either respond to it or they don't. If they want to do something, they know I can. You respond to it. It's biology. Nothing evil about it. You don't have to feel shame for choosing to go with it."

"Then why does it feel evil? Why do I feel the Holy Spirit convicting me right now?"

"Because you want to believe you're a child of God, but really you're a woman."

The silence that followed lingered in his ears. She curled up tighter. Nai curled into her. He slipped out of his sheath again.

"Get out."

Nai whined.

"Please, get out."

He rolled away from her and sat on the bed with his legs hanging off. Teth rose from the floor and stood. Camille's breathing indicated she was holding back tears. Nai turned his head toward her.

"If you feel bad about it—if you don't want to do it, all you have to do is stop asking me."

She wept a few times. Nai wanted to curl up to her again, but he knew from past experience it would only make her cry more. Everything worked backwards here. He stood up.

"You have not failed. Satan has not gripped you or your husband."

Camille did not respond. Teth touched his nose to Nai's chest, and they walked out. When Nai closed the door behind them, Camille cried without holding back.

Teth nudged Nai in the chest with his muzzle. Nai rubbed his muzzle back. He looked down realizing he had left his shorts in the bedroom. Now did not seem like a good time to go back for them.

Nai walked down the short hall and descended the flight of steps into the living room. He plopped down on the couch, facing the blank television. Teth lay on his stomach on the floor.

"It makes her so happy," Nai said, "but she insists on making herself feel miserable about it. How many times have I told her it's just sex? I'm not the devil, the devil is not working through me just to make her feel bad. This is normal. She didn't act this way at the hotel."

"She's back in her familiar environment," his raptor said. "Where she's expected to be a certain way. She maintains the look, but her scent..."

"I'm tired of this. I can't do it anymore, Teth. If she asks me again, I'm not sleeping with her, and we're not going back to church until we figure this out."

"I don't think they're ready to figure it out. They're not done communing with the Lord."

"Why hasn't He given them an answer yet?"

Footsteps came from down the hall. Anthony had a few pages in his hand. He looked up at them and smiled. His scent was not smiling.

"I'm glad you're done. I was hoping you could help me with part of this sermon. Everybody wants to know what they're supposed to make of aliens. I'm still figuring it out myself, so I don't think I'm qualified to write it."

Nai had finished scenting him from a distance. "That's not what you want to talk about."

The smile dropped halfway.

"We all need to talk about this," Teth said from the floor. "It's bothering Camille, and you are no better. You need to talk to her. Both Nai and I are confused about what exactly is upsetting both y'all."

"She's just a little confused. Why would God send us to you only to tempt us to sin?"

Nai growled as he rose from the couch. Anthony winced at the sight of Nai naked. "That's part of the problem! She thinks Satan is tempting her! You think God sent us to tempt you! Both y'all can't be right!"

"This actually ties into my sermon. I'm writing about what it means for morality. Do the laws of right and wrong apply to people who aren't children of God? What rules must they go by? Someone at church raised that question, and I think it's worth exploring. Will you tell me who makes your moral rules?"

"Why does someone have to make rules?" Nai said. "Why can't everyone decide what to do?"

"That's a good... Yes, a very good point. I believe the book of Kings says it clearly. During a time when Israel had no king, everyone did as he pleased. The result was crime, murder, rape, and no punishment. People need limits, or they will... Or they will be..." He began to sweat. "I... I really should get back to it."

"Anthony." Nai walked around the couch. "Why are you hiding it from yourself?"

Anthony's face flushed with blood. Nai stood close.

"What if God wants you to do this? What if He wants you to face this part of yourself? You've been denying it's there your whole life. My scent affects people. Nothing has to happen past that. Do you want it to happen?"

He breathed hard. Blood pooled in his groin. He didn't look at Nai. "I am a child of God. I shouldn't be tempted like this at all. I don't understand why God would do this to me."

Teth rose and drew the curtains. The sound seemed to give Anthony permission, for he dropped the papers, gripped Nai by the shoulders, and led him to the couch. Nai turned, leaned over the back, and raised his tail. Anthony was breathing so hard he could barely work his zipper. Nai waited eagerly, tail waving. He heard a bottle of lotion click open. Moments later Anthony was inside him, very moist. Nai smelled the body lotion from the hotel. Anthony had had it in his pocket.

3

Anthony knelt on the floor in his office, head bent low in prayer, Bible in both hands touching it to his forehead. He murmured the same prayer he had uttered a hundred times since the convention ended.

"Father, I beg for forgiveness. You have placed temptation in my way, and I have given in. A spirit of lust has come over me, and I cannot make it leave. Father, I am so sorry. I don't know what happens to me when I'm with Nai. Is he one of your creations, or is he something else? Is that why he can do this to me and my wife? Father, I feel so forgotten right now, and I know it must not be true, but I need guidance."

He paused, waiting for an answer to come to him, as it had many times before.

"Father, I approach you an unclean man. Please in the name of Jesus cleanse me in your eyes so I might receive guidance again. What am I supposed to do about this?"

He paused again, contemplated his next words, practically in tears.

"Please, Father, in the name of Jesus, I take command of this spirit of perversion, and I rebuke it! I rebuke it in the name of Jesus, and I declare it shall not have power over me as a child of God. I am born again, and no evil can touch me. My birthright is a place at the table of the Lord, and I hold you to that promise, Father."

Claws tapped the wood floor. "You've been in here for almost an hour," said a canine voice. "You keep repeating the same things over and over. Don't you think it's time to talk to people who can answer you?"

Anthony wept a little, composed himself, and answered without turning around. "This is something I need to work out with the Lord."

"Your wife is locked in your bedroom crying and pleading with God over what she and I did an hour ago."

"I need to spend some time with God."

"I think you and your wife could comfort each other a lot better than God seems to be. She's no better than you are, and she's called on the name of Jesus twice as much."

"We're both still looking for answers. When she's ready to talk about it, she will, and so will I."

Nai sighed. He walked back to the living room. The floor creaked as his raptor followed. Anthony clutched his Bible tighter, lowered his head and pressed it against the Holy Book harder. He communed with the Lord harder than he ever had.

Half an hour later, pastor Anthony ran out of things to say, and he felt in control again. He knew it wouldn't last, but for now, he felt like a man of God, a church leader with the power to take control of any spirit that tried to steal that from him again.

He stood up, set his Bible on the desk, and walked out of the office and into the living room. Teth stood in the kitchen, chomping on some of the raw hamburger from the refrigerator. Nai also held a package in his hand and munched on a hunk of it.

Anthony smiled. "Y'all didn't even heat it up."

"It tastes better uncooked, cold or not," said the raptor.

Anthony noticed the lines on his face and down his body. It seemed like a great way to introduce himself to the world again.

"You never did tell me how you got all those scars."

Teth met his eyes. "I like prey that fights back. What did God tell you?"

"I haven't received a Word yet. I may have to fast for a week."

"Fast?" Nai asked.

"The needs of the flesh often make it difficult to hear the Lord's voice. Denying the flesh its needs is a way to become sensitive to what the Lord is trying to say. A fast is denying the body food for a while until you hear from God."

"You're going to starve yourself until God speaks to you?" Nai said.

"Not necessarily starve. Some fasts allow juice or unleavened bread."

"Isn't God all powerful and can do anything He wants? How can His voice be drowned out by the needs of your body?"

"I don't know. God works in mysterious ways."

"Anthony," said the fox. "This is not evil spirits taking control of you! I have slept around with people from almost every species I've met! Male, female, other genders all y'all don't even have words for! God didn't punish them for it.

God hasn't punished me. What makes you so afraid He'll punish you?"

"Maybe not punish, but leave. If His spirit leaves me, the church will fall apart, and so will the community."

"Is that Satan's plan? Bring aliens to this planet just to tempt you to sin so God leaves you, and this little community falls apart without a church? Seems like a long way to go. Or is it God's plan? God is putting this temptation in front of you, knowing full well you can't handle it, and then punishing you for doing what He knew you would do. This doesn't make sense!"

"Can we please talk about it another time? It's been a long day, and I'm very tired."

"I—"

Teth held a hand up to Nai's muzzle. The fox looked at his raptor, then back at Anthony. He grunted, turned to his package of meat, and bit off another hunk.

A door opened. Footsteps came down the stairs. Camille walked to the couch, kissed her husband on the forehead.

"Hi, honey."

"Hi, Camille. Have a nice nap?"

She smiled. "Had a good talk with the Lord."

"I had to have a talk with the Lord a little while ago myself."

She laughed, turned, and sat in the recliner. "We seem to be doing it a lot these days."

"We do. We do..."

Camille's smile strained her face. "I was thinking... Just today... How much I love you, Anthony."

The pastor smiled. "I love you, too, Camille. That hasn't changed."

She nodded, smiled, faced the blank television. "How's the sermon? Will it be ready?"

"I don't know. At the rate I'm going, maybe not."

Camille laughed. "You'll pull through. You always do."

"I'm thinking about doing a fast. Would you like to join me?"

She did not face him. "Yes. I'll go through one with you. I could use a Word as well."

"The congregation Sunday needs one."

"What about Wednesday?"

"I have a few sermons I've been saving for a rainy day." She fidgeted with the buttons on her shirt.

Nai stood still, mouth open, hamburger spilling out. He turned to Teth, who stared back. Nai listened to them. He stuffed his muzzle full of ground beef to smother the agitated scents coming from the humans, and he turned away so he wouldn't have to see their happy faces.

4

The piano played. The pastor had just finished the weekly call for salvation, and the congregation sang hymn number two-thirteen, *Amazing Grace*, but with the word "wretch" replaced with "poor sinner." It wasn't written that way, but everyone sang it, which caught the two Relians by surprise.

A couple people had come to the alter, and pastor Anthony was speaking to them quietly now. He now prayed with them.

Teth and Nai sat in the front row. Teth was too large for the pews, so he lay in the aisle, Nai sitting next to him at the edge of the pew. He turned and observed the people. They sang their hearts out, and their eyes shined bright, but inside they were tired, or troubled, or worried. The disconnect between the emotions they put on display and the scents they gave off disturbed Nai. He was grateful Teth kept him from reverting because this was a situation that could cause it.

Now everyone moved about, shaking hands and meeting people. One man, brother Bernard, practically ran around the pews vigorously shaking hands with people, his face bright and full of the Lord, but his scent repulsed Nai. He wasn't happy. He didn't want to touch anybody. Something troubled him, but he shook hands with the aliens and asked them if they had let Jesus into their hearts yet. Teth spoke for them, as Nai didn't trust his voice right now. They wanted to learn more about it first before they said yes. Brother Bernard laughed, smiled, slapped Teth on the shoulder, and said after a few sermons, they'll give their hearts to Jesus, just y'all wait. He moved on, violently shaking every hand he could see, full of the Lord, and the zeal to share it with everyone.

Many people left church now, but quite a few others went downstairs to fellowship. As the pastor's "sons," everyone expected Teth and Nai to be there. Nai wanted to hide in the office, or the bathroom, or the car.

Pastor Anthony retreated to the curtain. Teth led Nai up to the stage in pursuit.

"Pastor Anthony," Teth called as they approached the curtain. He pushed it aside with his snout and slipped through the door, Nai right behind him. Anthony had gone through the other door and was just starting down the hall to the stairs that led to the kitchen.

He paused, turned to meet them. "Yes, what is it?"

"I had a few questions about your sermon."

He smiled. "Save them for fellowship."

"Actually I wanted to ask you alone."

Teth and Nai caught up to him. Anthony slowly walked toward the door. Nai caught up to him first.

"If God forgave humans of their sins because of Jesus, why not also stop the whole labor pain thing, and relieve men of the need to work the land?"

"Beg pardon?"

"Why does the blood of Jesus not forgive original sin as well?" Teth said. "Why didn't God remake the Garden of Eden after Jesus died?"

Anthony's paced slowed. "That's a good question. I don't think anybody's asked."

"Why did God need to send His son to die?" Nai said.

"That's an easy one. God couldn't forgive us until someone fulfilled the law."

"Why not just forgive everyone, since He wanted to do so anyway? Why did He need a blood sacrifice? He's God, so all He had to do was decide."

"Ah, I believe someone mentioned this in college. God knew man would never believe without a symbol of faith, and God had already created the law, so He could not simply forgive without someone fulfilling the laws He created."

"That's not what you said in your sermon." Nai's ears folded down. "You said God wouldn't forgive mankind until His son died. And if God is all-knowing, why did He create laws He knew you could never fulfill? Why was it necessary? Why not simply choose to forgive and then announce it?"

"These are wonderful questions, and I will be glad to discuss them in more detail at home. Right now, it's time for fellowship."

"Can I wait in the car instead?" Nai said.

They had reached the door. Anthony paused with his hand on the handle.

"Now why would you want to do that?"

"For the same reason I want to hide in the car when we're at home. Everyone's scents don't match their words."

"We're here to rejoice in the Lord's house, not dwell on our problems."

"This isn't that."

Anthony sighed. "We're still figuring it all out. Bear with us. Please."

He pushed the door, descended the stairs. Teth led his fox down the steps and into the kitchen. The fellowship was smaller than last week, presumably because there was only cheese and crackers with water down here on a single table.

Mary Kentworth walked about, without her husband. She noticed the Relians, excused herself from the elderly man she had been talking to, and walked straight for them, high heels clicking like she was about to attack.

"Teth, Nai, did y'all enjoy the sermon? I sure did." Her smile was wide enough to cross a timezone. "It was so wonderful to hear one again. Pastor Anthony has been away for the better part of a month. I'm so relieved he hasn't lost his touch."

Nai wanted to growl at her for acting so happy while smelling so worried.

"We wish to read more about this faith," Teth said. "I tried reading the Bible, but the text is very difficult to understand."

"That's because it's King James English."

"Who is King James?"

"English hasn't been spoken like that in five hundred years."

"Has the Bible not been updated?" Teth said, noticing Nai had been scenting the air coming off her much harder than he needed to.

"Oh, sugar, the King James version is the only true translation. It's the only one anyone needs."

"We will need more practice with..."

Nai's scenting had become panicked. Teth began to pull him away from her.

"Why are you lying to your husband?" Nai said.

Her smile dropped.

"He didn't father that child," Nai continued. "Brother Linus did. Where is he?"

She backed away. Nai slipped out of Teth's arm and followed her.

"Something is troubling you and that's not it. What's wrong? Please, tell me what's wrong and stop sounding so cheerful!"

She turned around, wanting to run away, but instead she walked away, looking in all directions, as if for a mirror to make sure she still looked composed.

"Please!" Nai shouted. "What's wrong?!"

All conversation stopped. All eyes focused on the fox. Teth dragged him back toward the kitchen. Nai struggled in his raptor's grip.

"I can't do this anymore! They smell wrong! Why? Stop it! Stop it! Stop!"

He broke free and dashed to the two men in the corner.

"Both y'all sleeping together! Y'all are terrified of someone finding out! Ashamed because y'all think God is going to punish all y'all! Is that it?"

They stood stunned.

"Y'all's smiles hide it from other humans, but I can smell what y'all are doing! Stop pretending it don't bother all y'all!"

He jumped out of the way just as Teth caught up to him, and Teth's arms grabbed empty air.

Nai's claws scratched the tile as he skid to a stop in front of a married couple chatting with sister Pam and a few others.

"Pam, you smell like you cried before you came here! I heard your husband today! He said the word bankruptcy! His business is failing! You don't have to act happy about it —you don't have to say praise the Lord!"

Teth gripped Nai by the shoulder and pulled him toward the door.

Pastor Anthony and Camille stood side by side in front of the kitchen entrance.

Nai screamed, burst forward, and ran to them. He slid to a stop, stood upright, and grabbed Anthony by the lapel.

"Talk to her! Stop pretending everything is all right! You fucked with me, she fucked with me, both y'all know it, so talk about it! There's no reason to be ashamed—I'll fuck everyone in this place if it'll make them feel better! And— I can't! I can't do it! You won't let me! I think I'm reverting! It's this—! It's this—!"

Teth jumped on him, flattening his fox on the floor. Nai screamed. The humans backed away. Camille disappeared through the kitchen. Pastor Anthony waited a few beats before following her.

"Talk to her!" Nai screamed. "Stop pretending nothing is wrong!"

The congregation hall emptied. Nai breathed Teth's comforting, normal scent. His heartbeat calmed down once the smells left his nose. Outside, cars started up and drove away fast.

5

The sphere opened onto the stage just behind the podium. A grey and tan raptor stepped through, scanned the room, scented it. A woman wearing professional clothes and carrying a briefcase followed him through the sphere a moment later, and then the way snapped closed. The pews were empty save for a single man dressed in a shirt and jeans and in bad need of a shave. He stood, walked down the aisle, and stepped onto the platform, hand outstretched toward CJ.

"Madame Secretary Rhine." He shook her hand.

"Pastor Curtis. We came as soon as we received your message."

"Never mind the pastor. I may not be one much longer."

"We read your story," Rive said. "Are Teth and Nai here?"

"They're around. Somewhere. I trust y'all can find them. They'll probably be the only scents you can pick up in here. There hasn't really been a congregation in months."

CJ walked to the podium and set her briefcase on it. She removed a document from the top and turned to face the pastor.

"Your message said it started three months ago when Nai lashed out and began accusing people of acts of immorality, including you and your wife?"

"Yes, that's the gist of it. Nai told everyone my wife and I had been sleeping with him. Needless to say, I was embarrassed. So was Camille. So was everyone."

He walked to the steps and sat down on the edge of the stage, facing the pews.

"So it was true?" Rive said.

"Yeah, but that's not the point. What we did in the privacy of our own home was between us and God. He had no right to blurt it out in public like that. I could have recovered, but the mood in the church was different after that Sunday. There was a lot less rejoicing. Less laughter. Eventually, less people. Camille tells me people don't feel comfortable here anymore, even though the Relians haven't shown up in all this time. Maybe they don't want to hear messages about God's love and righteousness from a man who was obviously living in sin himself. Maybe they don't want to risk the fox being there. Maybe he was telling the truth and they don't want him to blurt out their secrets, too."

"What did you say about it?"

"Nothing. I tried to go on like nothing had happened, but clearly nobody was willing to move on from that. The change in the mood got to me, too. It got to Camille. She's staying with other family. She mentioned divorce... unless the Relians go. Imagine that. She can't deal with the temptation, so she blames me for letting temptation into our lives. The church is behind on utilities. I'm behind on my mortgage. I'm out of options. That's why I called y'all. I can't keep the Relians anymore. They need a new home."

"Mr. Curtis," CJ said, looking down on him from the podium, "have you discussed this with Teth and Nai?"

"I told them I thought it would be better for them if they all left."

Rive stepped closer. "Better for them? Did they speak the truth?"

"They embarrassed me and my wife in front of my church. They humiliated brothers and sisters in Christ."

"Are you sure that's why they did not return to church, Mr. Curtis?"

"How can they show their faces again? I didn't want to stand at that pulpit again after being exposed. Camille didn't show her face for weeks after that. I heard people talking about her behind her back. I'm sure they're talking about everyone. This whole thing is a spirit of evil that has torn the community apart."

"Why aren't Teth and Nai here now?" Rive said.

"I told them to wait elsewhere. I wanted to talk to the two of you alone first."

"We'll need a word with them," CJ said. "I'm sure we can find a way to work this out."

"There's nothing to work out. They destroyed my church. My marriage. I don't want them in my house anymore. Pretty soon I won't have a house."

CJ closed her case and picked it up. "We're going to talk to the Relians. Feel free to come with us. Or you may wait here."

"I'm not going anywhere." Mr. Curtis stared over the empty rows of pews.

"Rive."

The metal raptor stepped off the stage and scented the air. He walked up the slanted aisle to the double doors. He bent low, scented the carpet, and then turned down the hallway to the left. They descended a flight of stairs to the church's lower level, and Rive followed the scent down the hall and around a corner to a large room.

The Relians lay on the tile floor. As Rive approached, they opened their eyes and stood to meet him. The raptors touched necks, and Rive nosed Nai with his snout.

"What happened?" Rive said.

The other theropod answered. "Nai has always had a difficult time in large groups of people, but I thought he would be fine while I was here. Something happened I didn't expect. These people... They kept a constant appearance of happiness and joy while their scents were in turmoil."

"Praise the Lord," continued the fox. "Glory to God, full of grace, Holy Spirit dwells within me! Their scents were full of everything but grace. It felt like I was drowning."

"Mr. Curtis wants us to find you a new home," Rive said. "Did he speak to you about this?"

"Yes," Nai said. "But there's a lot he hasn't said. He smells angry, his body language shows his anger, but he walks around with the same smile and calm voice all the time. I've tried to get him to talk, but he won't."

"What happened to the church?" CJ said. "Mr. Curtis says the church fell apart after you exposed his secret, as well as the secrets of a few other people."

"Secrets?" Nai said. "They weren't secret to me."

"Humans are not scent-based," Rive said.

Nai sighed. "I know."

The black raptor resumed for him. "After that, the church wasn't the same. We went a few times afterwards to try to mend relations, but nobody wanted to be near us again. Anthony told us to stay home on church nights. Then he told us to stop attending church events. We wanted to help. We wanted to be part of the community, but nobody would come near us. People stopped coming to anything associated with the church."

"Nobody wanted their secrets known," Nai said. "They wanted to stay hidden. They want the fake emotions —they want to pretend everything is all right! I can't... I don't understand what happened."

"We warned you about this," Rive said.

"I could've handled the church, but not Anthony and Camille. They were so excited about it at the convention, but once we came here, they changed."

"Do you think there's any chance of mending things?" CJ said. "We don't actually have a plan for finding a new home for someone. We have to make absolutely sure this is what everyone wants."

"I don't want it," Teth said. "Anthony and Camille are both compatible. They are wonderful people, but here, around the people of the church, they become somebody else. Anthony especially."

"I know who he is," Nai continued. "That's the person I want to be with. Same for Camille. The people they became once we got home are not the people we met at the convention. We all tried to get them to be real at home, with us and each other, but they hid behind praising the Lord. That's what drove them apart, not us."

CJ nodded. "Is there a chance Mrs. Curtis will come back?"

"Not a chance," Teth answered. "She says the devil was working through Nai. She blames her husband for letting evil into their lives. She wouldn't set foot in the same room with us again."

"What about Mr. Curtis?" she said. "Who does he blame?"

"He won't say."

Rive turned. "Let's go upstairs."

He led them out of the hall and up the stairs. CJ followed, briefcase in hand. They rounded the corner and entered the main worship hall. Mr. Curtis sat on the stage. A fire ax rested across his thighs. At the sight of it, Teth and Nai halted. CJ stopped behind them. Rive did not flinch as he descended the aisle to the podium, stopping in the aisle just a couple paces away from him.

"Mr. Curtis?" Rive said.

The human stared at the ax in his lap.

"Teth and Nai are here. We are prepared to take them away. Before we do, have you anything to say to them?"

He slowly turned his head up to Rive. "Me?" His eyes darted to the Relians at the door, and then back to the metal raptor. "No."

"Then I will speak for them." Rive straightened his neck. "We told you at the convention that Relians are accustomed to an environment of openness, inclusiveness, and honesty. Your exact words before agreeing to take them in were 'I run a Baptist church, so that won't be a problem'."

Anthony did not look up. "Yeah. I had a church. Everything was fine. Until they showed up."

"Mr. Curtis, they tell us that the people of the church presented false pretenses instead of seeking to get to know them. You and Camille were part of this, as well. Nai could not cope with that environment, especially at home. Have they told you this?"

"Yes, they all told me. What am I supposed to do about it? Force my congregation to divulge their personal lives in public for their sake?"

CJ squared her shoulders, pushed past Teth and Nai, and walked down the aisle. "Mr. Curtis, the primary complaint the Relians have is that you and Camille weren't open with them. They say the two of you refused to discuss anything, preferring to hide behind the same pretenses as your church members."

She slid behind a pew, set her briefcase down, and sat facing the former pastor, a single pew between them.

"What in particular did you not want to talk about?" she finished.

He hung his head. "Lord... Don't y'all have any idea how embarrassing this is? Y'all just want me to talk about the single most painful and embarrassing time in my life? Look my wife in the eye and admit I committed the sin of sodomy? Tell her to look me in the eye while she tells me she is consumed by a spirit of adultery right in my own house, and then go to church like nothing is wrong? What happened in that house was between me and God. Teth and Nai had no respect for that." He wrapped his fingers around the ax. "They drove my congregation away. They drove me and my wife apart. There's nothing left for us here. I'm leaving. Gonna try to start again somewhere else."

Rive opened his mouth, but CJ spoke first.

"Start another church, Mr. Curtis?"

He raised his head and met her eyes. "Maybe."

"When I went to church," CJ began, "I was told sin should never be hidden. Suffering and misfortune, as well. From what I've heard, the Relians only spoke aloud about things that everyone else wanted to stay hidden. Those same things will be under the surface no matter where you go. Perhaps God sent the Relians to show you that."

CJ turned her head slightly to Rive. He looked back at her, hands apart, stunned she had said it before he did. CJ smiled at him.

Anthony Curtis laughed. "So it's my fault? My fault! The Relians showed up, destroyed everything I loved, and y'all blame me? I told y'all I wasn't going to admit to my wife what I was doing. She didn't want to admit to me what she was doing. That we were both giving in to... That... I believed God had told us this is what we should do. God had called us to witness to these aliens and lead the community to welcome them. What happened? Everything is gone."

The former pastor hung his head and looked at his lap, catching his breath.

"Anger is not Godly," he continued. "He denied Moses the Promised Land because of it. As a man of God, it's important to manifest the Fruit of the Spirit. Love, joy, peace, patience, kindness, goodness, faithfulness, gentleness, and temperance. Galatians five. God knew my sin. That should have been enough."

"There's a difference between letting God forgive you," CJ said, "and ignoring reality. The Relians felt you ignored them. They wanted to live with who you really were, not the man of faith."

The former pastor's face cinched up, he rose to his feet, swung the ax, and brought the head down on the podium. It split in two easily, the ax head becoming wedged in the base. Mr. Curtis pulled it out, stumbled backwards on the stage a few steps, and stood looking over the pews.

"Is that better? Yeah. I'm angry. I'm pissed! I've been angry for months, but I did the Godly thing and rebuked that spirit of anger and handled things the way Jesus would have. With love and kindness and patience. Fruit of the Spirit... So..."

He raised the ax to the piano and brought it down on the lid. The ax head became wedged in the top. He yanked three times and pulled it free. CJ had risen and backed away to the door. Rive remained still.

Mr. Curtis jumped off the stairs, swung the ax, and chopped into the closest pew. The ax only penetrated an inch into the thick wood. He pulled it out, swung again, chopped another wedge into the pew, and then moved to the left. He chopped at the front row pew, kicking a few splinters in the air as he raised the ax. The noise echoed in the worship hall.

After a few minutes of hacking, he paused, panting. The sweat drops on his forehead were large enough to create a glare off the overhead lights. He stood at the end of an aisle, multiple chunks missing from it, and turned to Rive.

"I am a man of faith! Great men of faith trust God! Me...? I can't figure out why God would do this to me! Why God would send me aliens—why he would tell me it's my calling to witness to them! To show them how to live a life in Christ! Only for them to ruin my life! Why would God tempt me to sin and then—" He raised the ax and brought it down on the armrest at the end of this pew. "—punish me for it?"

The corner of the armrest flew off and bounced on the ground. The splintered crack made CJ wince. She stood at the top of the center aisle, between Anthony Curtis and the two Relians. Rive had not moved from his place.

Mr. Curtis walked down the aisle, swinging the ax overhead, hitting any part of the pew he could damage. The ax did little more than make lines in the seats, and this angered him, so he raised it again and again on the same spot until he had chopped a piece from the pew. He bent down, picked up the hunk of wood, and chucked it across the room. He crossed the aisle and chopped the pew on the other side as well.

"He's not supposed to put more on people than they can handle!"

The ax fell and chopped a seat.

"Well, He put more on me than I could!"

He raised it again.

"And He punished me for it!"

It came down and penetrated the seat. He swung again and again until a chunk came loose, then he stomped on it. Finally, a small segment of the pew came down and clacked on the floor.

"How am I supposed to act? I did the best I could, and God punished me for trying!"

"These are things you should have talked to the Relians about," Rive said. "Long before it came to this."

"This is between me and God! Me and God! God did this to me! He will answer for it!"

He chopped another pew, pausing to breathe only when he swung.

"They were my people! ... My community! ... I spent years ... cultivating it! ... Earning their respect! ... They left me! ... Didn't even ... ask me! ... Didn't ... Even ... Love and kindness! ... Forgiveness! ... Love thy neighbor! ... Turn the other ... Cheek! ... They! ... Did not! ... Believe! ... When I needed them!"

He had turned this row into a mess of splintered wood. The ax slid from his fingers, and he collapsed into a seat, facing the broken pulpit, panting.

"...did I? Did Camille? What happened to me? I had everything, and God took it away, just like Job. So what's next? What else can God do to me? What's the point? To prove I'm a sinner? Prove to who? He already knows that. I confessed it so many times."

He cried.

Rive turned, walked up the aisle, then down the pew. He picked up the ax and tossed it across the room. It clattered between two pews and fell to a rest on the floor. Rive crouched to be closer to his eye level. CJ stepped down the aisle toward the preacher. Teth and Nai ran past her, around the other side of the pew. Nai ran down the aisle above Mr. Curtis, Teth ran down the aisle below. They stopped on either side of him, Teth in front, Nai just behind. The raptor lowered his neck to meet the man's eyes, tail hanging over two pews.

"This is you," Teth said. "Your scent now... it's the man we smelled at the convention. This is who we wanted."

Mr. Curtis laughed. "This is not me."

"The three of you are an excellent match," Rive said. "There's no reason to find Teth and Nai a new home."

"Let me help you," Teth said. "I will prevent you from reverting, just like I do for my fox."

Mr. Curtis stared ahead. "Reverting into what?"

"Into what you think you have to be. I'm here to show you who you really are and help you become that. Stop fighting it. Call your wife. We can help her, too."

The man laughed. "Stop fighting it. Exactly what the devil told Jesus in the wilderness."

Teth growled. "We are not the devil! The devil didn't send us, and neither did God!"

"It's a new way to live," Nai said. "I promise you'll be happier than you were, faking it all the time. You don't have to now. Your congregation went to church because they believed they had to, not because of you."

Anthony Curtis looked up at the ceiling. He breathed deeply a few times. "Y'all tempt me into a life of sin. A life apart from God. Get behind me. You are a hindrance. He gave Job double his wealth after he pulled through his trial. I eagerly wait for God to do the same for me."

Rive backed away into the aisle. "Teth, Nai, let's go." He turned to the double doors.

The Relians walked down their aisles and joined Rive. They climbed the incline. CJ stood in the center, staring at the back of Mr. Curtis' head.

"If you change your mind, please call me."

"It's how it always works," Anthony said. "God breaks you so He can remake you. He works in mysterious ways, doesn't He?"

"Goodbye, Mr. Curtis."

She followed the tails of the Relians to the exit. She caught up to them on the front lawn, where Teth and Nai held one another in grief.

"You can't help everybody," Rive was saying.

"Now what?" CJ said as she neared.

Rive faced her. "I will make an offworld portal for them later."

"We're not going to find a new home for them?"

"This has been too much to ask them to go through it again."

"So much I could have done for him," Teth said.

"He's a great man of faith," CJ said. "Willing to stick to his beliefs no matter what. Well, how long until we have a portal back to Washington?"

"Less than a minute. I've been working on one since he started swinging the ax."

"Good. I told him he can change his mind. Would you go back if he asked you?"

"Yes," Nai said.

"Absolutely," Teth said at the same time.

"I don't think he will call, but you never know. What do you mean do for him, Teth?"

The raptor curled his neck. "I would have shown him all the things he fears are not sin. I would have shown him what real sin is. Now that the congregation is gone, I hoped he'd be open to it. Being a man of faith takes so much effort.

I wanted to free him from the pressure of feeling he needs to be this other person all the time."

CJ smiled. "One reason I stopped going to Mass. Faith like his should go down in history."

The sphere opened five paces away on the church lawn. Rive walked through, emerging in CJ's office. Teth and Nai walked through next. CJ took one last look at the church.

"Somehow."

She turned back and crossed the barrier to Washington DC. The portal closed a moment later.

Columbus

I

Malcolm turned on the bathroom light and stared at himself in the mirror. He looked like someone who had just stayed up all night fucking. He hadn't; it had all happened in the hour before his alarm went off. He giggled.

He had woken up with his head between Ratash's legs, face planted right on his slit, so he started licking. It didn't smell weird anymore. Now it was instant hard-on. Ratash had been at his lower body, licking his balls. A few position changes later, Malcolm ended up between Irus and Ratash. Ratash had gotten him first, and then Irus had fucked him afterwards.

Malcolm turned on the shower and waited for the water to heat up. Before these two moved in, he never showered in the morning, but since he came back from the convention three weeks ago, his entire routine had changed. At the same time, he felt like these two had always been here.

He stepped into the shower and began washing the sex off himself. They had told him no matter how hard he washed, he smelled like he'd been fucking around with a pair of Relians. Humans couldn't smell it, and Malcolm wished he knew what he was missing out on.

The raptor had been right about him. Malcolm had impulses to exploit he had never known. Ratash seemed to find a new one every couple of days. The day he had to start going to work again, he had come home and Ratash was on the living room floor, on his back, Irus buried to the hilt in him. He had stayed in that position even after Irus finished. The noises he made... The raptor never spoke an actual word, but the sounds coming out of his mouth were bizarre, like a wounded animal, and as Malcolm went about the kitchen making dinner for himself, he realized he was hard.

Finally he couldn't take it anymore. He had walked to the living room and stripped. Ratash kept making those noises. Malcolm rammed his ass for nearly an hour. By the time Malcolm was done with Ratash, dinner was ready. Irus had taken over in the kitchen.

Ratash had later explained what happened: he had been in a vulnerable position, making vulnerable noises. All prey species instinctually loved seeing predators wounded and helpless. Ratash had given that to Malcolm, and then twisted it into something new. Having power over a predator, becoming the hunter, and making the hunter the hunted, watching the mighty brought down and no longer a threat. Acting on this instinct was a rare experience.

Ratash had then reasserted his role as predator by pulling Malcolm to the floor and enclosing him in an embrace only a theropod could do. Malcolm could not move, and now he was the prey again, held in place by a predator four times his size. Ratash had somehow made that erotic without actual sex happening.

Malcolm smiled as he washed his legs. He could have it both ways with him. Predator and prey, dom and sub. Ratash could be either, and he could make Malcolm feel like either. Every time was different. Every orgasm special. He tried not to think about what would happen when the honeymoon ended, so he enjoyed it while it lasted.

He had taken them all around town when he wasn't working. North Market, the cultural district, several local conventions. Sometimes they just went downtown and walked around. So many people wanted to meet them, and body language must have given away they were close, because conversation always turned to sex. Ratash and Irus had no filter when it came to discussing it. The details would have been embarrassing if Malcolm hadn't yearned to be this open with people, too.

Gay bars had been especially interesting. Malcolm had a lot of friends who frequented them, and everyone had been eager to meet the aliens. Inevitably, Ratash divulged he loved mammals and their junk. Inevitably, his friends would show him theirs, and the raptor would be all over it. Even when Malcolm's friends thought they were in control, Ratash manipulated their instincts their whole time. Malcolm noticed it quickly, how the theropod made some people feel like the predator and indulged others making them feel like prey at the mercy of the predator who just caught him, sometimes figuratively, sometimes literally. The raptor somehow figured out exactly what anyone's fetish was, and he satisfied it.

To everyone's surprise, Ratash was the gentle one. Ratash could fuck hard, but he preferred to lie down and cuddle with his middle claw inside someone, taking it slow and easy. Irus fucked like an animal, which had its own appeal.

Ratash and Irus had become somewhat famous among the gay community in the city. His nickname was "Clever Girl," after the line from *Jurassic Park*. Onlookers just started saying it whenever Ratash convinced someone to play around. Ratash did not seem to mind. Not many people could actually handle Ratash, as the raptor was huge, but the few who had tried went around telling others there was nothing else like it.

Malcolm turned the knob. The shower shut off. He felt clean again. Still euphoric and weak in the knees, but at least presentable to society. He climbed out, dried himself off. He hadn't closed the bathroom door. He never did anymore, and he often did not bother wearing clothes around the apartment. There was no point in privacy, and the Relians were naked, so he felt he should be, too.

What had impressed Malcolm was just how well they behaved when they weren't having sex. It was like they knew certain places were good for certain kinds of talk and other places weren't. They became model citizens in the museums and restaurants. They talked about highbrow subjects when they weren't fucking, and Malcolm loved to hear about their adventures on other planets. Despite first impressions, it wasn't all sex. They had told him they could not fuck around with certain species either because of differences in culture or biology, but they enjoyed their company just the same. Sometimes it made Malcolm feel bad that Columbus was so confining and the apartment so small.

It really was like these two had always been here. They were so easy to live with, and neither felt like they had to keep up with Malcolm, nor did he feel obligated to keep up with them. At long last, he had found a perfect match for himself, not just sexually, but emotionally.

Now dry, he walked out of the bathroom and around the corner to the living room. He threw on a pair of sweat pants and a coat and opened the front door. Columbus winters sucked, but then again winter sucked everywhere Malcolm had been. He lit up and took a drag, stuffed the pack in his pocket. He breathed a sigh of relief. He'd had to smoke since he got faceful of slit.

He heard footsteps across the apartment. A three-clawed hand wrapped around the door and pulled it inward. Ratash walked outside and stood by Malcolm, Irus right behind him.

"You should shower," said the human. "You look like I did a few minutes ago."

"You used all the hot water," the raptor said.

"Oh, bullshit." Malcolm laughed. "If you can stand in sub-freezing weather and not bat an eye, you can shower in cold water. How the hell do you stand being outside like this?"

"All raptors teach their children how to control their metabolism so they can endure colder climates. They need to, since our foxes are always dragging us to cold, miserable places."

He nudged Irus's neck with his muzzle. The fox wagged his tail. He wore no shorts, so he grabbed his sheath and shook it in his raptor's direction. The gesture equaled "suck it" in their culture, but with a wag of the tail it was playful and not insulting.

Malcolm took a drag and exhaled the smoke away from them. "Can you teach me how to endure the cold like that?"

"Maybe," said the raptor. "I don't know if humans can, but we can try."

"Would come in handy. February is the worst month for winter."

"We learn as children. It takes years of practice. Not sure how long it will take you, but we'll find out if you're able."

"I'd love that." He took another puff, exhaled.

Ratash watched the smoke, stretched his muzzle into it and scented it. He snorted, shook it out of his muzzle. Malcolm smiled. It was as if the raptor had only just now noticed.

"You ever live anywhere this cold?" Malcolm asked.

"Actually, yes," said Irus. "We were on Jemum for a long time because of the disaster."

"What's Jemum?"

Ratash clicked his claws. "The mammals on that planet have the biggest balls in the contacted universe."

The human laughed, flicked the ash. "How big?"

"They look a little like raccoons," said the fox. "Shorter than you, and with a pair of basketballs between their legs."

"Holy shit. How is that possible?"

Irus answered. "They walk upright. In fact, that's why they do. Mating is communal in their society, so the more sperm a male releases, the better the chance of passing on his genes. It was a race for the largest balls, and it continued even after they reached sentience. That was pretty much all they lived for until they met their companion species. They're a species of insect, believe it or not. They're like dragonflies, about twice the size of your head, and when the Jemum realized they were intelligent, they stopped competing for mates and learned everything they could. Mating is still communal, but they're not competing anymore. And their balls are still huge."

"If you look at their jizz," said the raptor, "you can see all the sperm with the naked eye. There are so many squirming around that the semen actually moves on its own."

Malcolm had just inhaled. He coughed as he laughed. "That's fucked up! I wish I could see it! It's cold there?"

"In winter it's very cold," continued the fox. "The Jemum hide underground in burrows. The insects used to hibernate in trees, but to be with their companion race more they also took to moving underground in winter. Body heat keeps them warm. The sex also produces a lot of extra heat."

"I'll bet." He looked at Ratash. "So you must've been in paradise in that place."

"In a way." He clicked his claws and took another sniff of the cigarette smoke, resisting the coughing reflex. "The portals closed. Both of their Archeons died. It was winter when it happened, so everyone was underground."

"Oh. Shit..."

"It was hell for a long time. Even after winter, nobody knew what was going on. Then the portals came back for a while. We left to find out what happened but came back when nobody could tell us. The portals went out again. The second disaster. This time the Archeons did not remake the contacted universe. We were cut off. It wasn't until Deka and Rive portaled in that we went to Gaow and finally learned what happened. Meeting other Relians again for the first time in over two years... That was such a relief."

"I can't imagine. The Jemum were good company though, weren't they?"

"Very good," Ratash said. "Sex is completely communal among them. No rules, gender doesn't even matter. It helped them survive the winters, and it kept the species going. It's strange in that the females are still quadrupeds."

"Really? They walk on four legs? And the males walk upright because of their balls?"

"Yup. Evolution has a fucked up sense of humor."

"I'd love to see that."

"There's no light in their winter burrows," Irus said. "You get around by touch and scent. There isn't as much sex in summer, since it's out of season, but you can see them then."

"I'd love to."

Malcolm flicked the butt into the grass and then stepped back inside. The Relians followed, closing the door behind them. Malcolm removed the coat and tossed it on the couch as he walked to the kitchen.

"Malcolm," said Ratash. "Why do you smoke?"

He laughed as he packed lunch. "Started in high school. Bunch of friends got me into it."

He stood in the kitchen with Malcolm. "But why?"

"They were my friends. I wanted to be an adult. Bunch of them started drinking. Got me into beer, too."

Ratash stepped closer, sniffed Malcolm's mouth. "I don't like what it does to your scent."

Malcolm dropped a few granola bars into his lunch bag. "Oh? What's it do?"

"You smell normal only after you smoke. When you don't, you smell wrong."

"Makes sense."

"Why?"

"It's an addiction. Tried to quit a few times years ago. I turn into a fucking dragon when I'm off it. And I gain weight."

Ratash tilted his head. Suddenly Irus was behind Malcolm, arms around his stomach, muzzle tucked into his neck and sheath between his ass cheeks. Malcolm hadn't seen him come into the kitchen.

"Oh, God, you're so warm."

Irus whimpered.

Ratash had not broken eye contact. "May I see the cigarettes?"

Malcolm reached into his pocket and handed him the pack. The raptor took it, flipped the box open, sniffed it. He inhaled harder and harder. Malcolm smiled.

"Interesting?"

"Plants are something omnivores eat," he said. "I don't know of any species who burns and inhales a plant. Who had this idea?"

"I have no clue."

"Does it do anything for you?"

"Keeps me alert. And it's slowly killing me."

Ratash rose to full height. Malcolm zipped his lunch bag and shuffled out of the kitchen with the fox still holding him.

"How is it slowly killing you?"

Malcolm dropped the bag in the hall and walked himself and Irus to the bedroom. "That's a long story. I'll tell you when I get home."

He stopped at the dresser and opened the top drawer. The fox pushed himself harder against Malcolm's rear and growled a little. Malcolm leaned into it, scratched the canine's head.

"Sorry, foxie, work calls."

Irus growled again. "Call off."

"Already did that twice. Can't waste any more points."

Irus continued to growl, dry-humping Malcolm a few times. Malcolm grinned, slipped off the sweatpants. The fox continued humping him as Malcolm put on his work pants. He rubbed Irus's muzzle.

"That's a good fox. Keep me warm while I change clothes. How did I live without you?"

Irus whined. Malcolm smiled, opened the next drawer, and took out a shirt. He slipped it over his head, worked it down his torso again the fox's grip.

"All right, I'm dressed. Time to let go."

Irus whined again and humped him harder.

"Bad fox."

Irus let go and dropped to all fours, looking up at him and whining. Malcolm patted his head as he left the bedroom. Irus had watched how humans acted toward terrestrial dogs and he often imitated the behavior to put people at ease.

Ratash still stood in the hall, in an eager stance, as if he had just seen something dangerous, pack of cigarettes in hand. Malcolm took it from him and palmed it, then kissed the orange raptor on the cheek.

"See ya in eleven hours."

He grabbed his lunch bag on the way to the front door. The raptor did not say anything. Malcolm was already counting the days until the weekend, when he wouldn't be too tired and brain-dead to go anywhere.

2

Malcolm walked through the door and mentally subtracted one day from the countdown to the weekend. He enjoyed coming home to someone now. It forced his brain to wake up and stay active during the week. Before the raptor and fox arrived, he typically stayed brain-dead for the entire week as a defense mechanism, as it took far less effort to be in work mode all the time than switch back and forth every day.

Irus sat on the carpet in front of the television, Playstation controller in hand. Ratash lay on the floor, holding a book. Malcolm noticed the white mark on the spine.

"Hi, guys." He closed the door and kicked the snow off his shoes. "You went to the library?"

"Yeah," Irus said.

"How did you find it?"

"We started walking and asked someone on the street where the library was."

Malcolm untied his shoes. "And they gave you a card?"

"Sure. We have an address. We know the phone number."

"Oh... What did you borrow?"

Malcolm crossed the living room and stood over the raptor. Images of cigarettes and tar-filled lungs graced the covers of all four books. Ratash held one of these books now.

"You really wanted to know about tobacco, didn't you? How'd you find all of that?"

Ratash lowered the book and looked up at him. "The librarians were very helpful. As soon as we walked in, I told them what I wanted to learn about, and they showed me how to use the filing system."

"Sweet. Well, did you find what you wanted to know?"

"I read three books on the subject. The first two are at the library."

"No shit? You can read that fast?"

"Once I learn how, yes, I can."

"I thought only the Archeons could do that."

"They can read faster, and ten books at once, and listen to a roomful of people and respond to all of them. I'm not that good."

"I didn't know that. Interesting stuff?"

Ratash growled. For once it did not make Malcolm hard. "Why does this shit exist?"

Malcolm laughed. "Good question."

He turned and walked back to the door. He took off his coat and hung it up. He turned around and Ratash was standing right in front of him, nose to nose. Malcolm jumped.

"Jesus! You weigh seven hundred pounds—how the hell do you walk so quiet?"

"I read a history of tobacco. Everyone knows it's awful for you, and yet it's allowed to continue. Did you know tobacco companies once added antifreeze to make the tobacco taste cooler as it burned?"

"No, but I'm not surprised."

Malcolm walked down the hall, unbuttoning his shirt.

"Who knows what they're doing to it now! None of that has to be disclosed!"

"I know."

"You do?"

Malcolm entered the bedroom. He tossed his work shirt on the bed and picked up a casual shirt. It was too cold to be naked in the house.

"It's old news by now. Everyone knows the shit causes cancer and has all sorts of junk added to it."

"People don't smoke because they want to," Ratash said from the bedroom door. "They smoke because they have to. Why doesn't someone stop them?"

"I don't know."

He took his pants off and tossed them onto the bed. He slipped on a pair of sweatpants and turned around.

"Malcolm..." Ratash began. It was a few seconds before he continued. "You know there's a problem, but you still smoke. Why?"

"I told you. I tried quitting years ago."

"You said you turn into a dragon. Withdrawal is that hard for you?"

"Very. Almost lost my job I kept snapping at people. Even broke a machine at work. That's why I had to smoke again."

"Patch and gum didn't work?"

Malcolm smiled. "You really did your homework, did you? Yeah, I tried both. It's not the same. It gives you nicotine but there's no smoke. The habit of picking up a cigarette and inhaling. Nothing replaces that."

He walked out of the bedroom to the kitchen. Ratash followed close behind him.

"I am... horrified. I have been to over a hundred planets, and nothing like this exists. When someone realizes something causes harm, the first thing anyone does is stop. I don't mean quitting, I mean..."

Malcolm reached into the freezer, pulled out a TV dinner, and opened the box.

"Entire species had social rituals before they became sentient and joined the contacted universe. One I remember hearing about involved migrating to a particular river-head to breed. It was a species of aquatic people."

"Salmon?" Malcolm said, pulling the film off the tray.

"They did that long after they found their companion species. Then one day someone realized that when they did this, the entire species gathered in one place and predators picked them off easier, so they stopped doing it. The entire population changed its behavior. Why hasn't anyone done this for tobacco?"

The microwave whirled. Malcolm walked by Ratash to the front door. The raptor stayed at his heels, still talking.

"It's the best thing to do, but nobody's doing it! It doesn't make sense! Why would anyone not do what makes sense?"

"Good questions. You should ask the librarians. If I knew the answer, I wouldn't be working in an auto parts factory ten hours a day."

He reached into his coat and pulled out a pack of ciga-rettes. As soon as Ratash saw it, he reached out with his claws and knocked it out of Malcolm's hand. Malcolm looked at it on the floor, two large gashes torn through the box. He checked his hand and it wasn't bleeding, then he looked up at Ratash.

The raptor closed the distance, rubbed Malcolm's neck with his muzzle. "I can't let you kill yourself. You're quitting."

"Wha...? No, no, now's not a good time. I told you I turn into a dragon."

Ratash pulled back, looked Malcom in the eye. "I've given blowjobs to two dragons." He clicked his claws. "They don't scare me."

"No. Fuck no, Ratash, I can't quit now! I will snap! You'll hate me—I'll hate you! We get along great—I don't wanna ruin that."

"I will get you through this, even if I have to hold you down with my cock all day."

"Ah—"

Ratash pushed his muzzle into Malcolm's face. "Do you want to quit?"

Normally this kind of aggression made Malcolm hard, but something was different.

"Yeah, but—"

"Do you know you need to quit?"

"Look, I said—"

"You know what you need to do, and you're not doing it. You need help."

Malcolm couldn't find the words to argue anymore. "I will turn into something worse than a dragon. I will scream at you. I will break things. I may even get fired."

"I bring my fox back from the old ways. Whatever you become, it can't be worse."

Malcolm looked down at the cigarette box on the floor. He looked up at the raptor again. The theropod's breath was hot and smelled like raw hamburger. He felt it starting already, a dragon in his belly wiggling around, warning him that if he didn't smoke it would burst out and destroy the city.

"I'll show you what happens, but that's all I'm promising."

Ratash growled again. This growl did give Malcolm a bit of a rise, but the raptor's stance took it back down again.

3

Malcolm sat on the couch, Ratash's neck draped over his lap, watching Irus play Playstation. To Malcolm, it was just moving colors. His foot bounced up and down. He was rubbing his temples. Then he itched his neck. Several times he tried to stand up, but the raptor's neck held him down.

He hadn't smoked since the drive home from work, which meant his last cigarette was five hours ago. He clenched his hand.

"I can smell what it's doing to you," Ratash said. "English doesn't have words to describe it."

"Fuck."

"Yeah, that's a good word for it."

"Just fuck." He tried to stand up. Ratash held his neck over Malcolm's lap, forcing him to remain in the seat.

"I can't do this now! Not now!"

"There's no better time."

Malcolm remained seated, feet planted as if he wanted to leap up in an instant. He drummed the armrest with a finger. Faster. Faster.

"Don't hold it in. Don't pretend everything is all right. Humans expect you to hide it, but I don't."

"I don't want you to hate me."

Malcolm grabbed the remote and tapped it with his fingernail. Then he played with the battery cover, making it click louder and louder.

"The dragon is still hiding," said the raptor. "It wants to come out. Let him out. I wanna meet him."

"Ratash, don't tempt me."

"Don't pretend you're in control."

"Ratash, I told you I'd show you what happens. This is it. I get fidgety. I get anxious. Lighting up is all I can think about. It's instant relief. The longer I sit here..."

"That's it. Show me the dragon. I can't help you fight it if you don't show me."

"I don't wanna do this."

Malcolm tried to sit up, but the raptor held him down again. Malcolm grabbed his neck and tried to push him off, but Ratash had more muscle in his neck than Malcolm had in both arms it seemed.

Malcolm grabbed the back of the couch and pulled himself up and slithered out from under his neck. He climbed over the back of the couch and swung off just as Ratash raised himself.

"Where are you going?"

"You ruined my last pack. I'm going to the gas station. I can't fucking do this right now I got too much shit going on between you and fucking work and the motherfucking traffic and I got three more days of this before I get a fucking break!"

Malcolm stormed halfway to the door. A hand gripped his arm and yanked him backwards.

"Son of—!"

The human pulled back and went halfway down. The raptor walked on his stomach, flattening him to the floor and pinned him with one foot.

"What are you doing? Get off me!"

Ratash stood on him, killing claw poking his heart. Malcolm wiggled and writhed.

"This is what that shit is doing to you." The raptor lowered his snout to Malcolm's face. "Give it all to me. I can't kill it if it's hiding."

Malcolm couldn't struggle under the raptor's weight. He noticed Ratash was not dripping. After a minute under his foot, Malcolm collapsed and breathed. Ratash did not let up. The wave had passed. Malcolm cried a little. "Oh my God, it hasn't even been six hours."

"Tell me what it's doing to you."

"Getting a cigarette is all I can think about. There's no room in my head for any other thought. I hate feeling this way. Just one smoke and it's all gone. I'll feel like me again. I can do this gradually, just one cigarette a day or something."

Ratash nuzzled his cheek. "First anger, now pleading. You should smell yourself. This scares me."

"It's only gonna get worse. I can't work like this. They won't let me take time off to stop smoking. All the guys there smoke. I'll give in. I can't do this."

"You won't give in. I will go with you."

"What?" Malcolm raised his head. "They won't let you be there!"

"When they see what I'm doing, they will."

"This isn't going to—"

"Refuse to work if I can't be there."

Malcolm laughed. "Doesn't work that way. They'll just get rid of me."

Ratash snarled. "I'll make it work."

He scented Malcolm's armpit. It was a swamp under there. He raised his muzzle and stepped off of Malcolm, still looming over him.

"Don't run to the store." Ratash stood in attack stance pointed straight at Malcolm, a posture Malcolm had only seen one other time, during the dodge ball game. "Run to me. I will get you through this. Don't hold back. I wanna meet that dragon so I can fuck him to death."

The human sat up, held his head, felt his chest. Both ached. He panted. Another wave was coming. "You really want me to do this?"

"You know you need help. I want to help." He folded his hands. "I mean it when I say your scent terrifies me like this. I wish you knew how wrong it is."

Malcolm held his stare. In the movies this was always when the dinosaur pounced. The human climbed to his feet. "If you think you can get me through this, all right. Let's go. But I can't promise this will end with all of us being friends or even with me having a job."

The raptor clicked his claws. Irus's ears remained folded as he played.

4

Malcolm hoped his boss would say no. He prayed to God it wouldn't be allowed. Nobody was allowed to be on the factory floor if they weren't assigned to a station, but to Malcolm's surprise, Ratash went straight to the big boss, told him what he was doing, and that he was going to stick with Malcolm until the man was off cigarettes.

Maybe it was the fact that a fucking dinosaur was making demands. Maybe it was the audacity. Maybe it was out of pure curiosity to see what the hell happened next, but the boss gave Ratash and Irus earplugs and hardhats and let them follow Malcolm. He guessed he had told everyone what was going on, for even the other bosses who arrived later in the day simply walked by the Relians as if they belonged there. The one time the bosses talked to one another and cooperated on something...

So Malcolm walked from machine to machine, carrying parts from one to the other, the same motions every day, keeping up with the equipment, effectively becoming a machine himself. The raptor and his fox stood just off to the side, watching him. How they did not become bored out of their minds Malcolm did not know.

The bell sounded for his station's ten-minute break. Malcolm leaned on the die press and hung his head. This was where he broke down every time. Just enough time to smoke and nothing else. He felt a three-fingered hand on his shoulder.

"Go and sit down. You smell tired."

If anyone else had done that, Malcolm would have simply threw their arm off and walked away. But this was Ratash. Malcolm didn't feel the need to conceal his suffering.

"I'm not tired!" he screamed.

People at the next station heard him, even through their earplugs. Malcolm saw them staring out the corner of his eye.

Malcolm turned around and crossed the yellow line marking his machine's station. He heard claws clicking, and then something slammed into his back. He fell forward and hit the ground. Some instinct he didn't know he had made him look to the side so he didn't break his nose. A muzzle lowered to his ear.

"You're walking away to bum a smoke from one of them. Don't follow them. Let them kill themselves. You're better than that."

"Fucking snake! You have no idea what this is like!"

"Just lay here for a while. It'll be a good break."

"I don't need a break! I need a fucking smoke! It's the only good part of my day! The only goddamned relief I can get!"

"Don't run to them. Don't run to a cigarette. Run to me. Nothing you do scares me. I've seen far worse."

"Motherfucker! Fuck you and fuck this job and—."

"Yes, yes, let it out! Let it all out! Show me what that shit does to you!"

Malcolm lay under Ratah's foot for a minute. People gathered. Two managers had left their offices and stood on the factory floor, staring. Some of the machines had stopped. It was very quiet in the factory now.

Ratash turned his snout in all directions. "It's okay. I'm helping him quit smoking."

A few people laughed nervously. Three people gave a thumbs-up as they passed.

"Don't any of you tempt him, or you'll be next." He clicked his hand-claws, not caring how many people knew he was grinning.

Malcolm turned his head and found the boss who had given Ratash and Irus permission to be here. His mouth hung open, and then he slipped back into the offices, closing the door.

Slowly the people began to return to their stations. The machines started up again. Malcolm lay still on the concrete for five more minutes. The people came back from break. They stopped and stared at Ratash standing on Malcolm with his killing claw seemingly read to sink into his back and sever his spine.

"All of you can smoke if you want," he shouted to them as they stared. "Malcolm is quitting. I'm here to help."

They slowly migrated back to the machines and started them up again. Ratash released Malcolm. The human stood up and met the raptor's eyes.

"This is embarrassing."

Ratash clicked his claws, laughing. "It's entertaining for them."

"Now I know why nobody laughs in sitcoms."

"Your scent is an absolute mess. What's going on in your head?"

"Try going without food for a week. Ten times a minute I get a pang and I just want to smoke and it's pissing me off that I can't think of anything else."

His anger made him work faster than the machine, and having to wait for the damn thing to catch up to him made him even angrier. It was a nasty cycle that built over the next two hours of repetitive, mindless motions.

When his next break came up, he turned to Ratash and then sat down on the concrete. Ratash walked up to him, nuzzled his face. Malcolm pushed him away. Ratash came back. Malcolm pushed him away again. He came back again. Malcolm felt drained. He reached around and hugged the raptor around the neck.

"This is taking fucking forever," he said.

"It's what you needed to do."

"I know! This is why I couldn't quit!" He began tapping his palm with a finger.

"This is easy."

"How the fuck is this easy? This is torture and it's not even lunch!"

Ratash wiggled his muzzle under Malcolm's arm and inhaled. He breathed it for almost a minute, then raised his snout and met Malcolm's eyes.

"I can smell the chaos in your body. I have never smelled a mammal's scent do this before. It hurts me."

"Yeah, it hurts *you*."

"It really does. I have to kill it. I read smokers tend to snack to replace the habit. Don't run to the refrigerator. Run to me. I'll get you through this."

"Stop saying that!"

"I mean it. Food won't help you. I will."

Malcolm closed his eyes. He leaned against the machine and sobbed. He didn't care that everyone was watching. It didn't seem to matter now.

5

The first five days were always the hardest. Three days with Ratash and Irus at work looking over his shoulder were hellish, but it got him through the week. Now it was the weekend. He had planned to treat himself and the aliens in his apartment at a bar, mixing with all his friends.

All of that was on hold. Instead, Malcolm sat on the couch playing Playstation with Irus and Ratash on a Sunday afternoon. The fox sat on the floor in front of the television. The raptor lay sideways on the couch, neck draped over Malcolm's legs, head facing the screen. Malcolm was surprised the couch hadn't broken under their weight yet.

Malcolm had read their vision was so good they could see pixels dimming between blasts of the electron gun, and he didn't know how they tolerated the flickering screen, but somehow they did. He had a feeling they endured it to help him, which pissed him off. They went with Malcolm to the bathroom, to work, shopping—more like ghosts haunting him everywhere he went, and it pissed him off.

Every waking moment he thought about smoking, how long it had been, how long it would be, and every five minutes he wanted to get up, but Ratash could stop him with just a glance. That pissed him off.

Malcolm was pissed off all the time, and that pissed him off, too.

Ratash smelled it. He knew Malcolm's mood, and when Malcolm was about to lash out, so he prepared for it, which pissed Malcolm off even more. His suffering was out in the open, even when it was internal, and he hated it.

But after the second day he realized what Ratash was talking about. Don't run to the store, or the fridge, or anyone else. Run to him. Malcolm had been leaning on Ratash since the second day, and as long as the raptor was around, he had somewhere to go. On his own, he couldn't even make it past the jitters and anxiety on day two. It was working, and that also pissed him off.

Ratash leaned over and sniffed his armpit. Malcolm wasn't wearing clothes, so it was easy access. The human hadn't had a hard-on in days, and he hated not feeling like himself.

"You smell much better," Ratash said as he pulled away from Malcolm's arm. "You're a lot calmer."

"It won't last."

"You're coughing less."

"Less than a week."

"The dragon is still in there. I'm still waiting for him to come out. I will fuck him to death when he does."

"You know if you had a job, you wouldn't be able to do this. You'd be at work all the time and you'd have to let me go through this alone."

"That also puzzles me about this place. Nobody has time to help one another because they are too busy. Addiction like this would never happen in the contacted universe, but if it did, you'd have ten people around you helping you recover. Here, everyone turns the other way and says it's not my problem. If you're in pain, you're expected to hide it and keep going like nothing is wrong. Why?"

"I don't fucking know!"

"It's stupid."

"When you have to start working, you'll get it. You won't be able to stick with me twenty-four seven. Nobody has time to do anything else."

"Good thing my food is paid for."

"For now. Only a matter of time before it ends. You'll have to work sixteen hours a day seven days a week just to afford all that meat you eat."

"I'll hunt."

"In Columbus? Good luck."

"Plenty of animals outside the city. I can smell them when we drive. Easy to track, easy to take down."

"If it's not illegal now, I'm sure it will be."

"Why would it be illegal to hunt my own food?"

"Everything else is."

"Tobacco should be, but it isn't."

Malcolm clenched his fist. He threw the controller down. Ratash scented his underarm from a distance. Malcolm wanted to punch him so he'd leave him alone. Instead, Malcolm looked at him. He wanted to break something and collapse into fetal position and cry at the same time.

"I *like* smoking. I fucking love it. It makes me feel good. I can focus. I *hate* this."

"That's what you need help getting past." The raptor raised his head up to Malcolm's chin. "I gotta piss. Can I trust you by yourself for a minute?"

Malcolm panted a few times. "Yeah."

The raptor climbed off the couch, walked around it and down the hall to the bathroom. He didn't close the door or turn on the fan. Malcolm heard water hitting the toilet. He stared at the front door.

Malcolm leaped from the couch. He grabbed his keys and wallet, jumped into the sweatpants he'd left there, then ran outside. He fumbled the keys and cursed that such a simple thing as finding the right key was difficult. He found the right one and unlocked the door.

He backed out and had just left the subdivision when he saw a dinosaur outside the driver's side window. The raptor was keeping up with him on foot. Malcolm hit the gas. The raptor fell back and then caught up again, watching Malcolm as he ran. Malcolm floored it, doing fifty in a thirty-five. Still the raptor kept pace. He remembered the Relians never locked the passenger doors. Ratash threw one open and leaped inside, depressing the rear shocks and making the car swerve. Ratash rested a hand on Malcolm's shoulder. He felt the raptor's muzzle by his neck.

"If you're going out, we should get some burgers."

"Jesus Christ!"

Malcolm pulled over to the shoulder and threw the car in park. He held the steering wheel. The muzzle now rubbed his neck. Malcolm pounded the steering wheel, but instead of screaming, he crumpled. He began sobbing. He felt claws on his neck. Loving and tender caresses, just like the muzzle against his cheek.

"I can't do this! I want to be normal! I want to be happy! Can't we just go back to fucking all the time? Please can we just go back? I hate feeling this way please just let me smoke."

Malcolm felt teeth on his neck. He exposed more of his neck for the raptor, and Ratash mouthed him more. He had told the human long ago this was one of the most intimate things a prey species could let a predator do. Malcolm felt helpless but safe at the same time, even parked on the shoulder.

"Better?"

"Yeah," Malcolm said, thoroughly drained.

He sat for a few more minutes while Ratash mouthed his neck and rubbed his shoulder. Once he had control again, he pulled the car out of park and turned around.

Malcolm led the way back inside. Irus was still playing the game, sitting lower, ears still back. Ratash went straight to the bathroom. Malcolm heard water hitting the toilet again. Ratash hadn't finished pissing; he had been waiting for Malcolm to make a break for it. The human sat down on the couch, feeling defeated but surprisingly victorious. That was one of those moments he had caved in the past and then felt like the most pathetic person in the world for giving in and ruining his progress. Ratash had just saved him from that. He took a breath. He felt happy about it.

Irus had turned around on the floor and now sat like a dog looking at him, ears folded back.

"You've been very quiet lately," said the human.

Irus turned his eyes down to the carpet. "It's not polite to comment when a raptor brings a fox back."

"Huh?"

Irus now looked at him. "This is why raptors and foxes don't fuck around. It makes this process easier." He rose partway and nuzzled Malcolm's neck. "I know what you're going through. I become a monster without Ratash, too. He'll help you."

Malcolm stared silently. The fox sat back down and unpaused the game. The human picked up the controller where he had dropped it and joined.

A moment later, Ratash walked around the couch and lay on the floor in front of the empty cushions.

Malcolm kept thinking about how it would feel to smoke again. To have relief. To be himself again. He hadn't had sex in almost week, and that pissed him off. But he hadn't smoked this whole time. That was the goal. He kept reminding himself of that.

6

Malcolm had the presence of mind to realize he was in the second week. He now only thought about smoking ten times per hour instead of fifty. Progress. Agonizing but measurable. Ratash and Irus stood near him as he became one with the factory machine.

The raptor hadn't had to hold him down in six days. Malcolm still yelled at him, but Ratash didn't seem to mind. He was not scared of anything Malcolm said or did, and that had been so liberating. He could do anything short of grabbing a knife from the kitchen, and the reptile didn't hate him.

Instead of going to the fridge, Malcolm went to Ratash. The raptor kept him occupied. He had a storehouse of stories and experiences offworld. Either that, or more games, more long walks. Ratash had started doing that. Taking Malcolm on walks. Now Malcolm felt like he was on a leash, but he was in no shape to decide how to handle this, so he let it happen because he was two weeks in and hadn't gained any weight or picked up a single cigarette.

He wondered how long they would stick by his side. Once he was through the woods and could be trusted to say no on his own, they would have to sit at home again. Then what? Would they start looking for a job? He hadn't given much thought to the future of all this.

He was surprised Ratash had stopped dripping. Normally the raptor was a faucet, but since he had resolved to get Malcolm off tobacco, he hadn't dripped once. Malcolm wanted to ask him about it, but he didn't want to bring it up. He was just glad he didn't have to explain the puddle of lube on the concrete every day, or why his raptor had a maxi pad taped between his legs.

The bell rang for lunch. Malcolm finished the part, set it in the bin, and walked down the lane between the machines, raptor and fox at his heels. Malcolm clocked out for lunch. He pulled his earplugs out and turned to go to the lockers for his lunch bag.

"First I want you to go outside," Ratash said in his ear.

"What? Why?"

"Let's see if the dragon is still in there."

Malcolm's heart raced. "Shit, no. I just got through that."

"I'm here. Let's see how far you've come."

"Oh God please no."

Ratash nudged him with his head to the smoking area outside. Malcolm gulped, and after a few strides with a raptor leading him he walked by himself.

He pushed open the doors and emerged. There they were. All the smokers on first shift puffing away. The air was full of smoke. Something stirred inside Malcolm. Feelings he thought he buried last week.

Ratash sniffed his underarm though his uniform. "There it is." He clicked his claws. "There's the dragon."

"Not here. Not in front of everyone. Please."

"You'll have to deal with temptation soon enough. Don't let the dragon hide. Let him fly."

Several people had seen them. They waved.

"'Sup, Mal," said one of them. "Didn't think I'd see you again. Not with your dinosaur herding you around."

Malcolm growled. Ratash clicked his claws. The human walked over to them, stood beside them. Smoke blew in his face. It smelled horrible, and yet the dragon inside him stirred and writhed and moaned.

"Proud of you, Mal," someone else said. "About time you kicked it."

"It's all these idiots have been talking about," said one of the women. "Nobody can believe Joey lets those aliens stay."

Malcolm smiled. "I think he just wanted to see if it would work."

"Damn straight," said someone else. He bent over, coughed, then took another drag.

Malcolm had forgotten what it was like to spend half the time coughing and then smoking, knowing the cause and yet doing it again and again.

"There's a bet going," said someone in front of him. "Goes all the way out to three months."

"Make 'em all lose," said a lady. "They all don't think you'll last that long."

"He's already two weeks out," said someone else. "He'll make it. And the rest of us will still be here. Still burnin' a hundred dollars a week on these pieces of shit." She looked at Malcolm. "Don't give up. Don't let them tempt you."

The dragon roared. Malcolm squeezed his fists. Ratash's head rested on his shoulder. "There he is. Don't ignore it. Let him out."

"Not here," he whispered.

"Yes, right here. Show them what it's doing to you. Show them!"

"Fuck you, no!" Malcolm swatted Ratash away. He stumbled into someone and into the cloud of smoke. It smelled so good and yet it filled him with nauseating revulsion. The dragon kicked and screamed.

"Fuck all of you! Fuck all of you!"

Ratash crouched, splayed his claws, aimed his body at Malcolm.

"Up yours!" Malcolm screamed. "Why did you bring me out here? I was doing good and then you fucking made me come out here!"

Ratash stalked, raised his killing claws, and growled. "I knew he was hiding. Come out and play."

"You know what, fuck you!"

Malcolm snatched a cigarette from the nearest person's hand. Everyone backed away. Malcolm raised it to his lips but didn't even make it halfway to his mouth. Ratash bowled into him, shoving him backwards. Malcolm wrapped his arms around the raptor's neck and held on as he went to the concrete. He landed on his back, the raptor standing on him with both feet. The human was surprised Ratash didn't break his rib cage putting all his weight on him.

"You goddamned lizard! I was out of the fucking woods! Why'd you do this to me! Why the fuck did you—"

He was pounding on the raptor's thigh, reaching up trying to kick something. Ratash took it. He didn't flinch. He lowered his muzzle to Malcolm's face and screeched at him. It could have been the last sound on the face of the planet before the world ended. Nobody made a move or a sound for a solid minute.

Finally Malcolm took a breath. "Oh God."

Ratash stepped off him, holding his hand out. Malcolm took it, pulled himself up to his feet. Ratash nuzzled his neck as Malcolm stammered.

"I'm sorry. I'm so sorry. I didn't mean it. I'm sorry."

"Don't apologize. You don't have to keep him inside you."

Malcolm leaned on him as the raptor walked him back to the doors. Irus walked on Malcolm's other side, holding him around the waist. They had to pass through the cloud of smoke again. Malcolm held his breath but then realized he was hiding from the dragon again. He breathed it, forced his body to take it in and remember it.

Just before the door closed, he heard several people muttering "shit," "damn," "Jesus Christ," and "I need another smoke."

7

Malcolm looked in the mirror. The raptor's slit lube covered his face. He giggled at his reflection.

He had made it this far without a single smoke and without gaining a pound. He didn't hide from it anymore. He welcomed it when Ratash tackled him during a tantrum because it killed the dragon like nothing else ever had.

It was Saturday, and for the first time in as long as he could remember, he had woken up with morning wood instead of cigarette cravings. Ratash noticed. He had spent the last hour sucking on it. Meanwhile Irus had been behind the raptor, fucking his brains out.

Malcolm felt calm. Relaxed. He was sure the dragon was still there, smaller now, its voice weaker, but all it had to do was nag him a little and Malcolm would pick up a smoke again and then he would have to start all over. He shivered at the thought as he leaned over the sink.

Footsteps walked around the corner. A theropod filled the door. He had Malcolm's cum on his muzzle, and it looked adorable.

"Three months," Malcolm said to the mirror. "I can't believe it."

"You smell better every day."

"I feel a lot better. Don't get comfy now. It's not over. It's never over. You can't kill this dragon. It'll always be there, trying to get me to feed it again."

"I'll fuck it till it dies."

Ratash stepped into the bathroom and stood next to Malcolm. He looked at both of them in the mirror. Malcolm wrapped an arm around his neck.

"Fuck you. This was a nightmare." He pulled him closer, hugged him. "And I couldn't have done it without you."

"I know."

"Don't stop. Tackle me and rip my guts out before I smoke again."

"Don't stop running to me when you're tempted."

Malcolm released him, looked at himself in the mirror again. "You know you can never get rid of an addiction, right? You just replace it with something else."

"That was the plan."

"I don't know if this is good or bad."

He heard something wet drip on the tile floor. He smiled. Ratash hadn't done that in weeks. The raptor growled. This growl gave Malcolm a hard-on, and he leaned on the sink and bent over. Ratash climbed on top of him, still growling. It wasn't a growl of aggression. It proclaimed victory.

Malcolm sure felt victorious. "Oh, God, that feels so good. Wow..."

Ratash did not ride him hard. He never did unless he smelled the human wanted it hard. How he knew, Malcolm still hadn't figured out. Malcolm saw Irus in the mirror. He was standing at the door, rubbing himself, waiting for his turn on the human. As the raptor thrust, Malcolm thought of something for no apparent reason.

"So... Did you mean it... when you said you gave head to a couple dragons?"

Ratash couldn't laugh with his hands gripping Malcolm's shoulders, so he drummed his claws on them instead.

"I wasn't kidding. A Krone was in heat and he heard about me. Wanted me to work my magic on him. I made him cum so hard others heard us from the next mountain range. I've gone to see him a couple times since then. He won't be in heat again in my lifetime though. Then there was Norh." He growled. "Got him off eight times while we were on Gaow. He even let me fuck him. Whatever Stephen did to him, I like the change. Wish I could take more of his dick, but he's way too big for me."

"How do you give a blowjob to a dragon ... ooooohhh."

Ratash told him exactly how to give a blowjob to a dragon.

West of Mexico City

I

The building they approached was huge but apparently now in disuse, given the condition of the signs leading up to it. The road itself was lonely and overgrown, far enough outside the city to be isolated but not far enough to feel it.

Kylac sat in the passenger seat, a pair of black shorts covering himself. Deka and Sonjaa lay in the back. The seats had been removed, giving the raptors enough room to lie down comfortably. Jeff Morton drove, which surprised the Relians. Deka, Kylac, and Sonjaa had not seen Jeff drive or fly himself anywhere since they first met him in the White House four months ago. Now he was dressed for hot weather and doing things himself, obviously because he didn't want anyone to recognize him down here. A pointless effort, as the three Relians traveling with him would certainly give him away.

"I've been planning this since before you arrived in Boston," Jeff said as he drove up the bumpy road. He gestured with one finger from the steering wheel. "That up ahead used to be a factory. They made car parts for General Motors until the workforce shut it down and forced the factory to move elsewhere."

"How did they do that?" Sonjaa said.

"Went on strike. Demanded an eight-hour day and for someone to repair the machines. Said too many people were getting hurt. A friend of mine was part owner of that factory. He told me the changes they wanted would have put the place in the red for years. Had no choice but to close it down. Moved three towns over. People were much more grateful for employment there."

The Relians did not address that.

"He still owns the building. Had plans to do something with it in the future, but I asked him to lease it to me instead. This place is two football fields long, three wide. There's still power going to it, and it may look like crap from here, but inside it's in good shape."

Friend's muzzle appeared out of empty air and whispered in Deka's earhole. "Ask him about the guns under the spare tire." He grinned like a human. His muzzle did not disappear.

"Are you going to tell us what the guns are for?" Deka asked.

"Nothing gets by you, does it?" replied the human. "I promised I would take you on a hunting trip. I thought it might thaw the ice that seems to have formed over things in recent weeks."

They saw the main entrance. The cracked parking lot had saplings and grass poking out of it, but the concrete of the sidewalk and the building itself looked clean and well-kept. Jeff parked in front of the entrance, shut the engine off, and popped the trunk. Deka and Sonjaa crawled out. Jeff climbed out and removed his sunglasses, looking up at the building.

"No rules here. No laws. Couldn't do this anywhere in the states, not even Alaska. Too many people trying to tell me what I can and can't do."

He walked to the trunk, then pulled up the spare tire, reached under it, and removed a large box. He lay it lengthwise and opened it. Deka, Sonjaa, and Kylac gathered next to him. Friend manifested in the trunk on all fours, sitting like a terrestrial fox, wagging his tail. Sometimes it was difficult to believe Jeff could not see him.

A rifle and a forty-four magnum handgun lay inside the box, along with three boxes of ammunition for each. Jeff nodded, closed the case, and picked it up by the handle. He led them around the car to the front door. He pushed it open, and they entered a large reception hallway. A branch to the right led to offices and administration. Directly ahead, a closed set of double doors led to the factory floor.

Sounds of animals filled the building. Large animals. Animals with teeth and claws. The smell was overwhelming, not just the animals, but the fear and hatred and boredom. The Relians recognized some of these odors from the zoo: lion, jaguar, tiger, many others.

The raptor's hands sagged. Kylac's ear folded back. Friend manifested in front of the door, tail waving about. Jeff did not turn to face them, and Friend mouthed his words.

"I overheard you say you like to hunt other predators, Deka. The bigger the teeth, the longer the claws, the better it tastes." He stepped toward the double doors. Friend disappeared as Jeff's hand clamped the handle and threw the left side open, then the right. The doorstops dropped, holding them against the wall.

The interior was indeed as large as Jeff claimed. The building housed no factory equipment. Chain link fences ran the length and width of the building. The Archeons' eyes and ears measured it instantly and placed the scents of all the animals, matching them up to the noises they made.

They stood before the entrance to a chain link hedge maze. The fence formed a path that snaked between the twenty-three rectangular enclosures throughout the building. Fourteen lions lounged inside three of the fenced-off areas. Six tigers in six enclosures by themselves. Nine bears between eight other enclosures. Seventeen jaguars within four segments toward the rear. Two elephants and a rhinoceros were also in one enclosure at the very back.

The concrete floor was only visible on the walking path between the cages. Artificial grass covered the enclosures. The high ceilings of each cage had fencing covering them to keep the animals from jumping or climbing out.

Jeff set the case down, pulled out the rifle, and began loading it. Friend manifested himself in every enclosure at once. In some places he pretended to examine the animals. In others, he examined and feigned disgust at their dung piles. In the lion cages he pretended to hump the females or be humped by the males.

The Relians heard mechanical sounds. The lights had been recently installed. Some concealed cameras. They heard a couple of them pivoting right now.

Jeff was inserting rounds into the barrel. "These were the biggest predators I could get. They've been under my care for months. Cost a pretty penny to ship them from reserves and zoos who were looking to reduce expenses. Not to mention paying people to renovate this place and keep the animals fed." He gestured with the gun to the factory floor. "Now's your chance to hunt. Let's have some fun."

He smiled as he inserted the last shell. He cocked the gun and checked to make sure the safety was on. Now he loaded the magnum. The Relians scanned the factory floor again. It echoed with growls and cries of animals in great pain. Though blood covered a large percentage of the artificial grass, implying they had been fed recently, they were still hungry and miserable. There were no trees or rocks in the enclosures, so all of the animals were bored. The pachyderms in the back paced back and forth. Some of the animals walked with a limp. They had been crippled, probably by the handlers.

Loaded and ready, Jeff strapped on a holster for the magnum, shouldered the rifle, then led them into the cages. The first cage they walked to had six lions in it. A few paced the far end. Others stared at the newcomers. Jeff paused at the combination lock, turned the wheels, and popped it. The door swung inward. The lions glared at them. An instance of Friend sat on top of one, pretending to ride it like a rodeo bull.

Jeff faced Deka and gestured inside with his head. Deka turned to the lions and then back to Jeff.

"You really think we're stupid, don't you? All of these animals are endangered. Killing them is a crime."

"Not if they're outside a reserve."

Sonjaa stepped forward. "You thought we were desperate to hunt and would go insane at the sight of this!"

Jeff turned to face her. A manifestation of Friend threw himself against the cage right behind Jeff, snarling at him and wagging his tail but not moving the cage or making any noise.

"I would never think that."

Sonjaa growled. "I heard you talking to Penny! It's exactly what you thought would happen! Now it makes sense! You think we're voracious predators who can't control ourselves! How long have we been living with you and we've never acted like hunters! Predators are animals—that's all you can think when you see us! Why did I ever think you were getting to know us?"

Kylac finished: "Security cameras are recording us. You want to have video to hold over our heads so we'll agree to do work for your business friends."

Jeff's face remained impassive, but his scent betrayed intense frustration. He closed the gate, set the lock in place and latched it but did not turn the combination wheels.

"I'm giving you three a chance to do something you won't be able to do anywhere else. Hunt without restrictions. No laws here. No rules. This is a theme park for predators I built, and someday I want to build more like it. I understand raptors don't want to be fed. They want to kill their own food. There's a solution to that problem. The cameras are to observe how well the layout works and to make adjustments in the future."

Deka stretched his neck, touched noses with Jeff. "You should know by now you can't lie to us."

Jeff backed up, reaching into his shirt pocket and pulling out a pair of earplugs. He inserted them one at a time, raised his rifle, and aimed through the fence. The Relians backed away. Jeff fired. The shot echoed around the whole factory. The animals screamed and roared. The lioness Jeff aimed for fell, still breathing. Jeff cocked the gun, ejecting the case, and aimed again. He fired. This shot hit her exposed stomach. She screamed. Jeff removed the gun from between the links and pointed it upwards as he turned to the Relians.

"This is a playground. I'm already talking with people to make it legal in the states. Only a matter of time before it is. If you wanna pout in the bleachers, go right ahead. All I ask is you walk with me and listen."

He led the way to the next enclosure. This one had two tigers in it, both of them with hobbled legs. They smelled angry, hungry, bored, desperate. The cage was large enough for a raptor to build up to a run at full speed but not so large the animals would be able to hide in a corner.

Jeff paused at the fence, watching the tigers within.

"I think you've figured out your people are in a grace period. The food stamps mean they don't have to work for a living. It was not my idea. In spite of what you must think of me, I and all of my associates are looking out for what's best for people. I was one of the guys who wanted to make the Relians work for their food right out of the gate, but the politicians listened to the other guys, the people who wanted to ease them into American life. Hence the food stamps. I know the people who made it happen. They're liberals. God knows why."

He aimed his rifle and fired. One of the tigers fell, limbs flailing everywhere. Jeff had shot him in the shoulder. Jeff removed the rifle and continued talking into the enclosure.

"But people like me outnumber people like them. All we have to do is get together, make some calls, and suddenly the news will be filled with stories of Relians who aren't working. The press releases surveys they conducted that show the majority of people are angry Relians are getting all this food and don't have to work for it. People will believe it. The surveys will have questionable sample sizes and sources, but no one will notice. People will follow the crowd, and where no consensus existed before, now one does. People will cry out to make them provide for themselves, that it's not fair humans have to work for their food but the aliens don't, and suddenly the food stamp program will be cut off. Raptors and foxes will have to work, and if they want to eat what they normally eat, they'll have to work some very long hours. That's impossible, so eventually they will be forced to adapt to fast food, TV dinners, and so forth."

He turned around, faced Deka.

"But if the Archeons should loosen their attitudes and show some gratitude, the Relians will find their food stamp status preserved for the time being."

Deka and Sonjaa growled, but Jeff couldn't hear them over the bedlam the animals made. Jeff continued.

"I have been very generous and patient with the three of you. I have given you chance after chance to secure a good future for yourselves, and I'm starting to feel like you're spitting in my face. You were rude to my business partners, insulted my senator, dismissive of my wife, but worst of all, you have been lecturing me on morality. You've been here one year, but you proceed to tell me what's right and wrong."

He turned, raised the rifle, and took aim. Friend was standing in his line of sight. Jeff pulled the trigger. Friend caught the bullet in his teeth. Jeff looked past the sights, at the tiger he was aiming for.

"Damn."

He aimed again. Friend caught this round between his fingers. He flicked the next round off course with his tail and caught it as it flipped over his head. For the next one, he bent over, raised his tail, and caught it with his sphincter. He pulled it out and held it with the others. Jeff cursed as he emptied the gun and reloaded the rifle. Friend walked through the enclosure, carrying all the rounds. He phased through the fence, held them over Jeff's head, and showered him with them, laughing like a human.

Jeff jumped as the bullets flowed over him. He stood up, glaring at Deka.

"Are you messing with me?"

"You mess with us," Deka answered. "It's only fair."

"How did you do that?"

"I'm an Archeon."

Jeff's stare might have killed. He knelt and reloaded the rifle.

"Do you understand what I'm trying to tell you? I still want to believe all of this has been cultural differences. I brought you here to show you that I can make things happen, and if I can't, I know the people who can. Anything you want, I can get. The three of you are exceptionally smart. The question you need to ask yourselves is: do you want to be used, or do you want to be useful?"

He cocked the gun and stood.

"Because I am this close to asking you to leave and telling my friends the time has come to end the grace period. True, a bunch of people I know will fight it, saying it's too soon and it needs to happen gradually, but all I have to do is call the right people, and it will happen."

Jeff walked them to the next enclosure. It was a long walk, half a football field away. This one had bears in it. They smelled angry at the world and they wanted to make the world pay. Jeff raised his rifle, fired a round. Friend stood in front of it, paused time, grabbed the bullet, carried it back to Jeff, and placed it right next to the barrel of his gun. Time unpaused, the bullet resumed course and struck the rifle, knocking it from Jeff's hand. Jeff backed away as the gun clattered inside the chain links and fell to the concrete. It rested against the fence.

He turned and glared at Deka again. The red and blue raptor held Sonjaa's claws, sharing a laugh with her.

Jeff's face had turned red. "Please stop that."

"Would you believe me if I told you it wasn't any of us?" Deka said.

"No."

"That's part of the problem. You're not listening to us."

"I have heard every word you have said to me. Every word you have said to my friends. It has been one insult after another. One judgmental speech after another. I'm tired of it. So I'm going to put this plainly. Either work with us, or work against us. If you work with us, I promise your people will have a much easier time living in the United States. Maybe the world, but that's beyond my power. If you work against us, I promise life will be absolute hell, not just for them, but for you three as well. Do you want to spend your lives poor, or do you want to be happy? Do you want to be powerless, or do you want to make a difference? Do you want your people to be like everyone else? They're not, but they could be. The two of you," he looked at Deka and Kylac, "can start by starting that hedge fund with my good friend Mr. Sattle. It's a simple thing. Both of you already admitted it wouldn't be a strain for you, and showing you're willing to work with us will go a long way to making sure life is easier for your people. Can we at least agree to that? It's only fair. We're making the investment, and we're getting something in return."

Deka and Kylac looked at one another and then back to Jeff.

"People like you are holding your species back," said the canine.

Jeff sighed. "I think you don't know what you're talking about. People like me make the world go 'round. That's why I've been so patient with you three. I figured you didn't know that and you needed time to understand. You probably still thought the government was in charge, so you had to suck up to those people. Most of them take orders from us."

Time paused. The animals stopped making noise and rattling their cages, but this time Jeff did not stop moving. He noticed the silence. He pulled his earplugs out and looked around. Everything was still, animals suspended in mid-jump, some in the process of snarling. The drool in their mouths hung in the air.

Friend's muzzle appeared next to the Relians' ears. "I'm bored. I took down his guard. He's about to say some interesting stuff. Get ready!"

Deka stepped up to Jeff while the human's mouth still hung open.

"We know exactly how things work around here. It's because of people like you that mindless pursuit of money is rewarded while creativity and personal freedom are suppressed. You have money, you have influence, so the world works this way because of you. You may not have created the system, but you keep it going because it suits you."

Jeff backed away from Deka. When the raptor finished speaking, he recovered and stood his ground. "People are stupid. If they had brains, they wouldn't be where they are right now."

Sonjaa joined Deka at his side. "If people like you disappeared, human beings would be free."

"Here we go again. I never imagined aliens being so self-righteous."

"I have lived in other cultures!" Sonjaa jumped the distance and shoved her muzzle in his face. "Not just other people, other species! They understand what they are! They want to understand it, but you! You keep yourself willfully ignorant! You won't even learn Spanish so you can talk to the people in your house every day! Your housekeeper's name is Marissa! Why wouldn't you learn her language? Why do you want to treat her like she doesn't exist?"

"It's what America is about!" Jeff shouted. "Looking out for your own self-interest! That's what I should be free to do! Those people... They don't have a clue what's good for them! They want things for free. They don't want to work for anything. They want me to provide them with a good life, and what will I get? They make *me* the slave! They're not worth spending money on! There's no point helping them because they *can't* learn! You can put books in front of them but will they understand? Education is a new market we're just starting to tap! We made college required to get a decent job, which means everyone has to go and it's more profit for us after we took control of universities! All that profit went to waste before us! We're trying to privatize the lower grades, too. Once education is on the marketplace, quality will go up with tuition. The people who deserve it will get it. The rest can stay in the mud and work. If they don't like the jobs I create, they can work for someone else! Why do those people expect me to pay for their stuff?! They can take care of themselves! I've got my own problems to deal with!"

Jeff's face was very red. He mumbled a little until finally actual words came out. "I can't change things! This is how the world works! People are stupid! It's pointless to waste money on them. They'll fritter it away on beer and lottery tickets. They won't turn it into investments and make more. If everybody were investors, nobody would be working! There'd be nothing to invest in! There has to be people working! That's why they're called the masses. Their role is to work. My role is to invest in their work. If it wasn't for people like me, they wouldn't have a place to work and they'd destroy everything! History never remembers them, but it remembers the people in charge of them. The more desperate they are, the harder they work, and the more useful they are to the rest of us! They're in my way! They want to tell me what to do! Give me freedom and I'll build great things. Give them freedom and they'll burn the world down. That's why we privatized the prison system—they're going to get arrested anyway, someone should make money off that! I saw that market before it existed, I invested in it! I made money! Would they have? No! I did!"

Jeff held his head and screamed at them. "Why won't you listen to me?! All you want me to do is talk to my housekeeper, talk to my driver, meet their needs, think of the little people. I can get anyone to do those jobs but you can't get anyone else to do what I do! I matter! They're replaceable! What kind of joke is this that aliens land and they turn out to be communists who can't see who the best people in the world are!"

Deka snarled as he turned his muzzle up to the ceiling and yelled. "Friend!"

Jeff paused. Friend appeared next to him, tail waving. "Yes?"

"Friend..." Deka began. He breathed a few times, looking the fox up and down. "I need a portal to the hunting grounds on Beslos."

Friend's tail waved. He looked up at the ceiling, then back to Deka. "Sure. Do you want me to keep time still here?"

"Yes, please!" He turned to Kylac and Sonjaa. "Let's have some fun!"

Sonjaa growled, touching her claws to Deka's.

A sphere appeared behind Jeff. Deka could tell it really did lead to the southern continent on Beslos, where wild game roamed in herds that covered hundreds of square miles and predators could hunt them as they pleased. In Deka's case, he chased the hunters. Time moved normally on that side of the portal.

Jeff unfroze. Deka took off running. He plowed into Jeff and dove through the portal. Kylac and Sonjaa followed. The way closed behind them.

2

The Sikor hunted in family units of two to five individuals. They stood two stories tall with a neck as long as the body. They walked on two, digitigrade legs, ran on all fours, and attacked with their forelimbs and teeth. They had feathers along their neck, skull, and arms. The rest of their body was bare skin. Their feathers were sharp, meant to keep prey from retaliating, and other predators from challenging their kills. Jeff would comprehend them as a combination of a brontosaurus, a cat, and an eagle. They hunted multiple species of herbivore nearly as large as they were.

Deka and Sonjaa ran with a group of seven other carnivores, some of them theropods (with and without feathers), others hairy quadrupeds, and others had wings (feathered, fleshy, or furred), and could take to the air at a moment's notice. They had chased this individual from the family unit, and now they closed in.

Jeff ran to keep up with Kylac, naked, having been stripped of his clothes and sidearm an hour ago. The fox ran on all fours across the grassland, also naked. Centuries of hunters roaming these lands had kept large swaths of it free of vegetation, and the pack of carnivores drove the Sikor to one of these clearings. Kylac led Jeff into it ahead of the pack. He held Jeff back from venturing too far inside, and the human stood panting at the edge of the clearing.

The Sikor burst through the grass, long tail dragging on the ground to keep itself upright. The pack of carnivores poured out of the grass, surrounding it. Deka and Sonjaa ran side by side, claws splayed and mouths open, screeching at it. The Sikor raised a forelimb and swiped across the ground at the two Relians. Deka and Sonjaa both jumped over the clawed hand and landed on the Sikor's arm. Sonjaa landed higher up than Deka, and she climbed the arm. She drove a killing claw into its shoulder and slashed backwards. Blood flew from the Sikor. It swung its shoulder down, trying to throw Sonjaa off. She braced herself on the creature's flesh, gripping it with her hands and feet.

Deka couldn't run up the arm, so he slashed at the creature's wrist. He must have hit a good spot, as the creature flailed and the fingers went limp. Deka leaped off just as the Sikor pounded its fist.

Meanwhile the other five hunters dove for its legs, or flapped to the air and swooped its head. One of the flying carnivores covered in fur landed on the Sikor's face and shoved a clawed hand into its eye. The Sikor flailed and folded into itself as it knelt on the ground.

Sonjaa still held onto the shoulder, and now she let go and lunged for the throat. Its thick layer of feathers covering the most vulnerable parts were impossible to penetrate, so she climbed around them and stood on its hunched back. She dug in and hacked the flesh along its spine. The creature howled and dropped to the ground. It was about to roll, but Sonjaa had exposed its spine. Now she reached between two vertebrae with an arm. The creature snapped outwards and howled, then folded back up again and fell to the ground.

Deka ran for the flank and tore its abdomen open. The other hunters landed on it and began hacking it apart as the Sikor moaned and thrashed its head while the hunters devoured it. It couldn't seem to move anything from the neck down, and just seconds later, it stopped moving entirely. Within minutes, the hunters had torn off its skin.

Deka emerged from the carcass, scales dripping in blood, and scented the air. His nose turned him in Sonjaa's direction. He stalked up behind her, slit dripping lube the whole way. The green and yellow raptor was at one of the creature's arms, tearing muscle from it and gulping down whole chunks. He shoved his nose under her tail and scented her. She raised her muzzle, looked back at him and snarled, but not in an aggressive way. Deka climbed on top of her, gripped her shoulders and mounted her. Sonjaa opened her mouth and looked up at the sky as Deka thrust. He scented the blood on her. She scented the blood on him. Deka's hips moved faster.

Kylac turned to Jeff. He knelt in wet dirt, shaking. He had urinated. Kylac knelt beside the human and held him. Prey often had two reactions to witnessing a kill. Either he was satisfied seeing someone else fall, knowing he got away, or terrified of being next. Jeff seemed to be feeling both re-actions at once, and the impulses were so unfamiliar to him he could not decide which was better. Kylac held him around the shoulder, giving him comforting warmth. Jeff and Kylac weren't the only ones standing at the sidelines. Several people from other planets, herbivores and omni-vores and carnivores alike, had been watching. Jeff looked at all of them as if they would turn on him next, and yet he also smelled elated to be alive.

Deka climbed off her, dangling from his slit, dripping semen and lube. It would be another minute before it re-tracted completely. He turned his muzzle in Jeff's direction. If the human had had any more urine in his bladder, he would have ejected it right then. Deka turned his body to match his head and trotted to Jeff, neck parallel with the ground, bloody claws spread apart. Only Kylac's hand pre-vented Jeff from running away.

His scales were no longer dark blue but entirely red with Sikor blood. His muzzle dripped with it, his arms dripped at the elbows, and his claws had strings of blood connecting them. His penis still hadn't retracted. Jeff trem-bled harder as Deka neared. The raptor stopped nose to nose with the human.

"*That* was a carnivore theme park. No cages. No fences. No limping, starving, scared animals. It's an entire continent for carnivores to gather and take down animals ten times their size and then fuck over the body while the blood is still running down their mouths. Every planet with carnivores has a continent like this. I dare you to come here and try to charge us for it."

Deka raised a hand and palmed Jeff's face. Jeff gasped but held still. Deka smeared his face with Sikor blood and let it fall away. He tilted his head as he looked at the hu-man.

"Raptors used to cover themselves in the blood of their prey and parade around to show how powerful they were. We don't anymore because there's enough food for everyone, enough room for everyone, enough of everything. We don't keep other members of our species poor and hungry so they have to obey us. The people in the contacted universe use their talents to relieve everyone of the need to survive. Only when you satisfy that can a society advance beyond its animal ways."

Deka turned and sat down next to the human. Kylac removed his arm from Jeff's shoulder and approached the kill. Jeff began to stand and follow the fox, but Deka rested a bloody hand on his shoulder and held him in place.

Sonjaa now ran from the carcass and approached them. She passed Kylac, nuzzled his neck. Kylac licked some blood off her snout, and then ran to the kill. Sonjaa ran full speed and skidded to a stop in front of the human. She lowered her muzzle to his eye level.

"You may be covered in Sikor blood, but your piss reeks of fear." She clicked her claws. "I have a business proposal for you, Jeff. I want to keep you here for a few weeks to collect your piss and sweat and bottle them as perfume. I think people of all scent-based species would work twelve hours a day for a year just to know how you smell right now." She nosed him. Jeff looked away. Sonjaa nosed him again. "I want you to know how much I enjoy your scent like this. It's the real you. Finally."

Sonjaa sat down on Jeff's other side, facing the carcass. Jeff shivered harder than ever sitting between two carnivores as he watched other carnivores devour the giant animal. The others greeted Kylac, some taking pieces of the kill and feeding him. Kylac gulped them down, trying not to get his fur too bloody.

Friend manifested on Deka's other side. "When will you be ready to return?"

"A few more breaths. I think Jeff has seen enough. We'll clean him up, put him back in his clothes, and then we'll leave."

"Slight catch. I have to bring that piece of Earth back to where the rest of the universe is, so about two hours will be lost."

"Don't think it will be a problem. How is Jeff?"

"He will make those phone calls and end the grace period. You scared him too much. Now he knows you can't be reasoned with, so he perceives all Relians as a threat to the status quo. Right now he's imagining a worst case scenario: the Relians will refuse to join the workforce. Humans will then start to ask questions about why they're working so hard for so little, and the raptors will lead a revolt against him and his business cronies."

"I'm glad he finally realized it."

"Do you want me to give him a change of heart? I can."

Deka considered that. He inhaled Jeff's scent: awful, as it had always been, but now with fear in it. Primal fear.

"No more favors," Deka said. "Just send us home as soon as Kylac's had his fill and Jeff is dressed." Deka turned his head and looked at Friend. He wiggled his claws, trying to smile with one hand. "Thanks. It's... nice. To have you back. I'm starting to like this new you."

Friend's tail wagged. He leaned over and touched his nose to Deka's. It didn't feel like anything. Deka turned to Sonjaa, scented her. She was cleaning herself off as well she could. Deka wanted to help her, but that would only remind her Rupi was not here to clean her off. In spite of this, she smelled as she had before the disaster. He wondered if his fear had been misplaced and she would recover without having to face what happened to her in the Lake. Deka had been worried her mind would not be able to rebuild her subconscious strong enough to contain those memories, but perhaps it had.

Deka turned to the carcass. Kylac had left the body and was coming back, blood staining his muzzle and chest. Deka eagerly waited to clean him off. Kylac had also seemed more connected with reality since Friend arrived, and he considered the stimulus had been exactly what Kylac needed to complete his subconscious and settle into his new identity.

The fox stopped in front of Jeff. The human had just witnessed him gulping down raw pieces of animal. He could not look away from the people tearing this creature to pieces. Kylac lowered himself to Jeff's eye level.

"We knew from the start you didn't want us to live with you out of the goodness of your heart. All of your rich friends asked you to get close to us so you could try to influence us. They were hoping to control us, temping us with money and a position in society. It is how you mold the world to your advantage. You keep other people desperate and subservient to elevate yourselves higher. You can't imagine a society that doesn't need people like you. A society that allows its people to be free from the control of others. A society that doesn't need laws because there is no oppression to break out of, and nobody has to trample on someone else to survive. The Relians represent it, and that is sure to scare the hell out of all your associates. You can't change us, but maybe we can change some of you."

Jeff was looking Kylac in the eye. He opened his mouth and spoke for the first time since he realized where he was. "How?"

"You'll see," Kylac said. "If we're right, Relians won't be on Earth much longer. We can't stay. Not with your associates trying to make it illegal for us to live."

Deka stood. Sonjaa also rose to full height, and together they herded Jeff through the grass.

Chichen Itza

Stephen and Norh lay at the base of a Mayan pyramid, on their back, legs spread apart, letting the sun bake their underside. Norh fed Stephen a memory of a temperate planet full of tiny mammals and slithering reptiles. Almost the entire memory took place from the air.

The planet had many climate zones with so many different species evolved to survive in those environments. Norh was young then, still full of zeal to put his abilities to good use and help the Lost. He was sure one of these animals would attain sentience someday.

Norh had spent years flying across the planet, observing what lived on it. The Krone were generally patient, being so long-lived their temperament was spread out just as long, so it took conscious effort to remember most species lived much shorter lives and everything happened on a faster time scale for them.

Finally Norh came across something. It was buried in a rainforest, so he had passed it when he came this way several years earlier. It was made of stone, pyramid-shaped, not unlike the ancient structures at this site.

It took Norh hours to pull off all the vegetation that had grown over it and dig the pyramid out. When he had revealed it, Norh sat and beheld the ruins of the people who once lived here. They were gone. Norh had found no trace of any intelligent life on this world, so whatever happened to them, they were forever lost. Norh searched for days, sticking his head wherever it would fit, but he found no written language of any kind. Just stone structures and statues and the sound of flora slowly spreading its roots into the rock and breaking it apart.

Norh had remained there for months, mourning people he could never meet. Norh cried for them, wishing he had come here a century or two earlier. Back then, he believed he could have saved them.

The memory concluded. Now it existed between both of them. Stephen could recall it as if he had lived it himself, and if he thought about it long enough, he believed he had.

"It's remarkable," Norh said, "how many patterns you discover when you've visited enough planets."

"That place... It looked just like the Maya civilization. I wonder who they were."

"Everything I see on this world reminds me of something I witnessed on another."

Stephen spread their wings in a smile. "Everything?"

Norh spread their wings wider. "All right, cotton candy is new to me, but I still cannot eat it."

"Sometimes I miss eating things like that."

He rolled them to their side and raised their neck. The tourists snapped pictures of him, as well as the ruins just behind them. He lay as regal as possible for the tourists.

Norh had shared many memories since they started roaming the world. Planets where the people created technology, harnessed the electron, practiced agriculture. All of it resembled something humanity had done. Norh had left these worlds in defeat, returning many years later to confirm what he already knew would happen: they destroyed themselves in conflicts over resources, or territory, or mating rights.

"We really must stop," Norh said. "If we share too many memories, we'll lose ourselves."

"I like living your life, sad and lonely as it was."

"Full of defeat. Pointless. Your life is much more interesting. There are other people in it."

"I've only got thirty-four years of memories to share! I'll run out way before you will!"

Norh lay their neck down and sprawled out on the grass. "I do not want to stop either. Half a lifetime of experiences I cannot have is so interesting to explore. That is one of the hardships of being a Krone. I can observe people, but I cannot truly be part of their lives. Very few species are as large as we are. None can survive in the places we can. Even if I came to know any people, they could not go where I can."

"It's the feeling I get from many of these memories."

"I tried to use it to change the course of civilization while it was young and its direction easy to influence."

"Did you know all other Krone come to the same conclusion?"

"Not until I was middle-aged."

Norh opened himself up and shared a memory of himself in his cave. He had just thought to try doing what he did on other planets: fly around and observe the people on his own world. He spoke to the offworlders. He listened to them talk about the Krone casually. They knew what the Krone did, and yet Norh himself had been ignorant.

Norh had retreated to his cave and pondered this. He had spent his entire life traveling from one uncontacted planet to the next, searching for lone species on the brink of intelligence, or had just crossed it, trying to become their companion species. He had failed every time, and now he had just learned that every Krone tried this. They all failed.

Norh became more determined than ever to succeed. He picked up the pace, pondered the stars and the movement of the planets and found ones young enough to be a good place to search.

The memory expanded. Norh flooded Stephen with forty-seven planets at once—all of them in various stages of development, harboring lone species in equally diverse points in their societies. Stephen became aware of primitive species, advanced species, species with no spoken language, species who used steam for everything.

One race who possessed technology and used it to come up with ways for males to keep females tethered to the home, as was their nature.

Another of flying reptiles who convinced themselves flying was some kind of sin, so they clipped their wings upon hatching and lived on the ground.

Stephen gasped. Norh had given him the ability to handle multiple channels of information at once, so he did was not overwhelmed from that. He gasped because he forgot himself during that brief moment. For the duration of those memories filling him up, he didn't simply relive the memories of someone else. He became Norh.

Norh realized what he had done and retreated to his side of their mind. The line between them felt thinner. One memory at a time did not make a huge difference, but after so many at once, they felt a noticeable change.

"My apologies," Norh said. "I want you to know about all the worlds I visited. I almost gave you everything."

Stephen reached over and touched the hand Norh controlled. "Don't be sorry. That felt good. It's a lifetime of experiences I can't have."

Stephen felt obliged to give him something in return for all of that. He fed him the memory of the first time he met Brenda. Norh sprawled out and rolled to their back again. For some reason, Norh reacted to Stephen's memories much more than Stephen reacted to Norh's.

It was the personal contact. Meeting someone, feeling a connection to them, sharing experiences... It was so rare for a Krone. They were so evolved they often had no choice but to be above everyone they met. Norh relished being part of someone else's life. Parents. Childhood friends. School. Affection. Norh even cherished Stephen's memories of his wife's death because it was a kind of loss Norh had never experienced, and he never would. His mind did not work the way Stephen's did. He simply didn't feel this for his fellow creatures, so to experience life from this perspective was something a Krone wouldn't even think to dream of.

They couldn't stop. Now they were closer than ever to becoming one person, and the more of each other they shared, the less frightening it seemed.

Maryville

I

The sphere opened in an unused room of the hospital. The tan and grey raptor stepped through, followed immediately by CJ. As soon as she was through, the way closed, and three women and two men dressed in white hospital smocks approached them.

"Welcome to Missouri," said the black woman holding out her hand for CJ. "I almost didn't believe you when you said you were gonna beam in."

The secretary of Relian relations shook it and nodded to the other members of the staff.

"I don't think I'll ever fly again," CJ said.

The woman turned to Rive, met his eyes. "Nice to meet you, too. Wow. You are real, in the flesh."

Rive rubbed his claws. "Half of me is."

"You happen to be a doctor?"

"No. Where I come from, doctors are not often needed."

"You didn't bring a doctor from Walter Reed with you?"

CJ shook her head. "Rive insisted it would not be necessary."

"There is almost no disease among Relians," Rive continued. "Genetic deformities are so rare I can call them impossible. Environment is the only other factor."

"Well, I'm doctor Azure, physician in charge of their care. I went to the seminar about the aliens, so right now I'm the most qualified person in the state to look after these two. Follow me and I'll let y'all have a look at the patients."

They left the room, walking on either side of the doctor with the other men and women behind them.

"You tell me disease is rare among Relians?" Dr. Azure asked.

"That's right," Rive said.

"They said the same thing. They had no idea what was happening. Damn good thing they came. The fox was experiencing shortness of breath, fatigue, body aches, loss of fur accompanied by a spreading rash. Her throat began to close when she arrived. The raptor also had shortness of breath, body aches, and rash, but she had fluid leaking from the eyes."

"How long?" CJ said.

"They've been in and out of the hospital for weeks with one symptom or another. Now it's all at once, and they both had rashes all over their bodies. That's what really threw us off—what would do this to both a reptile and a canine? We admitted them yesterday. Did you read the faxes I sent?"

"I read them. Environment must be the cause."

"I'm open to suggestions. Nobody else is sick, their apartment is free of mold or fungus or anything you'd think would cause a reaction. Only about ten thousand people live here. We have a couple factories, a place that makes batteries. All have been here for years. Can't blame pollution."

"I need more details. Toxicology, blood analysis—"

"Maybe you should just call one of the doctors out there in the universe," she said, waving in his face. "Where do Relians go when they get sick?"

"Everyone learns medicine. Everyone is qualified to treat the sick and wounded. But for very rare cases when healing is beyond someone, they take a portal to Selta. The saber-toothed cats on that world are the best doctors among oxygen-breathers, and for serious events they will help off-worlders."

"I can't believe you just said that with a straight face."

"My face can't be anything but."

She smiled as she looked him up and down. "When this is done, I wanna look at that metal fused to your body. Every doctor wants to, so I suggest you don't fall asleep here or you'll wake up with an IV in your arm and a tube up your rear."

He clicked his claws. "I may endure it if you can tell me anything new."

"Maybe you should just take them to the cats. I'm to the point where I don't care what we have to do. I want to help these people, but I don't know enough about them to do it. The rest of the paperwork is waiting for you in their room. If y'all have any questions, get with me or any of the nurses on staff."

They rounded a couple more corners, and she stopped in a room with two beds. A raptor lay in the far bed on her side. The fox lay in the near bed on her back. Both were hooked up to IV units. Both were unconscious. Both had a tube down their throats hooked up to breathing machines.

Patches of fur had fallen off the canine, a red rash in its place. Some of these patches had bandages over them, which meant they had bled. The raptor's scales were white with orange spots of random sizes up and down her body. Her underbelly had no spots on it, but she also had rashes covering her scales. A human woman in her late twenties sat between the two beds.

"Jessica," said doctor Azure. "This is Secretary Rhine and Archeon Rive."

"You came," said the woman, standing up. "Oh, man, it must be bad if you showed up."

Rive stayed at full height and approached the beds. "We're here to help. Do you have their papers?"

She nodded, opened the drawer between the two beds and removed a stack of papers about an inch thick. She handed the whole thing to Rive.

"Thank you. Please tell Secretary Rhine what happened from your point of view. I will be listening as I read these."

CJ pulled up another chair and sat facing the young woman. Jessica sat down in hers. Doctor Azure and the other nurses and doctors had dispersed to resume their daily routines.

"It began about a week after we came back from the convention in Topeka. They started complaining about itching. They itched all over, all the time. We didn't know what to make of it. I thought it was fleas, but I checked them and nothing was biting them. We saw doctor Azure, and she couldn't find anything either. If it affected just the fox, that would be one thing, but this affected both of them. Canine and reptile skin... What irritates both?"

Rive stood at the foot of the raptor's bed, flipping through the pages at about one every three seconds. "Many things irritate scales as well as canine skin."

"We couldn't figure it out. Then they were tired all the time. Sraad, the raptor. She didn't feel like eating anymore. Then a week later the body aches began. I tried getting their food from different places, but that didn't help. I bought a filter for the water, no change. Then last week they told me they were having a hard time breathing. That's when the hospital admitted them. Had to put tubes down their throats or they'd suffocate. I was just looking into moving somewhere else. Would it help? Is anyone else having this problem?"

"Nobody," said CJ.

Jessica turned to Rive. "Don't stick around too long. It'll happen to you, too."

Rive did not look up from the papers. He was more than halfway through the pile. "If it does, I will know the signs."

"We need to get out of here," Jessica said. "There's something here that's killing them. I don't know what it is, but it's awful."

"We will probably transfer them to Walter Reed just in case," said CJ. "Will you be at home?"

"I will, or here."

"Thanks for your help. We'll get to the bottom of this. I'm sure Rive already has an idea. Don't you?"

Rive had just finished with the packet. He flipped the pile over as he handed it back to Jessica. "Several."

She took the papers and set them on the table between the beds.

"So do I. Let's go outside. Jessica, is there a place to rent a car around here?"

"No."

"Of course. I love small towns."

"Do you need a ride somewhere?"

"Probably to many places."

"Can't you make a hole in space and just jump through?" Jessica said.

"I'm on unfamiliar terrain," said the raptor. "I need detailed maps to go anywhere I have not been. Driving is easier for short distances than making spheres."

"I can drive you."

"Are you sure? It will take you away from here."

"I'll feel better if I'm busy. I'll just stay here worrying if I'm not."

She walked them out of the hospital and into the parking lot. Jessica had an old station wagon. Rive had plenty of room in the back. CJ climbed into the passenger seat, opened her briefcase on her lap, and flipped through the faxes from the hospital.

"Before you begin, Rive," she said, "let Watson stick in a few words. My husband was allergic to wheat, and he wasn't just a little allergic. If he smelled something with wheat in it, his nose would run. If he ate anything with wheat in it, he'd have pain all over his body. This sounds like a severe allergic reaction to something."

She paused, waited for Rive.

"Go on," said the raptor, rubbing and occasionally clicking his claws.

"Jessica said they changed their food and filtered the water, so it's not that. That leaves something in the air, and what is this town surrounded by?"

"You think they're allergic to corn?" said Jessica.

"Maybe. It's the most obvious place to start. Did you do any checking into that?"

"They don't eat the corn."

"My husband didn't have to eat wheat to react to it. Take us to your house, Jessica. Let's see what's growing nearby. I know people in the EPA who will run an analysis. A couple dozen Relians are living near cornfields as well, but they're not having this reaction, so if we can find out what strain this is and what's different about it, we should have an answer. What do you say, Rive?"

CJ heard him rubbing his claws. "I think it's a good place to start."

"Glad you agree." She looked back at him and smiled. She was nose to snout with him. "See, you're not the only one who can figure things out."

Jessica started the car and backed out of the parking spot.

Rive clicked his claws. "You figured out what law to use to bail out that fox who chased down a shoplifter."

"He thought he was doing the right thing. That had to count."

"Glad the judge thought so."

Jessica drove them a mere mile and a half from the hospital to a division of apartment buildings near the town's leading edge. Sure enough, corn grew everywhere, and it was already as high as the proverbial elephant's eye.

Jessica parked in front of one building. CJ stepped out of the car and began walking to the cornfield. Jessica opened the hatch for Rive, and the raptor slid out of the cargo hold and trotted to CJ. He matched her pace as she approached the farmland.

"Feel anything strange?" CJ said.

"The corn smells different from what I'm used to, but not strange."

"And you're an Archeon. Nothing gets by you."

"I am acutely aware of my surroundings. Nothing seems unusual about the corn here. The air is full of normal smells. Fewer chemicals."

"But other raptors and foxes don't have this reaction. I'm taking samples of the corn, the leaves, maybe the soil. I'll ask Jessica if she has any jars I can use. Anything that can tell us if something is different. I'll also find the farmer and get some information from him. Think you can make us a way to Aames in Iowa for a sample from the fields growing by that one guy's house?"

"I can have a way ready within the hour."

"Thanks."

Rive stopped ten feet from the cornstalks and observed the field as a whole. CJ walked up to a stalk. The corn stood half again as tall as she was. She reached for an ear close to eye level and pulled.

"Anybody else have domesticated crops on other worlds?" she said.

"Some do, in a way. Most of the time it is not necessary. Population is low enough people can find the food they need."

CJ pulled on the ear, but the corn did not budge. She pulled harder. The stalk did not lean, even at the base.

"But it's all scattered around," she said as she yanked on the ear again. "How can anyone live foraging for food all the time?"

"There tend to be clusters of editable plants growing together," Rive said.

The ear behaved like a clamshell welded to a steel wall. She raised a leg and braced her foot on the cornstalk and yanked the ear again.

"Archeons on each planet maintain ways to places where there's food so nobody has to forage far," Rive continued. "Most of the time people can wander in, pick what they need, and leave. If an area becomes used up, the Archeons make a portal to another place until the previous region grows again."

CJ yanked and pulled and twisted, but the ear would not come off. The stalk did not move. She let it go, gripped the stalk, and tried to pull it sideways. It was so rigid it could have passed as a sapling. She let go of the stalk and backed away, hands on hips, looking it up and down in bewilderment.

"Rive... I've only been near a cornfield a couple times in my life, but I'm pretty sure corn isn't supposed to do this."

Rive approached the plant cautiously, scented it. "I'm unfamiliar with this variety, but it smells as corn should."

"I should just be able to yank an ear off. You're the one with claws. Try cutting one."

The raptor stepped up to the stalk and slashed the corn stalk at the base. It made a solid thunking sound. It did not wobble.

Jessica joined them at the edge of the cornfield and stood next to CJ. "That's weird."

CJ turned to her. "You didn't notice this?"

"No... The farm next door grows corn every year. Never walked up to one and tried to take any. Looks like I couldn't even if I wanted to. What the hell?"

Rive crouched at the base, hacking away with his claws. The corn remained rigid and unyielding. His claws hadn't dented the plant at all.

"I've seen TV shows about people making crop circles," said Jessica. "All they need is a board and rope and they can flatten the stuff."

"It's like solid oak," CJ said as she watched Rive try to cut the stalk down.

After a couple minutes of slashing, he had made a hole in the stalk. He sawed the rest of the way through and finally, at last, the corn stalk fell.

CJ and Jessica approached the plant. Rive straightened up. He was breathing hard.

"What kind of corn is this?" he said.

"I don't know," said CJ, "but I'm getting Tim on the phone. This thing is going to the lab."

She bent at the knees and picked up one of the ends. It was much heavier than she expected. She began dragging it to the car. Jessica picked up the other end and they carried it between them to the car.

"Jeez!" Jessica shouted. "It must weigh a hundred pounds!"

"Makes me wonder what the corn is like." Rive walked beside them, looking the plant over, scenting it. He waited for them to walk on and scented the exposed base, which was still moist. "Something is familiar about it."

"What's familiar?" CJ said, straining to hold it up.

"I would rather not say until it is analyzed."

"Of course. Don't want to jinx it, as usual."

"This is not a cornstalk!" Jessica shouted. "Can't believe this was growing next to my house and I never noticed!"

Rive ran ahead of them and opened the trunk. CJ and Jessica shoved the plant inside. They leaned on the car to catch their breath.

CJ looked inside at their haul. She reached in, tried to twist an ear free, but again she couldn't twist it a millimeter to any side. It was as if the corn itself were encased within solid tree bark, and yet the leaves were shaped and formed as one would normally expect. CJ closed the trunk.

"While we're here, let's take samples of your water and some of the food you and the Relians ate."

"Can they analyze all of that so quick?" Jessica said.

"For me, they will. For anyone else it'll take months. Might be able to get someone over here for air samples, too."

"Wow. The whole nine yards."

"Two Relians are sick. They're the only two in the country, maybe the world. We should find out why. It's the whole reason the president made this a cabinet position. So we can get answers quickly. I want to know what this thing is."

Jessica led them up the driveway. CJ and the raptor followed. The building Jessica lived in had three other apartments in it. Hers was in the center, one of the upstairs units. She inserted a key, opened the door, and ascended the carpeted steps.

"How's the portal coming?"

"Another half hour."

"The sooner the better." She looked over her shoulder.

A light breeze drifted from over the field. The cornstalks did not blow majestically in the wind.

"That field makes me nervous," she said.

CJ and the metal raptor followed her through the door.

2

Tim Cadre wasn't the director, but he was pretty high up and could arrange emergency testing. The first thing she had shown him after Rive made the way to the EPA offices was the cornstalk from the field, and it was the first thing he had taken back to the lab.

Less than an hour later, three men and one woman walked around Jessica Byrne's apartment and the surrounding area with cotton swabs, glass beakers, and air sample machines. It only took them another half hour to gather the samples they needed, and then one by one they stepped through the sphere in Jessica's living room.

CJ stood in the living room with Tim Cadre as the team finished up.

"You have my cell," CJ said. "Make this the fastest rush job you ever did. I want every kind of analysis you can get on that. Get your local offices to take samples from that other field I mentioned."

"Yep, I'll get on it," he said. "I'll call you as soon as I have something."

"What do you think so far?"

"Way too soon to tell, but I'm intrigued. Give me at least a week. Meantime, talk to the farmer. Find out everything you can."

"I'll do that. Thank you, Tim."

"Not a problem, Chris. I'll be in touch."

He turned and walked through the sphere. Rive and Jessica waited by the top of the stairs. When he was safely through, the way closed, and the three of them stood alone in the living room.

"It's that easy," Jessica said.

"Impressive, isn't it?" CJ said. She walked to the door.

"How long will it take? Can you take Heze and Sraad to another hospital?"

CJ walked down the steps to the front door. "Probably, but first we need to know what's causing this."

She opened the door. Jessica and Rive followed her.

"How long until we have an answer?" Jessica said as she locked the door behind them.

CJ was already halfway to Jessica's car. "He said a week, but I think he'll put this on fast track. The air samples won't take too long to measure. That cornstalk might take a few days. They'll have to crosscheck all the samples." She turned and waited at the passenger door. "Normal clients take months. He can get it done in days. You saw how fast he got people here? Normally that would take a week by itself unless you mention arsenic or dioxin."

Rive had reached the car. He opened the trunk.

"How do you know him?" said the raptor.

"I worked with him when I needed tests done for a lawsuit back when I was in private practice in Texas."

Jessica sat in the driver's seat. CJ opened her door and sat down on her side. Rive had crawled into the cargo hold, closing the trunk behind him.

CJ continued: "I had several clients who claimed crop dusters kept spraying their houses. They didn't live near farmland, and they were upwind of any farms, so it should have been impossible. The local offices kept giving me the runaround, so I called the main office. I got Tim, told him what was going on, and he helped me cut through the red tape. Even used him as an expert witness for my clients."

"How did that turn out?" Jessica said, starting the car.

"Turns out their planes were malfunctioning. Faulty nozzles. They sprayed whether the pilot wanted them to or not. That might've been an accident if we didn't also get papers from the company that proved they knew about the faulty equipment and did nothing about it. My clients made videos of those planes leaking pesticide, the EPA tests proved it was the same chemical, we won, and that company had to make the repairs and pay for damage."

Jessica had driven out of the apartment division. She turned a corner and drove up the road. They saw the farmer's house just outside the field, a gravel road leading to it half a mile away.

"Now that you mention it..." Jessica said. "I haven't seen any crop dusters this year. I haven't seen anyone spraying anything."

"That cornstalk is thick as a tree. It probably doesn't need it."

Rive slithered up to the front seat and rested his muzzle next to CJ's ear. "It still puzzles me that it took your lawsuit to force them to do what they knew was right."

"It's called incentive, Rive. That's part of what I did. Hold people responsible. It's what lawyers are supposed to do. If there are no consequences for doing the wrong thing, nobody will do the right thing." She laughed. "I know what you're going to say. It's not like that in the rest of the universe. In a perfect world, they would have done proper maintenance and nobody would have to force them."

"In a perfect world, there is no maintenance to perform," Rive said, clicking his claws.

"No crops. No chemicals. I know."

"Some species do cultivate plants, as many cultivate herds of animals to hunt, just not to this extreme. There is no reason not to do the right thing because it does not cost less to do the wrong thing."

Jessica turned onto the gravel road. Rive held the back of the seat to keep from being tossed around on the bumpy road. A white man in his early sixties whose skin had been permanently damaged by many sunburns over the years stood on the porch, cigarette in hand, watching them. Jessica parked the car next to a truck that looked as if it had been on the farm since the seventies. CJ climbed out and held the door.

"Greetings, sir," she called to the man on the porch. "My name is CJ Rhine, White House Secretary of Relian Relations. We noticed you have some interesting crops on your field. May we ask you a few questions about them?"

The man flicked the ash as he took a couple lazy steps forward. He leaned on the railing. "From the White House?"

"That's right. I answer directly to the president of the United States."

He smiled. "I voted for Perot."

CJ smiled back. "Be that as it may, I'd like to know more about this corn. It's nothing personal. You're not in trouble. Did you know Relians were living in those apartments across from your field?"

Rive had climbed out the back and closed the hatch. He walked around the car and stood next to the secretary.

The man shook his head, but he was still smiling. "Jiminy Christmas." He finished the cigarette and extinguished it on the railing. "Why don't y'all come inside. We'll have a sit down."

CJ led the way up the steps and through the front door. The man gestured to the kitchen table, a round poker table that also looked leftover from the seventies, and then he walked to the kitchen.

"What'll y'all have? Coffee, soda?"

"Coffee please," CJ said, taking a seat.

Rive could not sit in the chairs, so he stood at the table.

Jessica sat next to CJ. "Coffee will be fine, thank you."

He poured three cups of coffee, carried them to the table, and set them at places. He paused at Rive.

"Nothing for you?"

"No, thank you."

He smiled. "Suit yourself. You look like you could use some meat on them bones." He addressed the women. "I'll be right back."

He walked down the hall and disappeared around a corner.

Jessica looked around absently. Rive took this opportunity to scent the house.

"Anything?" CJ said.

"The corn's scent is not as strong here, upwind of the field, but it does concern me."

"No itchy feeling yet?"

"Not yet."

Footsteps came from the other side of the house and grew louder. The man returned with a small packet of papers. He set them in front of CJ and then took a seat on the opposite side of the table, cradling his mug.

"That's all I have on them crops out there."

CJ leaned over it and flipped through a few pages. It looked like a sales portfolio, but it had phone numbers in it, a company name on every page, and a copyright notice at the bottom dated this year.

"My name is Ken Marko," the farmer began. "I own this farm. Wife and I ran it for thirty years until she died back in ninety-one. Just before planting season, I got a visit from some people. Now I buy seed, fertilizer, and pesticide from that company, Crescendo. I have to. They're the only ones left in town. They tell me and all of us here is gonna be planting a new crop this year. A hybrid, patented. Called it Crescendo Corn. C-Corn for short. Seemed normal enough when I first planted it, but then when it started to get tall, that's when I noticed it don't bend. I called them up, asked them what the hell this stuff was, and all I got was a warning not to talk to anybody about it."

"You're talking to us," CJ said.

"Right. I know you from TV, you answer to the president, and you got an honest-to-Jesus metal dinosaur with you. I start calling, I get a lawsuit slapped on me, just like all my neighbors who complained over the years. I hate being bullied. Bad enough I gotta go through them every year for everything I need. They raise the price, I can't go nowhere else. Now they tell me what to plant, how to plant it, who I buy from, and who I can talk to about it. They don't tell me what this plant is or what it's a hybrid of. Only that it don't need pesticides."

"Have you had any allergic reactions to it, Mr. Marko?"

"No, but something about it ain't right. And it gets worse. When I called them last month and asked how I'm supposed to harvest corn that don't bend, they told me there would be new equipment available for lease at the store. So I says fine, y'all gonna pay for it? They said no. They're charging me to lease the equipment I need to farm the crops they all want. I don't know how I'm gonna make that happen."

CJ slid the packet of papers over to the raptor, who began reading them one page every two seconds.

"Mr. Marko, have you tried to eat any of that corn outside?"

"I wouldn't put that stuff in my body if my pastor served it to me. Not till I know where it came from."

"My Relians are in the hospital with severe allergies," Jessica said. "We think the corn may have something to do with it. What do you think?"

"I think anything's possible. The stuff out there ain't natural. They won't tell me a damn thing about it, and that's what scares me. Now, I want you to take this to the president. Show him what's going on. Every farmer in this county is scared out of his mind. Not everyone is growing this stuff, just us around town, but Crescendo tells all of us what to do. We can't do a damn thing without them knowing. They probably got guys watching the place. They might've seen you come in. Don't make it look like I told you anything, please. If you talk to anyone about this, talk to the president. Tell him I'll vote for whoever runs for the Democrats next time if he'll do something about it."

"I promise," said CJ. "I had the EPA out here taking samples. I gave them one of your cornstalks. They'll figure out what that is."

"Oh, Jesus! Don't tell anyone else you did that! I signed a contract that said giving samples to anyone for any reason is not allowed."

"You didn't give us these samples."

"It's all property of Crescendo. Taking it without their permission is a violation of copyright law. I had to sign it. There's no one else left in four counties to buy seed and farming equipment. Bought 'em out or drove 'em out of business. Now there's an indestructible plant outside, and I don't know a thing about it. Please find out. Will you take my number?"

"Absolutely."

Rive had read the packet. CJ turned to him.

"Anything useful?"

"The terms Crescendo Corn and C-Corn have copyright symbols after them each instance they are used. It only states it's a new hybrid corn, doesn't need pesticide, and will survive harsh weather. It promises to grow even where corn is not supposed to grow. It is not very specific."

"Yep," said Mr. Marko. "That's the key selling point. It's supposed to grow everywhere. Y'all wanna know what I think? I think we're a test. Before they roll this stuff out worldwide, they're growing it here to see how well it does first. Then before you know it, the stuff is everywhere. They probably want to grow it in Alaska or something."

"Did someone tell you that, or are there other documents?" asked the raptor.

"The men told me that. Ain't written down yet."

"Is that specifically what they told you? What were the exact words they used?"

Mr. Marko thought about that for a moment while he cradled his cup. He hadn't taken a single sip from it since he sat down.

"They said it can grow in any climate. Cold, hot, wet, dry. The leaves are thick to keep bugs out. The stalks are durable to help it survive any weather."

Rive looked at CJ. "We need to get in touch with them. Find out more from them."

Mr. Marko chuckled. "They won't tell you a thing."

"Ms. Rhine is a cabinet secretary," Rive said. "They'll talk to her."

"Or just give her a sales pitch," Mr. Marko said. "Everything about what they do is protected as a trade secret. They don't give info to no one. You talk to them, they're gonna know you talked to one of us. They'll come for all of us, sue me, force me to sell my land."

"They wouldn't do that," Jessica said. "Who would farm it?"

"Crescendo will buy the land. Hire a bunch of Mexicans to work it. That's where this is all goin'. They don't need me or any of us. Bunch of us think they're trying to push us off our land so they can own it, too, and don't have to pay nobody to grow their corn."

"We'll be discreet," CJ said, standing up. She just now realized she hadn't taken a drink either. "We're getting to the bottom of this right now. We won't mention your name."

"Thanks," he said, also standing and extending his hand.

CJ shook it. Jessica stood, slipped the packet of papers under her shirt, and shook the farmer's hand as well. Rive bobbed his neck at him. Most humans did not like shaking a clawed hand, so this seemed to be the acceptable compromise. CJ led them to the door.

"We'll be in touch, Mr. Marko. Thanks for everything."

"Godspeed."

CJ crossed the porch and walked down the steps. As she opened the passenger door, she discreetly looked around. A yellow car was parked on the shoulder of the main road. She couldn't see if anyone was inside, but it made her neck hairs prickle.

"Let's not go back to your place yet," she said. "Let's find somewhere to eat. I have some calls to make."

3

CJ had weak roaming service in Maryville. She was talking on a cellular phone in a fast food restaurant, which drew some odd looks from people, and not because of Rive for a change.

"Right. Yes, I know. I am the secretary of Relian Relations, a cabinet position, answering directly to the president of the United States. Please let me speak to your supervisor."

She looked down at the table.

"They transferred me to you. Is there a local office I can visit? I'm in Maryville, Missouri."

Jessica opened her mouth and took a bite of her burger. She dipped a French fry in ketchup and ate it while she chewed the meat. CJ had chicken nuggets but had yet to touch them. Rive stood at the table, eager to go somewhere he could eat.

"Fine, what's the number?" She already had pen and paper ready. She scribbled down a number. "Thanks. Goodbye."

She pushed the end call button and slid the antenna back into the phone. She looked down at her food and sighed.

"I haven't gotten the runaround since I became a senator. Took me all this time just to get the number for their local office."

"Are we going there?" Jessica said.

"No. Local offices are a waste of time. We're going straight to their corporate headquarters. I'm gonna walk in there and demand to see somebody in charge."

"Where is it?" Rive said. "I'll need to study the map if it is somewhere we haven't been."

"Start on a way back to the DC office. We'll go from there."

"Are you leaving?" Jessica said.

"Maybe." She thought, picking up a nugget and dipping it in ketchup. She held it front of her mouth. "Yes. Yes, it's the only thing we can do right now until Tim gets back to me. What are you thinking, Rive? You seemed interested in what Mr. Marko had to say."

"I would rather not say until we have the analysis of that cornstalk."

CJ smiled as she took a bite and chewed. "Come on, Poirot, just this once let me in on your hunch."

Rive clicked his claws. "What you call a hunch is actually subconscious connections coming together and trying to rise into the conscious mind. I have no subconscious, therefore I do not have hunches."

"What do you know then?"

"I will know if it is correct when we hear from the EPA. Meanwhile, I am making a way back to the office."

"Do you really think you'll get answers from them?" Jessica said.

"No, but the questions they don't answer will be more informative than any answers they give."

"I'll have the way ready in half an hour."

Jessica slurped her soda. "So is this goodbye?"

"For now," CJ said. "Their corporate office is in Dallas, of all places. Taking a portal will be much faster."

"Can I come with you?"

"Not this time. The doctors will need you to make medical decisions for Sraad and Heze. You need to be in touch."

Jessica looked disappointed. "I want answers, too."

"You'll get them, and if we find what I think Rive thinks we'll find, they'll be in Walter Reed in a day or two, and Crescendo will have to turn over a few hundred boxes of paper to the Attorney General."

"Really?" Jessica said.

"It's why I'm here. To hold people accountable."

Rive clicked his claws.

4

Dallas, Texas, was the last place in the world CJ wanted to go, but thanks to the portals, it didn't matter where they had to go. When they first walked in and CJ showed her identification to the front desk, they only got a mid-level manager. Upon further inspection of her credentials, she moved higher up the chain, and now she and Rive sat in the office of the vice president of operations, which CJ took to mean she was speaking with someone who actually knew what was going on and was at liberty to discuss it.

Joseph Conch looked as though he had spent his whole life in an executive office chair. She had shown him the medical summaries of the two Relians. She had produced the information packet on C-Corn but claimed she obtained it by calling the corporate office with a request for information on the fields around Maryville.

"We would like to know what this C-Corn is and where it came from," CJ said.

The man on the other side of the desk was looking over his glasses at the medical summary. "I am not allowed to divulge that information. It's all covered under the law's trade secret provisions."

"Two Relians are in the hospital with severe allergic reactions. We have reason to believe C-Corn is the cause."

"As I understand it, the corn has not been harvested yet, so there is no evidence of that. I also understand there are several factories in that town. Have you checked into those possibilities?"

"Nobody else is sick, Mr. Conch, but there's a C-Corn field right next to where they live. We're exploring this possibility first. Is there anything else you can tell us that's not already in the packet?"

"All the information you need is there, Ms. Rhine."

"What is it a hybrid of, Mr. Conch?"

Finally he raised his eyes from the report and regarded CJ and Rive. "I cannot discuss that at this time."

"You can't tell me what your company crossbred the corn with?"

"That's correct."

"Why? It's just corn, isn't it?"

He folded his hands, squared his shoulders. "It is corn that is protected under recent copyright laws that cover gene splicing."

Finally, after twenty minutes of talking, he had said something new.

"Gene splicing. So it's not crossbred. It's genetically modified."

"That's correct."

"And you can't tell me what plant or animal it was spliced with?"

"That's also correct."

"But it was spliced with something that is supposed to allow the corn to grow in any environment. Why is that? What's the company's goal with C-Corn?"

That seemed to be a much more industry-friendly question, as Mr. Conch leaned back in his chair. "Our goal is to be the world leader in corn production. Our product will allow it to be cultivated on land that was previously thought to be unsuitable for it. I do not mean just here in the United States, but all over the world. Perhaps beyond, someday."

He smiled and nodded at Rive. Rive's hands remained apart. Mr. Conch continued.

"We feel our proprietary corn has the potential to end hunger worldwide by addressing the supply and longevity problem. Cold climates, hot climates, wet, dry. Even arctic. Corn will grow there now, and the world will have us to thank for it. Our competitors are still making bio-products that require use of herbicides and pesticides. We believe our patented product has an edge over our competitors in that it does not need either."

"Why Maryville, Missouri? If this is your first planting, why not start in Alaska, or somewhere in the Yukon?"

"Crescendo has multiple test fields across the nation. It is currently in the stage of testing performance in multiple climate zones."

"Testing? You have brochures and information packets. Your company claims it can do all these things, so hasn't it already been tested?"

"In laboratory conditions, yes. Maryville represents one of the first real-world plantings. When results come in, we will roll out on larger scale."

"What results are you looking for?"

"Crop yield, viability, durability."

"Taste?"

"Taste is a given."

"I see. And who created this hybrid? May we speak to some of the scientists who created C-Corn?"

"Not at this time."

"One last question, Mr. Conch, then I will let you get back to your day. If it can be proven your company's corn was responsible for the two Relians' condition, how will your company respond? Will you be prepared to withdraw C-Corn from the market?"

"Crescendo will cooperate fully with any authorities who may be called."

"Thank you, Mr.—"

"I have one question," Rive said. It was the first word he had spoken since CJ sat down in this office.

Mr. Conch looked surprised. He met Rive's eyes and nodded.

"How much has this company spent on research and development for C-Corn?"

The man considered his words carefully, probably assessing whether or not that was a trade secret, too. After half a minute, he reached a decision.

"Over two hundred million dollars, I believe."

"That's more than one third of your company's annual revenue. Thank you. We'll let you know if there's anything else."

CJ stood up, shook his hand, and saw themselves out the door and down the hallway to the elevator. CJ pushed the button and waited for the car. They did not speak. They had agreed not to speak until they were outside.

Minutes later, they walked out the door side by side into the dry heat of Dallas. After they had opened one block of distance between themselves and the building, Rive spoke.

"He has more incentive to move the project forward than consider how C-Corn may affect people."

"Two Relians are not enough to raise concern, not when the town itself is unaffected."

"I'm not convinced the town is unaffected."

"How do you mean?"

"Relians have a low tolerance for pollution. You'll recall the trouble many had adjusting to a city, being around car exhaust and the like. Relians may simply be the first to feel the effects."

"You think the Relians are the canaries in the coal mine?"

"Possibly. As exposure accumulates, humans will experience the effects as well. Will you call your colleague in the EPA and ask him how things are progressing?"

"Even he needs time to work. I'll call him in a day or so. Let's go home and get some sleep."

Rive paused on the sidewalk and looked around. CJ stopped and turned to him.

"I will send you home if you wish, but I do not want to sleep in the White House tonight. I have never been here before. I wish to explore."

CJ smiled. She looked around, too. "Yeah. We are in Dallas. It's been twenty years since I've been here. I suppose it is nice to be back."

Rive clicked his claws, started walking again. "What brought you to this part of the country before? Why have you not been back?"

CJ kept pace with the raptor. "My brother used to live here. I came for his wedding almost twenty years ago."

Rive curled his neck upwards. "I did not know you had a sibling."

CJ laughed. "Finally, something that surprises you. We're not really on speaking terms. I don't even know where he is now. He and his wife divorced six years after the wedding. I think my brother was at fault. No question. He was a jerk to her."

They walked a few paces. CJ looked around and sighed.

"We can find a hotel. Visit some sights while we're here."

Rive held his hands together in a smile, lowered his neck, and looked at her from a low angle. "You are from here?"

"South, actually. I never lived in Dallas, but my family drove up here often. Met Albert in Arlington, and that's where we set up our own practice."

"You don't have an accent."

CJ smiled. "Law school will do that to you. Get me drunk enough and I'll start talking like a Texan again."

Rive rubbed his claws as he raised his head. "May I buy you a drink?"

She laughed and blushed. They walked with the rush hour traffic.

5

The theater quickly emptied just after ten at night, and another line of people waited for the next showing. CJ and Rive walked out of the theater together. They stepped onto the sidewalk, veering toward the car CJ had rented a few hours before. People stared at Rive, but most did not notice him.

"Funny," CJ said, looking over her shoulder. "There was a real alien in a theater full of people watching a movie about first contact with alien life. You'd think they'd turn off the movie and watch you instead."

"I am glad they did not notice me."

"I remember Relians don't get much out of movies," CJ said, turning to meet Rive's eye. "What do you get out of them? And is it physically painful for you?"

Rive rubbed his claws. "My vision is good enough to see the spaces between the frames, so the illusion of a motion picture is lost on me, as it is for all Relians. Yes, they are difficult to watch, but they provide immense insight into your culture."

They stepped down from the sidewalk and into the parking lot.

"Dare I ask what you see when you watch a movie about first contact with aliens?"

"This movie in particular, or entertainment in general?"

CJ laughed. "Both, but first tell me what you thought of *Contact*."

"I think the same of this movie which I think of all entertainment, though this one was refreshing in that it featured a woman as the protagonist and she is not on screen to subconsciously stimulate the males in the audience."

"Ain't that the truth. It's a small miracle when a woman isn't on screen just to show her breasts or rear even when fully clothed."

Rive stepped over a median. The clanking of his metal foot on the asphalt stopped for a few steps as he walked through the mulch between the shrubs and then resumed when he dropped back down to the street. CJ noticed his head had remained at the same height the whole time.

"Even with that slight variation, the core of the movie is the same as all entertainment as an expression of base animal instincts and subconscious desires."

"Do tell."

"The presence of an enormous amount of fiction is characteristic of an unhealthy society." He turned his head and looked down his flank back at the theater. "Just look at all those movies playing, and this is only a tiny fraction of the whole." He turned back around and half-faced CJ as they passed the parked cars. "I've been in stores. Shelf after shelf of movies, books, and music. This is not a sign of great thinkers and imaginative people, but a symptom of unfulfilled desire. A society which is so repressed, so desperate for adventure and sex and happiness they must create fictional worlds in which those desires are met to feel better about their situation."

"People don't tell stories where you come from? People don't make music?"

"They do, but for a different reason. The best metaphor I can think of is mathematics. In the early centuries of civilization on your planet, it was used purely to solve practical problems. Land division, taxation, resource management, and so forth. Gradually, mathematics evolved into something that was also done for its own sake, apart from application to reality."

"So... Creativity isn't done to express anything in alien cultures?"

"Yes, it is, but the creative endeavors do not express the same things the people of Earth need to express. When I watch a movie or listen to your music, I see and hear a desire for freedom. Humans do not merely write about their petty wishes. They write about freedom—the one thing they do not have, which is of course the one thing they declare out loud they have in abundance. Human society organizes itself into a strict hierarchy with one person at the top telling the others what to do, and the others have no control over their lives. The subordinate humans yearn to break free of the control of the alpha while the alpha struggles to keep them under control for his own benefit. This conflict comprises the majority of the stories you tell."

They had reached the rental car. CJ opened the driver's side door, then reached to the back seat and unlocked it for Rive. The raptor pulled the door open and climbed inside. The rear end of the car sank a few inches and settled. CJ closed the door behind Rive and then sat in the driver's seat. A muzzle rested on the shoulder of the passenger seat, his mouth inches from her ear.

"Pulling a little further away from the subject, all of your fiction follows the same structure. It is set up to resemble sex."

"What? How?"

"Introduction, turning point, resolution. Foreplay, climax, afterglow. All stories follow this basic pattern. Scenes within those stories follow this pattern, conversations, character arcs, everything. The best stories are fractal patterns structured after intercourse. Would you believe plenty of species would not comprehend this structure because reproduction works differently for them?"

"I think I believe everything you say at this point."

"Furthermore, all fiction has one other thing in common: it imbues meaning onto existence. One of the rules of storytelling is that everything must mean something to the story. This is because significance is missing from most people's own lives. They strive for life itself to be meaningful and don't want to confront the idea that it is not, so they project that desire onto fictional characters; that's why everything in fiction must serve a purpose. They desire their lives to be interesting, so they derive that from empathy for others who experience what they wish they could, even if those people are not real."

CJ started the car. She had deliberately parked where she would not have to back out of a space, as it was difficult to see out the rear window with a large theropod in the back seat.

"The vicarious experience is what entertainment is all about," she said.

"It seems to be a good thing to you, but in your kind's case it is a symptom of oppression, a yearning to escape a dominant human who controls your lives and prevents you from living a life of your choosing. Everything is an expression of this yearning. Whenever I notice it manifest itself, I hear a species crying out for help."

CJ drove out of the parking lot and merged with traffic.

"I don't see oppressed people," she said. "We've got it pretty good in this country. People are free to do as they please, go where they please."

"I beg to differ. Even in this country people cannot go where they please and do as they please because they are tethered to their livelihoods. They must perform tasks for others to earn money so they can afford food and shelter. That is why they need entertainment in the first place. It serves a practical purpose."

"And you think it's because we still organize ourselves like primates?"

"The evidence is clear. Consider that most movies feature the same group: a dominant male, multiple subordinate males, and one female, who is always the love interest for the dominant male. The alpha usually does not have any special skills himself, but rather coordinates the people who do have special skills, which leaves unanswered the question of why the subordinates allow the dominant to order them around when clearly they are better than he is. It is bare naked animal instinct, and yet nobody here perceives it as such. Television also follows these patterns. The programs meant to appeal to men all feature this basic setup. Multiple males, one dominant, the others submissive, and one female in the group. The ideal social unit of primates. Stories revolve mostly around power struggles between males of the group fighting for more status, fighting to undermine the dominant male's authority, and so forth. Shows meant to appeal to women depict the same things.

Usually women struggling to break free from the dominance of a man and assert control over their own lives. Conflicts like this have been going on since before your species achieved sentience. Males struggling against one another for dominance may be the original form of entertainment for your kind. It is the only way you comprehend civilization."

CJ laughed. "I'd love to hear what you think of *The Three Stooges*."

Rive clicked his claws. "These struggles for dominance can also be played up for comedy. That is all humor is: recognizing when something does not have the expected consequences. More broadly, it is a reaction to an unexpected connection forming between two concepts. All species have a means of reacting to this, but not all of these reactions equate to what you call a sense of humor. Another form of this reaction is the concept of fun. Dangerous actions without consequences. Some species would not understand why humans watch violent movies or play violent games because they depict something so serious."

"So..." CJ continued. "If creativity does not express some sort of desire, why be creative? What is the purpose of telling stories or making music if it doesn't express anything?"

"The reason the alien being appeared to Jodie Foster's character as a human was so she would listen to his words and not be distracted by his appearance. He knew human beings are not able to comprehend something alien yet. It requires steps so no one is overwhelmed."

"Are you saying it's beyond our comprehension?"

"Yes, but not in a bad way."

"So you didn't enjoy the movie?"

"You first."

"I thought it was very well-done, but I also like Jodie Foster. It was very accurate how the press reacted, how people would react to news of a message from another world. The romance wasn't very strong, but it didn't need to be. I think if we ever did receive a message from the stars, that's exactly how people would act."

"You received much more than a message," Rive said, clicking his claws. He lifted his head from the other seat and looked around. "Are we going somewhere?"

"Yes, actually. I've only been there once, but I will never forget the way. This chance probably won't come again, so I should go back."

"Where?"

"Let me see if I can surprise you."

"Do you want me to act surprised when we arrive?"

"Of course not."

Traffic was light. Nothing to slow them down. CJ took an exit.

6

She pulled the car up to the curb and stopped in front of a house. It did not look any different from the other houses in the suburb. It had two stories, an attached garage big enough for two cars, a brick facing, and a plastic deer in the front yard. Rive rested his muzzle on CJ's shoulder and looked out the driver's side window with her.

"Surprised?" she said.

"No. You mentioned your brother earlier. I figured that's the only place you would want to go. For having been here only once, you knew your way around very well."

"I took enough phone calls from his wife. I felt like I lived here for years. Then it ended. Never heard from either of them again. This was their house."

"It's for sale."

CJ looked down at the lawn. A realtor sign stood half fallen over in the grass.

"Probably changed hands a dozen times by now."

She sat with both hands on the wheel for a moment. She shut the engine off and shifted the car to park while she unbuckled.

"I wonder..."

Rive lifted his snout as she opened the door and climbed out. She walked up the sidewalk and climbed the small flight of concrete stairs to the front door. The door-knob had a combination lock over it. Inside the combination lock would be a key to the front door. She turned the top wheel one click to the left and tried the button. Nothing. She turned it back, and then one space to the right. The lock popped, and she pulled the key out and unlocked the front door. Smiling to herself, she slipped the key in her pocket and turned around.

"Open house. Come in."

The car shifted, the rear shocks relaxed, and Rive slipped out the passenger side and closed the door. He trotted up the sidewalk and joined her.

"We're in luck," she said. "The last person left it so they could get in later."

CJ led the way in. Rive followed, closing the door behind them. The house was empty. A few lights lit the room so she could see everything had been painted beige. The walls, the ceiling, the doors, the fake wood trim. The staircase in front of them had real wooden steps and railing, but it had been painted white.

"That should be a crime," CJ said, walking up to the steps.

"What should?" Rive said, scenting the empty room.

"The last time I was here, every room was a different color. This room was blue. The dining room was light green. The trim was a complementary color. And the steps... The steps weren't painted at all. They were natural, beautiful, unvarnished oak. Now they're white. Why would anyone paint this white? Why white? Why paint real wood? Mother of God, this is hideous."

She shook her head as she walked by the steps into the living room. She paused at the end of the hall, one arm on the wall, the other at her side. Rive stood behind her and stretched his neck over her shoulder, looking around. The hall opened into a large, open living room joined to the kitchen, the two separated by a waist-high partition. The fireplace in the corner was real, not gas, and it had been used frequently over the years. Most of the hardwood floor had plastic spread over it. The kitchen was spacious but devoid of appliances. A single bulb over the island in the center of the kitchen provided the only light down here. CJ stood silent for almost a minute.

"They had the reception here. I remember the couch was over there." She pointed at the living room. "I sat in it. Talked to my brother and his wife for hours, whenever they weren't talking to other people. Met so much of her family. I was the only one from our side of the family to come. Both our parents died years before, and we barely knew our other relations."

She stepped into the room, crinkling the plastic, stopping over empty space.

"Right here. On the couch. It's where I first met her. They had the stereo on."

She turned to the empty wall and gestured to it.

"A record player. One of his friends was in charge of it. He played Patsy Cline, Elvis, Pink Floyd."

She turned back to the space where the couch would be and stared at it.

"She was so smitten by him. They met the year before, and now they were married. When they were together, she glowed. He glowed. And I was worried."

Rive now stepped into the room. Somehow he walked without crinkling the plastic. He stood beside her and faced the empty space where the couch would have been.

"Why were you worried?"

"Because I'd seen it before. With friends. They met someone, they glowed, they bubbled with enthusiasm, but it always happens. The enthusiasm fades, and reality sets in. I was afraid it would happen again."

"You may have noticed subconsciously they were not a good match."

"It was too late. They were married. Nothing left to do but hope I was just being cynical. My brother was always hard to get along with. He had no filter. Said the first thing that came to mind—no thought for how others might take it. I knew he'd need to find a girl who found that charming. She was a nice person, but she didn't strike me as someone who would tolerate it. In the long run. Best I can figure it, she found it exciting and new at the time, but the longer she had to put up with it, it just became annoying. And he didn't exactly try to meet her halfway. He was the kind of person who expected others to adapt to him." She laughed. "I warned him this might happen. He didn't believe me. Probably why I never heard from him again. He didn't want to admit I was right. I was always right. He hated that about me. Makes me wonder if he just wasn't capable of seeing it. The marriage lasted six years because he wanted to prove me wrong. Otherwise, she would have left him in the first year. That's the feeling I got from talking to her."

CJ turned to Rive. He held his hands apart.

"What else were you right about?"

"I was right about him not having the personality to make it in medicine. He dropped out in his second year. I was right about the other girls he dated. It was so obvious to me they weren't right for him, and he hated me every time they broke up. I kept telling him her personality was too close to his, or too different. Finally I told him it's not them, it's him. He still didn't believe it. I think he prevented us from talking until they were married so I couldn't tell him it wasn't going to work."

She turned away from the imaginary couch and wandered around the empty room, recreating the furniture in her mind as she went.

"I have to wonder why he couldn't see it. It was so obvious to everyone around him. All he had to do was make better choices, but he kept making the wrong choice over and over. It was like he was born to mess up. He told me that once. He was born to fail, and I was born to succeed. I didn't believe that, but now... looking back on it, I have to wonder. What do you think?"

She turned to Rive and met his eyes from across the room. The dim backlight made him look like a creature from a nightmare, but instead of fear, CJ stared in wonder. The raptor still held his hands apart.

"Perhaps he was." In this light, she could not see his mouth move.

"Is it really possible?"

"Genetics determines the connections that form in the brain the same as the blood vessels in the rest of the body. It is basically the same, but there will be subtle differences between individuals. Humans are willing to accept some people are born short, some tall, some with the temperament to succeed in a particular job while others are not. But they are not willing to accept some people are born without the right connections to survive in society itself. In short, that they are born to make the wrong choices. You are willing to accept animals enduring it, but humans have free will and can choose their own path. I hatched with the right mental connections required to be an Archeon. I accept that, and so does everyone else. Only people with the right kind of mind can do what I do. It is not a goal one can strive to achieve, which means we are not completely free to choose what we do in life. Each individual has a limited capacity, and a person cannot exceed it, physically or mentally."

"People can learn. Don't aliens believe in free will? How can you have a society without that?"

"Of course. Anyone can form new connections in the mind; they are easily shaped by environment and experience, especially when young, but that also happens within boundaries. Our foxes, for example, are born with an intense instinct to keep other scents away. With help, they can learn to redirect it to something equally intense but less destructive, allowing the higher mind to assert itself, but the urge never goes away no matter how hard they try. It implies no one has complete control. Your brother may have been born to make bad choices in this society, but perhaps there exists another society in which his bad choices would actually have been good. Where I come from, he would have been free to find the society that best suited himself. Human society forces some people to go against their nature to survive, and this is another source of strife. They must conform to one society's rules, and if they are lucky, they find a creative outlet to express their frustration while they survive where they do not belong."

"So... just another symptom of an oppressed society?"

"Almost everything on Earth is."

"He was born to screw up and fail?"

"With the way humanity does things, he probably was."

She leaned against the wall, staring at the theropod across the room. "That's not... That's not what I wanted to hear. I was hoping you'd tell me it's all his fault."

"One cannot be faulted for being what one is."

"All he had to do is listen. He could have made better choices."

"If he did not have the temperament to be a doctor, who is to say he did not have the temperament to survive in human society itself? He might have done better with a different species."

"Is that what you believe, Rive? Everyone just follows genetic programming?"

"The difference is human culture blames individuals for being individuals instead of acknowledging that some may not be suited for human society. Remember Ratash and Irus?"

"God, yes." She looked at the floor and laughed. CJ wandered around the room, meandering to one corner and then to another. Rive remained in place and followed her with his eyes.

"Ratash rarely associated with his own kind. He found the usual way of doing things too confining. He ended up living with multiple species of mammals. He liked their ways better. Imagine if he had been forced to live in Relian society. He would feel trapped, being unable to couple with his fox. He would spend his whole life denying what he is, made to feel guilty about it. If your brother could have chosen what society to live in, he would have found some-place he could be happy. This is another theme in enter-tainment: finding one's place. Everyone is certain their place must be out there, but most are not free to pursue it, forced to work to provide for themselves or a family in-stead. For some, there really is no place for them in society. They were born with the mental connections better suited for the rules of another species, which means they are con-demned to failure and misery here."

"I can't even imagine having that kind of freedom. Not just to move to a different country, but live by the rules of another species."

"People who are forced to pretend to be what society expects them to be spend their whole lives acting, going through the motions. After years and years of this... they might forget who they are, and then they might lash out in violent ways to escape it. So many people would be hurt, and all you can do is watch. A mature society allows people to be free to live the way they want. They should be free from people forcing them to become someone else."

Rive looked every which way. CJ waited for him to continue.

He turned to her again. "Watching movies is more than physically painful for me. It fills me with pain for humanity as a whole. When I watch a movie, I see people crying to be set free from these confines. I see entire lives wasted in oppression and the pointless pursuit of survival. To me, it is truly alien because it does not happen in the contacted universe. Or it shouldn't happen. A mature society recognizes when it is doing something wrong. It makes every effort to correct the wrong so no one gets hurt again."

CJ stopped, faced him. Smiled. "That is probably the most heartfelt thing I've ever heard you say."

He clicked his claws. "Biologically, I do not have a heart."

She smiled, crossed the room, and then held him by his real shoulder. "It's very late. Let's find a room and turn in for the night."

She walked to the hallway. Rive turned and followed a few paces behind her.

"You don't want to see the rest of the house?"

"I didn't go upstairs last time. No reason to now."

CJ reached for the doorknob and opened it for Rive. She stepped outside after him, pulling the key from her pocket. She locked the door, then replaced the key in the lockbox. She turned the top combination wheel one space to the right, and then followed Rive to the car, yawning. Rive had not locked the door, so he let himself into the back seat. CJ climbed in and buckled up.

"Any idea which society my brother might've done better in?"

"I need to know more about him. What is his name?"

She turned the key, lowered the brake, and pulled away from the curb.

7

At five in the morning, CJ's cell phone rang. She groped around the end table until she found it. She pulled the antenna out.

"Tim?"

"Chris, did I wake you?"

"Of course you did. What's going on?"

"Where are you? Can you come to the lab? I need to speak with you."

"I'm in Dallas, but I'm with Rive. I can be there in an hour or two."

"I'll wait for you where Rive made the door last time."

He hung up. CJ collapsed the antenna and sat up. The raptor was asleep on the floor. She nudged him with a foot.

"Wake up. Wake up, Rive. We need to get back to Washington. Tim just called. At five in the morning. It must be important."

"I heard," he said. "Even when I'm asleep my mind is paying attention."

"Did you hear him?"

"I did. I'm working on the way now."

"Good." CJ wrapped herself in the blanket, grabbed the rest of her clothes, and walked to the bathroom. Rive lay on the floor and thought about the way.

An hour later, they emerged through a sphere in the EPA lab. Tim was waiting for them against the wall.

"It's only been three days," CJ said. "Did you find something?"

The raptor joined her at her side as the sphere closed. Tim handed her some papers. He turned around and began walking. CJ and Rive kept up. Rive read the papers.

"The first thing I had them do was a DNA analysis of that cornstalk. It normally takes weeks. I wanted to know what the hell it was more than anyone. At the same time, they ran the atmosphere analysis and did the water sample. I think we found what your Relians reacted to."

He turned a corner and entered an office. Test tubes and petri dishes and DNA profiles covered the desk in the center of the room. Tim walked behind it, picking up a petri dish.

"We isolated it. Here's a blowup." He set that down as he picked up an oversized piece of paper. "It looks like pollen, but it isn't. It contains a soup of chemicals we're still trying to analyze. It doesn't come from the reproductive system, but from the leaves."

"The leaves?" said the secretary. "How?"

"We're working on it." He picked up a smaller piece of paper, this one showing an electron microscope scan of a leaf. "This is one of the leaves that encases the cob. These large holes are how normal plants breathe and vent water vapor. But these larger holes," he pointed to one, "do not correlate with anything we know. It's a new organ emitting this pollen-like substance, but it has no reproductive function that we can tell. In fact, we can't find this cornstalk's reproductive parts."

CJ met his eyes. "We talked to the—"

Tim held up his hand and walked around the desk. "Hold that thought; I'm almost done. This last thing..." He picked up two more papers. "DNA comparison between this stalk and the one in a field elsewhere in the country. There are differences, but look at this sequence here."

He pointed with a pen to a column of dots.

359

"This segment is not even made of the four chemicals of DNA, adenine, thymine, guanine, and cytosine. There's a fifth chemical in here. We're not sure what it is, or how it got there—"

"I am," said the raptor.

"Please?" Tim said.

"It's genetic material from a plant on Gaow."

"Gaow?" said Tim.

"During the disaster, I gathered the Relian survivors there. That's where we came to Earth from. I spent a lot of time on that world with my fox. Predation has yet to evolve, even among the plants. All of the animals still live in the ocean. The only thing they have to survive is the environment. Conditions in the ocean are stable, but on land the weather can be extreme. The temperature ranges from thirty below zero to one hundred and thirty above in a single day on your temperature scale. With that, the wind can exceed hundreds of miles per hour. Plants have evolved ways to adapt to these extremes. I settled the Relians on the most temperate area of the planet, but those species of plants still grew there."

"Are we looking at an invasive species? Did they bring any with them?"

"No. We know the dangers of invasive species."

"Then how did alien DNA get into corn?"

"It's a hybrid," said the raptor. "Owned and patented by a company named Crescendo."

"They gene spliced an alien plant into terrestrial crops?" Tim said. "Where did they get it if nobody brought anything with them?"

"I don't know," Rive said.

"Seeds," said the secretary. She leaned on the desk. "When the Relians first came here, some of them went through medical exams. They would've taken stool samples."

"I was watching," said Rive. "Nobody did."

"You think those toilets were hooked up to the sewer system? No, they went to a lab. Probably had some interns pick them apart, and what did they find? Seeds from an alien plant."

Rive looked at CJ. "The plants evolved on a world with no animals on it. Seeds are not adapted to pass through an animal's intestines."

"The plants are indestructible, so why not their seeds? Even if there were none, they would have found undigested plant matter."

"What plants did the foxes eat on Gaow?" Tim said.

Rive turned to him. "Many of them were edible. They haven't evolved any defense mechanisms because no animals have evolved to eat them yet. Some were seed-bearing, but they don't make anyone sick."

"Maybe they don't," said Tim, "but someone found they could survive anything and grow anywhere and shot those genes into corn."

"Seedling to patented product in one year," CJ said, shaking her head. "They couldn't have tested this. They couldn't have."

"Maryville *is* the test," Rive said.

"Wouldn't they do this before they released it into the real world?" Tim asked.

"Not when they have two hundred million dollars in research at stake," Rive replied.

"Do you have any idea what this pollen-like substance is?" said Tim.

"It is pollen for that species of plant."

"Well, the corn is making it, but it doesn't serve that function anymore. It's probably just extraneous now. So in addition to the desired traits, it also has some leftover traits from the alien plant, and those systems are broken. The DNA controlling them is incomplete. It's probably just producing random garbage. The pollen specks contain all sorts of chemicals. They're like little floating candies with liquid centers. It may not even be stable; it could produce different chemicals in subsequent generations."

"Is there a chance humans will be affected?" CJ said.

"There's a huge chance. Maybe not now, maybe not even this harvest, but with long term exposure, there will be side effects. This pollen is in the air, the water, the soil, it covers everything we tested. I think we can look forward to a health crisis in the coming years."

"Tim, write up a report now. I'll have it on the president's desk by the end of the day."

"Results aren't complete," he said. "I'd rather wait until we have everything. We're still working on what chemicals are in this pollen."

"Get started. May I take copies of your work so far?"

"I gave it all to you when you arrived."

"Perfect. Let me know if you learn anything else."

CJ turned and left the room. Rive followed, papers in hand.

"We need to get those Relians out of there," CJ said. "We'll take a cab to Walter Reed and make a way straight to the hospital."

"I'll work on it there. Then what?"

"We pay Mr. Conch a visit and show him what we found. There might be enough here to open an investigation. Let's see him weasel his way out of that."

Rive clicked his way across the floor, but it sounded different from what CJ normally heard. She looked down. Rive's killing claws were raised.

8

Jessica Byrne looked through the portal at her Relians on the other side. The doctors from the military hospital in

Bethesda had just transferred Sraad and Heze to their equipment. They switched it on, doctors watched the monitors, and one of them waved her through.

She looked at CJ. The secretary placed a hand on her shoulder. "They should recover quickly. You'll have to arrange to relocate soon."

"How will I do that?"

"You have my number. Call me when you're ready to leave. Rive will make a way for you to come back."

"Will you let me know what happens?"

"I'll be in touch. I promise. And don't worry about the bill. Either the federal government will pick it up, or someone responsible will."

"Thank you," she opened her arms. CJ embraced her, then she walked through the sphere.

A number of doctors and nurses watched from the other side. The sphere closed, and the hospital room was vacant. CJ turned to the raptor.

"Let's find a discreet place to go to Dallas."

She led them out of the room, down the hall and out of the hospital. CJ noticed Jessica's car. The keys were on the dashboard.

"On second thought, let's drive her car back to her house. Wouldn't be right to leave it here. She might be in Maryland for a while."

She walked over to it, opened the door, and climbed in. Rive opened the hatch and crawled in.

"All right. Here's the plan." She backed out of the parking spot. "We go to Dallas, march in, and demand to speak to Mr. Conch. If he won't talk to us, we'll go straight to their lawyer. With the papers we've got, it should be enough to get their attention."

She threw the car in drive, pulled out of the parking lot and onto the main road. She turned and began the short trip to Jessica's apartment building.

"It'll take them a few days to answer all this, at least, and maybe by then Tim will have something else."

"Shouldn't we wait until the research is complete before going to Crescendo with it?"

"We should hit 'em with this now and put a stop to it before they can clog up the process with litigation."

"We have still not proven C-Corn was the cause of their condition."

"I called Tim a few minutes ago and told him the Relians were at Walter Reed. Gave him authorization to take blood and whatever else he needs to prove pollen is present."

"They will create litigation no matter what the research shows."

"Of course they will, but this gets the process started."

She noticed something in her rearview mirror. The yellow car looked familiar. A quarter mile later, she placed it.

"I think we're being followed."

Rive bent his neck and looked through the hatch window.

"That's the car that was parked on the street in front of Mr. Marko's house."

"That's what I thought. He was right. They were watching his house. That means they know he spoke to us. Keep working on the way to Dallas. Looks like we have to deal with the local office first."

She drove the rest of the way to the apartment complex, turned and parked in front of Jessica's building. The yellow car parked right behind her, blocking her from backing out. CJ checked around. A few cars in the parking lot, but most people were at work this time of day, so the apartments were deserted.

Rive opened the hatch. He had just barely enough room to squeeze between Jessica's car and the front bumper of the yellow car. The secretary grabbed her briefcase, tossed the keys in the glove box, and then stepped out.

A white man dressed in business casual climbed out of the yellow car. He closed the door and took two steps forward. Rive walked around Jessica's car and took position next to the secretary.

"Crescendo local office, I presume?" she said.

"No," said the man. He looked at the apartment behind her. "Can we go inside?"

"Anything you have to say to me you can say here, mister?"

"I'd rather not give my name. You are Secretary Rhine, and Rive. You know what's going on?"

"That depends on what you mean."

"I mean that I also know what's going on. I work for Crescendo. I was on the C-Corn project."

"Can you show me some sort of ID?"

"How 'bout we go somewhere else? Somewhere they won't think to watch us."

"You were watching us the other day. Your car was parked by Mr. Marko's house."

"Word gets around fast in Crescendo about who the farmers are talking to. Word also gets around when the EPA takes unauthorized samples of patented corn. Let's at least go inside. The less pollen we're exposed to, the better."

CJ looked at Rive. The raptor turned to her. "I don't like his scent."

CJ looked at the man. "We talk here or not at all. If Crescendo's watching the farmers, they already know you're speaking to us."

The man looked frustrated. "Your call." He slipped his hands into his pockets and approached them.

"That's close enough," she said.

He hesitated, shrugged his shoulders, then removed his hands from his pockets. He held something in his right hand. Rive raised his killing claws, spread his hands, and stepped between him and CJ.

The man raised it all the way. Rive crouched and was about to jump when something shot from the man's hand. A wide cone of clear liquid covered Rive's face. Rive shrieked and dropped to the ground, the metal ringing like iron hitting asphalt, hands covering his eyes. He began convulsing. His eyes watered so much it dripped between his fingers. A deep red rash started spreading across his skin.

"Rive!" CJ raised her hands. The man aimed it at CJ now.

"There's my ID," he said.

Rive writhed. His screams died off as his voice gave out. He still convulsed, but silently and eerily still. CJ took a step closer to him. A cone of liquid came from whatever he was holding and hit her on the left side of her face. She dropped to her knees beside Rive, holding her head, but she only felt a slight burn through her closed eyelid.

"Concentrated C-Corn pollen," said the man. "This is a proof of concept weapon, not even a prototype. We had to use an empty can of air-duster. Takes about ten minutes to work on humans. Well, that's what I'm told. Now we know it works instantly on Relians."

CJ started to get a headache. She sat on the ground, placed a hand on Rive's skin. The raptor was overheated and shaking, his breathing deep and gasping.

"Now will you listen?"

She draped herself over Rive and looked up at the man. "Let me call the hospital!"

"Make a move and I will shoot you again. You won't live long enough to call anyone. If you listen, I promise not to take too long and you can get him and yourself to the hospital before his throat closes. And then yours."

"You just assaulted federal officials! This won't stop anyone from exposing your damn company!"

"I'm not here to snuff you out because you're too close to the truth. That only happens in movies. I'm here because you found the truth, and I've been told you need to know what happens next."

Rive had stopped convulsing. He was barely breathing. CJ turned to him. "Rive?" She shook him. "Oh, God. What the hell did you do?"

"The EPA's analysis is impressive. Crescendo's team didn't take a second look at the pollen. They knew about it but didn't bother to analyze it. Nobody anticipated this, but it opens a lot of possibilities. Now they know C-Corn has some major flaws, but that's okay because other companies can step in to correct those flaws. Ever hear of Apple computers?"

"Of course I have!"

"Ever wonder why they didn't become as big as Microsoft? Because they didn't let other companies stick their hands in the pot. They made products themselves, and those products had no problems. No other companies could come in and make products designed to address those problems. When C-Corn rolls out, it will be as-is. Its flaws are already being pitched as opportunities for other companies to make profit. The sturdiness creates need for new farming equipment. The health problems create more demand for medical services. The high cost of the seeds and farming equipment creates need for farmers to take out loans, which is good for banks. Oh, yes. The people running Crescendo have thought of all that. This is how they're fixing it."

"What is your point?" The rash spread quickly across the raptor's skin, and he didn't seem to be breathing at all now.

"Crescendo is the only company with an alien plant in its possession, so that gives them a way to crush the competition. They've invested a lot into this. They bred about a hundred different strains, and this was the best of all the splicing attempts. Dozens of people spent months isolating the sequence for the plant's durability. Those were the only genes they injected into corn, but it looks like that sequence also controlled other things." He laughed. "Now they have a new product to pitch to the military. The plan is to convince farmers to grow the corn in nations that happen to have what other industries need and the United States can get for them. Oil-producing nations, mineral-rich nations. Less resistance if the people are sick and need to go into debt to buy supplies just to eat."

Rive's skin was so warm CJ's hands were sweating. "How did Crescendo get the seeds? How do you know what the EPA found?"

"The company has many contacts in the senate and house, state and federal. They all owe Crescendo big time for campaign funding. Several of them pulled strings to make sure Crescendo got those seeds. Same for the research. In return, those politicians tell the people everything the company does is safe because as far as they know, it is."

"Why are you telling me all this?"

"I was sent to give you a chance to save your career. If you go forward with this, I promise Crescendo will ruin you. Mr. Cadre's findings will be discredited, and he will be dismissed from his post. Crescendo can produce a dozen studies to prove C-Corn is safe. They have two of them ready to go and can commission others any time. They have lots of friends in congress, not to mention judges throughout the country. Even if you go to the press with it, they will report on the other studies, the government will be thrown under the bus, and it will be business as usual."

He laughed, lowered his hand and stood with his arms to his side.

"Speaking personally, I'm surprised. You were a senator. You should know the government doesn't have the authority to shut down any business operation. Things like this are happening all over the world all the time. Politics just takes attention away from it. Eventually people will be able to accept corporations run the world, but until then they need it to look like government is running the show and messing everything up. That way people believe Crescendo is coming to save them. Makes people feel like they have some control over their lives when they elect people who vow to shrink the government."

CJ's hand had migrated to Rive's face. Her fingers felt the seam where the metal joined with his skin. She began to feel lightheaded, and she saw spots in her vision. Her breathing sped up, but she still felt out of breath.

The man looked at Rive and shook his head.

"Concentrated, this is what the pollen does, but in small enough doses, the effects are far more gradual. Could be decades before anything happens. Might be as small as an increase in asthma, or food allergies, or something. It means nothing can be linked directly to a cause, and hospitals will get lots more business treating the symptoms. Did you know members of Crescendo's board of directors also sit on a number of hospital boards? Ever wonder what people running hospitals are doing running a biotech company?"

CJ couldn't catch her breath. "I will expose you! I will make it my life's work to see your company crash and burn!"

"You won't be the first to try. You can scream it from the mountain all you want. Nobody will hear you."

He backed away, opened his car door, climbed in, and started the engine. He waved to her through the windshield as he backed out of the apartment complex.

She stood. Her face itched as if a thousand mosquitoes had bitten her. She threw open the car door and opened the glove box. In those few seconds, the itch spread to her entire body and made her double over. She grabbed the keys and stumbled as she ran to Jessica's front door. The itching reached through her skin and into her muscles, as if her skin was scratching itself raw down to the bone.

Her legs wobbled. She collapsed and crawled the last few steps to the front door. She groped with the key, found the lock, and turned it. Her hand had no strength. She raised herself halfway up, throwing her whole body into it. She twisted the knob and fell into the doorway. She reached hand over hand and climbed the stairs. She felt she was leaving her skin behind and crawling out of it. She gasped for air. The spots around her vision grew bigger and ricocheted faster.

She reached the top of the stairs, crawled across the carpet to the kitchen. Her body burned at the slightest movement. She tried to scream, but her voice was gone, and her vision was fading.

She saw the phone cord. She tried to stand up to reach the receiver, but her legs wouldn't move that way anymore. She grabbed the cord and pulled the whole phone off the counter. She barely heard the noise it made as it clattered on the stick-on flooring.

On her hands and knees, she found the keypad and pressed nine. Then one. Then one again. She heard ringing, but she couldn't find the receiver. The ringing came from everywhere. As her vision swam and flickered, she noticed her hands. They had swollen so thick she couldn't bend her fingers. Blood seeped out of the hair follicles.

Drops of blood fell from her face and splattered on the floor.

"Nine-one-one what's your emergency?"

"Ambulance!" CJ screamed.

"What's happening, ma'am?"

"I'm inside! He's... Outside!"

"Who is outside, ma'am?"

"Can't breathe... Get both ... us!"

She collapsed to her stomach and screamed but quickly ran out of air. She inhaled. Nothing happened.

"I have your address as ... Ma'am? ... I'm dispatching ... can you hear ... ma'am, are you still ..."

9

Rive was bodiless. He felt the Multitude touching him, and they were not happy. They flashed images at Rive. Images of pain and intensity.

Did you shut me down?

They flashed more painful images at Rive, induced feelings of dread and pain, and then receded, leaving Rive alone in the void.

I'm sorry. I didn't expect this.

The Multitude was used to Rive by now. They communicated with him often while he was sleeping. Rive had learned how to speak to them better, but it was still on his terms. He had yet to grasp how they perceived reality, let alone how to talk to them in their language.

Right now the Multitude was calling out for Sonjaa again in frustration.

When Sonjaa had recovered from the Lake, shortly after tearing Friend's body to pieces, Rive had asked her if she remembered anything about the language of the Multitude. Sonjaa had never spoken about her time in the Lake, but she told Rive she remembered what she did, even if not how.

Since Sonjaa had been a metal explorer and translated between them, Rive's relationship with the metal had been much calmer. The metal understood Rive's world a little better, and Rive understood theirs. They knew what Rive was and that he needed them as much as they needed him.

He had not even begun on the way that would move the entire mountain range from the destroyed planet Reth into the underground ocean caverns of Neben. The Dekanites would have to carve out the remainder of the caverns first before he could begin. It would be a complicated, non-spherical portal that would take many years to calculate, but it would be worth it for all species involved. The Multitude would have energy again, maybe even become companions with the Eich, who also needed free-flowing electrons to survive.

Rive sent the Multitude feelings of regret that Sonjaa could not intercede for them again. He sent them feelings of gratitude for sparing him the pain of whatever that man shot him with.

The Multitude sent him sounds of panicked voices, people asking for pulse rate, EKGs. They were sounds happening around him right now. The Multitude kept them from reaching his brain directly. Rive recognized them. He sent the metal reassurance.

They sent him a summary of the sensation of his skin being on fire and bleeding. Blood was seeping between almost every scale left on his body. Again, Rive sent them reassuring thoughts. This was a hospital, a place that helped people when things like this happened.

The Multitude sent thousands of images and sounds and feelings at the same time. All of it added up to a question: *is this what can happen to the body?*

Rive sent them thoughts he hoped would add up to *yes, the body can be harmed.*

Panicked mental noise came from the metal. They didn't want to be vulnerable. If something happened to Rive's flesh, the metal would die as well.

Rive drew the metal close to him and embraced it like a raptor. *These people know what's wrong. They know how to fix it.*

The metal was still scared, and now it huddled with Rive, connected him to their neural net. They swarmed Rive with impulses his brain did not know how to interpret. The metal did this frequently, trying to acclimate him to their reality, but despite enduring it nightly it had yet to become clear.

Rive was an Archeon. He could take in any information, find the patterns, and understand it instantly, but this wasn't merely language. It was reality as language. He never wanted them to stop, but he couldn't take in the impulses for very long without losing his mind.

Thanks to Sonjaa, the living metal understood the vast differences in mental processes that existed between them and could at least understand Rive's basic thoughts now. Sonjaa had not been able to imbue the same understanding of their language into Rive, so the talking had been maddeningly one-sided, but at least they understood one another now.

After an indeterminate amount of time, Rive disconnected. The metal receded from him, and Rive communicated to them in terms familiar to both of them.

Since he was here, Rive updated them on the status of the portal. He sent them images showing them how much of the caverns had been carved, and where their new home would be. The metal was excited. They could not understand how long it would be until they reunited with the entire mountain range, but they understood progress.

They gently wrapped Rive in their reality again. Rive took it, tried to find patterns and comprehend reality as they did.

10

Rive opened his eyes. He lay on his side in a hospital bed, arm hooked up to an IV unit. A tube was down his throat, and a machine breathed for him. Gauze covered his scales, and he lay on top of multiple towels, all stained with blood. He had bled through his skin.

He felt no pain. His head swam inside his skull, and he couldn't smell anything. His eyes still leaked fluid, which made his vision swimmy, and his inner eyelid tried to flick it away, but that only smeared it more. He could make out a watery image of Doctor Azure and three nurses. Doctor Azure shook her head.

"I was only kidding the other day. You know that, right? Can you hear me?"

Rive tried to click his claws, but his real hand responded in slow motion. He clicked his metal claws together, but the sound was too quiet to hear. He nodded with his snout a couple times.

All the nurses smiled. Doctor Azure also smiled. "Got you just in time. Ambulance crew had a hell of a time inserting that tube, but it kept you alive."

Rive tried to answer, but nothing came out.

"Don't speak, don't speak," Doctor Azure said. "Tube's gonna stay in for a bit longer. When we're sure you can breathe without it, we'll pull it out. The IV drip is to help with the pain. Whatever happened to y'all, it was ten times worse than the ladies we just sent to Walter Reed."

Rive raised his muzzle. Now he could see the bed next to him. CJ lay in it. She did not have a tube down her throat, but much of her face and arms had been bandaged.

What hadn't been wrapped in gauze was covered in a nasty-looking rash that made her look as though she'd been burned alive. The IV bag next to her bed dripped fast. She smiled at the sight of Rive's eyes, apparently grateful for every breath.

"The Madame Secretary was in bad shape, too," Doctor Azure continued. "Not as bad as you, but another five minutes and we'd have had to do a tracheotomy to get air to her lungs. Maybe skin grafts, as bad as that rash was."

Rive turned his muzzle back to the doctor and the nurses.

"Either y'all got any idea what hit ya?" said the doctor.

"I don't think you'd believe me," said CJ. Her voice sounded raspy and weak.

"I'd believe anything." She walked over to the wall and switched on the x-ray viewer. "Hope you don't mind. We needed to see what was going on in your throat. Thought you'd like to see what's going on with the rest of you, too."

She hung a few x-ray sheets against the light. Lungs, kidneys, stomach, much of it was there. What wasn't there showed up bright white. The metal had remade his missing organs, though probably just the physical form. His throat did indeed look swollen, even to an untrained eye.

Another x-ray showed his lower half. Rive clicked his claws in slow motion. He knew his penis hadn't survived the disaster, but he had never been able to tell if his gonads had. The area behind his slit showed up all white, and just behind it were two bight white ovals. The metal had remade his reproductive parts, too. They didn't work anymore, but it had copied his biological form exactly.

The other x-rays showed the metal twisting through him under his real skin like a phantom circulatory system. There were no isolated pieces. Even the parts of his outer body that looked isolated were connected internally.

Rive clicked his claws in thanks. Doctor Azure smiled as she took the x-rays down and switched off the light.

"You're laughing now, but wait till we take that tube out of your rear." She smiled, walked up to him, lay a hand on his real hand. The touch felt good, but also uncomfortable even through the painkiller. "You're stable. Both y'all are recovering, so it looks like whatever happened is being flushed from y'all's systems. Can I call the president and give him an update on y'all's status?"

CJ laughed. "He'll probably call you soon."

She grinned. "Love to talk to him. Can't believe I got a member of the president's cabinet in my care. Not to mention a space alien. I expect he'll want both y'all transferred to Walter Reed, too. As soon as the tubes are out of him, I'll okay it."

"Thanks, doctor. We'll be fine here. I don't think Rive is in shape to make a portal right now. Are you?"

Rive wished he could answer. He closed his eyes and curled up.

"That's what I thought," said the doctor. "Another day or so and both y'all should be feeling a lot better."

Doctor Azure walked out with the x-rays. The nurses followed, all smiles. Rive uncurled, turned his muzzle CJ's way. She reached over and held her hand between the beds. Rive couldn't seem to move his real body very much, so he reached out with his metal hand. She wrapped her fingers between his. Rive clutched her hand, rubbed her fingers with his claws. He was grateful the metal gave him feeling in his artificial claws. It felt so good to touch someone.

"I called Tim just before they woke you up. He's been fired. Government confiscated his analysis. Said it was unauthorized. Someone is going to have questions for us. I plan to tell them everything. Ambulance brought my briefcase. The papers are still in there. I checked. We didn't lose the research."

She smiled. Rive rubbed her fingers.

"He told me it's hopeless, Rive. I was welcome to expose them, but I would only be committing political suicide. That stuff he sprayed us with... It's the future. Little by little. C-Corn... They don't plan to fix it. They know it's dangerous, so they're selling the solutions to all of its defects."

Rive stopped rubbing. He wanted to speak so badly. He moaned in pain instead.

"I'm going to fight them. I don't care what it does to me. Someone will listen. It's my job to hold them responsible."

Rive squeezed her hand, then remembered his strength and loosened his grip. She squeezed his hand back. He wanted to tell her that this was the first time anyone had touched his metal without wincing or complaining about how cold it was. Instead, he closed his eyes and curled back into the egg.

Boston

The video wall had nine televisions on it. Some played VHS tapes of old TV shows or movies. Others showed broadcast. The rabbit ears needed adjusting on three of them, but Kylac filtered out the static in his mind so everything still made sense.

Deka and Sonjaa lay in front of the empty seats, on either side of Kylac's legs, also watching the televisions. Friend's projection sat next to Kylac. He focused on the set playing a tape of *The Twilight Zone*.

"You might dismiss them as an uncontacted race who can't understand where they are or what's going on," Friend began, "but many of them do know something is wrong. They express it in fiction like this, distorting reality just enough to help others see a larger point."

"If it really made a difference," Sonjaa said, "they wouldn't need to create things like that all."

"They express it because they don't know what to do about it," said the fox in the Lake. "They are powerless in their society, so they create little worlds of their own to feel better about it."

"Not too much different from what you want to do," Kylac said, scratching himself through his green shorts.

"How so?"

"You want to get out of the confines of this universe, but you don't know how, so you express it by bothering us." Kylac waved his tail, brushing it against Friend.

"I do know what to do about it. I'm just waiting for you."

Kylac turned to him. "You have not said how I can possibly help you understand where you are. How will me joining you in the Lake do anything?"

"We figured out quite a bit during our time together. If we continue, I'm sure we will take each other higher. Without our old ways, there's no risk."

Deka turned his head, set it on the armrest. "What do you know of the Lake so far?"

"You want me to just explain something I don't even understand?"

"You know the equations, don't you? That's what you and Kylac were trying to figure out. Start by telling us what the hell the antispheres were."

"Opening ways into the Lake without understanding where they led. The math worked, but understanding why took a long time to work out. Even after I figured it out, it left me with unanswered questions. The biggest still bothers me. I know how the universe is, what its equation is, but not what powers it so to speak. That's what the Lake does, I think. I know what the Lake is as a concept, but until I know how I can't venture too far from this universe."

"Describe what you see from where you are," Deka said.

Friend's tail waved. "I can't. No language has words to describe it. I don't have senses anymore. There is no perception the way you know it."

"Try," said Deka. "Use metaphors and fiction."

"What it's like... Well, try to imagine floating outside the universe. The universe is now the size of a planet to you. Stretching to infinity are incarnations of the universe. Snapshots of it as it moves through time. Each planet represents the universe at different increments of time as it travels across the Lake. Those versions of it fade after a few billion years but you can still calculate what they would have been. Now imagine you're aware of everything going on at each snapshot just as you're aware of what's happening on each of these televisions. You can project yourself into those screens and affect the events, but it takes a lot of effort. That's the kind of effort I'm expending just to come down to this level again."

"That's... how it was for me," said Sonjaa. "Except I was confused."

"If you had been an Archeon, you wouldn't have been. A conscious mind is the only thing that exists out here. The metaphor is imperfect; the Lake actually exists all around you, touching everything, not something that's somewhere out in space."

"Are you sure there's no one else with you?" Deka said.

"There probably is but I don't know how to perceive them yet. For all I know they're touching me, trying to get my attention, but I can't feel them. I hope to soon. Right now... I think I've reached an impasse. Something is holding me back."

Kylac and Deka heard Jeff at the bar by the window. He was on the phone with someone, yelling at them.

"When's he going to make those calls?" Sonjaa asked.

"He already has," Friend answered. "In fact, he's talking with one of them right now. It will take time before those people believe his story."

"Notice he hasn't changed," Kylac said. "We showed him a glimpse of life offworld, and it did not affect him at all."

Deka nudged his fox. "Remember when we took Stephen offworld? It's the complete opposite. I think we're right."

Kylac nudged Sonjaa. "Stephen wanted to go up to all the predators and talk to them while they were ripping the meat off the carcass."

"He wasn't scared?" she asked.

Deka reached over. "Stephen's fear filled him with wonder. Nothing like Jeff." He wiggled his fingers. "I like your business idea, Sonjaa."

She reached to Deka and clicked his claws. "I never thought the market would have something I wanted." She took a deep breath. "It was a unique, satisfying scent, and I want to share it with everyone in the contacted universe."

Deka played her claws faster. "Mass production would be a problem, but maybe we could collect a surplus and store it for later. We'll try aging it. It might get better."

Sonjaa couldn't remember the last time she had laughed like this. "We'll find someone to synthesize it and make candles."

Friend wagged his tail. "You'd be rich."

"I'd give them away for free just to blow Jeff's mind," Sonjaa said. The hunt and the laughter had been a tremendous relief. She was breathing easy for the first time in years. She turned to Friend. "So what will you do once you create a universe of your own?"

"I plan to do things right. No more letting life forms rise from the mud and battle it out for survival. No more old ways. Nobody should have to deal with their animal nature underneath a higher mind. I will start with fully developed and conscious life forms. I will tell them exactly what their purpose in life is. No more wandering about struggling to survive, untold billions dying alone and confused."

"Sounds familiar," said Deka. "Like a certain story a certain human now in a Krone's body once told us."

"Whoever that god was did a lousy job explaining himself. I plan to do things right."

The doorbell rang. Today was Marissa's day off, so Jeff left the drawing room and walked to the front.

"And what will be the purpose of life in this new universe?" Sonjaa asked.

"I haven't gotten that far."

"That should be the first thing you decide before you create a universe!" She clicked her claws.

Friend's tail wagged.

Jeff screamed from the front door. All four Relians in the drawing room stood up. Deka and Sonjaa ran around the couch. Kylac vaulted the back of the couch, and they ran to the door.

A pangolin-like creature the size of a bear stood on the landing almost on all four limbs but slightly raised on her hind legs. The Archeon from Neben. Jeff had dropped the phone and was staring.

"Qan?" Deka said, in English. "What are you doing here? How did you get here?"

Qan answered in perfect English. "Rive has come to Neben a few times. He told me where to find you."

Footsteps came halfway down the stairs and stopped. Penny gasped. The children screamed. Penny hid them behind herself. The young girl tried to see around her arms and get a look. The teenager had already broken away from her mother and ventured further down the steps. Penny whispered for her to stay up here.

Kylac turned to Jeff and Penny. "Everyone, this is Qan. She's the Archeon of the planet Neben."

"Qan," said Sonjaa. "This is Jeff and Penny Morton. They are letting us stay with them while we become acquainted with human civilization."

"Nice to meet you, but I'm here on an urgent matter. I volunteered to come here and speak to you about it. The three of you might know more than anyone."

"Come inside," Deka said. "We'll talk."

Jeff suddenly came to life. "No... No! Do not bring that in my house!"

Everyone stared at him. Penny appeared to be on the brink of tears. The two girls looked full of wonder.

"Get out!" Jeff yelled. "Get out! All of you! I've had enough of this crap! Out of my house! Now! Never come back!"

They walked out the open door and stood on the landing.

"If you're not out of the gate in five minutes, I am calling the police! And you can forget about your people! They're as good as zoo animals now!"

Deka wanted to urinate on the front lawn and walk away, but the gesture would mean nothing to him. Jeff slammed the door. Just down the road, they heard the gate opening. Deka walked them to the yard and into the trees.

Qan plodded along after him. "What was that?"

"Long story. What brings you here?"

He stopped just inside the small forest surrounding the helipad. Friend's muzzle appeared next to his earhole.

"I slowed time in the yard. You have all the time you need to talk."

"Thanks."

The muzzle vanished.

"Numerous people on a dozen worlds have reported it," Qan said. "There is an antisphere moving about, and it is killing people."

Deka said nothing. Nobody spoke.

"Yes," Qan continued. "It happened on Neben, too. I came to you because people on my world actually saw what caused it. Or what it seemed to be. Three people approached something. They said it looked like an antisphere, but when they neared, it moved."

"An antisphere moved?" Kylac said.

"Not just that. It moved as though it were alive. They said it resembled the silhouette of a Relian canine, but it had no depth. When they walked up to it, it leaped at them like a fox as well. Its claws grew to ridiculous proportions, and so did its arms and legs. They managed to avoid injury.

Then the canine-shaped antisphere folded into itself and disappeared."

Sonjaa's hands sagged. Kylac's tail tucked between his legs, and his ear turned backwards.

"On other planets," Qan continued, "there were deaths and damage to the land. Nobody could see what was actually causing it until now. Does this sound familiar to any of you?"

Deka was snarling. He raised himself on his hind legs and yelled. "Friend!"

Qan paused. Friend manifested next to her.

"What?"

Deka growled at him, crouched, spread his claws.

"I don't know what she's talking about," said the old fox.

Deka dashed to him, claws raised. He knocked him down and stood on him, killing claw about to sink into his chest. Friend acted unfazed being under Deka's feet.

"I sent my old ways outside the universe. They can't go anywhere."

"Where are they now?"

"I... I don't know."

"You don't know where your own fucking old ways are?" Sonjaa said, the curse word rolling off her tongue like a tulip going over a waterfall. She crouched and raised her claws, too.

"I'm separated from them! I can't sense them! I'm not even aware of them..." He gasped.

Deka had done nothing. "What is it?"

Friend hesitated three times before he finally spoke. "There's another hole in the universe. No... I don't know who it is. I can't perceive it. But it's been to Neben and Craio... It's changing things. I didn't notice it before! How did I miss it?!"

Deka screeched at him, shoved his killing claw into Friend's chest and swiping back. No blood. Friend's body was unaffected, even though Deka had felt the claw pierce flesh. Deka jumped off him and stood in attack stance, facing him.

"I think it's time you revealed yourself."

"To Qan?" Friend was now standing on two legs.

"Yes! To her!"

"She has..." He stared at the motionless pangolin. "Her numbers changed. She's not supposed to be here. What's happening? Numbers are changing all over the universe. This is..."

Qan unpaused. She looked around and finally found everyone standing behind her. She tilted her head at the sight of Friend, who was still muttering.

"This isn't right. My old ways are in the Lake, and they are changing the future! They're a collection of animal instincts! They couldn't have found a way back!"

"You..." Qan said. "You should be dead."

"We tried," Sonjaa answered, "but he moved his consciousness into the Lake just before I finished eating him."

"I couldn't find my way back!" Friend continued. "How are they here? I made sure it couldn't happen! They have no mind of their own!"

"Yes, they do," said Kylac, walking up to the projected fox. "Old ways know how to survive. They know scent anxiety. It's all they care about. And now there's a creature made of pure instinct roaming the universe trying to find somewhere to satisfy its needs."

"It has no sense of smell! It has no body! It can't be doing this!"

Kylac was now nose to nose with Friend. "Your old ways are doing exactly what you would be doing if they were still part of you. But why haven't they destroyed the universe by now?"

"I don't know."

Kylac opened his mouth and clamped his teeth on Friend's neck. His jaws passed right through his body and snapped shut. Kylac snarled and backed up a step, fur raised. Deka walked up to his side and held Kylac at the shoulder.

"I believed you!" Kylac screamed. "I was ready to forgive you for the people you killed—for the misery you put me through!"

"Can they be stopped?" Qan said.

"Good question," said Deka. "Friend? Do you have any ideas?"

Friend stood still, looking at everybody.

Deka lunged. "Find your old ways and destroy them!"

Friend was shaking. "I can't."

Deka snarled again, raising his killing claws.

Friend did not react. "If I go near them, they will find me. If they find me they will merge with me, and if they do I will revert. Remember how I was when you ate me? That's what I will become out here."

"Aren't you everywhere all the time?" Deka said. "Find the extra hole in the universe and plug it!"

"They're in the Lake, not here! I'm not everywhere in the Lake! If they find me here... No. If they find one of my projections, they can follow it to me. I can't let it happen."

Deka lunged again, swiped at Friend's head with his hand. His claws went right through him. Deka snarled as he swung his tail to stay standing.

"I was just starting to like you again. If you won't clean up your mess, we will!"

"What?" Friend said.

"We're going to find your old ways and destroy them."

"They'll kill you! You can't—!"

"Kylac," Deka turned to him. "If we get you close enough, do you think you can block the ways it makes?"

Now Kylac shivered. "That would mean—"

"You'll have to tear down that new subconscious of yours. Fuck."

"I ca... I can't..."

"We'll figure that out on the way." He faced Friend. "Looks like things are working just as you wanted. We're chasing the Lake now, and the only way to stop it is for Kylac to do what you want him to do. Did you plan this?"

Friend was silent.

Deka was about to charge again, but Kylac dropped to all fours and pounced on him first. Friend went down. Kylac tore into his neck. This time his body came apart as expected, with blood and internal organs and the scent of wounded flesh. Friend did not move as Kylac tore him apart and ate him. After a minute, he met Friend's eyes.

"Did you plan this?!" Kylac screamed.

"No." Friend's voice sounded perfectly normal, despite him having no throat. "I thought I was rid of my old ways. I thought they would stay inert in the Lake forever. They're searching the Lake for me. They don't know the Lake from the normal universe. That's why they're jumping from one to the other. This wasn't my intent."

Kylac jumped off Friend, rose to his hind legs, suddenly no blood on his muzzle or chest. He walked to a tree and leaned against it, hanging his head.

"I can't do it. I walled those memories off for a reason. I'm not sure I can handle it without reverting. I will be worse than Friend if I do." He turned. Looked back at the throatless fox. "The only thing that kept me from reverting last time and killing everyone in the universe was not wanting to become like you."

"Hold on to that thought," Deka said. "You might be the only thing that can stop his old ways. Friend can't hide from himself forever."

"Where are they now?" said Kylac.

"They're in the Lake," answered the other fox. "I don't know where they're going to emerge next."

Deka turned to Qan. "Then let's go to Neben. We'll talk to the people who saw it happen, follow it everywhere it's been. Maybe it left something behind. Qan, would you like to make the way?"

"I... I can't seem to make one right now."

"Oh, right," Deka said. "Friend, unpause time. We'll show you around Boston until you open the way. I'll warn you nobody's seen a mammal from Neben before."

The wind began blowing again. The trees began moving. Deka led them down the driveway to the gate. It was wide open for them. Friend appeared in front of it.

"It's been longer than ten minutes in the rest of the world. The police will be here. If you walk around Boston with Qan, someone will shoot her. This has... This has caught me off guard even more than all of you. Allow me."

A sphere leading directly to an oasis on a desert planet appeared next to him. Birds and mammals walked about on the other side, and a creature of living crystal swam just under the surface of one of the ponds. It zapped lighting at one of the birds, but the bird did not seem to mind. The Eich must have learned how to lower their voices.

"I also showed Rive and Norh the conversation we just had. They know what's happening and that all of you will be gone. Rive wants you to know that he will take care of the Relians on Earth, and Norh wants me to tell you to wait for him on Neben. He and Stephen want to join you."

Sonjaa growled. She walked to the portal and stepped through, sinking slightly into the sand. Qan followed her. Her feet were adapted to walk on loose sand, so it didn't slow her down at all. Kylac and Deka stood still, staring at the projected fox.

"It's going to happen," the raptor said. "Kylac will eventually join you. What about me and Sonjaa? What will happen to us?"

"I don't know," said Friend. "You might be ripped apart in the Lake when my instincts find you."

"Or I might," the other fox answered.

"Kylac, just let me show you how to separate your old ways. You might stand a chance of destroying them if you're in the Lake. That's where they are. Trapping them in this universe won't help."

Kylac growled at him. "That worked so well for you."

He stretched his shorts out and let them fall down his legs. He stepped out of them and into the sphere. Deka huffed in Friend's face and then walked through as well. Friend disappeared, and the way closed. A police car was just pulling into the driveway, lights flashing. The gate shut behind it.

About the Author

James L. Steele has had the idea for the Archeon series in his head since the mid-1990s.

He has been published in various anthologies and magazines, including: *Solarcide, Allasso, Different Worlds, Different Skins: V.2, Tall Tales with Short Cocks V.2, Bourbon Penn, Gods with Fur, Claw the Way to Victory, The Reclamation Project*, and *Fictionvale*.

His sci-fi novel *Huvek* is published through Argyll Productions.

He lives in Ohio, where he pursues his hobby of becoming a wine connoisseur while having multiple micro-existential crisis per day.

Blog: DaydreamingInText.blogspot.com

Twitter: @JLSteeleAuthor